D1566977

Philip McBride

Redeeming Honor

To Wallace & Celeta

Enjoy

Philip McBride

Philip McBride

Philip McBride

Philip McBride has asserted his right under the Copyright Designs and Patents Act of 1988 to be identified as the author of this work.

Redeeming Honor is a work of historical fiction and except for the well-known historical people, events, and places that are included in the work, all names, places, and incidents are from the author's imagination or are used fictitiously. Any resemblance to actual persons, living, or dead, is purely coincidental.

Copyright © 2015 Philip McBride

All rights reserved.

ISBN 13: 978-1515300250

ISBN: 1515300250

Dedication

This novel is dedicated to my daughters-in-law, Maggie and Meredith, because they are both history nerds, they make our sons happy, and they provide Nita and me with beautiful grandchildren.

Philip McBride

Acknowledgements

The cover photograph is courtesy of Tom Bender Images of New Braunfels, Texas.

The cover design is by graphic designer Karen Phillips.

Other Books by Philip McBride

Whittled Away: A Novel of the Alamo Rifles

Tangled Honor: 1862

Philip McBride

Chapter 1

January 2, 1863
Winter Camp of the Fifth Texas Infantry Regiment
On the Rappahannock River, Virginia

Confederate Captain John McBee yelped when the flat blade of the wooden sword landed hard on his ribcage. He stepped back and glared at Lieutenant Campbell Wood, who glared right back.

"Close your line, Captain. How many times do I have to tell you?" Woods scolded the older officer.

McBee was sweating, even though the winter air was cold enough for the two officers to see their breath, and both men were coatless, only wearing vests over their shirts. They faced each other standing on the edge of the regimental drill field, the dried grass beaten down from the daily fencing lessons given by Lieutenant Wood to the other thirty officers in the Fifth Texas Infantry Regiment.

Captain McBee took a deep breath and resumed his *en garde* position, front foot, shoulders, and sword arm pointed at his opponent, knees flexed. Wood did likewise and for a few seconds the two Texans slashed and parried in mock combat. The wooden swords blades rapped against each other until the lieutenant slipped his practice weapon past the captain's guard and jabbed him in the chest with his weapon's blunt point.

"You failed to bind my blade when you should have, Captain."

"And I'm again dead on the field," McBee concluded. "You know, Campbell, if I ever get in real sword fight with some Yankee officer..."

"You better shoot him," Wood said, interrupting his student.

"I'll keep that in mind, but I was going to say that if I ever do cross blades with another company officer, he's no more liable to be a schooled fencer than I am. All those academy graduates who've learned to sword fight the French way wind up leading regiments and brigades, not companies."

"Captain, you malign me!" Wood said in mock alarm.

"Wood, the backwater military school in Texas that let you in doesn't count. Besides, you're barely shaving and already the regiment's adjutant. And sword master."

"Hardly a master. I'm only a drill instructor whose students learned to use blades fighting Comanches or in barroom brawls," Wood replied.

"Well, you were right about my leaving my right flank open, not *closing my line,* as you said. And every knife fighter knows he better lock up the other man's blade."

"Those are two of the basics, Captain. Maybe in another few weeks of practice, it'll start coming naturally."

"That may be, but I can't say I'm enjoying getting whacked and poked by a lieutenant half my age. Not sure it's something my men need to be seeing. But captains follow the colonel's orders. Isn't it about time for your next victim?"

"Not yet. *En garde, mon capitaine!* I must avenge the insult you cast upon my back water academy!" Wood assumed the position, stomped his front foot, and attacked to McBee's left.

The middle-aged captain with the salt and pepper beard barely raised his sword in time to protect himself from another whack to his ribs. While McBee's first clumsy parry was successful, Wood slid his sword down and delivered a blow to his opponent's calf before the captain could respond with his own slashing attack.

"Can you duel from your knees, Sir?" Wood stepped back.

"They taught you to cheat at that military academy." McBee rubbed his stinging leg. "Maybe I should just rush you, chance a wound from your blade if I must, and break your nose with my sword's brass fist guard. Then stomp your face into the dirt."

"Captain, in melees with your men and the enemy all mashed in together, that might be your best chance of staying alive," Wood said without smiling. "But if it's just you and that Yankee captain…"

"I know, I heard you the first time. *Shoot him.*"

"Captain McBee, Sir!" Lieutenant Absalom Daniels called from several feet away.

"What?"

"Sir, the new men, the recruits from Texas are here," Daniels reported.

"Very well, Absalom, let's go see what sort of men we're going to turn into soldiers," McBee said. The captain looked at Lieutenant Wood and shrugged an insincere apology, glad for the excuse to cut his hour of fencing instruction short.

* * *

McBee paced slowly from one end of the line to the other, his scowl settling on each man's face, wanting to see how many of the new recruits would look him in the eye.

"Welcome to the Army of Northern Virginia, Gentlemen. I'm Captain John McBee, your commanding officer."

The line of new soldiers studied the man. His gray frock coat hung loosely from his shoulders, was patched at the elbows, and the hem was fraying. A brown leather waist belt snugged up to the last notch supported a polished metal scabbard and sword.

A year of warring had hardened McBee's countenance and that of the two sergeants standing near him. All three stood erect, but dark shadows under their eyes betrayed a deep-set weariness. Their cheek bones protruded and all were rail-thin after the hard marches and limited rations of the previous year.

McBee had spent his forty-second birthday recuperating from a bullet wound in his shoulder, a memento of the battle at Manassas Junction the prior August. His graying beard was shorter than those worn by most of the officers, as he had impulsively shaved it off three weeks earlier to surprise a woman named Faith. But there was no indication to the thirty-six recruits that their captain was a man smitten by a woman's affections. They saw a lean, dark-eyed officer whose appearance scared some of them, even though his next words lessened their fears, briefly.

"Since ya'all are still more civilian than soldier, if you have a question, ask me now, because after today, you'll be in the hands of your sergeants and corporals, and they will be the only ranks above private you'll be talking to."

After a silence that lasted several seconds, a voice in the second rank said, "What about uniforms, Captain? Don't we get uniforms? My shoe soles from home got more holes than leather and my coat's coming to pieces."

"After you show us you got the makings of a soldier, deserving to wear the uniform of the Confederacy, you'll get one. We don't have uniforms to waste on weaklings or shirkers. For now, you will drill wearing the clothes on your back."

The man with holes in his shoes sighed, but not so loudly that the sergeants or captain heard him.

"Tomorrow you will receive an Enfield rifled-musket so the sergeants can teach you to load and shoot it," McBee said.

A nasal twangy voice came, full of swagger, "I kin already shoot squirrels off'n a branch thirty feet up. Whyn't cha jest give me the danged rifle now and point me towards the bluebellies?" A spattering of chuckles came from the other recruits.

McBee glanced towards Sergeant Stephens, who moved quickly behind the second rank and grabbed the collar of the young man who spoke, pulling him out of line and around the formation to stand before the captain.

"What's your name, Mister?" Captain McBee softly asked.

"Asbury Lawson," the man answered loudly, the bravado in his voice only slightly less.

"Fetch Private Lawson an Enfield, Sergeant. A loaded Enfield, please. Private, take off your coat and hat. Corporal Hodges, would you be so kind as to take the private's hat and coat down to the tree line out yonder by the creek. Nail them to a tree trunk where we can see them, then make yourself small somewhere so you can bring Private Lawson's clothes back after he takes his shot." McBee directed.

"Private, you say you can hit a little squirrel thirty feet up an oak tree. If you can hit your own coat or hat out there, at about the distance we start shooting at the enemy, I'll put a new uniform on your back and you can keep the Enfield and help teach the rest of these fellas to shoot. How's that sound?" McBee asked pleasantly.

The young man smiled broadly and said, "Sounds mighty fine, Captain." And with a smirk in his tone, he added, "You might as well send for that new uniform now."

Sergeant Hubbard, who had been standing at the end of the formation, flowed over the space separating him from the private. Without hesitating, he grabbed the man's shoulder, swung him around and smashed him in the mouth with a fist. Blood gushed from the recruit's mouth as he staggered backwards.

Sergeant Hubbard said, "He's your captain, boy. Show respect." Turning away from the line of recruits to face McBee, Sergeant Hubbard winked and added, "Sorry about that, Sir. Won't happen again."

McBee frowned at the man's bleeding mouth, pulled a dirty handkerchief from a pocket, and handed it to him as he said, "Private Lawson, before I bother the quartermaster, I think I'll wait for you to back up your bragging with your marksmanship."

Soon Lawson held the Enfield and Corporal Hodges had hidden behind the biggest tree trunk near the creek bed.

"There you are, Private. Now put a hole in that Yankee squirrel with your Enfield. That's close to two hundred yards, about where we start firing during a battle. You put a hole through your hat or the chest of your coat, and you'll get your new uniform today, and as a bonus, I'll give all you new recruits the rest of the afternoon to lie in the shade," the captain said.

The young man hefted the Enfield in his hands, trying to get a feel for its weight and balance. He started to sit down so he could brace his elbows on his knees, but Sergeant Stephens stopped him by saying, "Sonny boy, we ain't fit a battle yet sittin' down. Stand up and shoot offhand like a soldier."

Much less confident than when he first spoke, and with throbbing teeth, Lawson put the Enfield to shoulder and lined up the sights to center on his own brown coat, a dark spot on the tree trunk that he could barely see at the distance. He decided to raise the barrel ever so slightly to aim at the even darker shadow of his black hat, in case the bullet dropped some. The nine-pound weight of the weapon was pushing his left arm down, so he shifted his grip back about six inches and aimed again.

Finally, Lawson let out his breath and squeezed the trigger, his view instantly blocked by smoke from the Enfield's discharge.

Five minutes later, Corporal Hodges held out the coat to Captain McBee, who said, "Let's see where you shot your first Yankee squirrel." No hole was found in the coat or hat.

Five minutes after that, the three dozen recruits were on the drill field, under the direction of Sergeant Hubbard, learning that even the simple of act of turning left or right while in formation took all their attention. Private Lawson was wearing his brown coat and was never told his shot had knocked bark off the tree right in the gap between his hat and coat collar, a shot that impressed his captain and the sergeants. The recruits drilled for three hours before they were put in four-man messes to cook their first meal together.

During their rushed travel from Galveston to Virginia, the men had been fed hard crackers and cold boiled beef stew, and were not expected to cook. Most of them had never cooked at home, and few had any idea what to do with the coarsely ground cornmeal and lumps of fatty pork they were given. Even fewer men had brought cooking pots or fry pans.

Quickly realizing his new charges were about to toss or burn the meager rations issued to them, Sergeant Hubbard gathered his corporals and further divided the new messes into pairs. He told his corporals to spread the pairs of recruits among the veterans to make sure the food was not wasted and the new recruits each ate something. Then he went looking for George.

"Sa'geant, is you tellin' me I gots to find nine pots an' nine frying pans tonight? Dat's mo' what Levi do, him bein' the captain's man," George answered.

14

"That's what I said, George. I know Levi is off somewheres taking care of the captain's ma, and you're the lieutenant's boy. You got pull with the other darkies. You can find the tin-ware someplace. We ain't got half the men we did back in the spring. Where'd all their pots and pans get to? I need nine pots and nine fry pans by tomorrow morning. No less, no later." With that, Hubbard walked away.

George rubbed the back of his neck as he considered where he was going to beg, borrow, or steal nine sets of cookware. He wasn't particularly pleased about being handed the sergeant's problem, but he couldn't protest or complain to the lieutenant without unpleasant consequences. Beyond that, the challenge secretly appealed to him. Within minutes he was off to see what he could pry away from the other officers' man-servants and was sorting out the answer to just where the cooking supplies of dead men wound up.

* * *

Privates Jason Smith and Cal Gilbert had mixed emotions as they greeted the two recruits assigned to them. Smith spoke first. "Now look here, you men are goin' to have to figure out how to cook cornmeal without burnin' it black as soot, but not today. Today you just watch me an' Cal."

"I can cook," the heavier and taller of the two recruits said. His partner stayed silent, but nodded.

"All right. Here," Smith said, tossing the fry pan at their feet. "Just use your half of the rations. After you make a mess of yours, I'll cook our half. You got names?"

"I'm Edward Bell, he's my brother Zebulon," the shorter, slimmer recruit answered. The dark-haired siblings shared similar facial features, Zebulon looking older and rougher than Edward, who appeared to have been pulled into the army straight from a school desk.

"Pleased to meet you, Edward and Zebulon. Ed and Zeb, huh? I'm Jason Smith, the homely one over there is Cal Gilbert," Smith said pointing to his messmate who, even though filthy with greasy hair bedeviled by lice, was still the more handsome of the pair.

Zebulon Bell knelt by the fire and soon had half the salt pork sizzling, making a pool of melted grease in the fry pan. While the pork cooked, he poured half the cornmeal into a tin cup and added just enough water and a few drops of the hot grease to make yellow dough. He shaped six round gooey balls and slipped them into the grease-filled skillet and cooked the corn dodgers, nudging them over a couple of times with his pocket knife, until they were a uniform golden brown.

Smith and Gilbert glanced at each other and quickly picked up the corn dodgers and chunks of cooked salt pork. With a full mouth, Smith pointed at the other pile of cornmeal and uncooked salt pork, and said, "Go ahead. Cook y'orn, now."

* * *

"Absalom, you did a fine job," McBee said that evening as he scanned the roster of new recruits by the light of a lantern. "You enlisted more men than any of the other officers. Company C is now the largest company in the regiment."

"That fifty-dollar bounty brought them out of the river bottoms, all right. Some of them came from Madison County, but they all signed on in Centerville. And you saw that at least one of them can shoot," the lieutenant answered.

"Well, it's bound to be a mixed bag. Hell, here's one who's older than I am, Andrew Dunlap. Forty-four," McBee noted. "I wonder how his knees and feet are going to hold up once we start campaigning again."

"I made a tally, John. There are four old coots in their forties, and seven more between thirty and forty. Fifteen are in their twenties, and ten of them ain't even twenty. And I doubt two of those boys ever even shaved yet," Daniels said.

McBee looked up to say, "Alamo and Napoleon Brashear? They must be brothers. There can't be any two men would name their sons such. And these two Greens are likely a father and son. Damn, I hate that, 'cause you can just bet one or the other is likely to get killed before this is all over. Are any of them jailbirds that the sheriff persuaded to enlist to get rid of them?"

"None that I know of. But Sergeant Moss caught one trying to pinch a new shirt out of another man's blanket roll."

"What'd you do?" McBee asked.

"Moss thumped him good. Left him a swollen black eye so the rest of them would take notice."

"Hmm. Sergeant Hubbard did similar to that boy this afternoon. And he still shot like he was born to it. Be sure the other sergeants know which one's the thief. Drill them hard all morning tomorrow. Then issue the Enfields," the captain directed the lieutenant. "There's no time to waste. We don't know how long we'll be here."

When the Daniels left his tent, McBee started to call for his man-servant, Levi, but caught himself just in time. He had left Levi in Lexington, so the captain picked up his own chamber pot from under his cot and tossed the morning's urine out the back of his tent.

Chapter 2

The McBee Home
Lexington, Virginia
January 2, 1863

The two-story McBee house sat at the end of a side street that narrowed into a trail up a ridge just past the McBee property. Two other homes of prosperous families shared the street. All three houses had carriage houses, which included rooms at the back for the house slaves.

Doctor Barton sat by Elizabeth McBee's bed and stared at the hexagon shaped bullet exactly like the one that the ruffian had fired in the cemetery. Sheriff Cain had collected the unusual bullet from the pocket of the dead man's jacket and passed it along to the doctor, thinking that seeing the projectile might be helpful to his treatment of Mrs. McBee.

Gently unwinding the bandage from her head, the doctor worriedly studied the irregular furrow that snaked across the side of her skull and nipped the skin from the top of her left ear lobe. He dipped a wash cloth in a shallow dish of water and squeezed a trickle onto his patient's lips. Not knowing if she heard him or not, the doctor breathed, "You should be dead, Elizabeth McBee. But here you are, a week later, still sleeping like a baby." He returned the washcloth to the dish and put his hand on Mrs. McBee's bony shoulder and patted it.

While Dr. Barton's hand still touched her shoulder, Mrs. McBee shivered suddenly, and before the doctor could react, she opened her eyes. Without moving her head, she squinted in the afternoon sunlight from the window.

"Too bright," she whispered barely loud enough to be heard.

"Great God in Heaven, you're back," the doctor exclaimed, forgetting his normally austere bedside manner. Grinning like a little boy, he instructed the woman sitting on the other side of the bed, "Mrs. Samuelson, would you please pull the curtains."

Faith Samuelson sat near the window, her chin resting on her chest, softly snoring, with her hands linked under her extended abdomen. She jerked awake at the doctor's voice, and turned to see the older woman's open eyes. Realizing what the doctor had said, she pushed herself out of the chair and pulled the heavy curtain across the window. Then, smiling with relief, she stepped to the bedside where she took Elizabeth's gnarled fingers into her hand. The younger woman noted by touch what she had noticed by sight earlier, that Elizabeth's finger joints were hard and knotty from a half century of hand-sewing and embroidery work.

"Elizabeth, can you hear me?" Dr. Barton asked.

"Water…be lovely," the patient croaked softly.

As Faith held a tiny cup to Elizabeth's chapped lips, Dr. Barton, having regained his normal focus, asked, "Elizabeth, this is important. Do you know where you are?"

Mrs. McBee rolled her eyes around the room again, and said, "Home."

"Good. Do remember what happened to you? Do you know why you are in bed?" the doctor asked.

"Shot."

"That's right, Elizabeth, you were shot. Do you remember where you were when you were shot?"

Elizabeth hesitated before saying slowly, "Cemetery. I was hiding behind little Betsy's tombstone. Is it ruined?"

"No, it has a chip out of it, but Betsy's marker is still upright," Faith answered.

Instead of replying, Elizabeth said, "My head hurts terribly. Am I dying?"

Doctor Barton smiled at the older woman, thinking Mrs. McBee had been a vibrant personality he'd known all his life, "No, Ma'am, you are not dying. The bullet cut a groove in your scalp and nicked the top of your ear. You bled quite a bit, but head wounds do that. You've been asleep for several days while your wound decided whether or not it was going to heal. This young lady has kept it cleaned and bandaged, rather expertly, I might add. The skin is pink and puckering up nicely along the cut. Just what I wanted to see. Now that you're awake, I can give you some powder for the pain."

As soon as she swallowed a bit of water with medicinal powder derived from the sap of willow trees stirred into it, Mrs. McBee fell back to sleep.

Levi and Sally sat eating at the kitchen table when Faith came through the door to announce the news they'd all been hoping for. "Elizabeth woke up. Dr. Barton talked to her before he left. She knows where she is and remembers that she was shot in the cemetery."

"Praise the Lord," Sally said, while her son Levi kept silent but nodded his head vigorously up and down.

"She'll be hungry as a wolf when she wakes up again," Sally said as she stood up. "I'll have some chicken soup ready for her. Maybe some mashed red potatoes, too."

"Thank you, Sally," Faith said.

"No thankin' me, Miz Faith. Miz 'lizabeth would have my hide if I didn't have proper food ready for a sick one," Sally spoke while she poured water from the big wooden bucket into a pot to boil some red potatoes.

"Levi, fetch me a good plump chicken from the coop. Plucked right, mind you. I don't want no feathers a'tall left on that bird," Sally pointedly instructed Levi.

"Sure, Mama," Levi answered. He picked up the large Remington pistol from the table and stuck it into the waist of his trousers, pulling his shirt tail over the exposed pistol grip.

Levi went straight to the wooden chicken coop, pulled out a brown hen, and wrung its neck. He carried the carcass to the big stump that served as a chopping block and work table, where he used a knife to slit the dead bird's throat and drain the blood into a pan.

Levi sat on a stool to gut, pluck and trim the bird with an efficiency that came from his childhood years as his mother's kitchen helper.

He chafed at the discomfort of the pistol barrel poking his leg, but he never considered removing the pistol and setting it on the stump. When he was outside, Levi kept the pistol hidden, even if he was in his own backyard behind a fence. He knew that regardless of the circumstance, a slave caught with a pistol was apt to be hanged without further investigation.

After he took the bird to his mother, Levi returned to the chopping block to split some firewood. He was on his third piece of sawn oak when Sally called his name sharply from the backdoor and waved him in.

"Levi, they's Home Guard men at the front door. You stash that gun in the flour bin right now, and go back to choppin' wood. Hurry now, boy, I gots to open the door." Levi quickly did as his mother directed.

Sally parted the curtain in the front door window, acknowledged the two men with a nod, and pulled the door open.

"Yes, Suhs?" she asked them in subdued voice.

"We'll be coming in," said the man with a lieutenant's bar on the folded down collar of his civilian sack coat, as he stepped past the house servant. Both men held pistols.

"Suh, this ain't proper. The missus is ailin' and ain't receivin' visitors."

"Shut up, woman. We ain't no damned visitors. We're the Home Guard, and we been told things ain't right in this house. Now get out of our way. How many other darkies are here?" the officer asked.

"Suh, ain't no coloreds here but me an' my boy Levi. He's out back splittin' firewood," Sally said with as much dignity as she could muster when facing two men she had heard were harsh with slaves.

"Go see who's in the yard and carriage house, Paul," the lieutenant said to his companion, sending him hurrying through the house to the backyard.

"What about that lame boy? Ain't there a little gimp legged nigger living here?" the surly lieutenant asked.

21

Sally stood tall, and forced her voice not to quiver as she said, "He died nigh on two weeks back."

"Did he? Too bad for the missus, even a gimp boy is worth hard money these days."

As he walked through the three downstairs rooms of the house followed by Sally, he asked, "What's wrong with your missus? Don't she have sons off in the army?"

"Yes, Suh, she do. One a capt'n and the other a sergeant," Sally answered, hoping the mention of McBee's rank as a captain would soften the provost's harsh manner.

"What about the pregnant woman? Folks say there's a pregnant gal living here," the lieutenant asked as he opened the door to look down into the root cellar.

"Suh, she's upstairs sittin' with the missus."

"Why's she here?"

"Don't know, Suh. White folk business," Sarah answered looking at the floor.

"Don't you sass me, girl. Don't you sass me. Now what's ailing the missus?" the lieutenant spat out.

"Her head, Suh. Her head is cut open real bad."

Private Paul returned from the backyard to say, "It's like she said, Lieutenant, just one buck out there splitting oak logs. Nobody's in the carriage barn."

"That so? If there's a pregnant gal here who don't belong, it may just be that her husband run from the army to be with her. I'm goin' upstairs to look around. Paul, you stay here with the darkie," the lieutenant said.

"Sure, I'll keep her company," the private answered. As soon as the lieutenant clumped up the stairs, Paul walked close to Sally and put his pistol barrel under one of her breasts and pushed up, saying nothing, but leering at her.

Levi stood in the open door to the dining room, holding an armload of split oak. He saw the man's weapon touching his mother's chest. Enraged, Levi dropped the wood and stooped to pick up one piece. He looked up towards the parlor as the man slid the weapon down Sally's dress front and pushed the barrel between her legs.

With frozen eyes, Sally looked past the soldier and saw Levi holding the oak limb. She shook her head NO, and the man laughed as he looked at the young Negro staring at him. He reached out with his other hand and pulled up the back of her dress to pat

Sally's bare buttocks. Then he pointed his pistol at Levi. Sally kept hers eyes open, riveted on her son, silently pleading with him until he dropped the piece of firewood.

Lieutenant Blomerth stood in the door to Elizabeth McBee's bedroom and studied the lined face of the bandaged woman in bed. She was sleeping, so he shifted his gaze to the pregnant young woman sitting by the window.

"Where's your husband, Mrs. …uh, what's your last name?" the lieutenant asked, still loosely holding his pistol pointed down at his side. He picked at his teeth with a dirty fingernail while he listened to her answer.

"My husband is at war, where you should be, and my last name is none of your business," Faith Samuelson said, looking him in the eyes.

"Oh, I'm at war all right, and you are saucy. Who's the father of the child in your belly?" he asked, now scratching his rump through his trousers.

"The father is an officer in the Confederate Army, and a man you should fear," she replied. "You would do well to leave this house and never return."

"That so? You're the wife of an officer, huh? Maybe…" he started saying when he heard a loud voice downstairs.

"Dammit all, Blomerth, come down here, and put your man on a leash," Sheriff Cain called, looking up and seeing Blomerth's back in the bedroom doorway. To Private Paul he said, "Take your hands off the darkie, Paul. She ain't yours to paw all over. And holster your Colt. Levi ain't doing nothing but bringing in firewood." The sheriff looked sharply at Levi, who backed quickly into the kitchen.

"What are you doing here, Sheriff?" asked Blomerth as he came down the stairs.

"I'm asking you the same. No call for the Home Guard here. It's just a house filled with women and darkies," Sheriff Cain curtly answered. He kept looking at Paul who had dropped his hand from Sally's buttock, but was still holding his pistol. "Paul, I told you to put your pistol away. Ain't any deserters here for you to shoot. Do it now."

Paul looked towards the sheriff and said, "The buck in there picked up a club to use on me. I may shoot him for that."

The sheriff answered, with anger in his voice, "You do and I'll make sure the judge fines you a thousand dollars to pay Mrs. McBee for her lost property. Then he'll throw you in my jail for a year for not paying, 'cause you ain't seen such money in your whole life. Now holster your gun."

Lieutenant Blomerth gestured for Paul to do as the sheriff ordered. Private Paul stomped out the front door.

"That man's dangerous, Hiram. He's not right in the head," the sheriff said to the provost lieutenant.

"Why do you think the army cut him loose? And who else is still here to back me up? The deserters and bushwackers hiding out in the hills are damned dangerous themselves. I need a dangerous man with me."

"You keep him close while you're in town. Take him to see a whore while he's here, maybe then he'll leave the old ladies' house servants alone. Now, why are you at Elizabeth McBee's house? Her two sons are trustworthy. Hell, one's a sergeant with Jeb Stuart and the other one's a captain from Texas. Ain't neither one a runner."

"Yeah, that's what the nigger said. I heard a woman is here to have a baby. Came to find out who sired her pup. It ain't uncommon for a scared young soldier to walk out of camp in the night to go see a newborn. I'm looking ahead. Makes my job easier."

"All right, you've looked. I know you aren't from around here, that you were sent out here from Richmond to round up deserters. I'm vouching for the McBees. They've been in this valley for nearly a hundred years. Let'em be," the sheriff warned.

"What about that young gal? You never said which McBee is her husband."

The sheriff sighed and said, "Neither one. It's complicated, but it doesn't concern the Home Guard."

Home Guard Lieutenant Blomerth raised one eyebrow as he said, "Then who's the daddy? He a soldier? He might concern me."

"He's another officer. Like I said, it's no concern of yours. The Yankees have taken over the county where she's from. She's here to have a safe place to have her baby, a place where her husband, who is a Confederate officer, can come see his new child. That's all it is."

"Hell, Sheriff, if that's all it is, that ain't complicated. You holding out on me?"

"I said I vouch for the McBees. Now get out so I can go upstairs to pay my respects to Mrs. McBee."

"You never said what that gal's last name is."

"I don't know her last name. I'll ask and let you know later on. Now leave."

"Sure thing, Sheriff."

Levi stood by the corner of the house behind a tall shrub and watched the two men ride away. He was beside himself with fury at the white man who had used his pistol to molest his mother while he watched. After the men were gone, Levi remained hidden with his hand wrapped around the handle of the big Remington revolver that Captain McBee had given him. He knew that the captain had given him the pistol only to protect Mrs. McBee and Mrs. Samuelson from the pregnant woman's own husband or his thugs, but Levi now intended the weapon as a means to avenge his mother.

Chapter 3

Winter Camp of the Texas Brigade
On the Rappahannock River, Virginia
Late January, 1863

The veterans hadn't expected the thirty-six new recruits. The old hands were glad to see their number of riflemen more than double, yet they did not personally embrace the fresh fish. Sergeant Stephens quickly saw that the survivors didn't want the yoke of friendship with the replacements. When he had forced the new men into the veterans' cooking messes, no one challenged him, but little campfire talk took place. Stephens had expected the new men to be pestered with questions about things at home back in Leon County, but even gregarious men like Cal Gilbert held back, waiting to see the mettle of the men who had joined them in the ranks.

Lieutenant Daniel's man-servant George successfully carried out Sergeant Stephens' order to collect pots and frying pans, allowing the first sergeant to regroup the new men into their own messes. Brothers Zebulon and Edward Bell were paired with Polaski Phillips, already labelled a thief, and marksman Asbury Lawson. Wiley and Samuel Green, who turned out to be uncle and nephew, shared cooking duties with brothers Alamo and Napoleon Brashears.

Asbury Lawson knelt by the fire, poking at a chunk of gristle-laced beef that sizzled in a fry pan of nearly rancid bacon grease. Lawson decided after only two days of drill that the army was not what he expected, and he wasn't too sure how long he would stick around. Even though he had quickly spent his bounty money back in Texas, leaving him broke again, and he was in Virginia, with no idea how he would get home, Lawson wasn't worried. He had never lacked self-confidence and he fully expected that both funds and opportunity would come his way soon enough. He thought when the time came, he might go somewhere besides Texas, maybe further west, or even north.

The Bell brothers lay on their blankets under the stretched canvas tent fly, waiting for Lawson to finish cooking their supper. Zeb Bell wanted to do all the cooking for the foursome with his brother helping him, but Ed Bell held him back, insisting the other two men take a turn. Ed had quickly seen that their assigned mess partners were lazy men who had no cooking skills and no interest in cleaning pots. He figured if Zeb and he volunteered to cook all the meals, they would also wind up gathering firewood and filling canteens for all four of them. Ed Bell thought if Phillips and Lawson each took just one turn cooking and ruined their already scant daily rations, that they would willingly let the Bells cook, and would themselves accept the chores of washing up afterwards and refilling canteens.

While the Bells watched Lawson keep the frying pan over the hottest part of the fire until the slab of beef turned into a crisp board, Phillips wandered through the camp on his way back from the sinks. He nodded to other recruits and noted which men left their gear unwatched.

Back at their fire, Phillips held his hunk of charred beef in both hands as he gnawed a small piece loose. He half-chewed it and choked down the stringy gob only by taking a long draw from his canteen. "That was the sorriest bite of meat I ever put in my mouth, an' I ain't particular 'bout my meals," he said as he flipped the rest of his beef portion into the fire.

Lawson narrowed his eyes at the older man, but said nothing because he'd only eaten two bites of his own portion before giving up. The fried cornbread mush was even worse.

Zeb Bell managed to swallow whole all five bites of his piece before he accepted his brother's offer of his burned beef. He spent the evening working it like a piece of hardtack, patiently softening a small bit with his saliva before he tried to chew it. Zeb Bell had a large frame and a belly that had always pooched out, even during the lean times on their parents' hardscrabble homestead on the Trinity River. Being hungry was a way of life for him, and he welcomed anyone's left-overs, burned or not.

The next afternoon, neither Lawson nor Phillips objected when Zeb Bell cooked their new rations of beans and salt pork over the fire Ed Bell built.

"Asbury, you might want to get down to the creek for the washing water before all the coals turn to ash," Ed suggested in a friendly tone once the four of them had finished eating.

"Nah, I reckon not. You do it, or just turn the pot upside down over the coals. That's all the cleanin' it needs," Lawson answered without moving from his half-lying down position.

"Yup, your brother makes a fine cook, and you can take care of the pot as you see fit. I done told you last night, I ain't particular," added Phillips. "And if you do go down to the creek, my canteen's about empty. Take it with you."

Ed Bell stood up, nudged his brother Zeb to get up, and pointed at the firewood on the ground near the fire pit. Zeb Bell stooped over and pulled two wrist-thick limbs off the pile and handed one to Ed, who said to Lawson and Phillips, "I thought it would come to this, just not so soon."

Seeing their two messmates were now listening, Zeb Bell took over from his brother, "After you eat my cooking, one of you turds will wash the pot with hot water, ever time, and fetch the washing water, and the other piece of crap will fill all our canteens. Ed will see to the fire. That's the way it's going to be. Lawson, you take the pot down the creek, and Phillips, you take all four canteens. Me and Ed can either start whopping you two with these sticks or put'em on the fire to heat the wash water. How you boys going to have it?"

Zebulon Bell's size was noteworthy, yet the pair's willingness to brawl surprised Lawson and Phillips. After a brief hesitation to decide if the portly boy was bluffing, Phillips reached for his belt knife, while Lawson looked for a palm-sized rock.

From his own campfire, Third Sergeant Moss saw the two brothers brandishing firewood clubs, but the sergeant was too far away to hear what Zebulon Bell said. Moss muttered to himself, "Dammit, I shoulda seen this one coming." He then loudly called for Corporal Hodges.

The two NCO's reached the imminent fight barely in time for Moss to bellow, "No weapons! Drop it all, boys. If you gotta work out a disagreement, it's bare fists only."

Asbury Lawson let go of his rock and was snake quick moving towards little Ed Bell, who was standing straight up and took two clumsy steps backwards, his arms bent at the elbows, palms out, his eyes wide, all indications that the slender man was scared now that he didn't have a weapon.

Phillips had no choice but to square off with Zeb Bell, whose height and girth exceeded his own. Polaski Phillips had been in fights, but he preferred to egg others on from the side. He didn't want to take on Zeb Bell alone, so he moved more slowly towards the large Bell brother, waiting for Lawson to quickly dispatch the smaller Bell and then assist him.

As Lawson reached Ed Bell and drew back a fist to smash into his face, Bell kicked out with his right leg, driving his foot straight up into his opponent's groin. Lawson doubled over in pain, as Bell clasped his fists together and delivered a hard blow down across his exposed shoulders and neck. Lawson collapsed, groaning.

Phillips watched Lawson surge forward, only to see him get beaten down without landing a blow. He froze, staring at Lawson who was crumpled on the ground. While Phillips was distracted, Zeb Bell simply reached out and jerked him forward, wrapping his arms around the man's chest and squeezing. After ten or fifteen seconds, Phillips head leaned to one side and his eyes rolled up. Ed looked over and said, "He's out." Zebulon Bell released Phillips who fell limply, breathing hoarsely.

Moss stood still with his hands on his hips and quietly wondered, "Why was I worried about you two?" Looking at Ed Bell he asked, "Where'd you learn that scared mouse act? It sure worked."

Bell shrugged, and said to the sergeant, "I'm not a big man, and this ain't the first time. Do we have to stay in a cooking mess with these two?"

Moss shrugged before he answered. "Don't know who else would take them, especially now. Besides, I think you Bell brothers done persuaded these two to get along with you."

Moss picked up a canteen and poured a stream of water onto Polaski Phillips' head. When the man stirred and sat up, Moss dropped the empty canteen into his lap. Moss then stepped over to Asbury Lawson and pulled him up.

"Phillips, you and Lawson listen. I don't know or care who said what to set off this little fracas, but it's done and over now. You're in my platoon, and you'll damn well do what I tell you until this war's over or you get killed. Just now you both got whipped in a fair fight. If you try to even the score, I'll find out, and you won't like what'll happen to you next. You got that? Nod if you understand."

Phillips and Lawson both nodded.

* * *

Alamo Brashears and his younger brother Napoleon stopped eating to watch the fight. "Kicking like that ain't fair fighting," Alamo said before he shoveled another spoon of white beans into his mouth. Alamo was lean, with straight sandy hair, worn short and badly cut.

Napoleon, whose cheeks and nose were spotted with freckles under his curly red hair, replied, "Aw, Al, look at him, he's a skinny little guy. His butt's the only thing on him with any meat. What you want him to do, stand there and get pummeled senseless? I say hoorah for a little man what can use his feet to bring down somebody about to bash him. Glad it weren't my nuts, though."

Samuel Green, a balding man who considered himself a student of human nature, poured canteen water into the cook pot. He intended to let the burned beans stuck to the bottom soak for a few minutes before he scraped them loose with his knife blade and then wiped the insides of the pot with straw.

"I'd say watch out for Phillips and that Lawson boy. Lawson showed us he can shoot, but he ain't worth spit otherwise. Same for Phillips." The other three men in the mess knew it was Sam Green's shirt that Phillips had been caught trying to snitch out of Green's bedroll on the train coming to Virginia.

"Uncle Sam, why you sayin' that about Asbury? He seems a good feller to me," young Wiley Green asked.

"Wiley, you'd do well to keep your distance from Asbury Lawson. He's the sort won't ever be anywhere close when you need a pard. You stick with your kin and the Brashears here."

"He's right next to me the whole time we're drilling," Wiley protested. "I still don't see what makes you think that."

"You'll learn soon enough. For now, you just remember your uncle's warning."

* * *

For a week the sergeants and corporals in Company C drilled the new recruits as a separate platoon. The first day or two the old hands watched, enjoying the entertainment of their NCO's yelling, and making bets as to which recruits would be formed into an *awkward squad* targeted for additional drill sessions.

Starting the second week in the Confederate camps along the Rappahannock River, each regiment in the Texas Brigade began a morning routine of company drill for an hour, followed by regimental drill for two more hours. Twice a week the routine expanded to include brigade drill when all four regiments maneuvered together. Afternoons were generally left to the men to gather firewood, cook, rest, and tend to their equipment. An evening parade ended each day, a time when the brigade officers made a cursory inspection of each regiment and the orders for the next day were read aloud by the brigade adjutant.

At a parade in early February the adjutant read the order that the brigade would form at noon the next day to witness the punishment of a private who had been absent without permission for several weeks. He was to receive thirty-nine lashes administered to his bare back, one stroke per day of his absence.

The buzz started among the men immediately after the order was read. As soon as the regiments were back in their camps, nearly every man bent his sergeant's ear about the harshness of the punishment awaiting the private, who had, after all, returned on his own. Most of the sergeants agreed with their men and passed along to their officers news of a growing anger in the ranks about the thirty-nine lashes. Many of the company commanders shared that information with their colonels, along with their own disagreement with the severity of the scheduled punishment. No one knew just when the tipping point of discontent was reached that evening, but no parade was formed at noon the next day, and nothing more was officially said about punishing the private for his extended absence by applying thirty-nine lashes.

Chapter 4

The McBee Home
Lexington, Virginia
February 4, 1863

The crown of the first baby's head appeared near midnight. The midwife gently pulled as soon as she could see enough of the skull cap to grasp it, while Sally pressed down on Faith's abdomen and exhorted her to push. The midwife worked the shoulders one at a time through the portal from womb to world, until without warning, the dark-haired boy-infant almost leapt into the midwife's waiting hands. The sudden completion of his birth was caused in part by his fair-haired sister who was right behind, apparently eager to join her twin brother. Sally had to scramble around the mother's leg to catch the girl-infant.

Faith yelled at the pain of her son's birth, her screams turning to sobbing groans when her slightly larger daughter followed. Faith's forehead and cheeks were mottled with red spots, her hair lank and wet, her face glowing with sweat from her birthing exertions. The midwife wiped both babies clean and cut their umbilical cords before placing them at their mother's breasts. Both immediately began to suckle.

Levi paced in the hallway and cringed at Faith Samuelson's screams of pain. When he heard a baby cry, he couldn't hold back any longer and called, "Mama, did the capt'n get a boy?"

Sally called back, "Glory be, yes he did, Levi. A strong boy chile is on Miz Faith's right side, an' a straw-haired girl chile is on her left. Glory be!"

Elizabeth McBee stood to the side, the scar from the gunshot wound above her ear still pink, eyes sparkling at the sight of her new twin grandchildren. She reflected that these two were the first children to be born in the McBee home in Lexington, since all three of her sons and little Betsy had been born at the farmhouse she sold after her husband died years ago.

* * *

The next day, Elizabeth came into Faith's room, this time with a purposeful walk. She had already placed an inkwell, a sharpened quill, and a large Bible on the table by the window. The two infants were feeding in Faith's arms, eyes trying to focus and tiny fingers reaching to touch the adoring face that sang softly to them.

After taking her seat, Elizabeth opened the Bible to the page on which five generations of McBee family marriages, births, and deaths were recorded. She watched her new grandchildren for a moment, before saying gently to Faith, "I never thought I would have reason to fill in the page under John's name."

Faith looked at her and nodded without words.

Putting on her reading glasses before picking up the quill and dipping it in the inkwell, Elizabeth asked, "Now, dear Faith, what is your maiden name, your name before your first marriage to Lieutenant Samuelson? The brute who killed a child in my home, who abused and abandoned his wife, and tried to murder my son. I will not sully our family tree with the name of such an evil man. Besides, Samuelson sounds Jewish. So, what is your parents' last name?"

"Cohen," Faith said as she looked sidelong at Elizabeth and tried to suppress a sly grin.

"Cohen? Isn't that a Je…"

"Yes, Elizabeth, I'm from a Jewish family, as was Adam. Our parents were members of the same synagogue in Richmond. That's where I met Adam."

Somewhat stiffly, Elizabeth said, "Well, you seem comfortable enough in Reverend Brown's Presbyterian Church."

"Put your mind at ease, Elizabeth. I'll cheerfully follow the religion of my husband, John. I've not been a very good Jew," Faith said. "I've long admired the story of Jesus and Mary Magdaline, and have no qualms about attending Reverend Brown's church."

"Oh, Faith, I'm so glad. You won't be sorry," she said as she began to write under John's name, *Married to Faith C-o-l-l-i-n-s.*

"Now dear, there is the delicate matter of your wedding date. There must be a date. There can't be a McBee marriage without a wedding date. May I sugge…"

"May the Eighth, 1862," Faith said, interrupting Elizabeth, but not taking her eyes from her children.

Elizabeth looked up sharply, and was about to speak, but closed her mouth and wrote the date.

"Elizabeth, May the eighth was the night I met your son, the night I mended his bloody feet, the night God sent me to John to…to create these two beautiful children. John's children, his children of our marriage. Even if we hadn't said vows, and even if I was still living under Adam's spell."

"Faith, you can't exchange the Christian vows of marriage with John while Lieutenant Samuelson, evil or not, is still alive."

"I know that, Elizabeth. I think about it all the time. May the Lord forgive me, but I often wish Adam would get killed in the war. But, I doubt that will happen as long as he works in Richmond."

"And what are my grandchildren's names? Have you decided?" Elizabeth pressed on, eager to move away from such an unchristian thought, especially since she shared Faith's spoken death wish for Adam Samuelson.

"Your granddaughter is Betsy Miriam. Your grandson is John Jacob McBee."

"Oh, Faith," Elizabeth rejoiced, through instant tears, "Oh Faith, you needn't."

"My mother is named Miriam, and she will be pleased; and I don't know how better to thank you, than to remember little Betsy."

Elizabeth reached out and squeezed Faith's shoulder, "Sally will be honored, too. Jacob's death is very hard on her."

Mrs. McBee wrote the names in the Bible, closed it, and said, "Another thing, Faith. You need to hire or buy a wet nurse very soon. Those two hungry mouths will keep you drained and sore. Betsy and John Junior will grow fast and need two more nipples to keep them full. I'm afraid Sally is past her prime, and I keep her busy in the house, even if she is able to provide milk. My other two women are rented out to the hotel and too old."

Elizabeth continued on a different line of thought, "I can ask around and find out if there's a white woman, maybe some soldier's young wife or widow, who's about to wean her own. But a hired wet nurse wouldn't be dependable. She'd have to come and go from her own home, and take care of her own children, usually when she's needed here."

"No, I think it's time for me to contact the auction house and find out what's available. I know Johnny's been successful in his business in Texas, since he offered to pay me for Levi's use. Even if this confounded war is driving up the price of everything, including healthy Negroes, I'm sure he can afford to buy you a wet nurse. And she can live here with Sally. She can share Levi's bed, and Johnny can get back his investment through a young one."

Faith listened with growing indignation and dismay until she sternly said, "Elizabeth, you told me that day in the cemetery that slavery is *complicated*. Going to an auction house to buy a young African woman to suckle my children and to breed with Levi is not complicated. It's barbaric. I won't do it. I will not be party to dealing in human cargo."

Nonplussed, Elizabeth tried a new tack by saying, "But, dear, what about your lovely bosoms? The children will destroy them. One child at a time puts a strain on them, but at least the baby can switch and give one a rest, but two at the same time…"

"We will buy a milk cow. Levi can build another stall in the carriage house," Faith said with conviction.

"But the babies are too little to drink from a glass. They need a nipple," Elizabeth countered.

"I know that," Faith said, wincing as Betsy gummed too vigorously. "I've seen advertisements in the Richmond newspaper and *Harpers* magazine for glass bottles with soft leather or India rubber tops designed especially for infant feeding."

"But, Faith, we're in Lexington, and there is a war going on. We can't send for anything from New York, and the blockade is shutting off everything that used to come into Richmond."

"Elizabeth, we will use towels dipped in the milk if we must, but my children will not feed from the breast of a woman in bondage, so help me God. These two can drain me dry every day until my bosoms are stretched and prodded until they are unrecognizable... and John no longer likes them," she added with a sob, "but I will not buy a slave. Never."

In a low, breaking voice, Faith hissed, *"Find a damned milk cow!"*

Chapter 5

Winter Camp of the Fifth Texas Infantry Regiment
On the Rappahannock River, Virginia
February 20, 1863

After spending nearly two months in winter camp training their new recruits, while the army commanders waited for spring weather, General's Hood's Division received orders to march to the southern border of Virginia.

Captain McBee stood in a semi-circle with the other nine company commanders, listening to the lieutenant colonel. Most of the officers wore heavy wool great coats, some civilian, some military. The civilian coats were an array of styles and muted colors. The military coats were both Confederate gray and Union blue, the latter mostly stripped from the dead at Fredericksburg the previous December.

A few minutes later, after the captains had been dismissed by the colonel, McBee gathered his lieutenants and sergeants around the campfire in front of his tent. Lieutenant Daniels' man-servant George listened from the shadows, just beyond the firelight.

McBee summarized to the lieutenants and sergeants, "That's it then. We draw three days rations from the commissary wagons, strike the tents, and start the march at dawn. The darkies will bring the wagons along behind like always. We're headed southeast of

Richmond, back near where we fought last summer. There's a whole passel of Yanks around Suffolk making folks nervous."

* * *

"Dammit, Lawson, ain't you ever folded a tent in your whole life? Ain't you ever folded anything in your whole life? Do you even know what the word *square* means?" Corporal Hodges berated Ambrose Lawson. "You gotta lay out the tent on its side, square-like, before you start folding in the flaps."

The new private kept silent, but made no particular effort to find the crease where the ridge of the tent had been, to pull the jumbled heap into a two-layered square. He just grabbed handfuls of canvas and shoved them towards the middle of the wet pile that the tent had become. He was partly stooped over, reaching for a new handful of canvas, when he toppled onto the tent, shoved in the rump by a muddy shoe.

"Lawson, you are a slow, slow learner, boy. I thought I got your attention the first day you mouthed off to the captain," Second Sergeant Hubbard said. "Now get up and stretch that canvas into a square with sharp edges. Then you fold in the sides. You don't get it into a flat square, I'll have you carryin' it all the way to Richmond."

Private Lawson got up and slowly started looking for a corner of the tent to start a square. While he worked, he mentally put Hubbard on the top of his list of men he would even the score with right before he took off one night.

Hodges glared at the sergeant for interfering, at the same time realizing that the daylight was fading fast, and Lawson had been dogging it since they started. *All right, Sarge, lesson learned. Sometimes the boot works better than words. Just don't do it again,* he thought but didn't say. Instead, Hodges bellowed at Private Phillips, who was loitering near the wagon, "Get over here, Phillips. Grab these tent poles and take them to the wagon. Now!"

Zeb Bell kept two frying pans full of fatty bacon sizzling while the others struck the tents. Watching the bacon with one eye, Zeb used a flat rock as a table to roll cornmeal dough into balls that he meant to fry in the bacon grease. He was cooking the rations for all four men, for three days, although to him, it looked like enough for two small men for two days, at most.

Meanwhile, Ed Bell tugged at the leather straps on top of Zeb's knapsack, trying to cinch the buckles tight enough that the blanket roll would stay in place. Ed finished getting his and Zeb's gear ready, then headed to the creek to fill the canteens. He took all four of them, since Lawson and Phillips were under the watch of the NCO's, learning to fold heavy wet canvas tents into compact squares that could be stored in the company wagon.

* * *

The drum roll beckoned the fifty-six riflemen of Company C into formation an hour before dawn. Men groggy with sleep clumsily rolled their damp blankets and tied them into horseshoe collars to drape over one shoulder, or strapped them to their knapsacks. Some, including the Bell brothers, had slept without their blankets, so they could simply put on their packs and not fumble around in the dark while the sergeants and corporals pestered them to hurry up.

Zeb Bell leaned on his musket, watching Lawson and Phillips struggle with their gear. Zeb gnawed a piece of near-frozen raw bacon, and suddenly shivered from the cold. He wondered if trying to sleep several hours without cover had been a good trade-off for not having to roll and tie his blanket with numb fingers in the dark. Either way, he knew they all would be warming up on the march soon enough. He also noticed a few snowflakes begin to fall, landing wetly on his hands.

Captain McBee brooded over the fact that a dozen of his surviving veterans were missing from the roll call. He wanted those men back, but couldn't protest them being put on other duties. Having a number of healthy men detached from the company to serve as guards, hospital stewards and commissary helpers was a fact of life that all company commanders had to accept.

Then McBee remembered the letter he'd received just the day before. He put his hand to his chest and patted his great coat over the pocket where he'd put the carefully folded letter. The letter made him smile in satisfaction and joy one minute, and frown in worry the next. He also rubbed his bullet wound near one shoulder. Even six months later, his shoulder still ached, especially when a morning was this cold.

"I swear, I'm gonna ditch this knapsack. These damned straps are cutting plumb through my shoulders," Ambrose Lawson said.

"Me too. Look around. How many of them old fellers do you see carrying 'em? Not too damn many, that's what I see," added Polaski Phillips. "I'm with you. This is my last day to be a damned pack mule. Hodges, why you still have yours anyway?"

Corporal Hodges, who'd kept his knapsack for over a year of campaigning, and was marching next to Phillips, replied, "Because I need what's in it. Even got a spare shirt. Before you get rid of your packs, you best consider how you gonna tote what's in 'em. Or be ready to live without."

"Huh, live without what? Anything I need I can stuff in a blanket roll or my pockets," Lawson answered.

* * *

Snow fell all morning and covered the fields bordering the road. The only breaks in the sea of white to either side of the column were the bottoms of the wooden fence rails that lined the road. The four thousand pairs of feet of the soldiers in Hood's Division turned the road bed to icy slush. The sun stayed hidden behind the gray clouds, and the snow kept falling into the afternoon.

Captain McBee's blistered feet were healed and he wore two pairs of socks inside his old boots, but he still couldn't say he actually felt his toes. McBee carried his sheathed sword on his left shoulder to keep it off his healing right shoulder as he walked in his place on the edge of the road.

Private Fulton marched next to McBee, his musket slung upside down on one shoulder to keep snow out of the open end of the barrel. McBee broke a long silence with the news he was eager to tell someone.

"Rafe, I'm a father. Letter came just a day ago. Twins, by God. Twins. A boy and a girl."

Fulton shook his head in feigned disbelief. "Ain't you a little long in the tooth to be startin' a family, John? Captain John. Father John. Hee, hee. I like that, *Father John.* Here we are on a freezin', muddy road to hell, led by Father John McBee. Did you pray over us 'fore we started marchin'?"

"I prayed that you would stay with the company this time and not fall out straggling. I suspect I'm going to need you before long to help keep the new boys moving in this damned snowstorm. About the letter and the twins, just keep all that to yourself. And your teeth are long as mine, Private Fulton. So don't be getting saucy with me. It's still *Captain* McBee to you and everybody else. Until we clear Virginia from the Union scourge, I reckon fatherhood will have to wait," McBee said, and thought wistfully to himself, *Faith will have to wait.*

"Damn, John, to be so old, you are one sad smitten sonofabitch. Sometimes you talk like a fifteen year old pinin' over the memory of that first titty he grabbed a'holt of the night before."

McBee smiled with one side of his mouth and answered, "I'm not that bad, but like I said, Rafe, just keep all this between you and me," the captain reminded his old friend, before he muttered one more time, "Twins, by God."

Rafe Fulton nodded and kept marching without saying anything else. But he was worried about his old friend, his captain. He knew that McBee's fatherhood only complicated a situation that was already dangerous and mixed up enough. Fulton wondered where the lady's legal husband was these days. He wondered if perhaps the man was a war casualty, but prudently decided not to ask.

Zeb Bell was shivering uncontrollably as he walked. He considered unpacking his wool blanket at the next rest and draping it over his shoulders for another layer of protection from the snow. Yet, he knew Ed would fuss at him for getting his only cover wet, and he didn't know if the blanket would even fit over his knapsack. But he sure wished the shivering would stop. It was bad enough that the hours of marching had made him sweat through his shirt. Now the snow had penetrated his wool jacket, letting the wet snow from the sky meet the wet sweat from within, resulting in a growing, numbing cold across his shoulders, chest, and back.

Since the company formed by height, tallest to shortest, and he was one of the shorter men, Ed Bell was near the back of the company column, and he too was suffering in the wet freezing weather. Neither Bell brother was aware of the other's condition, but both were thinking back to Ed's insistence that they keep their blankets rolled on their knapsacks the night before. What seemed last night a clever way to be among the first men ready to march this morning, seemed foolish now. They had started the march cold, damp, and shivering instead of reasonably warm and dry. Worse, the expected warmth coming with the exertion of marching had eluded them both.

* * *

General Hood hated to slow or stop a march early because of bad weather or bad roads or bad Yankees. He also considered straggling to be one of the most preventable problems of the army. He firmly believed tired men could maintain the prescribed marching pace even when they thought they were played out. Therefore, he was strict in his discipline to keep his troops from leaving the column when they began to lag back.

As he rode back along the column in the early afternoon, even Hood had to acknowledge that the weather was winning this day. His column had already lost hundreds of men during the first morning, a time when he expected no stragglers, everyone having started fresh just a few hours before. Yet, the general was dismayed to pass men alone and in pairs, and even in small groups, sitting under trees near the road, waiting to gather the strength to rise and walk a bit farther before they stopped once more. A few men had their shoes and socks off, massaging feet turning blue from the cold, trying to work the circulation back into their toes before they turned black from frostbite.

By two o'clock Hood ordered the column to stop and bivouac for the night. Corporals badgered the men to gather firewood. Sergeants set their best woodsmen to work with tinder boxes, striking chips of flint against steel, showering sparks onto wads of lint, charred cloth, or dry wood shavings. Here and there men successfully coaxed flames from the tinder and fed their tiny fires bigger and bigger twigs and sticks until the snow-soaked wood finally caught fire. Flaming sticks were carried to frustrated men who lacked the skills or luck to start their own fires.

Within an hour the woods on both sides of the road were dotted with circles of men huddled closely around fires that sputtered and crackled. It seemed that the gray sky was sucking up the heat along with the smoke as shivering men inched closer and closer, seeking from the orange flames the warmth they desperately needed.

Just inches from the glowing coals, Ed and Zeb Bell held their place by Zeb standing with his legs spread far enough apart for Ed to squeeze in between them. Both had their wool blankets draped over their heads and shoulders, stiff, gloveless hands holding the edges of the blankets closed across their chests.

Ed kept his crossed legs over the top of Zeb's shoes, and wiggled his own toes as much as he could. For all that, both men were trembling in the cold, with no intention of leaving the fire to sleep. Yet, by dusk their fire was going out and the pair lay down, now somewhat warm, each wrapped in his blanket, heads on cartridge boxes for pillows, and feet still in their shoes, stuck under their nearly empty knapsacks.

A few yards away, Napoleon and Alamo Brashears, who were experienced winter campers, were spooning with their heads nestled on a knapsack, still dangerously close to the coals of their fire. They had one brother's blanket under them and the other's blanket over them. Both had pulled their hats down to their ears, and Alamo's arm was draped over Napoleon, pulling him close. The second knapsack was under their feet, and against commonly held logic, they had taken off their wet shoes, and each wore instead a treasured second pair of wool socks, topped by their wet socks. They had tucked their wet shoes up against their stomachs, hoping their body heat would dry them by morning.

Ambrose Lawson and Polaski Phillips slept half-wrapped around a fire. When Phillips rolled over in his restless sleep, he shoved the corner of his blanket into the hot ashes. The wool cloth smoldered during the night, but was too wet to spread.

Captain McBee and First Lieutenant Daniels slept across the fire from each other, Second Lieutenant Anderson and First Sergeant Stephens completing the square of blanket-covered men, who were no warmer and slept no better than the men they commanded.

When the division was rousted out at dawn the next morning, every blanket was covered in snow. There was no wood, wet or dry, left to rekindle fires, so the troops stumbled, cold and stiff, into formation and began the march without strength-restoring food or feet-warming fires. By eight o'clock the snow was turning to sleet as the temperature barely rose above the freezing point.

The second day's march in the sleet and half-frozen mud was worse than the day before in the snow. By noon, not hundreds, but thousands of men straggled behind their companies, the column barely half its original length. Around four in the afternoon the head of the column reached the railway station at Hanover Junction, ten miles north of the intended campsite on the other side of Richmond.

* * *

Captain McBee and Colonel Powell, the commander of the Fifth Texas Regiment, stood on the warped boards of the loading platform next to the train track. They watched a long line of sick and limping soldiers slowly climbing up into the passenger and box cars of a six-car train.

"Colonel, with no disrespect intended, are you sure you got that order right?" Captain McBee asked in disbelief.

"Yes, John, that's straight from General Hood's own mouth. The weather ain't breaking, and nearly a third of the division is straggling. The general has appropriated that train right there to haul the worst cases to Richmond. Meanwhile, you, Sir, are to command the thousand or so stragglers who can't keep up, but won't fit on the train. You are allotted three days to get them all, all of them, John, no one left behind, to the capitol city.

"Colonel," McBee protested, "I'm a captain, a company commander. I've never even commanded one wing of our regiment, much less a brigade-sized group. Why me? Why doesn't General Hood assign one of his staff officers who's accustomed to large commands?"

"John, did you see me climb out of General Hood's head? Hell, I don't know why he wants you to lead the stragglers. They ain't but a bunch of lame, shirking, and sick men. Likely half of them are the new recruits that ain't ever been on a campaign march before." Colonel Powell saw the look of dismay had not left McBee's face. His thin mouth and flashing eyes told the colonel that the captain was still angry and confused over the assignment.

"Look, John, it's General Hood's business to know about his officers, even captains. He knows you're older than danged near all the other walking officers. He knows you got wounded bad back at Manassas last summer. Maybe he's trying to do you a favor. Keep you healthy enough to lead your company in the next battle."

"Yes, Sir," McBee said as he straightened his posture. His confusion was washed away with the thought that Hood had singled him out for his age, General Hood himself being barely over thirty, ten years younger than McBee.

"If the commanding general believes I'm only fit to lead a column of broken-down shirkers, then, by God, I will march those sad sonsofbitches to Richmond, and it won't take any three damn days. It's only ten miles."

Chapter 6

Hanover Junction
Ten Miles North of Richmond
February 23, 1863

Private Jason Smith looked at his captain with disbelief. "You want me to take this note and report to George? Lieutenant Daniels' George? *Nigger* George?"

"That's right, Private. I didn't think I was unclear. But I'll say it again. You get on this mule, sorry there's no saddle, and report to Daniels' man-servant George. You give him the note and do what you must to make sure he promptly, I mean immediately, follows the orders in the note. You help him with the manual labor if you must. If you have to, cuff him to speed him up. You clear the road by threat of using your Enfield or bayonet if that's what it takes. Do you understand?"

"Can I read the note?" Smith asked. "Sir?"

"Certainly. It simply says for George and the other servants to empty our two company wagons of all cargo and bring the wagons here by dawn. You will be the one responsible to make that happen. George is old and can be cranky sometimes. This is not the time when his contrariness will be tolerated. Do you understand?"

"Yes, Sir. But what about the supplies in the wagons? That's all your personal belongings. And the men's tents and most of our cooking pots."

"You make sure George leaves one darkie to stay with the gear. I'll do all I can to see it reaches us. Regardless, I'll be looking for you and George before dawn. Now go. And don't spare the mule."

* * *

Rafe Fulton didn't like responsibilities, especially those that required him to assert himself to other soldiers. The fact that Fulton was tall and possessed a natural military bearing didn't matter. He was still reluctant to tell any other man to *hurry up*, to *keep going*, to not falter on the march.

His first reply to Captain McBee's "request" had been blasphemous, bearing no regard for his old friend's rank of captain and position as commanding officer of their company. Rather than rage back at Fulton, McBee had simply ignored the profane refusal and thanked him for taking on such an onerous chore, a chore that went far beyond his normal duties as a private. The captain assured Fulton that there was no one else he trusted more for such a crucial task, not his sergeants or corporals, and certainly not his young lieutenants.

McBee concluded by telling Fulton, "Rafe, it'll be no different than herding beeves down a road back home. Some you'll be able to move along with a soft touch or a soothing word. Some will take a prod with a sharpened stick, and some you may have to jerk their tails to straighten them out. And you got the good sense to know when to do which. Stephens, Moss, and Hubbard are good men, but they're too full of bluster for this one. And Daniels, well, he still looks like he's sixteen. You know that strung-out men from other regiments who don't know him wouldn't pay him any mind. He'd wind up pulling his pistol and shooting one of them. Can't have that."

Fulton gave in, knowing when McBee reverted to praise, he really was in need. Nonetheless, for the sake of appearance, and some practicality, Fulton replied, "All right, Father John, on one condition. I need a greatcoat before we start tomorrow morning. That train is full of men who are gonna spend the day sittin' on a warm bench ridin' the rails. Get me one of their greatcoats, so those *beeves* I'll be herdin' to Suffolk tomorrow won't see I got no stripes on my jacket. They'll *gee and haw* better if they think I'm a mean ole sergeant."

"Done. Thanks, Rafe. There'll be corporal stripes for you after this if we make it to Suffolk by dark."

"Keep the corporal stripes for some feller who wants to work ever' day. That ain't me. This is for you, Father John, a gift on account of them new twins you're so proud of. A one-time only gift. Don't do this to me again, or I'll lite out for home next full moon."

Fulton said the last bit to McBee's back, as the captain had already turned and moved on to find his NCO's to give them their instructions for tomorrow's march. They would provide the flankers for the column, keeping tired and hurting men from drifting into the woods to hide or sleep. McBee knew his NCO's would do well berating those men and even man-handling them back into the column, relying on their rank if nothing else worked. McBee also knew a string of men would drift further and further back until they seemed to simply fade away behind the end of the column. That's why he had gone to Fulton. McBee had not forgotten the morning he had watched his old neighbor soft-talk a sober teamster into buying a lame mule. He just had the way to make men ashamed to not do what he suggested. If Fulton couldn't keep those rearward drifters from fading away behind the column, no one could, not even a squad of heavy-handed provosts.

McBee's ace, about which he'd told no one, not even Fulton yet, were the company's two supply wagons, emptied of all their cargo. Those empty wagons would give Fulton the leverage he'd need by the afternoon when the pleas of the most crippled men became too clearly credible for even Fulton to ignore. McBee knew Fulton to be a good poker player, and he'd get the last mile out of any man, even those who he would finally let finish the trek in the back of a wagon.

"Absalom, our command tomorrow is going to include men from a dozen regiments and a hundred and twenty companies. Danged few of the men will recognize you, so keep your temper in check. Don't go off all wild-eyed if some tough old bird ignores you. Your duty will be to keep our NCO's doing their jobs on the flanks, especially late in the day, when men will want to give up. You're going to use those young legs of yours moving up and down the column checking on our flankers. But you remember you're an officer. Remember our sergeants are the guard dogs, not you. You're the guard dogs' handler."

"Yes, Sir. I'm on board. Where will you be?"

"At the head of the column, of course. Setting the pace so we'll reach Richmond by dark. We're not going to take three damn days to go barely ten miles. No, Sir. I'll check on Fulton at the midday break, but otherwise I'll be up front if you need to report."

Lieutenant Daniels nodded before he started to salute and leave, but stopped when McBee said, "Absalom, we're not going into battle tomorrow, but it's going to take all our command skills to keep the column moving. I'm depending on you. It's just us and a whole lot of weary and ailing men, who are looking to us for leadership. There's no colonel or support staff to help us, there's no back-up, so use your head."

"Captain…John, are your feet and shoulder up to it? I can find you a horse. The men will see you better if you are above them on the back of a horse."

"You pegged it, Absalom. They'd see me above them, sitting while they're walking, when they'd give anything to sit, even for a few minutes. No, I'll march at the head of my command. Even *this* command. Especially *this* command. Word will get around that their captain is on his feet with them."

* * *

Zebulon Bell stumbled, but his brother grabbed his elbow and used all his weight to lean back and keep Zeb from going to the ground.

"Sorry," Zeb mumbled without looking up.

"Hand me your musket," Ed replied as he reached out to pull the Enfield's sling off Zeb's shoulder. Zeb didn't protest as the musket slipped down his arm and Ed lifted it from him. The extra nine pounds of weight felt like more, but he willingly took on the extra burden to keep Zeb going a little further.

When the column had stopped earlier for a short rest, Zeb was shaking and sweating and his forehead was burning hot. Ed saw Sergeant Moss and waved him over.

"Zeb's got the fever and the shakes real bad, Sergeant. If he goes on now, he's likely to overheat and die."

Moss knew the Bell brothers by sight and had seen the fight at their campfire. He respected the small young man who had taken on the bigger recruit, but he had clear orders.

"Bell, your brother has to get up and keep moving. Every man in our company is being watched to see if Captain McBee goes easier on us than all the rest of these men. He's gotta get up. Take off Zeb's knapsack and leave it. Maybe that will help him."

Ed Bell sighed deeply, but didn't protest. Instead, he nodded, and bent over to unbuckle Zeb's pack. When they started again, Ed left both his and Zeb's knapsacks, muskets, and leather accouterments in a neat pile, half-hidden under the low branches of a fir tree. With Zeb's arm draped across Ed's shoulder the pair resumed the march.

Sergeant Moss didn't say anything when he saw the Bell brothers had abandoned their weapons and gear. Instead, he pulled a filthy handkerchief from his pocket and tied it to a tree limb to mark the location of their belongings. After Moss resumed his own march, a sneezing, shivering soldier from another regiment pulled the handkerchief from the limb and gratefully blew his nose into it before stuffing it into his pocket.

* * *

"Private Fulton, have you sent men to both the wagons yet?" Lieutenant Daniels asked as he joined Fulton at the back of the column.

"Nah, it's still early. But I ain't left anybody sittin' on the side of the road." After a few more steps, Fulton added, "That damned John mighta seen fit to tell me he had the wagons comin'."

"Since when did captains start telling privates their plans?" Daniels replied.

"Since he twisted his old friend's arm to be the broom at the back of this column of stragglers and sweep these no-accounts along."

"And you are doing a noble job of it, Private Fulton," Daniels said. Then the lieutenant saw one of their own new men sitting near the road, leaning against a boulder.

"Lawson, get up!" Daniels hollered at him.

"Can't. I'm played out. Need to rest a while," Asbury Lawson called back.

The lieutenant took a step towards Lawson, and ignored Fulton when he said, "I got him, Lieutenant. My job."

"Nah, Fulton, it's mine."

Lieutenant Daniels stopped next to Private Lawson, and growled, "You call me Lieutenant, or Sir. Now get up."

"Can't, *Sir*. I'm give out," Lawson answered

Daniels unsnapped his holster, pulled his pistol, put it an inch from Lawson's left arm, cocked it, and pulled the trigger. The round ball went through Lawson's coat sleeve and dug a bloody furrow across his upper arm.

"Damn! You shot me!" Lawson cried, slapping his right hand over the wound.

"Yeah. Now get up and walk."

"But I'm bleeding!"

"Yeah. In this weather it'll crust up soon enough. Now move!"

Daniels didn't re-holster his pistol as he turned and resumed walking. When he reached Fulton, Daniels asked, "Is he walking?"

Fulton looked back, grinned and said, "Yeah, and these other laggards seem to be getting' along a mite faster, too. I like your style, Lieutenant."

"I've always had a way with words," Daniels said as he angled away to check on his flank guards further up the column.

* * *

Captain McBee's command of the thousand stragglers reached Richmond just before dusk. McBee led the column himself, until he was obliged to step off the road to greet General Hood. The division commander had been informed of the column's arrival two full days before he expected it, and had ridden out to meet them.

"Thank you, General. It was my honor, Sir," McBee said when Hood dismounted and insisted on shaking his hand for a job well done.

"I understand you were wounded at Manassas last summer when we drove those red-legged bastards," the general said. "I believe today demonstrated that your recovery is complete. The South needs men like you, Captain. Leaders who will keep the men going forward."

"Thank you, Sir. As a company commander, I've not led such a large body of troops before today," McBee responded, trying to nudge the general into saying why he had been selected to lead the stragglers.

Sensing McBee's unspoken request, on a whim, General Hood decided to answer truthfully. "I'm told, Captain, that last month your company received the most new recruits of any company, in not just your regiment, or the Texas Brigade, but the most in the entire division. How many men was it?" Hood asked.

"Thirty-six, Sir. All from Leon County."

"Thirty-six green recruits to replace those brave veterans you lost in last year's campaigns. That's an excellent result. But it's also far more recruits to arrive at one time than in any other company. Therefore, far more drill instruction needed. To be honest, Captain, I was concerned that the new men would slow your company, with so many recruits not yet conditioned to the rigors of the march. I confess I feared that your company would be a drag on the whole brigade. I couldn't allow that. Not in my old brigade, not my Texans. But I am gratified I needn't have been concerned. You have performed a laudable service to the division today."

Captain McBee was flummoxed, unsure whether he should stand tall and proud, or resent what the general had unexpectedly admitted.

Hood saw the captain's confusion, and asked, "Tell me, Captain, have you roots in Texas? Did your father take part in the battles that tore Texas loose from Santa Anna's iron grip? Were you with the army in Mexico? You look old as I am."

"My father was a militia colonel with General Jackson against the British before I was born. I was raised here in Virginia, near Lexington. I went to Texas in time to fight the Comanches as a young man, but I fear I missed the Mexican War."

"Too bad. Many a good officer cut his teeth killing Mexicans. But the Comanche are also a worthy adversary. I commanded a troop of the Second Cavalry and killed two of the red heathens myself with my Remington. Close work, that day. You're a native Virginian, heh? Back now to defend Old Dominion. I trust we'll drive the northerners out before they can harm Lexington. Too many of Virginia's fine towns have been subjected to their *visitations*."

McBee hadn't considered the possibility that Lexington might fall under occupation of the Federal army, and the thought made him very uncomfortable.

General Hood ended the encounter by saying, "Carry on, Captain. I shall certainly let your colonel know you've gained my respect this day. I won't forget Captain McBee of the Fifth Texas."

Chapter 7

Lexington, Virginia
February 27, 1863

Private Paul's status as a provost held no sway with the barkeep, who had lost a foot working a cannon in the first big battle of the war. When Paul demanded his second glass of whiskey, the old vet poured it. But when the provost tapped his empty glass on the bar for a third, the barkeep held out his palm for payment. Paul flipped his last dollar on the bar and stomped towards the door as the barkeep demanded another dollar, which Paul didn't have.

Private Paul growled when he bumped into an older man going in the door. He shoved the man sideways and cursed as he stumbled onto the boardwalk. The provost leaned against the wall while several foggy thoughts competed for his whiskey-soaked attention. First, he knew he couldn't go back in the saloon with no money, but he vaguely remembered that he had completely emptied the bottle in his saddlebag. The trouble was Paul couldn't remember where he had tied his horse to a hitching rail. He'd have to go looking for the nag.

Third, he wanted a woman. The two prostitutes working the saloon had stirred him up with their husky hello's, but had disappeared when he used his only coins for the two shots of cheap whiskey. Paul hadn't had a woman since the day a gaunt dark-haired, hawk-nosed wife of a deserter offered herself to keep him from searching her horse shed.

He smiled at the memory of taking her on the table in the shack, and laughed out loud at the memory of her following him outside, yelling for him to leave, that she'd paid his price. She only stopped protesting when he turned and punched her in the face, breaking off a front tooth and knocking her to the ground. When the shed door creaked open behind him, Paul was standing over the moaning woman, staring at her bare legs, not even noticing her bleeding mouth.

Her husband barreled out in a rush with a rusty pitchfork, but Paul had been stone-cold-sober that day and swirled at the sound, pulling and cocking his pistol. The deserter took half an hour to bleed out from the two bullets in his stomach, while his wife endured a second assault, her head twisted sideways, her unfocused eyes glued to her dying husband's helpless stare. After Paul finished and rode away, she used her hands and a big knife to scrape out a shallow trench next to her husband's body and rolled him in, pushing some loose dirt over his face.

When Private Paul returned a week later, he found the husband's corpse half-eaten by hogs and dogs and the woman's bloated corpse lying in a pool of dried blood on the bed, wrists gashed by a butcher knife.

Paul shook his head to clear the hazy memory, and stood straight as he could. He stepped gingerly off the boardwalk and started walking with a drunken purpose. He made it to the corner, where he turned in a slow circle looking for a horse rump that seemed familiar.

"Get out the road, you drunk!" The man in the buggy yelled as he popped his whip near Paul's head and pulled on the reins to encourage his horse to move further from the tottering figure.

Nearly being run down by the buggy horse coming from a side street caused Paul to look down the street. He vaguely remembered that some days back, he gone with the lieutenant to visit a house at the end of this street, a house where he'd groped the darkie woman house servant. A house that had a carriage barn with a room at the back where he'd seen a bed, a bed where he bet the slave woman slept. Paul moved to the side of the street and headed towards the far end of the street.

The big house was dark when Paul approached. He saw the driveway and made his way to the barn in the back. He rattled the latch on the locked double doors at the front before he went to the side door. It too was locked, but he easily pried it open with his belt knife.

Faith finished her midnight nursing and carried the twins back to their bed. She saw the shadow as she wrapped herself in a shawl, idly glancing out the wavy glass window panes. She swallowed hard as the shape lurched towards the stable house, and she didn't move until she heard the latch being shaken.

She walked quickly to her bedroom door and opened it to find Levi in his nest of blankets, stretched across the doorway. "Levi, wake up!" Faith whispered as she shook his shoulder. "Someone's trying to break into the stable house."

The young man blinked and reached under the blankets for the big pistol Captain McBee had forced on him right before he returned to his regiment. He sat up and looked in question at his master's woman.

"Sally's sleeping there," Faith said.

Levi squinted his eyes as understanding broke through. He was silent as he rolled out of the blankets and descended the stairs in his stocking feet.

Private Paul pulled the wood slat door open and stepped inside. The room was so small the foot of the bed almost touched where the intruder stood. Moonlight from the open door behind him revealed the just-awakened woman staring at him with wide eyes. She shouted for him to get out.

Instead, Paul jumped on the bed, landing on his knees, falling forward, his chest pressing against the woman under the covers, his hands grabbing her wrists. He released one of her arms and fumbled with the quilt to pull it off the woman. She struggled under him and screamed until he slapped her hard on her face.

Paul couldn't see the moon shadow of the figure in the doorway and never heard the two soft steps the man took. He did hear the pistol cock and jerked his head around as the muzzle flashed an inch from his back. The lead ball went through Paul's jacket and shirt, through the skin and meat to the right of his spine, through a lung, then through more flesh and cloth, and lodged in the heart of the woman lying beneath him.

* * *

As soon as Levi started down the stairs, Faith hurried across the hall where she shook Elizabeth awake and then pulled the loaded shotgun from the corner. With a few words Faith told Mrs. McBee of seeing a man in the driveway and having sent Levi to the carriage house. The two women moved to the second floor landing where they waited, Faith holding the cocked shotgun pointing down the stairwell.

They heard a dim shout, then one muffled gun shot, and no further sound. The pair stayed frozen still, desperately wanting to know what was happening in the stable house, but determined to hold their place at the top of the stairs, keeping the loaded shotgun between any intruder and the newborns. Finally, they heard the back door slam and a familiar voice.

"Miz Faith, Miz McBee, help me."

"Levi, is that you? Come to the stairs! I can't leave the twins, come here!"

Levi walked slowly into the entry hall and looked up the stairwell.

"That's alright, Miz Faith. He's dead,"

"Who's dead, Levi?" Mrs. McBee asked, alarm in her voice.

"He is. The man who…the man who broke in the stable house. The man who broke into the room where Mama sleeps," Levi softly replied.

"You shot him?" Faith blurted out. "Did you shoot the man, Levi? Did you shoot him? We heard a gunshot. Was that you?"

"Yes'm. I shot him," Levi said in the same soft voice. Then he sobbed, "An' I shot my mama."

"Levi! We just heard one shot. Did you shoot the man who broke in?" Mrs. McBee injected.

"Yes, Ma'am. I done said I did," Levi hoarsely whispered back.

"But you just said you shot Sally," the older woman said, confused.

Levi didn't answer immediately, but slumped down to sit on the bottom step of the stairs, his back now to the women.

Slowly, with a stuttering quivering voice, Levi explained. "He was... on top of Mama... He was about to, to...hurt her. I held out the gun right behind him and shot him," Levi said slowly, as he wiped a tear off his cheek.

In sudden realization of what Levi couldn't say, Faith handed the shotgun to Elizabeth, saying, "Stay here. Shoot any man who tries to come up these stairs. Elizabeth, can you do that?"

Not sharing Faith's sudden understanding of Levi's behavior, Mrs. McBee took the gun and said, "Those are my grandchildren, Faith, and they are in my house. You go see what Levi is trying to tell us."

Faith hurried down the stairs. She stopped to pull the pistol from Levi's grip. She grabbed the barrel, noted it was warm, and stopped again in the parlor to light a small oil lamp. With a weapon and light, Faith walked steadily through the house and pushed open the back door. Swallowing hard, she cocked the pistol and held it out as she went into the backyard. She moved directly to the side door of the stable house, the door that opened into the small room where Sally slept.

Inside, the lamplight revealed a white man lying on his stomach on top of the quilt. Under his torso was a second body, a Negro woman whose lifeless eyes seemed to stare at the ceiling. Blood was pooling under the man, saturating the cover. Faith steeled herself and knelt down to hold the lamp close to the man's face. She recognized him as one of the provosts who had been in the house just a few days before. She stood and hurried back into the house, not even slowing down to close the door.

For the next half-hour, Faith Samuelson and Elizabeth McBee had a tense conversation, while Levi remained sitting on the bottom step of the stairs, lost in his guilt and grief.

"But, Faith, there's no one left but Levi to go fetch the sheriff. Jacob's gone and now Sally's dead," Mrs. McBee concluded.

"But can he? Can Levi face the sheriff and lie? I don't think so. No, I must go myself," Faith countered.

"The sheriff will wonder why you didn't send Levi," Elizabeth protested.

"His mother just died, isn't that good reason for him to stay here?" Faith said.

"Do you think the sheriff will believe that you shot that foul man?"

"He has to. You have to support my story. Do you want Levi hanged?"

"No, of course not. I'm going to need him when this cursed war is over," Elizabeth reasoned.

"Elizabeth, you know the sheriff. Will he put me in jail for saying I shot the provost? Will he see I did it to protect Sally?"

"He might see it as you protecting my property and let you go," Mrs. McBee said. "Or he might not. I don't really know. I've known Sheriff Cain for a long time, but you, Faith, you are a new card in the deck. I don't think he really believes that Johnny sent you here just because the Yankees have occupied your parents' town. And then there's that English rifle with your husband's name engraved on it... " she said as she touched the long, puckered scar on her scalp.

Elizabeth's words broke Faith's confidence, so she asked, "What if we tell the truth, that Levi shot the provost because he was about to violate Sally?"

"You were right the first time, Faith. The provost lieutenant would hang Levi before the sun sets. No, the truth won't do. Can we hide the man's body? Drop him down the well?" Mrs. McBee asked.

Faith almost smiled as she said, "And then what would we drink? And what about poor Sally? What would we tell the sheriff then? No, the sheriff needs to see them both, just like they are now. The only question can be who pulled the trigger. And it has to be me."

"I'll walk to the sheriff's office as soon as it's daylight. I'll be waiting at his door when he gets there. Once he sees the bodies in the stable house, what can he do but believe me? He knows you would never trust Levi with a pistol. It's illegal and not even imaginable. If he asks about the pistol, I'll tell him John left it for me in case Levi gets out of line, and for protection in case some kinfolk of the hooligan who shot you come looking for revenge. I can convince Sheriff Cain it was me who shot the provost."

"What should I do with Levi?" Elizabeth asked, accepting that Faith had chosen the only path open to them.

"The sheriff will expect him to be upset about his mother, so I guess we should give him a blanket and put him on the back stoop until the sheriff gets here. Sheriff Cain can't learn he's been sleeping in the big house. I'll put his blankets in a stall in the stable. I'll talk to him about how he must remain silent. Levi may be distraught over Sally's death. He many never get over how that happened, what he did. But he's not stupid. He'll tell the sheriff that the gunshot woke him up in the stable, that I fired the shot."

Elizabeth took both Faith's hands in hers and asked, "A little while ago, you asked me if I could guard the children. Now I'm asking you, can you do this? Can we do this together?"

Faith leaned forward and kissed the older woman's cheek, and answered, "*I* shot that man because I heard Sally's scream. *I* took the pistol with me for protection. *I* walked in on the man trying to violate Sally- your property. *I* shot him to protect that property. She sheriff *will* believe me. And afterwards we'll bury Sally."

Chapter 8

The McBee House
Lexington, Virginia
February 28, 1863

Sheriff Cain stared at the body of Provost Private Paul, noting the position of the corpse's arms and legs as it lay on top of Mrs. McBee's house-servant, Sally. With some effort he shoved Paul's stiff corpse onto its side. Cain saw that the dead man's trousers were unbuttoned and his member jutted out, now grotesquely swollen and turned blue-black.

"Hmmph," the sheriff grunted as he considered that either Paul was about to violate this poor darkie when he was shot, or he was bushwacked while relieving himself and brought here. He didn't think the second option was credible, but at least it was a possibility to be weighed.

He stooped over Sally's body and gently lifted and shifted it sideways to see if the mattress was blood stained. Cain couldn't see any dark stains or feel any stickiness, so without examining the corpse's back he concluded the bullet was still in her. That meant he would need the doctor to dig it out so he could see what caliber it was, if the lead ball wasn't too misshapen. He wondered if the doctor would protest having to probe into a dead Negro's remains.

On his way back to the big house, Sheriff Cain saw a young black man sitting and leaning against the trunk of the big beechnut tree, the empty branches spreading above the yard. His eyes were shut. The sheriff walked to him and said, "You're Sally's boy. I'm sorry about your mammy."

Levi looked up and nodded.

The white man studied Levi's face, and asked, not unkindly, "What's your name, boy?"

"I'm Levi."

"I thought you went to war with your missus's son. That captain from Texas."

Levi nodded and answered, "Yes, Suh."

"I hear the captain's wound is healed and he went back to his regiment," the sheriff went on. "Why are you still here?"

"The capt'n said I was to help Mama since my brother Jacob's gone," Levi said without hesitation.

"Ahh, that's right. How was it that little Jacob died?

"A white man hit him with his gun."

"What white man was that?"

Levi paused a few seconds, then answered truthfully, "My mama said it was Mizz Sam'lson's husband when he come to fetch her home."

"Why would he hit Jacob?"

Levi was suddenly scared of the sheriff's questions, so he just shrugged in reply.

The sheriff saw Levi would likely dissemble if he pressed further, so he shifted his questioning to last night's shooting.

"Where do you sleep, Levi?"

"In the stable next to the missus's horse."

"Did you hear anything from Sally's room?"

Levi shook his head.

"Are you telling me that you didn't hear the provost opening the door? You didn't hear Sally scream?"

Levi shook his head.

"Mrs. Samuelson said she heard the scream from upstairs in the house. You were just on the other side of the wall from your mammy's room."

"Maybe I heard something, but I was too scared to move," Levi muttered.

"A big buck like you? A strong boy like you, too scared? Too scared to go see why your mammy screamed in the night?"

"Maybe I got up and saw the white man in Mama's room," Levi said, then added quickly, "But then Miz Sam'lson come from the big house…and she saw the man on top of Mama and shot him…and Mama."

The sheriff looked at Levi for a long moment, then said, "Levi, that white man was onto your mammy like a hound on a bitch in heat once he smelled her up the other day. It doesn't surprise me he came back. But you did right last night, not to hit him, not to try to stop him."

Levi nodded again without looking up.

The sheriff went on, "On the other hand, I seem to remember stopping you from taking a piece of firewood to Paul the first time he came around. He would've shot you, most likely, back then and last night. I reckon you got smarter in the past few days. Yessir, you're a smart darkie, now. Too bad about your mammy though."

Levi didn't take the bait, but just nodded in agreement, still looking down.

* * *

Faith Samuelson and Mrs. McBee sat next to each other on the sofa, holding hands. The twin infants squirmed in their wraps on a blanket in front of the sofa.

"Yes, Sheriff, I can only repeat what I told you at your office. I had just put the twins back in the crib after their midnight feeding. I heard noises and looked out the window and saw a man in the driveway. Captain McBee had left a pistol here, and I took it with me to see who was creeping around our home in the middle of the night."

Mrs. McBee cut her eyes sharply towards Faith when the young woman said, *our* home.

"I went out the backdoor and heard noise from Sally's room and found a man on top of her. She was screaming and I shot him to protect her. To protect the property of my hostess. I'm heartbroken that the bullet went all the way through him and killed Sally, too. I had no idea a pistol bullet could do that."

"Yeah, those big army pistol bullets can go right through a board. What about Levi? Where was he? Did you see him?"

"Well, I don't know, Sheriff. I suppose he was in the barn."

"The same barn as where his mammy was sleeping?"

Suddenly apprehensive, Faith answered, "Under the same roof, but Levi was in the stable with the horse and buggy, not near Sally's room."

"Did you see Levi before you, huh, used the pistol?"

"It was dark, Sheriff, but, no, I don't remember seeing Levi until afterwards."

Everyone sat quietly and watched the twins for a moment or two before the sheriff turned his attention back to the ladies on the settee and said, "Levi said that your husband, Lieutenant Samuelson, hit little Jacob and that's what killed him. That right?"

Elizabeth McBee answered immediately before Faith could speak, "I don't know, I had just been shot myself, hiding behind my little daughter's tombstone, like a scared cottontail. Praise the Lord for Johnny."

"Indeed," answered the sheriff, "Praise the Lord for Johnny. But back to little Jacob, was it your husband who hit him, Mrs. Samuelson?"

Again, Mrs. McBee spoke before Faith could. "Sally saw it. She was standing right there at the foot of the stairs. She just said it was a man. A soldier. Sally, bless her soul, was just a darkie who didn't know an officer's uniform from a private's. Maybe it was the same soldier who attacked Sally. The evil man who Faith shot."

The sheriff kept his gaze on Faith, but spoke to Elizabeth, "I have a rifle in my office, an expensive English rifle, with the name *Adam Samuelson* engraved on it. The rifle that Captain McBee gave me and said was the rifle that nearly killed you, Elizabeth. Is there a connection?"

"I can't see one, Sheriff. I really cannot," Elizabeth answered stiffly.

"What about you, Mrs. Samuelson?"

"I, I..."

"That's all right, Ma'am. I'm not asking you to speak ill of your husband. Let me ask something else. I wired a friend who is a lawman up your way, Mrs. Samuelson. I asked him about your husband. He said Lieutenant Samuelson owns a river freight business. A business that has suffered since the Yankees closed off the rivers and shut down trade between Virginia and Baltimore and Washington."

"Yes, that's correct. But why…"

"Bear with me. I found a teamster's work pass in the pants pocket of the man Captain McBee killed. Your near-assassin, Elizabeth. The name on it was David Rankin. Mrs. Samuelson, did Mr. Rankin work for your husband?"

"My husband employs many men, Sheriff. I don't recognize the name."

"How do you think Rankin came to use your husband's fine English rifle against Elizabeth?"

"Maybe he stole it. If Mr. Rankin did work for my husband, maybe he knew where our house is, and knew when we were both gone. We've both been away from our farmhouse for some time now. Of course, Lieutenant Samuelson is usually away with his duties, and I was in Richmond working at a soldiers' hospital."

"When I became aware of my condition, my own mother's home was under Yankee occupation. Captain McBee was recovering in that hospital, and struck me as a gentleman. So I accepted his kind offer that I come here, where his mother and Sally could care for me."

The sheriff sat back in his chair and sighed before he said, "Ladies, I'll be straight with you. I have no interest in prosecuting Captain McBee for shooting Mr. Rankin. He was defending himself, and you, Elizabeth. I don't really care how the little darkie or Sally died. I don't care that Sally's assault was stopped with deadly force. Paul needed killing. No loss there. I do regret that Elizabeth has lost two valuable slaves.

"All that aside, I do care that two people have been killed in my jurisdiction."

"Four people, Sheriff. You forgot Sally and Jacob," Faith said.

"Yes, of course," the sheriff said, looking miffed at the correction by the young woman. "Two people, *and two darkies*, have been killed, three of them shot with Captain McBee's pistol. Even if the two men were both ruffians, even if the rifle *may* have been stolen from a house a hundred miles from here, it's a stretch for me to believe there's no connection."

Both women remained silent.

"Which requires me to ask, Mrs. Samuelson, why didn't you go home with your husband?"

"What do you mean? I didn't know Adam was in Lexington," Faith said.

"He stayed at a hotel on Main Street. The hotel that's just up the street and around the corner," the sheriff said.

"Oh?" Faith said, pointedly watching her children.

"He rented a room the night before Rankin shot Elizabeth and Captain McBee killed Rankin, and the night before little Jacob was killed."

The sheriff went on softly. "The hotel clerk said there was another man with Lieutenant Samuelson. A big rough looking man. Like Mr. Rankin. I think perhaps you two ladies are not being forthright with me."

"Sheriff…" Elizabeth started, but was cut off by the sheriff who held up his hand.

"Don't say a word, Elizabeth. Just a few minutes ago, Levi told me that his mammy said Samuelson was the man who pistol-whipped Jacob, not Private Paul," Cain explained.

"Mrs. Samuelson, I don't know why you really are here. I don't know why your husband came to Lexington, or why his companion shot at Elizabeth and her two soldier sons. However, if Levi is correct that Lieutenant Samuelson came here to this house, then clearly there is a connection. I suspect Rankin was shooting at Captain McBee, not you, Elizabeth."

Elizabeth nervously pulled at the folds of her skirt, while Faith quickly looked away from the sheriff's eyes.

"Mrs. Samuelson, since you did *not* go with your husband when, *if*, he came to fetch you, as Levi said, I think it would be a good idea for you to write to your husband and suggest he remain in Richmond, or where ever else his duties take him. Anywhere but Lexington. Because if I find him here, I will question him as an accomplice to Elizabeth's shooting. If you care for your husband, Ma'am, when you return to your own home with your children, you travel to him. Don't ask him to come to Lexington, *to fetch you.*

Faith nodded ever so slightly in acknowledgement.

"Elizabeth, I'm done here. I don't plan to come back. I'll send men with a wagon to take Private Paul's body away. I assume you will take care of Sally's remains?" the sheriff said.

"Of course," Mrs. McBee answered. "Let me see you out."

When the sheriff went through the front door, Elizabeth followed him onto the porch, shutting the door behind her.

She looked the sheriff in the eyes and said very softly, "Thank you, Abner."

The sheriff looked at her and said, "Elizabeth, it's been thirty years since Isaiah died, thirty years you've been a widow woman. Thirty years that I've kept an eye on your welfare, because I promised your husband I would."

"I know you've watched over me, Abner. You've come around with news and questions like clockwork during every one of those thirty years. I'm grateful for that. More grateful than you know."

"Elizabeth, I don't know why that young woman is really here, but I've a good idea that her children may be your kin. Your grandchildren," Cain said.

Elizabeth looked at the floorboards and stayed silent.

"You were almost killed by a man sent by that woman's husband. The pieces just don't fit any other way. I think that pretty young woman in your parlor strayed with your son. I think she's here to hide from her husband. But he found her and came after her and tried to kill the man who stole his wife. But his thug missed and hit you instead. Elizabeth, that boy of yours from Texas brought you a peck of trouble."

Elizabeth wiped a tear from one eye and sat down in one of the two rocking chairs on the porch.

"Sit with me, Abner." Nodding to the other chair, she said, "Sit with me."

He sat, leaning forward on the seat of the other rocking chair.

"I can't deny anything you said. All I can add is that Faith's husband is an evil man. Isaiah was weak, loving his bottle and the black girls more than me. But if Faith has spoken truthfully to me, Lieutenant Samuelson is evil. He's certainly not weak. Faith said he beat her and violated her. Sally told me that he killed little Jacob with one blow of his pistol barrel, while the little boy was trying to protect Faith from him. He took Faith away, and Johnny brought her back."

The sheriff rocked and studied Elizabeth's face, waiting for her to go on.

"Yes, those beautiful twins are my grandchildren. And I will keep doing all I can to protect them. And their mother. Because even though she is legally bound to another man, an evil man, she loves my son. I will not abandon her," Elizabeth concluded looking hard at the sheriff, her eyes shining.

Sheriff Cain rocked and thought before he said, "I meant it when I urged the young woman to advise her husband not to return to Lexington. You might tell her that again, yourself. If he comes back to my town, I will arrest Samuelson as an accomplice to Rankin in your attempted murder. And it would be an ugly trial, a trial that he might well win. As an army officer who has been cuckolded by another officer, a jury might just overlook the evidence that links him to Rankin shooting you. And I don't know what the army would do with your son. Yep, it would be ugly all around if that man returns to Lexington."

"Thank you, Abner. I'll tell her to write a letter right away. What about that dead man who Faith killed? Will the provost lieutenant accept Faith's right to shoot the man? He was trespassing and violating Sally."

"I think I can persuade Blomerth to let it go. But he's an arrogant man, and used to bullying people, so I would not let Mrs. Samuelson go shopping alone."

"Abner, we've no help now that Sally's gone. Faith will be busy all day every day in the house with her babies," Elizabeth assured the sheriff.

The sheriff nodded before he hesitantly said, "Elizabeth, this is more talking than we've done in thirty years. I'm sorry to be on your porch as sheriff, but I'm glad to hear your voice and have a reason to look at you and you look back at me."

Elizabeth McBee sat straighter and stopped rocking.

Twisting his hat in his hands, the silver haired sheriff then said, "There's more, Elizabeth. For every one of those thirty years I've wondered if you'd welcome my interest in becoming your second husband."

Elizabeth patted her hair, touched her scar, and looked up the street as tangled joy and regret bit at her. After a long pause to gather her thoughts, she answered, "I would have, Abner. I would have. Even after a few years of mourning, I was still young enough to have more babies. You know Isaiah was not the kindest or most affectionate man. Yes, I would have welcomed your interest. Why didn't you court me? Propose to me?"

Abner Cain looked at the small woman with gray hair and a scar over her ear, and felt every one of his sixty-two years.

"Elizabeth, I was the new sheriff. Men were trying me, testing me. For years I didn't know what dark night some drunken fool might use a shotgun or an iron bar on me. Remember what your overseer did to your cousin McChesney twenty years ago? Killed him with a piece of iron during a stupid argument. When I arrested him, it took three of us to wrestle him down. Sheriffing's dangerous work," Cain concluded.

"Yes, I pined for you, I surely did, but I couldn't put you in position to be a widow woman a second time. No, I couldn't do that."

Elizabeth held her clinched fist to her mouth, and then folded her hands into her lap.

"Oh, Abner, here you sit on my porch speaking such things now. There's a war on, my prodigal son has returned and put himself in a pickle. My home has become a refuge for a wayward woman, who has presented me with twin grandchildren. My darkies are dying faster than I can replace them. And you and I both have gray hair and weak eyes. I'm looking back at thirty empty years. Half a life wasted. Why are you men so stubborn and so, so dumb when it comes to women?"

The two kept rocking a few more minutes without Abner replying, so Elizabeth finally added, "Abner, once we get Sally in the ground, I'd be pleased if you would join Faith and me for Sunday dinner sometime soon. I'll see if I can remember how to cook a decent meal, although I may burn the biscuits."

"I'd like that, Elizabeth. Yes, I would. And a burned biscuit from your stove would be just fine."

The sheriff rose, nodded to Elizabeth, then put out his hand. She put her fingers on his and he grasped them and squeezed. Not knowing what else to do or say, Abner Cain put on his hat and rode back to his office, happier than he had been in a long time.

* * *

That same afternoon, Faith wrote two letters. First, she forced herself to follow the sheriff's instructions to write her husband a warning to stay away from Lexington. It was a short terse message.

Second, she penned a lengthy letter to Captain McBee, informing him of Sally's death and the sheriff's visit. Without being specific about who shot Private Paul, she suggested that Levi would finish his grieving sooner if he returned to the captain's service, away from the place where his mother died. She also assured the captain that the twins were healthy and growing. She added that Elizabeth had bought a milk cow and, with Sally's death, she would soon learn to squeeze milk from a teat, not so unlike their hungry babes.

Chapter 9

Camp of the Fifth Texas Infantry
Six Miles South of Richmond, Virginia
March 12, 1863

L ieutenant Daniels was unexpectedly anxious as he approached the captain's tent late in the afternoon. He found the captain holding a shiny tin plate as a mirror with one hand while he trimmed his own beard with scissors in the other hand.

"What do you think, Absalom? Am I now less a hairy bear?" McBee asked his subordinate.

"Yessir, you are the picture of dignification." Daniels replied, discreetly ignoring his captain's uneven whiskers.

"You do stretch the truth, but I must say I feel better," McBee said as he set down the tin plate and scissors.

"Sir, I have a message from the hospital in Richmond. The doctor says three more of our men have expired from their illnesses."

"Damn, damn, damn. Who are they? Let me see," McBee replied, as he held out his hand out for the paper.

"Sir, it's one of the Bell brothers, the older Green, and Stuart. Pneumonia got Bell, and yellow fever for the other two. But there's something else in the message, Captain. Something worse."

"What could be worse news from the hospital than three more of our soldiers dying?" McBee asked in exasperation.

"Well, Sir, it's about the younger Bell brother. He's still alive...but it seems *he* is actually Zebulon Bell's sister. He's a she, Sir. Ed Bell, Edwina Bell, that is. She was uncovered at the hospital." Daniels blushed as he pictured what he'd just related.

McBee sat down on a crate and rubbed his forehead. "Wasn't Ed Bell the little man, the new recruit who whipped Phillips in a fair fight?"

Daniels nodded.

"Is she dying of pneumonia too?"

"No, Sir. The doctor says he, I mean, she, came out of it."

"Thank goodness. But that means for all these weeks, a scrawny girl has been masquerading as a man on our company street? Right under our noses? And we never caught on? Is the doctor sure?"

"Well, I reckon he must be, Captain. That's not something he'd make up, and it'd be hard to hide when it's time for a bedpan."

"Yeah, sure. But what about her..." McBee held his hands up to his chest, "her bosoms?"

Daniels shrugged and blushed again, "I never noticed anything up top when she was with us, but I wasn't looking either. What happens to her now?"

"The army will boot her out when she's strong enough to walk. How she's going to get back to Texas is anyone's guess," McBee mused as he tapped the paper on his knee.

"Let me be for a while, Absalom," McBee continued. "I need to read the doctor's whole report, and then I may send you to the hospital with a note for the doctor. I've a mind to have you bring Bell back here. He, she, had the makings for a good soldier. We can do better than leave her alone, on her own in Richmond. I may make her a cook for us. That'd please Levi and George."

"Yessir, I've mail to deliver to the men. Oh, Captain, here's one for you from Lexington. Your mother certainly has a fine hand, if you don't mind my saying so," Daniels said as he held out the letter.

McBee shook his head at his lieutenant's familiarity, but decided it signaled a new level of trust between them, something he'd been looking for. "Thank you, Lieutenant. Yes, I still remember her making me sit at the kitchen table and fill pages with lines of properly formed letters. Especially the capital letters. The Q gave me fits, but she did insist on proper capitals."

McBee was silently pleased to see the handwriting wasn't that of his mother, but was Faith's hand. He sat in his camp chair, unfolded the sealed letter and began reading.

"Oh, no. Not Sally. Not Sally, too," he mumbled. McBee thought a moment more, then asked himself, *Who killed the provost? Faith never wrote who shot the provost.*

McBee pulled out a half-sheet of paper that had already been used on one side and quickly wrote a request for a week-long furlough to attend to his injured mother. He was vague about the cause of injury, but asserted that as her oldest surviving son he needed to look after some important banking matters related to her estate.

March 14, 1863

Asbury Lawson hated standing guard duty in the camp. Being a guard entailed all the things he despised about the army. Saluting high and mighty officers. Standing at attention for a long time. Polishing his musket barrel and bayonet to a shine. Staying quiet unless addressed by an officer. But there was one good point about guard duty. Unlike company drill or mess duty, standing guard did allow him time to think and plan how and when he was going to excuse himself, quietly and unobserved, from the army.

Guard duty also offered uninterrupted time to mentally refine and rehearse his retribution to Lieutenant Absalom Daniels for shooting him in the arm. Lawson had been dismayed that no one but Polanski Phillips took his side when he complained, and was especially angered that the NCO's, whose job it was to stand up for the men, had turned their backs on him. He wished he could include every sergeant in Company C in his plan for revenge, but he accepted that Daniels would have to serve as their whipping boy.

* * *

Edwina Bell stood quietly waiting for the captain to finish whatever he was writing. He looked up, noted she was dressed in black civilian trousers and a checked shirt, and motioned her to sit on the box a few feet from him.

"You're not a soldier any longer Miss Bell. Please have a seat." When she made no move, he said again, "Please. It's expected. You're a lady."

"No, Sir, I'm a woman, but no belle. But, yessir, I'll sit," the gaunt figure said as she perched on the edge of the box. Her suspender straps ran straight up her flat chest and her hair hung straight down covering her ears. McBee thought that she still looked more like a young man than a young woman,

"I am deeply regretful of your brother's death. Illness has taken a terrible toll of our soldiers, and I know how hard it is to lose a family member," McBee began.

"Have you ever lost a brother?" the young woman asked.

"Yes, I have. My older brother, Robert, the same year the war started. Yellow fever. He had a wife and two little children."

"Were you close?"

"Well, I lived in Texas and he was in Virginia. I hadn't seen him in many years. So, honestly? No, we weren't close. Not like you and Zebulon."

She looked away then back at him, wiping away a tear as she nodded.

"What will you do now?" the captain asked. "The Texas Hospital always needs nurses. I can write the doctor and vouch for you."

She shook her head sideways. "No, not where Zeb died."

"Another hospital then? There are many of them in Richmond." The captain then added with a candor that surprised Bell, "Sometimes I wonder how we still have men in the field, so many are in the hospitals."

"No. I thought maybe I'd find a job in a café as a cook. I'm a good cook, even if I am all skin and bones."

McBee sat back and smiled at her self-deprecating manner. He stroked his beard as if in thought, although he knew exactly what he was about say.

"I have a different offer for you, if you're interested in leaving Richmond," he said.

"Yes, Sir?"

"My mother is a widow in Lexington, eighty miles from here. Her house servant just died in an accident, and she needs a housekeeper and cook. She, uh, has a young lady with twin infants as a houseguest until the war ends."

Bell looked straight at him. "Yessir, the men are aware of your new twins. Congratulations."

Stunned by her words, McBee reacted by leaning against his chair back, and nearly fell backwards. In the instant of surprise he forgot that he was perched on a box, using a board for a lap desk. He took the board off his lap and set it next to him, giving himself time to recover before slogging on.

"Well, uh, yes, thank you. I've not yet seen them. However, I'm leaving today on a week's furlough to Lexington to assist my mother, who is recovering from a head wou…fall. That is, in fact, why I sent for you. Would you be willing to accompany me as my servant, my man-servant, on my trip to Lexington, with the intent to stay and work for my mother?"

"As her man-servant, or her housekeeper?" Bell asked, seeking clarification to an issue that was still unresolved in her own mind.

"Her cook, either as a man or woman. The meat and potatoes don't care who makes the stew. If a man, you would be her stable hand and driver. If a woman, you'd change the beds, do the laundry, and help with the babies."

Having no idea if he had just lost his senses, McBee concluded, "You decide which role fits."

He added, "Either way, whether you wear a skirt or trousers, I will expect you to protect my children and both the ladies. There is an army pistol in the home at Lexington which I will show you how to load and handle."

"You mean protect Mrs. Samuelson from her husband?" Bell asked sharply.

Again flustered, entirely taken back by her apparent knowledge of his most intimate affairs, McBee blurted out, "*How* do you know these things?"

"I've become friends with Private Smith. Don't worry, Captain, I'm good with secrets," she said with a straight face.

McBee sighed and said, "Yes, I grant you that. You are very good with secrets. And with your feet and fists, which is one reason I'm offering you this job. But I need to speak with Private Smith. I do mean protecting Mrs. Samuelson from her husband, with whom she is disaffected. He beat her and should he come around or send someone for her, I would expect you to stop the villain."

The young woman squinted her eyes and tilted her head as she said, "Captain, are you sure you aren't the villain?"

McBee started to bluster at her, but held it, instead saying, "That's a fair question given that I've just asked you to do violence upon anyone who threatens my family. I am a father of twins because of a shameful moment of weakness. No, I am not the villain. Human weakness leads to stupidity. I was stupid, but I'm not evil. I do not beat women, I do not kidnap others. I do not pistol whip small darkies to death. I do not hire thugs to shoot elderly women. Mrs. Samuelson's estranged husband has done all these things. Is that answer enough?"

Edwina Bell nodded, and surprised him again by saying, "Captain, you need a body-servant. Excuse me for saying so, Sir, but your beard makes you look like an old bear. It needs trimming. I could stay and cook for you and the other officers, and be the company barber."

McBee scratched his beard and thought, *So Absalom was just being polite to the old man.*

He looked at young Bell and said, "I thought at first to offer you just such a position, Miss Bell. But I'm not for two reasons: First, everyone in the company knows by now that you are a woman. I cannot have a young female tending to me. In fact, the whole camp is no place for a woman. You would be accosted every day by lonely men, now that your secret is out."

Bell sat still, hands in her lap, mouth firmly shut, and kept her gaze on the captain's face.

"Second, with the passing of my mother's housekeeper, I have a greater need in Lexington. Moreover, I'm bringing my man-servant back with me from Lexington. He is, was, the housekeeper's son, and, as you observed, I need him here."

77

"So, are you game to become part of the McBee household in Lexington?" the captain asked.

Instead of answering, Bell asked the question that had been growing in her mind since the conversation began. "Captain, why are you being so nice to me? Why are you so willing for me to work for Mrs. McBee? To live in your mother's home, dressed as either a man or a woman?"

McBee was now beyond surprise and answered truthfully, "Damned if I know. You had the makings of a good rifleman. You were loyal to your brother until he died. I heard how you practically carried him the last miles on that frozen march to Richmond."

She shrugged. "He was my family."

"Miss Bell, my family is now two women and two babies in a house in Lexington." *And maybe one mulatto man-servant,* McBee thought but didn't say.

"There is a bad man who has reason to hurt me and mine, and he knows where that house is. My heart is there, but my duty must be here. Company C is also my responsibility. I can't stay in Lexington, so I desperately need someone who can be rough as a cob protecting my family if the day comes, and also help run the household."

McBee admitted, "Bell, you baffle me. You are different than anyone I've ever met. You appear able to live as a man or a woman. I'm truly sorry that you came to my attention through your own misfortune, but if you turn me down, I've no one else to turn to. I've no idea how I will do my duty to my mother and my children."

"And Mrs. Samuelson?"

"Yes, Mrs. Samuelson, too," the captain conceded.

Edwina Bell shut her eyes for a long moment before she looked up and said, "I'll do it. Eleven dollars a month, plus room and board, same as private's pay. Hard coin, not Confederate notes. "

McBee exhaled a deep breath and held out his hand to shake. "Done. When can you leave?"

"Now. I'm wearing my belongings. All of them. Do you have an extra coat and hat?"

"A man's coat and hat, or a woman's?" McBee impulsively asked.

"I'm still thinking on that," Bell answered and smiled.

Chapter 10

The McBee House
Lexington, Virginia
March 20, 1863

Elizabeth McBee gaped at her son, confusion clouding her expression. The elderly woman started to speak, but clamped her jaw shut waiting for further explanation.

"It's not that unusual, Mother. In fact, Edward is the second woman to be discovered in our regiment. The other was even an officer, a lieutenant. A woman whose real name was Williams led her - his - company of riflemen in one of the first fights of the war and by all reports she fought well."

"What does that have to do with me?" Mrs. McBee asked.

"I thought you'd be interested that other women have snuck into the army by pretending to be men. After that first battle the woman lieutenant's company was assigned to our regiment since the company was from Texas," her son said, pacing in front of his mother.

"What's happened to her?"

"When Lieutenant Benford was found out to be a woman, she was sent home. The point is that Bell isn't the first or only woman to serve as a soldier, even in our regiment. There must be dozens or maybe hundreds of women in our army, living as men."

"All right," Mrs. McBee conceded. "Women can be patriotic, too. I remember the story of Molly Pitcher during the Revolution. Go on."

"Mother, Edward – Edwina – Bell has no money and nowhere to go. She can't stay with the regiment, now that her secret is out."

"But why here, with me?" Elizabeth protested.

"Levi shouldn't stay here after what happened to his mother. Those memories have to be eating at him. And I need him with me. I'm asking you to switch Levi for Edward Bell. I'm getting back my servant, and you're getting a good soldier to protect your household. Bell will be a better guard than Levi. He – she – is a fighter."

"Was this Bell person ever in a battle?"

"No, she and her brother arrived with a lot of other new men after Fredericksburg, and we've been in winter camp since then."

"So you don't really know if she is, as you say, a fighter."

"I saw her flatten a bigger soldier, a tough man, with just her feet and fists. She's a fighter, all right. My sergeant told me she carried her brother's rifle and knapsack along with hers in a snowstorm when he was too sick to carry his own."

"Can she shoot your pistol better than Levi?" Elizabeth asked pointedly. Then in a melancholy tone she added, "Oh, John, I do so miss Sally. Is this war going to snatch everyone from me? Are you and James going to come home when this *unpleasantness* finally runs its course? Am I going to lose my last two sons too?"

"I'll teach Edward about my pistol before I leave tomorrow," John promised, knowing better than to offer any assurance of his and his brother James' future well-being.

With a sigh, Elizabeth sat up and acquiesced, "Do as you must. Men always do anyway. Leave the man – woman – here. With Levi gone, we'll need a cook and a driver. And someone to do the laundry and split firewood. Might she be a wet nurse?"

"Why don't you ask Edward?" Captain McBee smiled in relief, saying, "He's on the porch. And thank you, Mother."

* * *

While Edward Bell and Elizabeth McBee talked in the parlor, John and Faith sat side-by-side on their bed while she nursed Betsy.

"John, I must make a confession to you. I had no idea that mothering, that rocking and nursing and changing dirty diapers of two little babies, would be so... so unrelenting. Sleeping through a whole night without two feedings would be a gift from God."

"Don't tell me you now regret mending my bloody feet last year?" John asked, smiling at Faith's wan face.

"No, my love, I certainly don't regret it, and don't you even suggest such a thought. Your bloody blisters opened the door for my new life. No, I'm not sorry about that."

"But you're discovering that being a mother is harder than you thought it would be."

Faith nodded, then to reassure him, and herself, she said, "But, I would never consider trading a whole night's sleep for the health of our precious twins. Never!"

"I never dreamed otherwise." John leaned forward to kiss Faith's forehead, his torso pressing Betsy's head into her mother's breast, causing both to grunt loudly.

"Oh, sorry, Betsy. I'll tell you my great secret now, Faith. Being a captain in this damned war is much harder than I ever thought it would be. I fear we're both committed to duties that are pushing us far beyond what we were the night you bandaged my feet."

Faith raised her eyebrows. "You mean the night I first lifted my nightgown for you."

The captain blushed. "Yes, that night." Then he leaned over and whispered in her ear, "That night was an age ago. I've almost forgotten how you managed to get past my defenses. Might you show me again later?"

In the middle of the night, with the twins sleeping in their cradles, her nightgown forgotten on the floor, the couple lay side-by-side in a warm after-glow.

"I need to leave tomorrow," he said.

"I know. There's a war, and you're a captain. Duty calls." She rolled onto her side to pat his chest and kiss his cheek, her long brunette hair falling loosely over John's face.

He twirled a length of her hair around one finger as he asked, "What do you think of Edward Bell? I've finally persuaded Mother to accept him."

"John McBee, I think you're a wonderful husband and a fine captain to have brought a competent and acceptable soldier to guard your family."

Hearing his mother's voice, John Junior whimpered in the dark, offering a gentle reminder that he was hungry.

"Can this woman soldier milk the cow to give me some relief?" Faith asked with a sigh.

John lay still while Faith sat up, retrieved her nightgown from the floor and pulled it over her head. She then fetched John Junior and put him on her breast, sitting on the edge of the bed facing away from the captain.

81

Philip McBride

"Faith, I remember word for word what you told me the night you mended my feet. I mean, what you told me about wanting a baby so badly that you would commit a sin with a man you'd only met a few hours before."

"I'm glad you remember. I'd never want you to think I was just a lonely woman. After eleven years of marriage, I had to try the last thing that might work. I did so desperately want a child. I truly thought Adam would never know. I thought I'd never see you again after that one night. I knew you'd leave the next morning, fight your war, and go home to faraway Texas. I truly thought if I gave Adam a son, he'd come home more often, stay home longer."

"I'm not questioning that. I agree, I don't think a marriage is complete without children."

"Good, because we're going to have a house full of sons and daughters."

She couldn't see John smile at that image. "It's not you, or your motive for that first night. It's me. It's that I came back to your house. I was a thirsty man who came back to the well to drink another man's water."

"Oh, John, I so loved you for that. Don't forget all those horrible things Adam did to us."

"Faith, all those things he did to us were after he found us together in his bed."

"Not all the things he did to me. Those started before…you returned to the well. Adam changed into an animal and beat me when he learned about the Negroes in the barn. I told you that."

"Yes, you did. Did you know then that your husband was a smuggler? That he was using his freight company, his wagons and his boat, to ship tobacco to the north?"

"After the war started, I hardly saw Adam. He rarely came home at all. Of course I knew he owned a freight company, that's how he supported us before the war. He even took me on his boat to Baltimore a few times to shop and go to the opera. But smuggling after the war started? No, I didn't know that."

Faith returned John Junior to his bed and the couple now lay on their sides facing each other, one of Faith's arms draped across John's rib cage.

"What about using the barn as a stopover for runaway slaves? When did you start doing that?" John asked softly.

"Even before the war started, I wanted to help those poor people, but Adam would never have allowed it, and I dared not do such a thing without his permission. It wasn't until after the first big battle of the war that I approached the preacher. By then, Adam was in the army and gone all the time."

"Faith, my family's owned slaves since…forever. You think it's not God's will for the white man to rule over the black man? For the civilized to have dominion over the savages?"

82

"No, and I haven't for a long time. Maybe when I was a little girl it seemed natural, just the ways things were. But then I turned ten. On that birthday, our mother took my older sister and me to the stream behind our house to swim. That day was the first time I was allowed to jump off the rope swing into the deep pool. I had to be ten, that was Mother's rule."

"And I bet you gave a shrill Rebel yell when you let go of the rope, and made a big splash," John said.

She smiled in the dark room. "I don't remember doing that, but I probably did. I do remember that after my very first jump from the rope my mother all of a sudden got scared and waded into the pool and pulled us out and wrapped us up in towels and shooed us back to the house."

"She see a water moccasin?" John asked, wiggling his finger up and down Faith's stomach.

"No, how I wish it had only been a poisonous snake. No, she saw something more vile, more dangerous. She saw two young Negro boys watching us from the other side of the stream, where our neighbor watered his animals. One of them was older than me, older than my sister. The other boy was probably close to my age."

"Mother told Father, and Father went to our neighbor demanding justice. I saw Father leave our house, John. My two uncles went with him, and he took a rope."

"Faith, you don't have to finish. I know what happened next." John lay on his back and locked his hands behind his head on the pillow.

"They did it. They killed the older boy. The next day my mother drove me and Sister to see his body still hanging from the tree. She stopped the buggy and made us look. I remember to this day exactly what she said. She said, 'You girls look at that. Any time a black buck puts his eyes on you, you tell your father, or your husband, or any white man, and he'll make it right.' She said, 'make it right,' like squeezing the life from a boy because he unknowingly went to the shared stream at the wrong time, would set the world right again."

"What about the little boy?" John asked.

"Oh, they were kinder to him. They tied him to the same tree and Father used his belt buckle on his back until 'he near bled out.' Those are the words I heard him say to my mother."

"Faith…"

"No, you asked me, my love. Let me finish. I knew from the day I saw that poor African boy's body hanging, twisting back and forth in the wind, that slavery was evil. Even a ten-year old girl could see the devil's hand at work. Even I could see that one person was never intended to own another person. That one race of people having such power over another whole race does terrible things to good people like my parents."

83

"Faith…"

"John," Faith sat up, and looked down at him with narrowed eyes, "What do you call Levi? What color is he?"

"Well, he's sort of light brown. He's a mulatto."

Faith reached out and set her palm on John's chest. "What's a mulatto, my love?

"A mulatto is a Negro with a white father. You know that."

"Yes, I do. It's a common term, mulatto, isn't it? What do you call a Negro with a white mother?" Faith asked.

"Well… there aren't any. No white woman would lie with a Negro man."

"That's right. Why, then, if the races are not to mingle that way, do so many white men lie with Negro women? So many that there's a distinct, common name for the children that are made by white men and Negro women? Why is that?"

"I don't know. A man's primal urge to couple with a woman, any woman, I suppose."

"I agree. Coupling is a deep-seated natural instinct in men. What are we white women to make of that? You men can couple with Negro slaves in the barn, and simply call your offspring 'mulattos' and be done with it. Returning to our beds with no guilt, no sin committed."

Faith tapped John's chest with her fist. "That *primal urge* ruined Elizabeth's love for your father. That one hour with Sally haunted you for twenty-five years. Both because *civilized* white men hold dominion over the savages of the world."

A cry came from the cradle and with another sigh Faith rolled off the bed to feed little Betsy. John said nothing more. Instead he listened to Faith humming softly to the infant while he mused over what Faith had said, and the fervor with which she spoke.

Chapter 11

Near Suffolk, Virginia
April 14, 1863

Because they were the same height, Private Smith stood in formation right behind Asbury Lawson, which comforted Smith, but also caused him stress, since Lawson was viewed as the best shot and the worst soldier in Company C. Smith didn't like Lawson, but there was nothing he could do about it. Smith at least thought he could count on Lawson to shoot straight, and that did matter, since they would be partners, moving and covering each other as skirmishers.

The five cannons in the little fort, named Fort Huger, had been a Confederate battery until just a few hours ago. In the dark of night a regiment of Federal infantry had quietly disembarked from a riverboat, theatrically using a black canvas screen to shield their movement from boat to shore. The deception worked, and within an hour the Federal troops stormed the fort, undetected until the last moment, and captured the artillery crewmen and the infantrymen who were garrisoned there to protect the cannons from just such an attack.

By dawn the artillery had been repositioned to face nearby Confederate positions along the river to either side of the fort, and the riverboat had carried away the newly captured Rebs.

Eighteen hours later, Lieutenant Daniels echoed Captain McBee's instructions that they were on a night reconnaissance. He made it clear that they were not a night assault force.

They were on a fact-finding mission, facts to be learned by gauging the amount of firepower in the fort once the blue skirmishers outside the earthworks retreated back to the safety of the walls.

"Use your cover, boys. There will be a lot of muskets aimed our way. You new fellas, listen to your pards who've done this before. As soon as you shoot, get behind cover or move away from that spot. The Yanks will be shooting at your muzzle flash. Move or hide before you reload."

Daniels made his speech to his platoon right before they marched. He didn't remind the thirty surviving new recruits in Company C that they would be loading their muskets in the dark, working only by feel, something they had never practiced.

The whole company moved away from camp, slogging through a mile of bottomland bordering the river. The thick scrub brush and tall bulrushes made for slow going, the leading men breaking a trail.

Company C was the first of three companies from the Fifth Texas on the night march, and Lieutenant Daniels was glad Captain McBee and the major were at the front of the column. Daniels swallowed in surprise when he saw the tall figure of General Hood join the Fifth Texas officers. Daniels thought, *This must be important for the general himself to join a night reconnaissance effort.*

An hour later, in complete darkness, the rising moon only a sliver, Lieutenant Daniels hoarsely whispered the order, "On the center file, as skirmishers, forward, march."

As Private Smith understood things, they were moving towards a fortified artillery battery overlooking the Nansemond River. They would likely find a line of rifle pits, and they were going to force the Union soldiers out of them, back into the main fort.

As Smith and Lawson moved forward in the dark, Smith quickly lost sight of the men on either side of them. When he paused he could hear men making their way through the brush, but his eyes were useless. Smith was ahead of Private Lawson, and when he turned to look back, he could barely make out Lawson's pale face catching a splash of dim moonlight. Otherwise, Lawson, even just a few yards behind him, was invisible in the darkness. Keyed up tight, Smith strained his eyes and ears for any indication of the Union pickets.

Soon, off to the right, Smith heard shooting, and a few seconds later the young Texan heard nervous voices to his front, where only the enemy should be. Without waiting for the Yankees to shoot, Smith pointed his musket toward the voices and pulled the trigger. He immediately fell to the ground and rolled behind a small tree. As expected, he saw two muzzle flashes not far ahead of him and heard a Minié ball whiz by, pruning leaves off the sapling above him.

As Private Smith clumsily reloaded in the dark while lying on his back, not able to see what he was doing, he listened for Lawson's return fire. He wanted Lawson to shoot, but didn't want to call out and draw more fire their way. Smith finished reloading and rose to his knees, using the slender tree for cover. He vainly looked back for Lawson. Nothing.

Just as Smith turned back around, ready to fire at the next sound, he heard a musket discharge behind him. Still fearing enemy fire, Smith remained silent. A second later, he saw a bright muzzle flash ahead of him. He quickly fired at it before he collapsed behind his tree to reload. While Smith was busy with his ramrod, a dark figure ran past him, bent over low. Smith glanced up as the running man passed within a few feet of him. The hard-running shadow shape, without hat or musket, going unarmed toward the enemy, confused Private Smith. He immediately discounted what he thought he had seen, thinking it absurd.

Smith remained still, listening to the sounds of men pushing through brambles and brush, the sounds moving away from him. Fearful of being separated from the other men in his company and snatched up by the Federal soldiers with his weapon unloaded, Smith didn't fire again. He didn't move even when he heard Sergeant Stephens' penetrating voice rallying the company to him.

Smith hugged the ground tighter and called for Lawson. He called a second time, more loudly, and waited. Finally, he gave up on Lawson and started moving back the way he had come.

Smith cursed as he stumbled and fell, losing his grip on his musket. He almost panicked when he realized that he had tripped over a body, a body too far back to be a Yank. This had to be Lawson, which meant the running figure had been a Yank who had let Smith pass by, then shot his partner. Damn.

Still alone and too scared to shout for assistance, Smith slung his rifle and awkwardly pulled the warm body to a sitting position, got his left shoulder under the torso, and staggered to his feet with his heavy burden. His foot kicked something metal which rattled at the contact. Smith instantly knew it was a sword scabbard, and with that came the awareness that he must be carrying Lieutenant Daniels, not Lawson.

Smith was worn out and about to kneel and slide Daniels off his shoulder when he saw candle light ahead. He staggered on towards the light, dropped to his knees and let Daniels fall on his back in front of the company. Sergeant Stephens knelt and held the candle close to Daniel's chest, illuminating the bullet wound that went right through the center button of Daniel's frock coat. The lieutenant was dead.

"Lucky shot. I bet the Yank never saw the lieutenant, was just pointing his musket towards his voice," Stephens said.

"Sergeant, can I speak with you, over there?" Smith said pointing to the side.

"Now, Private? We need to move." When he saw the Smith stepping away, he said, "All right. Corporal, get four men to carry poor Daniels back." Stephens followed Smith a few yards away.

"Sergeant, Lawson is missing. He ran right past me. Going towards the Yanks, Sergeant."

Stephens replied, "Hold on, Smith. Are you telling me that Private Lawson deserted? That he ran to the enemy?"

"I'm just telling you what I saw, Sergeant. It was real dark, and I was busy loading when Lawson rushed by me. But he didn't have his musket or his hat. That was just after somebody shot from behind me. I was looking forward, but the night lit up from the muzzle flash. But there weren't no Yanks behind me, Sergeant. Only Lawson. And the lieutenant."

"Damnation. That two-faced little prick." Stephens realized what Smith meant and wanted evidence. "Take me back there. Let's you and me find Lawson's musket and hat to back up your story,"

* * *

The Federal command assumed the Confederates would soon attack the earthworks next to the river with an overwhelming force to retake the artillery battery. Therefore, the next day the Union garrison abandoned Fort Huger, after spiking the cannons so they couldn't be used again.

* * *

Four days later Captain McBee and Colonel Powell studied the Union position across from Fort Huger, careful to keep their heads down. They were near the spot where Captain Isaac Turner had been killed the previous day by a Union sharpshooter firing across the river. All the officers in the Fifth Texas were depressed by Turner's death. He had been an outgoing young officer, about the same age as Lieutenant Daniels. Moreover, it was rumored that General Hood had intended to appoint Turner to lead a company of sharpshooters, crack shots pulled from all the regiments in the brigade.

After looking across the river until the first Minié ball thunked into the log near them, McBee and Powell, the commander of the Fifth Texas, slid down to squat on the parapet.

"Captain, you deploy your whole company to the right of the earthworks. Have your men crawl out to the river bank and start shooting at those damned sharpshooters."

"Yessir, But you saw how much cover there is across the river. That tall grass, cane, and bulrushes along the bank hide the Yanks just as well as they will hide my men. We'll be shooting blind."

"Maybe, but your boys might see enough smoke puffs to aim at to make a difference. Maybe just an hour of concentrated musket fire will give them cause to pull back too far to keep up their infernal sharpshooting."

"I'll bring the men up now, Sir. The river can't be more than two hundred feet wide, we'll make it hot for them," McBee promised.

The captain returned to his company which he'd left under the watch of Second Lieutenant Aaron Anderson. With the death of First Lieutenant Daniels, Anderson was temporarily the company's only subaltern. Anderson was also a very young man, but he had been serving as the second lieutenant for Company C since they left Texas. While Daniels' death greatly saddened McBee, he approved Anderson stepping into the role of first lieutenant. The captain had already submitted his recommendations for the promotion of Second Sergeant Hubbard to second lieutenant, Corporal Hodges as the newest sergeant, and Private Jason Smith to take Hodges position as corporal.

McBee had intentionally bypassed First Sergeant Stephens, viewing him as a man well suited to the top spot among the enlisted ranks, but a man who would chafe at being the lowest ranking junior officer. McBee had talked with Stephens about his decision, and the first sergeant was glad to remain as he was.

After crawling up to the river bank, McBee's men spent an hour firing twenty rounds each across the river. Captain McBee ordered his troops to cease fire, and wasn't very surprised that within ten minutes the Union sharpshooters on the far side of the river resumed their carefully aimed fire at the men inside Fort Huger.

McBee had just sent four men back to fetch another case of cartridges to distribute among his riflemen. The major hadn't told him to quit firing, so his men were busy running wet cloth patches down their Enfields, cleaning the black powder grit left inside the barrels. The captain jumped when Lieutenant Anderson touched his shoulder from behind.

"Damn it, Lieutenant, start announcing yourself some other way. What is it?"

"Captain, back home when we wanted to clear out the cane along the Trinity River to build a new boat dock, we set fire to the cane. Let's do that here. Let's burn out the bastards."

"Aaron, that's an idea with merit, but we're on the wrong side of the river," McBee said. "And those Yank sharpshooters are pretty good shots. They'd kill anybody in a boat before it gets across."

"Sir, they quit firing and hid when we were shooting before," Anderson elaborated to convince his superior. "When the men refill their cartridge boxes, we could start shooting again to keep the Yanks heads down while one of our men swims the river and starts a fire. Bulrushes are thick along the shore over there. It'll be easy for him to light a lucifer and get a good blaze going in no time. Private Green has already volunteered. He says he swam the Trinity lots of times back home to go sparking his girl. This river ain't any wider,"

"Wet matches don't strike, Lieutenant," McBee said.

"Yessir, that's why Sergeant Moss is cutting up a rubberized blanket to wrap a tin match safe inside, after we seal the safe with candle wax," Anderson said, his pride showing through.

"Water will still seep through," McBee concluded.

"Not if the match safe is out of the water in a little basket tied to Green's head. He'll keep his head above the water while he swims. Says he won't turn his body side to side and his arms will stay under the water. Only his head will be visible."

"With a basket on top," McBee said skeptically.

"Sir, Isaac Turner was a friend of mine back home. I want to do something that'll run those bastards out of there. We'll just be putting one man, a volunteer, at risk. I think it's a worthwhile plan."

"If you think it's a worthwhile plan, Lieutenant, and only one man, a volunteer, is endangered, go ahead," McBee conceded. "We're planning to start shooting that way again, anyhow."

Private Green left on his trousers and shirt when he slipped into the cold water, keeping low. The basket idea had been abandoned in favor of the box wrapped in rubberized canvas being strapped to his head with a belt cinched tight under his chin. The lieutenant then pushed an extra-large slouch hat down hard over Green's forehead and temples until the hat brim bent his ear lobes out. Green kept his head straight, trying not to jerk or nod, as he pushed off from the muddy bank, both legs and both arms making wide sweeping strokes under the water.

The forty riflemen kept firing over Green's head, doing their best to discourage the Federal sharpshooters. Nevertheless, when Green was halfway across the river, the first bullet splashed into the water behind him. Soon more rounds came his way. The one he remembered forever skipped off the surface of the water like a well-thrown flat rock. The Minié ball was on a slightly upward trajectory when it hit the front brim of his hat. He felt the whoosh and heard the wool felt tear when the lead bullet sliced through it.

Shaking from the cold water and the near-misses, Green crawled onto the bank and disappeared into the tall bulrushes. His company mates saw where he burrowed into the reeds and they kept firing to either side of where Green was last seen.

Within a minute smoke began rising and then flames emerged above the bulrushes. Green hit the water in a running dive, no hat on his head. He surfaced, and kicking wildly with feet and doing an arcing arm stroke, he swam as fast as he could back across the river. A few shots landed near him, then the Union riflemen abandoned the effort and pulled back from the rapidly spreading brush fire.

The fire burned out after it had cleaned the bank of vegetation for a hundred yards. Without cover to hide them, the Union sharpshooters gave up harassing the artillery crewmen. The Confederate battery and a garrison of infantry remained in Fort Huger for another two weeks without any further casualties.

* * *

"Men, you may not know it, but our Minié balls have two rings around the base, and the Yanks shoot Minié balls that have three rings. The doc dug the bullet out of Lieutenant Daniels. Here it is," McBee said to his sergeants as he handed the misshapen slug of lead to Stephens.

First Sergeant Stephens was skeptical. "How do we know that's the same Minié ball? We found Lawson's musket not twenty yards from where Daniels fell. Bullets shot that close go all the way through."

McBee answered, miffed that his first sergeant would question, rather than back up the find. "We know it's the same bullet because the doctor said it's the one he dug out of the body. Daniels' coat button and this Minié ball were both mangled up against poor Daniels' backbone. The brass button slowed it down and the backbone stopped it. Is that enough for you, Sergeant?"

Mildly chastened, Stephens said, "Two rings. The bullet is all mushed up, but I see two rings, not three. It's ours."

"That's right, Sergeant," McBee said. "It confirms that Lawson shot Daniels and lit out to the other side. Deserted. I hope they shot the bastard, but no one's found any bodies, ours, theirs, or civilian. Either the Yanks took Lawson away as a prisoner, or the little turd snuck off in the night and is hiding out somewhere around Suffolk."

"Piss on him," Sergeant Hubbard said. "I sure hope he's gone to ground and we catch the asshole."

"Tell the men about the Minié ball. I want them to know, so they'll not protect Lawson should we ever see him," McBee added.

Continuing, McBee said, "But that ain't real likely, since we're moving down into North Carolina and leaving Suffolk behind. We're going after food. Word is that North Carolina is ripe with beef, bacon, and corn, not like Virginia which has been picked clean by two armies. Longstreet's whole corps is going foraging on a grand scale. We're been assigned to feed Lee's army," the captain said.

"Well, it sure beats doing nothing but drilling in camp. Maybe we'll all get fat," Sergeant Hubbard reflected.

Chapter 12

Near the Virginia-North Carolina Border
Tidewater Region
Late April, 1863

Private John Hailey grimaced, as he did every time he had to climb onto the wagon seat. Hailey had injured his left ankle the previous summer during the fight at Freeman's Ford. He remembered his terror, frantically trying to free his foot from the grip of a bottom root and reach the bank before a bullet hit him. He made it out of the river without being wounded, but he severely twisted his ankle. At times like this he wished he could trade the fickle ankle for a quick-healing bullet hole.

Private Andrew Dunlap was already on the wagon bench seat. Dunlap was the oldest man in the company, a fact he told anyone who'd listen. "Yup, boy, you know th' capt'n and old red-headed Rafe was still on they's mamas' tits whenst I was on th' ground chasin' after lizards and yard hens. I'm too old to be here fightin' this war"

Hailey was tired of Dunlap's self-absorbed whining, so without turning his head, he asked, "Then why are you here, Mr. Dunlap? You're too old to be conscripted. Why did you join?"

"You ain't ever met my wife, have ya', boy?"

Hailey shook his head.

"Iffin' you had, you'd know why I put five states and the Mississippi River 'tween me and her."

Hailey shook his head again, and snapped the reins to get the team moving. The two horses leaned into their harnesses, and the wheels slowly turned to lift the wagon out of the muddy puddles. Standing next to one of the rear wheels, Acting Sergeant Hodges gratefully patted the back of the wagon, thanking it for rolling forward without the squad of walking men having to help loosen the big spoke wheels from the mud.

"I'm sure glad those nags still got some muscle, instead of just rawhide and bones like most of the stock in the army train," Private Dunlap said. He'd dreaded the prospect of climbing back to the ground and pushing on a wheel once they'd loaded the wagon with sacks of ground corn, loose ears of dried corn, slabs of bacon and several smoked hams.

Dunlap was particularly happy with the hen eggs he'd found stashed behind a loose bottom board at the back of a barn. He didn't mind that the load of food in the wagon bed was bound north, beyond Richmond, to Lee's army. He didn't mind that two of Longstreet's three divisions were tasked with emptying the northeast counties of North Carolina of all the food that could be found and hauled away.

Dunlap really didn't care about any of that. Let the farmers take care of themselves. He did care about the nine eggs that were now nestled in grass in the crown of his battered hat, the upside down hat resting on the bench between Hailey and him. Dunlap thought that bacon and corn were fine rations, but eggs, glorious fried eggs, white as pearls and yellow yolks running like the sunrise over a calm sea, made a meal worth going to war over. Fried eggs didn't hurt a man's teeth like hardtack did, and they didn't cause a man's stomach to curdle like raw bacon did. Yessir, fried eggs were the way a prince started the day, and tomorrow he'd breakfast like a prince.

Moreover, Dunlap was pleased beyond words that it was his turn to ride shotgun next to Hailey. While Hodges and the others trudged along next to the wagon and Hailey kept the mules headed back towards the growing brigade commissary camp, he could sit and bask in the afternoon sun.

It was clear to Hodges' whole squad that the good folks of North Carolina were not happy when the war arrived at their spreads, especially those farmers who hacked out a life far back in the coastal swamps. Yet, as far as they knew, only a few shots had been fired at any of Longstreet's foragers. They all figured those had been nothing more than harmless random shots of anger fired from a safe distance, shots taken by men who had just lost all their livestock or last fall's harvest.

The first bullet missed Hailey, going low, hitting the front board of the wagon. The second bullet struck Private Dunlap in the groin, causing him to instantly slump over and crumple into the foot space at Hailey's feet, howling in pain.

Acting Sergeant Hodges immediately went forward with his other five men to root out the ambushers, but they found no one. Instructing four of the five riflemen to fan out across the road and stay fifty yards ahead of the wagon, he returned to find Dunlap passed out, his head thrown back against the sideboard. Hailey had stuffed his jacket into the blood flowing from Dunlap's wound, and was trying to hold it in place to staunch the bleeding. Hodges could see blood seeping through the material, and figured it was useless, that Dunlap was about to bleed out. Still, he was a sergeant now and was expected to try and save his men.

"Come on Hailey, let's stretch out his legs and cut his trousers off so we can see the wound," Hodges ordered. They found that the round ball had torn through Dunlap's scrotum, but nothing more.

After studying the wound and gauging the amount of blood flow, Hodges said, "It's not as bad as I thought, but we need something to plug the hole in his sack. Oh man, the recruiter never said nothin' 'bout stuff like this. You got a handkerchief or a rag?"

"Nah, Sergeant, but here's some grass that Dunlap packed around his eggs. Will that work?"

"No, I need something solid to stick inside, up against the end of the blood vessels that are bleeding," Hodges answered.

"How about an egg? Got a hatful of fresh eggs here," Dailey said.

"What the hell, I don't know what else to do. Give me a little one. He was hit by a musket ball, not a cannon ball. That ain't a big hole." Using his thumb and forefinger, Hodges gently opened up the bullet wound in the loose skin of Dunlap's scrotum and pushed the small end of the egg into it. The first part of the egg slipped in easily, but stopped, so Hodges flipped open his pocket knife and slit the skin sack open a little further. He then put pressure on the exposed end of the egg until the whole elliptical shaped shell was out of sight, wedged up tight against whatever connected Dunlap's sack to his lower belly. In a few seconds the bleeding stopped.

"Holy Jesus," Hailey said reverently, staring at the huge round lump inside Dunlap's scrotum, trying not to look at the wounded man's member.

Hailey drove the team for three hours back to the commissary camp. When they ever-so-carefully lifted Dunlap out of the wagon, he moaned piteously. Word spread quickly about Dunlap's wound and the egg, so men crowded around while a surgeon knelt next between Dunlap's legs. With a towel ready in one hand, the doctor gently pulled the egg from Dunlap's sack. The bleeding did not start again.

One man said what all were thinking, "Would you look at that, the old man laid an egg."

"This can't be," the surgeon said as he held up the sticky dark pink egg, crusted with Dunlap's blood and juices. "It's heavy and firm like it's been boiled in a pot of water. "Give me a canteen."

He poured water over the egg shell, and it remained pink, darker on one side than the other. Next, he tapped the egg on the side of the canteen, and popped it open. The egg-white was the color of lips and the yolk was orange as a sunset.

"Anybody hungry?" the surgeon asked, causing two men to bend over and vomit.

* * *

"That's right, Major, at least a hundred thousand pounds of bacon, all at one farm. Some of it was hidden in a dugout cellar under a big corn crib," Captain McBee reported to his wing commander. "Sir, we're going to need fifty or more freight wagons to haul all that pork."

"The mother lode, huh? I'll send riders out, Captain, but you know our wagons are spread out all over the countryside. It'll take a day or two to get word out to all of them.

I'll need a dozen maps showing where this cache is. A hundred thousand pounds. I can't even imagine that much bacon in one place."

"Figured you'd need maps, I've got a lieutenant working on them right now," McBee assured the major.

Then McBee added, "My sergeant said he searched the pig farmer's desk and found a contract with the Union quartermaster for two hundred and fifty thousand pounds, that's twice what we've found so far. We may even find more before we're done."

Major Rogers answered, "Damn. I know the Federal cavalry controlled this whole region for months before we came, but have people no sense of loyalty? What kind of man would sell out his state for a stack of greenbacks? Damn."

"You know, Major," McBee, himself a dealer in cotton back in Texas, said to temper his major's anger, "The Yanks may not have given that pig farmer any choice. They could have just taken all his pork. Can we blame a man for doing what he can to protect his property? He told my sergeant that they threatened to burn him out if he didn't do business with 'em."

"I suppose that's one way to look at. A business man's viewpoint," the major grudgingly conceded. "Well, we'll take every scrap of that bacon and leave that money-grubbing farmer a paper receipt he can take to Richmond for payment. Let him explain to some colonel in the War Department just why he was selling every pig in this part of North Carolina to the damyankees. Damn. I still think we should hang the bastard for selling a mountain of bacon to the enemy."

Chapter 13

Office of the Army Quartermaster Department
Richmond, Virginia
May 10, 1863

Colonel Treadway motioned for Lieutenant Samuelson to sit in the chair facing his desk. The colonel oversaw Samuelson's duties as a contract liaison officer, and the two had known each other since before the war, as banker and aspiring young businessman.

The colonel studied the younger lieutenant, assessing if Samuelson was indeed the right man for the duty he needed to assign. The handsome blond lieutenant sat somewhat slouched in his chair, a posture of casual self-confidence that the colonel often thought bordered on arrogance. Some days that irked the older officer, but for this job he figured a bit of arrogance would be just the thing.

"Adam, I need you to take a special assignment for a week or so," the colonel began without the customary pleasantries.

Samuelson shifted in his chair to sit more erectly and said, "What would that be, Sir?"

"You, of course, know that the city is in the midst of preparing for General Jackson's funeral. My department is responsible for transporting the general's remains."

"Yes Sir. How may I assist, Colonel?" Samuelson asked.

"Plans for getting the body to Richmond are done. But you may not know that General Jackson is having two funerals. The first one will be here in Richmond. The second one will be in Lexington, where the general lived for ten years before the war."

"Yes Sir, he was a teacher at the military school there, if I recall."

"Right. His widow and infant daughter still live in Lexington, and that's where she plans to bury his remains, in the family plot in the city cemetery."

"Yes Sir. That seems a reasonable request by Mrs. Jackson," Samuelson said, his mind racing ahead to what his assigned duty might be.

"So it is, but it means we must transport the remains to Lexington from Richmond," the colonel continued. "That's where I need your services. I understand that you were in Lexington just a few months ago."

"I visited a contractor in Charlottesville, which is closer to Lexington than we are here in Richmond, but it's still a day's ride from Lexington."

"Yes, I know that, Lieutenant. I meant that after you finished your army business in Charlottesville, you went on to Lexington on personal business." The colonel spoke in a curt manner, not understanding why the lieutenant didn't immediately acknowledge he'd gone on to Lexington from Charlottesville. That was no crime, after all.

"Yes Sir, I did visit Lexington briefly," Samuelson admitted, without adding any explanation.

"That means you know more about the town than anyone else in my office, so I'm sending you to hire a boat to take the general's remains from the train station at Lynchburg, up the Kanawha Canal to Lexington."

"Sir?"

"Adam, no train goes to Lexington. You know that, since you've been there. However, the North Fork of the James joins the Maury River, which is now a canal complete with locks. And that canal goes right into the middle of Lexington. So, rather than put Jackson's coffin on a wagon for the last leg of the trip, we are going to send it up the Maury in a mule-towed packet boat. That's your job, Lieutenant. Hire an appropriate boat and be the watchdog over the casket until it is unloaded onto an artillery caisson in Lexington. I'm informed that the *Marshall* is the finest packet boat on the canal. I'm told its appointments are mahogany and velvet, most appropriate for well-heeled passengers and important cargo."

"Yes Sir."

"I'm further informed that General Jackson's widow and child are travelling on the train with the general's remains. That means they may desire to stay with the coffin on the boat ride from Lynchburg to Lexington. You will make every effort necessary to see to their comfort, should the widow choose to accompany the remains on the boat."

"Yes Sir."

Leaning forward in his chair, the colonel stressed to the lieutenant, "Adam, we are talking about the earthly remains of the second most popular man in the Confederacy. There will be crowds of adoring citizens wanting to be a part of every phase of his transfer from here to Lexington. His funeral in Lexington will involve a second parade and service, then the interment in the cemetery."

"Yes Sir."

"Your duty is only to insure that the general's remains are efficiently transferred from train to boat, and that the boat trip goes without a hitch. If the widow does want to ride the boat with her deceased husband, you will make her comfortable and remain prepared to deal with any unforeseen exigency. But I expect none of that, since you will plan each detail, and leave nothing to chance. Am I being clear, Lieutenant?"

"Yes Sir."

"Once in Lexington, you will attend the services and be in the entourage that follows the casket to the cemetery. Full dress uniform, to represent this department. Do you understand what your duty is? If you have any questions, ask me now."

"I understand my assignment, Sir. No questions. Transporting freight by river is how I've made a living since your bank loaned me the money to buy my first boat. A casket is only cargo, after all."

"Exactly why I thought of you for this duty. Just don't overlook Mrs. Jackson's comfort. She would be a most important passenger," the colonel reminded him.

"Yes Sir. Colonel, there is one thing," Samuelson said with visible reluctance.

"What's that?" the colonel asked.

"Might this be too important an assignment for a lieutenant? Being responsible for General Jackson's remains, and being so close to his widow, I mean?"

"I considered that before I called for you. Take this as a compliment, Adam. I have every confidence in your abilities, regardless of your rank."

"Thank you, Sir. I was just thinking of the reputation of the department, that a man of captain's rank might be better, more appropriate, to the solemnity of the occasion…"

Colonel Treadway's brow went from lines of bemusement, to sudden understanding. "I think a lieutenant in his dress uniform will be sufficiently solemn for the occasion," Treadway said to the young man, noting Samuelson's mouth tighten at his words.

Remembering that Samuelson was always diligent in discretely passing him envelopes of cash after his trips to contractors' factories, the colonel decided to toss the young man a bone.

"You've served the Confederacy well these two years, Adam. Complete this assignment with your customary efficiency, and when you return, I'll pass along a recommendation for your promotion. That would be *after* General Jackson's last boat ride, and *after* his widow has been appropriately coddled from Lynchburg to Lexington."

First Lieutenant Adam Samuelson smiled as he stood, saluted, and gave a final, "Yes Sir." Then he turned and left the colonel's office, heading directly to the telegraph room to send a message impressing the canal packet boat *Marshall* for a brief, but critical army assignment.

As the lieutenant spent the day working on the details of his assignment, he never gave a thought to the short note he had received in the mail from Lexington three months earlier: the note written by his runaway wife warning him that if he returned to Lexington he would be arrested. From the note, Samuelson gathered that Bull Rankin, the tough he'd hired to kill Captain McBee, had instead severely wounded the man's mother when he'd missed his intended victim in the ambush. The note indicated the sheriff had discovered the link between him and Rankin, and worst of all, the sheriff had in his possession physical evidence of that link, his expensive Whitworth rifle with his name elaborately engraved on the lock plate.

Not being a man to brood over past missteps, Samuelson had reflected on the handwritten message only very briefly. The debacle in Lexington the previous December had galled him, but he was a practical man and had already decided to simply let his wife go. He was again enjoying a bachelor's lifestyle after a dozen years of marriage that had borne no children. As lovely and willing as Faith had been, he now relished the pleasures available from the soiled doves in Richmond establishments like Mulberry Grove and the Haystack.

Further, in regards to Faith's terse letter of warning, there weren't any army contractors in Lexington to require his presence. At the time, he'd seen no reason why he might need to go to Lexington again, so he'd dropped the paper into the fire and forgotten it.

Lexington, Virginia
May 13, 1863

Captain McBee stood on the porch of his mother's home and briefly thought back to the day he'd stood on these same floorboards just over a year ago, anxious about seeing his mother after nearly two decades away. In the fifteen months since that day, McBee felt like he'd aged fifteen years.

He'd tried the doorknob, and found it locked. *Good,* he'd thought, *they've learned that not every visitor is a friend.* After knocking, he'd noticed the curtains at the front window part slightly as someone inside checked to see who had come calling. Just seconds later, Faith nearly knocked McBee backwards as she flung the door open, wrapped her arms around his neck and kissed him hard on the mouth

"Faith, we're outside, and I was just here a few weeks ago," McBee said when she pulled her head back, but kept him in her embrace.

"I've missed you terribly, and the twins have been crying for their papa," she answered.

"Can we go in now, before we're the scandal of Lexington?" he said, pulling her arms from his neck.

"Pooh. We're already the scandal of Lexington. We could make another baby right now, right here on this porch, and Mrs. Upright across the street wouldn't be any more scandalized than she is now."

"Mrs. Upright is not the name of the fine lady who lives across the road," McBee said.

"Oh, but it is," Faith said, pulling McBee in with one hand, and waving to the empty porch across the street.

Inside, McBee hugged his mother before he went up the stairs two steps at a time to see his infant children in the nursery. Faith came in behind him, picked up John Junior and handed him to his father, then did the same with little Betsy. Elizabeth came in, making a crowd in the small bedroom.

"It's the funeral, isn't it? General Jackson's funeral," Faith asked.

"Yes, it is," McBee confirmed. "General Hood remembered that I was raised here, and sent me to represent his command at the funeral tomorrow. He had great respect for General Jackson. I have a note of condolences from General Hood to pass along to Mrs. Jackson."

"She's a lovely young woman, Anna Jackson is," Elizabeth McBee said. "Her husband being a high-ranking general, none of us thought he was in danger of being killed in battle."

"It was after the battle, Mother. It was dusk and the general was out beyond where he should have been, doing a personal scout, and our own men thought his escort was a Yank cavalry patrol and opened fire on them."

"What a shame," Faith said. "And him with a wife and a baby daughter."

"It was a mistake that could cost the Confederacy dearly, I'm afraid," the captain added. "Jackson was Lee's right arm. He got more out of his men than any other general could, except maybe General Hood."

"Children," Mrs. McBee urged, "let's leave further talk of the war outside this house for the rest of the day. Faith, please take Betsy and let Johnny hold his son a bit longer. I suggest we go downstairs and see if our new cook is up to adding another plate to the supper table."

* * *

John McBee pulled out Faith's dining room chair after they had deposited the two infants in a shared day crib in the corner. Betsy was fussy while John Junior gurgled for a moment, then drifted to sleep. At four months old, the boy had caught and passed his sister in weight, even though she'd been larger at birth.

"John Junior has accepted the cow's milk. He even seems to prefer it, but little Betsy still spits it out until I put her on my breast," Faith told John, with a hint of concern.

"The cow has more fat. You, dear Faith, are slender as a reed, I expect from going up and down the stairs all day with the children in your arms. The cow just stands all day in its stall. I should hope her milk has more cream in it. Maybe that's why Junior likes it and Betsy doesn't," McBee suggested with a grin.

"John, hush that talk," Elizabeth rebuked her son. "You are not in your army camp. Consider your surroundings, please."

At that moment Edwina Bell came through the kitchen door carrying a steaming ceramic soup urn and wearing an apron over brown trousers and tan shirt. Her hair remained cut just below her ear.

"It's very good to see you looking so well, Ed..." McBee hesitated.

"It's Edward, Captain. My sister Edwina has returned to Texas," she said winking at the captain.

"Edward it is. I think you have made the prudent choice, Edward."

"I'm good with the horse and outside chores. I never did have a knack for washing the bed sheets back home," Edward said.

"But Edward is an excellent cook," Faith added as she stood to ladle the aromatic soup into their bowls.

As Edward returned to the kitchen, McBee saw the handle of a pocket revolver tucked into her trousers at the small of her back.

After an evening of conversation, that was in turn cheerful and melancholy, the family retired to their rooms. Before Faith joined John in the bed, she sat in the rocking chair by the crib and nursed the twins, one at a time. She left the lamp burning and made no effort to cover herself, as McBee sat with his back against the headboard and watched. Faith kept him engaged in conversation during the feeding, and was amused that while he shared stories from the army camp, he kept his eyes glued to her breasts, especially whichever one did not have an infant suckling at it.

Chapter 14

Lexington, Virginia
May 15, 1863

Edward Bell drove Captain McBee and his mother to Jordon Point, the river landing where the *Marshall* was expected within the hour. Faith had brushed most of the mud stains from the captain's frock coat, and had held his weather beaten felt hat in the steam over the tea kettle, doing her best to reshape it into a respectable appearance. Bell had blackened the captain's boots, as well as rubbed a shine back to the captain's tarnished sword scabbard and the brass buttons of his coat. Elizabeth had proudly presented her son with a scarlet waist sash which she had fashioned from a red silk shawl she hadn't worn in the two decades since her husband died. She'd deftly sewn a dark red curtain cord tassel on each end of the sash, the colors almost matching the red silk.

Sheriff Cain was already at the wharf, dressed in his Sunday suit. He didn't expect any problems more serious than a few crippled soldiers coming to town for the funeral and getting drunk and rowdy. He hated maudlin drunks, but found them easy enough to manage. Still, the sheriff knew today would bring out the largest crowd ever in the streets of Lexington, so he wore his pistol belt beneath his long black frock coat. His one deputy was nearby, carrying the riot gun that seemed permanently attached to his arm.

The sheriff had hired four more temporary deputies for the day, local men with war injuries that had forced them out of the army. Their job would be to keep the crowd out of the street, away from the artillery caisson that would carry General Jackson's remains from Jordon's Point to the cemetery, about a mile distant. The sheriff himself intended to join the procession following the caisson.

Elizabeth McBee directed Edward to stop the carriage near the sheriff and waited for Sheriff Cain to offer his hand before she climbed down. She wore the same black dress and bonnet that she'd bought for her oldest son's funeral two years earlier.

John McBee was secretly relieved that Faith had to stay home with the twins. He was not yet prepared to walk arm-in-arm with her at this most public and solemn occasion. Yet, he did regret that she would miss the event, knowing she'd want to hear about every detail. After his mother stepped out of the carriage, the captain joined the growing cluster of uniformed men who waited for the arrival of the *Marshall.*

Edward Bell drove the carriage back to the McBee home as instructed. Captain McBee had been emphatic that Faith not be left alone in the house any longer than absolutely necessary. It worried the captain that the large crowd expected for the funeral would provide an ideal cover, should Lieutenant Samuelson choose this day to try to forcibly take Faith away or harm her or the babies.

* * *

Lieutenant Samuelson was exhausted. Since receiving his orders from Colonel Treadway and indulging in a celebration with his favorite prostitute, he had slept little. He'd travelled to Lynchburg the next morning to find that the owners of the *Marshall* were loyal Virginians who were glad for their best vessel to be used for such a high profile purpose. Nonetheless, they quickly informed Samuelson that they expected full and ample payment in advance for disrupting the *Marshall's* schedule to accommodate General Jackson's funeral. Surely, they explained to him, as the owner of a freight company himself, the lieutenant understood they would incur extra expenses rerouting the cargo of the *Marshall's* regular clients.

More issues followed, creating obstacles to what first seemed a simple task. Finally, at 6:30 the next evening, in view of the thousands of spectators who lined the canal, the casket was stoutly secured by ropes atop the passenger cabin and covered with the Confederate national flag. General Jackson's widow and baby were settled into the plush cabin beneath the casket, accompanied by a number of grieving family members and close friends. Some were family and friends who lived in Lexington and had insisted on taking the *Marshall* from Lexington to Lynchburg that same morning so they could join the grieving widow for the return boat ride. Lieutenant Samuelson slumped in a seat at the far end of the long narrow cabin, Mrs. Jackson in his sight.

The trip took all night, the mule team twice switched out to maintain a steady pace of two miles an hour. The mules were led by a teamster who carried a lantern, and sometimes even in the middle of night, had to cuss people to get them off the mule path when they crowded too close, eager to see the *Marshall's* famous cargo.

Samuelson lingered at the back of the passenger cabin until Mrs. Jackson and her family had disembarked from the *Marshall*. On his way up the aisle, he paused at one of the windows, parted the curtain and looked out. He wasn't surprised to see the crowd of civilians on the wharf, nor the group of uniformed officers among them. Hearing the sound of boots just over his head, Samuelson hurried up the steps to observe the boat's crew freeing the general's casket from the ropes that had secured it to the cabin roof.

Samuelson had to push past an honor guard of eight senior cadets from the military institute who stood next to the cabin and effectively blocked his passage. The young men leaned in when he squeezed behind them, but would not move their feet as they solemnly faced the flag draped casket of the famous general, the same man who just twenty-four months before had been their professor of natural science and artillery.

* * *

Captain McBee waited patiently in the last rank of the Confederate officers who would march behind the family and the VMI cadets, all trailing the artillery caisson bearing the casket and a saddled, but riderless, horse led by Jackson's body-servant. Elizabeth McBee joined the gaggle of ladies from Lexington's close knit social circles who constituted the last component of the procession. Sheriff Cain positioned himself several paces behind

Mrs. McBee, trailing the procession, his eyes habitually roving back and forth, alert for anything that didn't seem right.

"Sheriff, it's a fine morning, ain't it?" Provost Lieutenant Blomerth said as he strode up to the sheriff and joined him in his slow pace at the back of the funeral procession.

"What's so fine about a funeral?" the sheriff retorted.

"It's a fine day 'cause the saloons are gonna fill up with folks from thirty miles in ever' direction, and they's gonna git drunk and say things 'bout them what's hidin' out in the hills and hollers. I'm gonna be a busy man over the next week or so rootin' out them skunks."

"Just keep your gun holstered, Lieutenant, while you're in my town," the sheriff warned him.

"Oh, don't you fret, Sheriff, I'm gonna be a rabbit tonight. A rabbit with great big ears. Don't you worry none 'bout me."

* * *

The hair on the back of Captain McBee's neck bristled when he saw Lieutenant Samuelson join the front row of officers. McBee ground his teeth and squeezed his sword hilt in a white-knuckled grip as he fought back the black fury that the sight of Samuelson brought on.

When they reached the cemetery the procession stopped, and the orderly ranks of officers broke apart as the hundreds of people slowly squeezed through the few gates in the fence that surrounded the graveyard. McBee maneuvered to put himself right next to Samuelson, who had moved off to the side of the crowd, waiting a few steps away from anyone else.

"If you or your thug put one foot onto my property, I will shoot you dead before your other foot hits the ground," McBee hissed into Samuelson's ear.

Samuelson tensed, then said in a low voice, "How can you do that, Captain, when you are here with me, on the other side of town from your mother's home. My man may be driving Faith away right now."

"Do you think I'd leave Faith unguarded? Whatever wharf trash you send will be no more successful than the other two I killed."

"Captain, I'm on duty today, an important duty until that casket is planted. So get the hell away from me."

"Just so you don't forget, Faith is staying here with her children. My children."

Samuelson snorted in derision. "I'm done with Faith. When the war is over, take her and your brats back to whatever hovel in Texas you came from. I wouldn't stay in Lexington, however."

"Is that a threat?"

"No threat, Captain. That's merely my observation that the devout Presbyterians of Lexington won't welcome a philanderer into their pious little town once the war ends and they return to meddling in their neighbors' lives. Even a battle-scarred warrior like you will not be tolerated living openly with another man's legal wife."

Since McBee agreed with what Samuelson just said, he remained silent, allowing Samuelson to say in an unexpectedly friendly tone, "I urge you to start tying Faith to the bed. I swear she enjoyed it. And you. Did you like watching your new woman being had that way by her real husband?"

Before McBee could reply, Samuelson jerked from a tap on his shoulder. He twisted around only to have the muzzle of Sheriff Cain's pistol pressed against his stomach.

"If you are Lieutenant Samuelson, you and I have business at the jail," the sheriff calmly said. "John, is this Samuelson?"

"Yeah, Sheriff, that's him,"

"If you'll excuse us, then, the lieutenant and I are going to take a stroll to my office," the sheriff said, prodding Samuelson with his pistol to start walking away from the crowd.

Speaking over his shoulder, the sheriff said to McBee, "Let my deputy know I'm at the jail, and tell him to stay here until the crowd breaks up. That may be quite a while."

Chapter 15

Lexington, Virginia
May 15, 1863

As soon as the pair moved around a corner, Sheriff Cain handed Samuelson a cleverly knotted piece of rope that had two loops in it.

"Put a hand in each loop, and pull it tight with your teeth," the sheriff directed.

The lieutenant glowered at the sheriff as he hobbled his own hands.

"Sheriff…" Samuelson began.

"Shut up. Stay quiet until we get to the jail."

Once inside the sheriff's building, Cain pointed at the chair in front of his desk. Samuelson sat down on the edge of the seat, back straight.

"Tell me about David Rankin," the sheriff said as he sat behind his desk, facing Samuelson.

"Who?"

"Tell me why Rankin, who was a deck hand on one of your boats, used an expensive English rifle with your name engraved on it to shoot a sixty year-old woman from ambush."

"A fine Whitworth rifle was stolen from my home months ago. Thank you for recovering it," Samuelson answered as he nodded towards his rifle on the wall rack behind the sheriff.

Sheriff Cain leaned forward and said, "That woman almost died, and she is a friend of mine." He rose and turned to pull the Whitworth off the rack, intending to shove the engraved lock plate into the lieutenant's face.

When the sheriff turned, Samuelson stood and smoothly picked up a rusty iron railroad spike off a stack of papers on the desk. The heavy spike was nearly a foot long, and as the sheriff began to turn back with the rifle, Samuelson slammed Cain's head with the blunt end of the spike as hard as he could. The sheriff dropped like a sack of rocks to the floor, his head bleeding profusely.

Samuelson looked down at Cain and muttered, "Sorry, Sheriff, but I wasn't liking where this conversation was going."

* * *

Two hours later Deputy Jones stepped through the front door of the jail. He saw the sheriff lying on the floor behind his desk, not moving, a trickle of blood running from a gash on his head and a heavy iron railroad spike laying next to him. A few feet away from the sheriff lay a wadded up Confederate uniform coat with the insignia of a First Lieutenant on the collar. The deputy did not at first realize that the sheriff's coat and hat were missing, as was the expensive English rifle that had been in the rack on the wall.

An hour later, the doctor had come and gone, and a small group of men waited on the undertaker. The deputy filled the silence with the obvious. "He must have bludgeoned the sheriff with the railroad spike."

"What the hell was the sheriff doing with a railroad spike on his desk?" Provost Lieutenant Blomerth asked.

"He kept it there as a paperweight," the deputy answered. "He'd pick it up and tell me at least once a month how glad he was the train don't come through Lexington. He said trains bring nothing but trouble to a peaceful town."

"Hmmph. Looks like the damned railroad got him anyway," Blomerth said.

"Me and two of the boys the sheriff deputized for the funeral are going after him," Deputy Jones told the group. He looked at Blomerth, "You're the hound dog who chases men all over three counties. Which way you reckon this lieutenant went?"

Blomerth rubbed his balding head and looked up as he thought. "He can't go back east to Richmond. The provosts would be waiting on him at the railroad station. Same for Charlottesville. Has the packet boat left Jordan Point yet?"

Someone told him he'd seen it pull away loaded with mourners and crates headed to Lynchburg.

"He could be on it, goin' south towards Tennessee. Lots of Unionists down that way. But it's a long ride to the Tennessee border. Or he could go up the valley, that'd be easy riding, but the telegraph would get ahead of him, just like goin' towards Richmond.

"Nah, if I was runnin' from killin'a sheriff, I'd head northwest toward the mountains, towards that part of Virgini' that stayed with the Union. Beckley, then on to Charleston. That'd be hard riding too, but shorter and safer than Tennessee onest he gets there. And I sure don't look for no Yank provost or sheriff to help us catch him."

"You goin' with us then?" the deputy asked Blomerth.

"He's an army officer on the run. Yeah, I'll take you fellas over some trails he won't know. May be we can get ahead of him before he gets to a Union town. But I ain't goin' into West Virgini'. I'm not goin' to get swept up by a Yank cavalry patrol and spend the next year in some Yankee prison camp. It's gonna be some hard riding, though, to get ahead of that piece of shit. He's got a three-four hour lead on us. We gotta move. Now."

* * *

Adam Samuelson huddled under the painted canvas cloth slicker the sheriff kept tied behind his saddle. It was drizzling and cold and Samuelson seethed in his misery. When the moon set and it was too dark to see the horse's ears, he moved off the trail to wait until first light to continue. He left the horse saddled and finally nodded off in short stints of fitful sleep.

He jerked awake in dim light when yet another trickle of cold water dripping from his hat brim seeped under his collar. It had quit raining, but everything was wet. He stood, stretched, urinated, and rummaged through the sheriff's saddlebag looking for food. Finding nothing he could eat, he sat down with the sheriff's pistol. He pulled the cylinder and used his pocket knife to carefully remove the round lead ball from one firing chamber. He then very carefully poured the loose black powder from that chamber down the barrel of the Whitworth. He repeated the process with the ball and powder from a second chamber in the cylinder. That left him three shots in the pistol, which he thought would be enough in an emergency.

Finally, he dug into his trouser pocket and pulled out his "lucky" hexagonal Whitworth bullet. He stuck his fingers into his ears, digging out as much ear wax as he could. He rubbed the wax mixed with spit all over the bottom half of the bullet, quickly slipped it into the mouth of the musket barrel and with some difficulty rammed it down. Finally, he took a priming cap off the pistol, and with the point of his knife, split the copper on opposite sides and worked it onto the nipple of the Whitworth. It wasn't a real snug fit, but Samuelson thought it would still send a spark to the powder well enough.

* * *

After a few more hours of riding, always taking any fork that took him more up than down, while trying to always keep his back to the rising sun, the lieutenant came to a crossroad. Samuelson was no tracker, but the intersecting muddy ruts were clean of fresh horseshoe prints, so he relaxed a bit as he considered which way to go. Two of the muddy wagon tracks both seemed to go generally in the direction he wanted, so he again chose the path that sloped uphill.

He reached the first bend past the crossroad and looked back. He didn't see anything, but when his horse stood still, Samuelson heard voices. He kicked his horse beyond the bend and slid from the saddle, keeping the reins in his grip. He looped the reins loosely over a fallen tree branch, and with the Whitworth in hand, he leaned against a large tree and watched four men ride into view. One man dismounted and studied the ground at the intersection.

Samuelson raised the rifle and put his eye to the scope, centering his aim on the man in front who wore a shabby army jacket with two bars visible on the collar. Just as that man pointed up the hill, smiling at his success at intersecting the fugitive's path, Samuelson squeezed the trigger, sending the spinning bullet through the center of Blomerth's chest and out his back.

The other three men jumped off their horses, the one-armed veteran falling in his haste when his phantom arm failed to grab the saddle horn to swing off. His head landed on a half-buried root knob and knocked him unconscious. With half his force down, Deputy Jones decided they had taken enough casualties and would prudently refrain from further pursuit.

Not knowing if he would be chased, Samuelson moved quickly back to his horse, mounted, and galloped away, keeping the horse at a run for as long as he dared.

In the late afternoon, Samuelson stopped to read a large crudely painted sign that leaned against a tree trunk:

> *This here is the border of the New state of Western Virginia.*
> *Rebel Trash go back or get Shot!*

Chapter 16

Camp of the Army of Northern Virginia
Near Brandy Station, Virginia
June 8, 1863

*S*abers, *thousands of sabers, really do rattle in their scabbards,* Captain McBee thought, as he and his men breathed dust and watched the endless ranks of horsemen trot past. *More creaking and clatter than rattle,* he mused further, *but maybe that's all the other trappings the horses have strapped on them.*

McBee was in his position at the right end of the front rank of Company C, directly in front of First Sergeant Stevens. Private Rafe Fulton was just a foot or two away, in his spot among the tallest men, and McBee could clearly hear Fulton's running commentary.

"I don't mind marching from camp to a battle, or from camp to another camp. But, marching two hours to watch a bunch of Virginia dandies on their prancin' ponies is a waste of my time."

"Rafe, when did your time become so valuable that it could be wasted?" came a voice near Fulton.

"When I started makin' a soldier's pay of eleven dollars a month, plus board and keep, that's when," Fulton retorted.

"Quiet in the ranks!" Sergeant Stevens growled.

In spite of frowning on General Hood's somewhat brash request to bring his entire infantry division of 6,000 men to the parade of General Stuart's massed cavalry command, General Lee had allowed it. Lee was painfully aware of the hardships that the two years of war on Virginia soil had brought to his state, and he knew that the Richmond newspaper reporters would fully report the day's spectacle. He'd decided an audience of several thousand foot troops in formation would add to the martial impression for the civilians who would be attending.

Nonetheless, Lee strongly cautioned Hood that upright behavior was expected. As a result of Hood's promise to General Lee, and backed by the threats of sergeants, the infantrymen held back from shouting, "Hey Mister, where's your mule?" or other epitaphs they commonly called to passing cavalrymen whenever the infantry columns had to yield the road to them.

Hood's men were stretched along a slight ridge with a panoramic view of the 5,000 cavalrymen demonstrating their maneuvers. The climax of the cavalry demonstration was an all-out charge towards Stuart's horse artillery, which had earlier rumbled across the field and unlimbered their cannons on a hillside to face back the way they had come.

The four long lines of horsemen galloped in ragged lines, pointing their curved sabers forwards. Most of the officers wore uniform jackets that were trimmed with faded yellow collars and cuffs of the cavalry, even if the enlisted horse soldiers were as haphazardly clothed as were Hood's infantrymen. In the simulated charge against the artillery batteries, hundreds of mounted troopers lost their hats, a temptation that proved too much for many of Hood's soldiers to resist.

"Hold my rifle," was heard up and down the infantry line, as dozens of slender men broke ranks and ran into the churned up field, racing for hats, especially the hats of officers that had feather plumes stuck in the hatbands.

General Hood was smiling in amusement at his men's antics until he saw General Longstreet turn to glare his way under his wide hat brim. Beyond Longstreet, General Lee was staring forward, stone-faced, with his chin tilted up, a sure sign of his displeasure. Hood quickly turned to his staff officers who sat on their horses behind him and loudly told them to make sure they collected the cavalrymen's hats and returned them. Then he winked.

Captain McBee sighed when two of his new men darted out of line to join the race. Without looking back, the captain told his sergeant to make sure those two privates were detailed to deepen the company sink back at camp that evening. *They can shovel shit for an hour or two in exchange for their frivolity in front of General Lee,* McBee thought.

The seven mile march back to the camp was filled with stories of flying hats and observations that several thousand horses all in one place left a lot of manure on the field. There were also grudging acknowledgements that several thousand cavalrymen all charging at once shook the earth and were a darned impressive sight to behold. Even Rafe Fulton had to agree it was an enjoyable day, even if he had to march fourteen miles for the entertainment.

Texas Brigade Camp near Culpeper, Virginia
June 9, 1863

Levi lowered the tin dipper down to the bottom of the iron pot and pulled up the biggest chunk of meat he could fish out of the brown stew. He surrounded the beef with pieces of potato and onions and put a thick slice of bread covered in molasses on the side.

When he set the plate on the crate in front of Captain McBee, Levi took a step back and waited without saying anything. Only when the captain looked from the Richmond newspaper to the plate did he notice Levi still standing near. McBee cocked his head to the side and pointed questioningly at the plate.

"I decided you ain't been eatin' right, so I went foragin'," Levi said in a matter of fact tone.

"You decided?"

"That's right, I decided. Me and George, that is."

"You and George."

"Yessir."

"It looks and smells wonderful. Let George know I'm grateful for his concern for my eating habits. Is George over his grieving for Lieutenant Daniels?" McBee asked.

"No, Sir. I reckon not. He misses the lieutenant something terrible, Capt'n. George and his wife raised the lieutenant from a baby."

"I know. Absalom thought of George as family. And you? Are you over your grieving?"

"No, Sir. Can't say that I'll ever be over grieving for Mama," Levi answered.

Three months earlier McBee had been horrified to learn that Levi, in rescuing his mother from a rapist, had accidentally killed her. The captain's own history with Levi's mother remained a dim, but guilt-ridden memory, leaving him no more capable of talking of the tragedy than Levi.

"Time, Levi. Time will do its healing work, but not in a week or a month or even a year."

At that moment, the drum beat for officers' call came from the colonel's tent. McBee hurried that way, leaving his stew untouched, but he carried the molasses-slathered bread with him. In just a few minutes he was back, letting his lieutenants and sergeants know they were moving out immediately to march back to Brandy Station.

"It seems Stuarts' whole cavalry division, all those boys we watched yesterday, are fightin' all the Yankee cavalry in Virginia, just five or six miles from here," McBee said as Levi handed him his sword belt. "We're going to help. Right now!"

Hood's Division marched back towards Brandy Station, but arrived too late to affect the outcome of the battle. After a day spent fighting the largest cavalry engagement ever on American soil, the Union cavalry moved back across the river, having learned where the bulk of the Confederate army was.

Texas Brigade Camp at the Cedar Mountain Battlefield
June 14, 1863

"Capt'n, are we staying here long?" Levi asked as he finished setting up his master's cot. "We ain't but a few miles from the other camp. Ain't we moving further? If the Yankees are this close to us, I don't see why we moved a'tall, "

"What do you care, Levi? One camp's pretty much like another," McBee answered while he lit the lantern that hung from the tent ridgepole.

"Excepting this one, Capt'n. This camp is haunted. There's so many dead men in this field that a body can't even fetch firewood without bringing back a load of legs and arm bones. Look like sticks in the dark. Ain't right, camping on top of all these bones. George, he bent over to pick up a limb and saw a hand sticking out of the ground. Capt'n, we ain't supposed to be here."

"I have to agree with you there," McBee said. "Sergeant Stevens told me he counted forty-nine skulls in one ditch. Hogs and dogs been at them for a year now. This is a pretty grisly place. I figure we'll move on tomorrow. But not tonight."

"Well that's all right then. But me, I'll be staying in the wagon all night, not under it. Ain't no dead hands gonna grab holt of sleeping Levi and pull him down to Lucifer's boneyard."

June 15, 1863

"Captain, do you remember that freezing march to Richmond last winter?" Private Fulton asked McBee. "The day you put me at the back of the column to sweep up the stragglers?"

"Sure, Rafe. I was in command of a whole brigade of limping, worn-out, half-frozen soldiers. My first independent command. We did a two or three day march in one. Really surprised and pleased General Hood. I'm grateful to you for your good work. It was a pretty miserable day, though."

"Well, Father John, as bad as that was, I'd trade today for it. We got more men dropping out from heat than we did from the cold."

"Particular. I'm surrounded by men who've become particular about where we sleep, and now, when we march," McBee said as he shook his head in mock dismay. He then wiped his face with a handkerchief already soggy with his sweat.

Hood's Division marched twenty-five miles towards the Shenandoah Valley that day, causing two hundred men to fall out by the roadside, as more and more men were unable to continue in the extreme heat. Another three hundred men reached camp on their own, but long after dark, straggling from sheer exhaustion.

June 16, 1863

As Hood's Division continued marching another twenty miles in the scorching heat, Captain McBee tried to keep his mind off his aching feet and creaking knees by thinking about his last night in Lexington with Faith, nearly a month ago. After he watched her breastfeed the twins, she had joined him in the bed, eager to shift her attention from two hungry children to the man she hungered for. The activities of the next hour left the captain wondering if he might next return to Lexington as father of a third child. The possibility pleased McBee and he began to daydream about life in Texas as a family man after the war.

Regretfully, after just a few minutes of such pleasant thoughts, the specter of Faith's husband interrupted his musings, turning his ruminations dark: *Yes, Samuelson fled Lexington and is most likely even gone from Virginia, escaping to a place that is not part of the Confederacy. Yes, he is now a criminal who will hang for murdering a respected sheriff, if he's caught. But, dammitall, he is still alive and is still legally married to Faith, and still is a potential threat to Faith and our children.*

Those thoughts depressed the captain as he marched sweating and aching, but he couldn't help but take the thread further: *If I live through the war, either I will have to take Faith and our children to Texas, or I will have to find Samuelson myself and haul him to Lexington to stand trial for killing Sheriff Cain. The first choice is cowardly and immoral, and the second will shame me and my family in my mother's hometown, because my inexcusable relationship with Samuelson's legal wife will become public knowledge during the trial.*

John McBee came to the conclusion that he needed Adam Samuelson dead, but not executed in Lexington, a conclusion that was deeply unsettling. Shaking himself from those bleak speculations, he thought, *Thank goodness I have a war to fight and don't have to confront this predicament today.*

June 17, 1863

Hood's Division marched only fourteen miles before making camp early, to allow the large number of straggling soldiers to catch up before dark and providing a few extra hours of rest for the men who had kept up.

Chapter 17

The Upper Shenandoah Valley, Virginia
June 18, 1863

New Sergeant Joshua Hodges stood in the deep water of the Shenandoah River, awkwardly holding his musket and leather accoutrements over his head with only one hand. The river was flowing fast enough to put a risk of falling in every step a man took, but Hodges was still enjoying the invigorating coolness. He reached out with his free arm to steady the soldier nearest him.

"Damn, Dickson," Hodges warned, "if you step in a hole, you're gonna be over your head."

Nineteen year-old Private Joseph Dickson, who stood five feet, four inches tall, was in water that reached his armpits. "Sergeant, I don't swim so good. If this gets any deeper, I've gotta go back or I'll drown," Dickson blurted in wide-eyed fear.

"Naw, you're not going back," Hodges assured the teenage soldier as he grabbed Dickson's collar. "Shuffle your feet, Joseph, don't raise them up. Just slide along, you'll be fine."

After several treacherous yards, the two men felt the bottom begin to slope up towards the bank. Soon the water was only to Hodges' waist, so he let go of Dickson. At that point, the private put one foot in a hole and lost his balance. He fell, his head going under, but the barrel of his musket poked out of the water. Hodges grabbed the musket barrel and held on until Dickson's head popped up. The private coughed and spat out water, but kept moving towards the bank.

"I thought ever boy in Leon County learned to swim in Keechi Creek," Hodges said to Dickson.

"Not me, Sergeant. My big brother William got bit by a cottonmouth in the Keechi. His arm turned black and he died the next day. Ma wouldn't let us near the creek after that."

"Well, you did good to hold on to your Enfield just now. I reckon you'll still have a bite like a moccasin yourself," Hodges said.

June 26, 1863

After three days guarding Snicker's Gap in the Blue Ridge Mountains, Captain McBee was glad to be moving again, even if the brigade was about to ford another wide river, the Potomac this time. *The men will be glad this one's only knee deep*, the captain thought, looking forward himself to the crossing.

"Lieutenant Anderson, would you just look at that," McBee exclaimed, as his first lieutenant walked over to stand next to him on the crest of the ridge that looked down on the river. The approach to the bridge and the wooden span itself was locked up with wagons and artillery caissons, leaving the long columns of infantrymen to ford the river upstream of the bridge. What caught the captain's eye were four buggies across the river that had been forced by the jam of army vehicles to abandon the road and cross the river at the same ford the infantry were using.

"Captain, am I seeing four carriages full of women? Young women? Handsome young women?"

"I believe you are seeing just that, Mr. Anderson,"

"Am I seeing a river full of soldiers without their trousers?"

"That you are, Lieutenant."

"Sir, it appears to me that some of those soldiers have also taken off their drawers for the crossing."

"It appears so, Aaron."

"You think our brigade is going to disrobe also, Sir? I mean with the ladies right there?" the lieutenant asked.

"You know General Robertson, I think, from before the war," McBee answered.

"Yes Sir. Fine man."

"Do you think our general would endanger his men by crossing that river overburdened by extra pounds of wet cloth?"

As Anderson opened his mouth, the call echoed down the brigade column to fall out and prepare to ford the Potomac. Immediately, most of the seventeen hundred men of the Texas Brigade began shucking their pants, and about half of those had no drawers beneath their trousers. The men, many of them carrying their trousers and leather belts, reformed into the forty companies of the four regiments, ready to wade into the Potomac. Most of the soldiers wore shirts with long tails that provided a modicum of modesty, but more than a few knotted up their shirttails to keep them dry.

The Texans and the thirteen young women from Maryland passed by each other in the knee deep water, the men whooping and waving hats at the carriages, while the ladies, some of them at least, averted their eyes. Try as the women might to maintain a detached dignity while in close proximity to a thousand men without trousers, it was obvious that the pride of Texas had come to Maryland.

Inside the Southern Border of Pennsylvania
June 27, 1863

"The men are drunk, Capt'n," Levi told his captain who had been at the sinks for some time trying to empty his nervous bowels.

"All the men? What about the ones that don't take strong spirits?" McBee asked.

"Don't look like there's many good Methodists in the company, but them that ain't drinking, look to be selling or giving their cups to those that do. I'd say that the Leon Hunters are now the Drunk Hunters."

McBee scowled at his man-servant. "Go get both lieutenants and Sergeant Stevens, right now."

Levi left immediately, having done his job to let the captain know how things had changed in the hour McBee had been away from camp.

"If you've had more than one gill of whiskey tonight, don't tell me," McBee warned the trio. "Get the other sergeants and find every man who's had too much whiskey and take them to the creek. Douse each man underwater. Baptize every drunk bastard in the company 'til he finds Jesus. We may march into battle tomorrow morning, and I will NOT be leading a company of riflemen still feeling tonight's whiskey."

After his subalterns left his tent, McBee made his own way through camp, wanting to see for himself if Levi had exaggerated the intoxicated condition of the men. He almost stumbled over young Joseph Dickson, who was on his knees trying to puke. Next to him Private John Haley was sitting cross-legged, sipping and singing to himself. The captain looked at the two, thinking soldiers or not, they are still just boys. He shook his head, and wondered why the hell General Hood had been so generous with the wooden casks of Pennsylvania whiskey he'd distributed among the regiments in his division.

McBee bent over, pulled up both privates by their elbows, and walked them down the hill to the creek. He didn't pause at the bank but just walked them into the water until it was waist high. He let go of each soldier's arm, put his palms on their heads, shoved them under the surface of the cold water, and held them there while he counted to five, looking up at the bright moon.

The two young men came up sputtering just as Lieutenants Anderson and Hubbard reached the creek with their first candidates for dunking.

"What took you so long?" McBee said, grinning behind his beard. "Bring those fellas in to join these two converts, and go fetch some more. I'll watch these." With that he shoved Dickson and Haley back under the surface.

Lieutenant Hubbard was glad to see the captain waist-deep in the creek and called to him, "Captain, Rafe Fulton has his own keg of whiskey and he's got his big damn knife out. He's pouring ample portions into the cup of any man who comes by, but he takes the first slug of ever' cup. I'll bring him along, but it'll likely take three or four of us to take the keg and his knife away without getting poked or slashed. I remember Rafe could be a mean drunk back home."

McBee sighed and asked, "Lieutenant, are you asking your captain to escort Private Fulton to the creek?"

"Yes Sir. That's exactly what the lieutenant is asking. You and Rafe go way back. Me and Sergeant Moss will be right behind you."

Private Fulton was teary-eyed and hugging the near-empty whiskey keg when he saw McBee walk up. He started babbling what a good commander McBee was to his company, and how the captain could count on him to back him up whenever he needed him. McBee didn't say anything, but gently unwrapped his old friend's arms from the keg and pulled him to his feet. The captain hooked an arm with Fulton's and together they walked to the creek and waded to the middle.

McBee repeated the same routine he had done with Dickson and Hailey. Fulton's head went under half a dozen times before he came up proclaiming his intention to never let hard liquor cross his lips again.

"Uh Huh, I'll remember that, Rafe," McBee said, shoving his friend's head under water once more to be sure.

It was a crowded creek for a while, but within the hour the Leon Hunters constituted the largest body of sober men in the Fifth Texas Regiment.

Chapter 18

Charleston, West Virginia
June 30, 1863

Confederate Lieutenant Adam Samuelson stirred when the noise of the jangling keys on the jailer's belt cut through the snoring of the man on the bunk over his head. Samuelson opened his eyes as the cell door swung open and a finger pointed his way, motioning for him to get up.

Two guards led Samuelson into a stifling office where a major sat behind a small desk, writing. Beads of sweat dotted the seated man's bald head and a fringe of gray hair stuck damply to his ears. Dark circles under his eyes gave him the look of a snapping turtle. The guards pushed the prisoner onto a straight back chair then stood a few steps behind him.

"We've had a man in Richmond checking out your story," the major signed the document in front of him without looking up.

"I expected you would."

"Your superior in the war office regrets your disappearance. His income seems to have dropped with your absence. He was easily persuaded by a stack of Union greenbacks to visit with our man at some length."

"About me?"

"You and a few other things that don't concern you," the major replied. "You are an interesting find, but not so interesting that we'd spend what we did just to verify your duties as a contract liaison officer."

Samuelson immediately wondered how much had been in that stack of greenbacks, and what else Colonel Treadway had told the spy in Richmond, but he prudently stayed silent.

"You say you want to serve the Union, you want a commission in exchange for what you've told me about your duties in Richmond. After spending, what, six weeks in a cell, are you still of a mind to switch allegiances?"

"I am."

"After doing nothing for six weeks but pacing seven steps and brooding over your situation, tell me again why that is, other than the fact you're wanted for murdering the sheriff of Lexington." The major leaned back and put his pen beside the ink well.

"The Confederacy isn't going to win the war. When I gamble, I like to win."

"Do you cheat to win?"

Samuelson smirked. "You know I do, and I know you do. Men like us hedge every bet."

The major patted his brow with a dirty handkerchief, at the same time saying, "And I'm about to hedge my bet on you. I'll pave the way for you to have a lieutenant's commission in a new regiment, an infantry regiment, not a staff job in Washington or any place else."

Samuelson smiled and nodded. *He'll hedge his bet by squeezing me for even more details about the inner workings of the supply department, and which contractors pay me to overlook the corners they cut. Which other liaison officers take bribes.*

The major smiled back. "I won't be keeping you long. I'm not going to grill you anymore about your army duties in Richmond, or your smuggling business."

Samuelson was stunned but didn't shift his gaze from the bald officer or otherwise betray his surprise. He was an accomplished card player and realized the major had just raised the stakes of their game, and his captor held the high hand.

"You want to bring something out of Virginia on my boat?"

"No, Lieutenant, we have boats, and we have other smugglers. Moreover, Northern Virginia has little besides tobacco that we want. After more than a year of the blockade, the South is gasping for air. Virginia really has very little of anything."

"How, then, are you hedging your bet on me?"

"By sending you back to Virginia to complete a task. Something that will be mildly helpful towards ending the rebellion. Something that will prove your new-found loyalty to the Union. Something you've done before."

Samuelson shifted to the edge of chair, unable to restrain his interest. "What?"

The major looked past Samuelson and motioned for the two guards to leave the room. When the door closed behind them, he said one word.

"Assassination."

"Who? Where?"

The major clucked his tongue. "You ask questions like a newspaper reporter."

"I can't kill a man if I'm blindfolded."

"Ah, quite so. All right. Your target is in Virginia, a member of the Confederate Cabinet. An important man. Maybe none more important than President Davis himself."

Samuelson needed only an instant to consider who that might be. "You must mean Benjamin, Davis's pet Jew."

"Perceptive. That's encouraging. Yes, Secretary of State Judah P. Benjamin is your target."

"Again, when? Where? Not Richmond, I hope."

"When? Soon. Where? We're arranging for Benjamin to find a need to travel to Lynchburg, far from Richmond, but just a few miles from Lexington, where your wife is ensconced with the mother of her lover."

Samuelson leapt up and glared down at the man, again surprised by the reach of the major's information network.

"Sit down, Lieutenant. You are not a man I choose to look up to," the major tartly ordered.

"I'm familiar with Lynchburg," Samuelson muttered as he sat down again. "How?"

"Not with your fine English Whitworth sporting rifle. I'm afraid you'll be without the beautiful weapon on which your name is so stupidly and exquisitely engraved. No, this time you will be closer, much closer, to your victim."

"Benjamin is said to be smart, the smartest man in the government," Samuelson leaned towards the major, his hands cupping his knees. "How are you going to get me close enough to take him down and escape, even outside of Richmond?"

"Because you're young and handsome. And even though your hair is blond and your complexion's pale, most importantly, you were born a Jew. Few men know that Judah P. Benjamin has a secret affection for young and handsome Jews. Maybe it's the circumcision. I'm assured by the guards that your foreskin is nothing but a wrinkled band of puckered flesh. Sounds rather hideous to me."

Samuelson was speechless as he put one ankle over the other knee and pressed against the back of his chair.

"You can't be serious," he finally said after an interminable ten seconds of silence, during which the major started writing another document.

The pen scratching on the paper continued for several more seconds before the Union officer looked straight at Samuelson and answered, "Why wouldn't I be? You don't have to actually perform perversions with the man. Just entice him to a private place to, ah, taste your, ah, circumcised fruit, and then stab the fat bastard and leave. How hard can that be to a resourceful officer like you?"

"Benjamin is married. He even has a child, a daughter, I think. Your information is wrong. I've seen the man in sporting houses in Richmond. Maybe you should hire a whore." Samuelson waved his hand dismissively.

"Very clever, Lieutenant. I enjoy cleverness. Usually." The major answered setting his quill carefully on the desktop.

"Benjamin's wife is a Creole, a Catholic married to a Jew. Offered to Benjamin by her desperate, but rich, father as nothing more than a marriage of convenience. An impossible marriage to rid the man of a tempestuous daughter; and for Benjamin, an open door into the Louisiana planter society. His wife has been in France for years, separated from the Secretary."

Samuelson was at a loss. "But that doesn't mean he's a...nancyboy."

"Please don't be so naïve as to offer judgment on the accuracy of my information. If I learned so easily of you being a cuckold, don't even imagine that I wouldn't as easily learn of the boudoir proclivities of one of the Confederacy's most influential men. Do you not think that Richmond's sporting houses cater to all manner of tastes? Do you not understand that silence is easily bought by a rich man?"

"But Benjamin has the president's ear. He dines with European royalty. He can't be..."

"Come now, Lieutenant, you're beginning to disappoint me. You gave the first impression of a worldly gentleman. I was thinking you have the look of an Alexander about you, a look that would catch the eye of Secretary Benjamin. I was hoping you wouldn't need a tutor in the sins of the Greeks."

Lieutenant Adam Samuelson slumped his shoulders, sagging against the hardwood chair. He felt revulsion, but he knew he'd do it.

Chapter 19

Near Gettysburg, Pennsylvania
July 1, 1863

McBee studied the lush farmland with no less amazement than did his men. They marched past two-story stone and timber barns that were as big as Texas courthouses. Rail and rock fences lined the roads. Beyond the neat borders, green cornstalks reached up eight feet high and bright red fruit hung heavy in the apple trees. Fields of yellow grain blanketed hillsides, adding to the bold primary colors of the landscape, shaming the browns and muted greens of the fields and forests back home.

"Captain, do these people even know there's a war?" Second Lieutenant Hubbard asked McBee when the captain dropped back to walk next to Hubbard at the rear of the company.

"Hmph, before today, I doubt they did. A lot of soldier-age men must work these fields, and there're no Africans up here to do it. Look at that barn and house there. Makes my place in Texas look like a shack," McBee answered.

"Yep. If all of Yankeedom is this rich, I don't know what they want with Texas, or any of the south," Hubbard said. "I don't know why they don't just let us split off. Even the farms we saw in the Shenandoah Valley don't hold up to these we're marching past. These people don't need us."

"The same thought has crossed my mind, Lieutenant."

133

"You know where we're headed, Sir?"

"To find the Yankee army, I imagine. Or maybe to find a nice ridge between the Yankee army and their capital city. I reckon we won't know until the colonel orders the regiment into battle formation," McBee answered.

"Wherever it is, I hope we wind up on a hill behind a nice steep wall of dirt and logs like at Fredericksburg last winter," Hubbard said. "That's the way to fight these damned bluebellies. Make them come right at our guns."

McBee was in good humor and goaded Hubbard a little by saying, "You mean you didn't like charging that hill outside Richmond last June, or chasing that bunch of red-legged Zouaves at Manassas, or fighting in the woods in Maryland after that?"

"Begging your pardon, Captain, but I recall you 'bout got killed at Manassas by those Zouave bastards. Weren't it more pleasurable to shoot Yankees from behind that big dirt wall at Fredericksburg?"

"Yeah, you're right," McBee said absently rubbing his shoulder. "I didn't like being shot. Besides hurting like hades, I lost my damned sword. Levi was so worried about getting me to the hospital he left my sword on the ground. I had to buy a new one in Richmond. Cost me dearly, too."

Mention of last year's battle wound took McBee's thoughts back to the long weeks he had spent recovering, and how Levi had nursed him at the Texas Hospital in Richmond until he went to his mother's house in Lexington. Then, as happened more and more often, his thoughts settled on Faith, of the pleasures of being in bed with her and, now, warm thoughts of their children, the twin infants she had borne.

Both men carried scabbarded swords resting on their shoulders while they marched. McBee's comment about his expensive new sword reminded Hubbard how relieved he was that McBee offered him Daniels' sword until he could afford to buy his own.

After they walked a bit in silence, McBee forced his thoughts away from Faith and said, "Lieutenant, I do share your preference for logs and dirt between me and the Yanks. But we both know we'll fight where we meet them. And General Lee didn't bring us up here to wait on the Yankee generals to come knocking, much as you and me take to the notion."

Hubbard nodded, pleased the captain agreed with his sensible perspective on waging war.

As the column marched closer to the town of Gettysburg, signs of a raging battle ahead became all too evident. Young John Hailey gagged at the nauseating stench and vomited when they passed by a pile of blood-crusted amputated arms and legs outside a field hospital. Flies swarmed over the severed limbs and in the hot afternoon air, the smell of feces and fear radiated from the hospital tent.

McBee sighed in relief when his company rounded a bend in the road, leaving behind the gruesome sights and nauseating smells of what battle does to fragile flesh.

"Father John, half your new boys turned a mite green around the gills back there at the hospital," Private Fulton said as Captain McBee strode up next to him. "You reckon they're up to a big fight today?"

"I'd say they're about as ready as we were outside Richmond last summer. We were all green as grass, no different than our new men now," McBee replied.

Rafe Fulton barely nodded as he walked on, wondering how many of the new recruits would fake wounds or rush to help a slightly wounded man to the rear. Fulton's attention returned to the present as they passed more and more injured men who had yielded the road to the column marching towards the battle. The thunder of artillery became nearly constant. Yet, the Texans did not reach the battle that day.

At dusk the order came to leave the roadway and bivouac without campfires. The men in McBee's company ate what food was in their haversacks, generally the raw bacon and corn that had been issued to them the previous day. As the light faded, men stretched out on the ground, used their blanket rolls and knapsacks as pillows, and enjoyed the cooling evening temperature. Most of them mused on what tomorrow would bring until they drifted into sleep. More than a few men woke up sweating from the same nightmare of a wild-eyed surgeon sawing off their arm or leg while they thrashed helplessly on a blood-slick table.

July 2, 1863

Hours before dawn, the sergeants kicked men awake and formed their companies. The order came to take off their knapsacks and blanket rolls, that the supply wagons that followed would retrieve them. General Robertson ordered only a small detail from each regiment be detached to guard the long rows of personal gear. A young lieutenant from his headquarters staff oversaw the twenty guards, and he had orders to find and rejoin the brigade as soon as the wagons arrived.

By midday the regiment's supply wagons reached the abandoned personal gear. Levi tossed knapsacks and blanket rolls up to George in the back of the wagon. When they finished, Levi told George he was going to follow the guard detail with the apples they had gathered that morning He meant to take the fresh fruit forward to his master's men and asked George to carry one of the sacks of apples.

Middle-aged George was still mourning the death, bare weeks ago, of his young master, Lieutenant Absalom Daniels, who he and his wife had practically raised since Absalom's birth. Moreover, with Daniels gone, George wasn't about to put himself any closer to the shooting than he had to, even if Levi asked, so he morosely shook his head, chin wrinkled, bottom lip stuck out over his top one.

Since George wouldn't leave the wagons, Levi slung the two bulging sacks and five spare canteens of water over the back of a mule and followed the guard detail at a discreet distance.

* * *

After their successes during yesterday's fighting, General Longstreet knew it would be hard to persuade General Lee to change his battle plan from attacking to a plan of defense. Lee ignored Longstreet's repeated pleas to find good high ground to defend between Washington City and the Union army. Longstreet stressed that much of Meade's army had to be in disarray after being driven through the town of Gettysburg the day before. Longstreet assured his commander that the enemy would be unable to interfere as Lee disengaged and moved his army east towards Washington. Longstreet even informed Lee about the ridgeline he'd found that would be the perfect place to force the

Yanks to attack them uphill, like they had at Fredericksburg seven months earlier. Lee didn't budge.

The corps commander grudgingly admired Lee's tenacity to stay with his instincts, but Longstreet was a stubborn man too, and throughout the morning he continued his efforts to dissuade his commander from the orders he'd been given. Meanwhile, Longstreet followed Lee's orders and started two of his three infantry divisions, some 12,000 soldiers, on a slow, circuitous movement to reach the far right flank of the Confederate army without being detected by the Union observers on Cemetery Ridge.

* * *

Well into the hot afternoon, the Fifth Texas Infantry Regiment stopped yet again. The infantry column waited while scouts went further ahead to insure the road didn't cut through open fields, where there were no trees to hide the column from the Union observers on the ridge. McBee stood in the shade, grateful to be out of the sun but regretting that a good captain must project an image of indefatigable strength by not sitting during the stops.

"Captain McBee, how are your men faring?" asked Colonel Powell as he reined in his horse next to the captain of Company C.

"Foot sore, but eager, Colonel. They're eager to do more than march."

Private Fulton and Sergeant Hodges heard McBee and gave each other lopsided grins. The two veterans knew their captain was preening for the colonel and stretching the likelihood that the men would rather attack the Yankees than march behind the screen of skirmishers off to their left. Even if amused by McBee's posturing for the colonel, Fulton and Hodges both thought that the day's march would end in the grim work of battle. The colonel confirmed their suspicions.

"Not much longer, I think, John," Colonel Powell replied. "We're about opposite the two big hills where the Yankee line ends. That's where we will go in and roll 'em up. The god-awful slow pace has been to make sure they ain't watching us and find reason to reinforce their flank."

"Yes Sir. Sounds like just the job for us."

"My Texans always move them. Ain't that what General Lee said last year? I expect he's depending on us to move them off those hills today. Look for it to be confusing, John. Keep your boys together and don't stop until we're at the top. Company C is the biggest company in the Fifth, but watch your flanks." With that caution, Colonel Powell moved on to encourage the next company, making the most of the brief stop.

* * *

As Sergeant Hodges marched next to the column, keeping one eye on several of the new men who seemed on the verge of straggling, he looked to his left at the distant hill covered by immense boulders. Even though a farm house and barn stood between the Texans and the hill, Hodges could see the dark shapes of cannons on the crest and make out the roughly triangular shape of a rock fence that enclosed a field on the near slope of the hill. He was glad the Fifth was moving around that hill and didn't seem to be moving into position to attack straight at it, as the First regiment was doing. Hodges thought that maybe the Fifth was going to loop around to the back of the hill and take the defenders in the rear.

After another half hour of marching, the regiment rested under a canopy of trees on a hillside, while all the company commanders gathered around the colonel. As most of the men sat and took swigs of water from their canteens, Hodges climbed onto a wagon-sized boulder and peered through a gap in the trees. He saw he was wrong in his first assumption about where they were headed. The Fifth Texas Regiment had not angled to the left to strike the back side of the boulder-strewn hill. Instead they had moved into the woods on an even higher hill, and were going across the slope. It looked like they were going to come out of the trees into a valley behind the first hill and in front of a long rocky ridge. Hodges asked himself how anyone ever farmed the land here with all the rocks. The ground looked as if God Himself had just splashed a big handful of giant stones down from the heavens right here.

Chapter 20

On the Slope of Big Round Top
Near Gettysburg, Pennsylvania
Mid-afternoon, July 2, 1863

Colonel Powell spoke to his company commanders with an intensity that hid his nervousness. "Gentlemen, we are going to dislodge the enemy from yonder ridge. We have the Fourth Regiment to our left and Law's Alabamians to our right. The First Regiment and the Arkansas boys have taken the rocky hill where the cannons were raising hell. A courier just told me they captured one of the pieces, and they're turning it towards the ridge to support us. Remember, Texans always move them. That's all."

As the regiment marched out of the trees and formed their long thin battle line, Hodges saw that the big rocks in the valley protected large numbers of Union skirmishers, some in blue and some wearing dark green coats. Puffs of smoke from musket muzzle blasts were appearing all across the valley. Straining to look far to his left, Hodges could only see that the first granite-topped hill was covered in smoke. He couldn't tell if friend or foe held the position.

Then Colonel Powell walked out in front of the color guard that had unfurled the Texas flag and the red Confederate battle flag. The bearded colonel waved his sword

139

over his head and shouted, "Forward, my Texans! For home, for country, for Texas! Forward!"

The jumbled terrain in the valley immediately caused the two Texas regiments to lose their tight formation, as small groups of men scrambled over and between boulders. A creek split the valley floor, and the brambles covering the marshy ground tore the soldiers' clothing. Beyond the creek a low rock fence ran the length of the valley. Behind the fence, Union skirmishers kept up a sharp fire. The Texans didn't know that many of the skirmishers were proven marksmen in the 2nd US Sharpshooter Regiment, armed with breech-loading rifles that they could reload in just a few seconds, without having to force bullets down the fouled muzzles of their weapons.

Captain McBee, his two lieutenants, and the five sergeants tried in vain to keep a semblance of order among the fifty riflemen in Company C. The Union positions were all high uphill, allowing Union soldiers to see behind all but the largest boulders. With casualties mounting the attackers were quick to seek cover behind large rocks to shoot and reload, reluctant to expose themselves by moving onward.

* * *

The lieutenant of the guard detail approached the cluster of mounted officers. A junior staff officer at the back of the group pointed towards the gap between two hills and assured the lieutenant that General Robertson could be found in that direction. Levi was still behind the returning guard detail, but even at a distance he recognized General Hood in his gold-braided uniform coat.

The general sat alertly and leaned forward in his saddle, watching the forward brigades of his division launch their attacks. He was particularly intent on the progress of the Texans against the first hill where the Federal battery was located. Hood was near bursting with eagerness for his men to overrun the battery so they might turn and use the Yanks' own cannons against them.

To his right, Hood couldn't see the rest of Robertson's Texans, but he had watched them and Law's Alabamians enter the critical gap between the first hill and the big forested mountain that dominated the terrain. Those six regiments, half the strength of his division, were his strike force, the spear point that would carry the second rocky ridge and turn the flank of the whole Yankee army. It was a prospect that was so close, so tantalizing, he could taste it.

Hood decided to observe the attack on the boulder-topped hill just a minute longer before he would ride forward to his right, into the gap to oversee the attack up the second ridge. His scouts had reported hundreds of unguarded wagons full of supplies just behind that ridge. When his troops topped the crest, Hood wanted to be there with his men, for he intended to personally lead the final phase of the attack that would ruin the Federal's position and win the day.

Sitting on his horse, watching his beloved soldiers move inexorably forward, and reflecting that he commanded the finest division in Lee's army, Hood's thoughts drifted to an Old Testament verse from the book of Esther. It was the one verse that had stuck in his mind since he was a young officer fighting Comanches on the plains of Texas: *"For just such a time."* *For just a such a time God put me here, now, at this moment, with my division in the one place where the Union army's backside is exposed, where we can turn the tide. Once we get over that second ridge, my division may just win the whole war.*

General Hood was about to snap his horse's reins when the spherical shell from a Union rifled cannon exploded thirty feet overhead. A piece of shrapnel tore through his uniform, lacerating his left arm, which immediately began bleeding like the throat of a butchered shoat. The general stayed in his saddle, slumped over, in shock and silent from the sudden pain.

Hood's staff officers quickly eased him off his injured and wild-eyed gelding. Finding the general's wound to be severe, potentially fatal if not treated, the officers quickly wrapped the wound with a major's silk waist sash, lifted their general to sit in front of an aide who rode a large gentle mare, and headed towards the field hospital. Command of Hood's division fell on the shoulders of his senior brigade commander, General Law, who first had to be located.

* * *

Captain John McBee heard a bullet smash against a tall boulder inches from his head and felt grains of rock strike his cheek. Sergeant Hodges was kneeling next to McBee and grabbed the captain's coattail to pull him down. McBee dropped to his knees behind the same rock that sheltered Hodges.

"Hot, ain't it, Sergeant?" McBee wheezed as he took a deep breath.

"Yup," Hodges replied. "Looks like they got a line of men on the other side of that creek up ahead, and more of 'em up yonder in those big rocks. Them uphill fellers got the bead on us."

"Good reason not to stay here. Let's get over that creek and drive them," McBee replied as he stood, raised his sword, and yelled, "Leon Hunters! Now, Forward!"

Another bullet whizzed by McBee, cutting threads from the coat sleeve of his raised arm. All of the riflemen in Company C, some roughly shoved by sergeants and corporals, left their cover and ran forward, screaming like banshees, fear shoved aside, replaced by an urgency to push the enemy skirmishers back and reach the cover of the rocks uphill from them. Men from other companies joined the surge, as nearly four hundred Rebel riflemen rushed across the low ground to the little stream that split the valley floor.

When the oncoming Texas soldiers were fifty yards away, the Union skirmishers abandoned their positions. In pairs, the sharpshooters hastily retired further up the hill, under the protective musket fire of the thin line of riflemen from Michigan and New York who held the ridge crest.

Colonel Powell didn't let his regiment pause at the stream. He stepped into the shallow water, waving his sword in his right hand, while he pulled the sleeve of the standard bearer with his left. The young man carrying the Texas flag clumsily clambered over the wet rocks, trying not to entangle the flag staff in the blackberry vines growing on the edge of the creek.

Twenty yards beyond the creek Lieutenant Harper, one of Powell's aides, staggered backwards, shot in the shoulder. Powell dropped his sword and grasped Harper, easing him to the ground. As Powell started to stand, he felt hot metal pierce his side. He tried to go on, but instead slumped next to Harper.

Lieutenant Colonel King Bryan crossed the killing ground searching for Colonel Powell. Bryan commanded the left wing of the regiment, and his five companies were jumbled and stalled on the hillside, unable to go further upwards. He needed more riflemen.

Bryan caught Colonel Powell's eye and rushed towards his commander, just as the colonel keeled over, still holding the wounded lieutenant. He and a corporal from the color guard lifted Powell and dragged him behind a large boulder.

Bryan saw that Powell was hurt too badly to continue fighting, so he patted his senior officer on the shoulder, saying, "Colonel, I'm assuming command of the Fifth. We are going up this hill." Colonel Powell nodded, unable or unwilling to speak through his pain, and remained where he was on the ground.

Lieutenant Colonel Bryan looked around, waved for the color guard to go with him, and took three strides up the slope before he was struck in the arm by a Minié bullet. Bryan quickly knelt behind a rock, clasping his hand over the wound. He was panting as he watched bright red blood pulse between his fingers, the mangled blood vessels in his arm hemorrhaging badly.

Surprised by the coppery smell of his life fluid, Bryan remained lucid as he called to the color sergeant, "Find Major Rogers and tell him he is in command of the regiment."

Then Bryan began his stumbling trek back down the hillside, supported by a private who was thankful for a reason to retire, even if it meant leaving the protection of the stones he had folded himself behind.

McBee looked right and left, seeing only a dozen or so of his fifty men among the rocks and brush. Private Fulton trailed a few feet behind McBee watching for sudden threats to his old friend. Sergeant Hodges stayed close to protect his captain and stand ready as a reliable runner should McBee need to contact the colonel.

Captain McBee worried that most of his command was out of sight. Knowing he couldn't direct men he couldn't see, he peered across the slope to find more of his company and lead them further upward. The enemy fire was still hot, but they were now too far up the ridge for the Federal cannons to target them. It was *only* musket fire,

McBee told himself. His men should be able to punch through one line of damyankees on the crest.

Major Rogers saw McBee and made his way to him.

"Captain, both the colonels, Powell and King are wounded and out of the fight. Command of the regiment has passed to me. Your men look to be further up this damned rocky hill than any of the other companies. You've got to press now. Get your boys up to the top. We're depending on you."

McBee nodded wordlessly.

"I'm heading to the right to get the other companies moving, get them up with your boys," Rogers said. "John, get up this damned hill!"

The major moved away, leaving the captain to his work. Rafe Fulton was a step behind McBee when the captain pointed uphill with his free hand. "There, Rafe, there. That officer. Shoot him."

Fulton's eyes trained on the Union officer who stood tall on a stone outcropping above the brush, exposed and silhouetted. Fulton had a clear view, could even see the man had red hair, a full mustache, and wore a double breasted coat with shoulder straps that flashed silver in the sun. The Union officer was looking back, gesturing at a line of blue coated soldiers who were visible behind him moving quickly into position, muskets on their shoulders.

The private from Texas pulled back the hammer of his Enfield as he raised the weapon to his shoulder, aimed, and fired. He couldn't see through the muzzle smoke if he hit the officer.

"Good work, Rafe," McBee shouted. "Maybe you bought us enough time to reach the top of this crag before his men get organized up there."

Both men took another few steps upward as Fulton pulled a fresh paper cartridge from the leather box at his waist. McBee was still hopeful his company had the numbers and the will to carry them to the top.

McBee had not made his way more than a dozen yards further before the musket fire from the ridge crest changed from a light rain of bullets to a hail storm that threatened every man who dared continue up the steep slope. The sudden increase told the captain that a new regiment was now deployed on the top of the ridge and maybe hundreds more riflemen were adding their fire to that of the original defenders.

McBee knelt behind a rock and counted six men, his men, wounded or dead on the ground, and couldn't suppress the thought that the odds of their carrying the ridge had just changed for the worse. Behind him, a bugle sounded the notes to rally on the color guard.

"Dammit," McBee muttered as he motioned for his men to disengage and move back down the hill.

The captain, Fulton, and Hodges joined the cloud of gray-clad men who descended back down the face of the ridge much faster than they had climbed it. The Union riflemen continued to find targets, inflicting more casualties as the Rebs tried to dart from rock to rock, or abandoned all cover and bounded recklessly downhill. McBee forced himself to walk, not run; to stand straight, not stooped over, as he descended, ignoring the bullets landing near him.

Major Rogers reformed the Fifth Regiment in a rough line at the base of the ridge. Fewer men were now being hit by musket fire from the crest, but he could still hear bullets passing overhead. Rogers didn't take the time for the companies to fully sort themselves out before he ordered the regiment to once again advance up the rocky slope.

The second assault up the hill went almost as far as the first one did before the men stopped and would go no farther. Rogers sent orders left and right to hold their position and wait for the next wave of Confederates to join them before they made the final push to the crest.

"Sir, can you point me to Colonel Powell?" a courier breathlessly said as he reached Major Rogers.

"Colonel Powell is severely wounded, but remains on the field," the major answered with strained courtesy. "He passed the regiment to Lieutenant Colonel Bryan, who is wounded and has retired to the field hospital. Command now rests with me. What does General Robertson have to say?"

"General Robertson is a casualty," the courier grimaced and continued, "Colonel Work is now in command of the brigade. Colonel Work says not to expect reinforcements, and to press the attack vigorously, Sir."

Barely hiding his dismay that his command was now on its own, Major Rogers swallowed the bad news, saying, "Please assure Colonel Work that the Fifth Texas Regiment will take this damned ridge."

The courier dismissed, Rogers reluctantly sent the regiment's adjutant, Lieutenant Wood, to start the right wing of the regiment forward for the third time. He sent the sergeant-major to order the companies in the left wing to resume the attack.

Lieutenant Campbell Wood scrambled across the hillside and soon encountered Lieutenant Hubbard from Company C. He repeated Major Rogers' orders and was turning to seek out the next company when a bullet slammed into his foot. Woods yelped and hopped on his other foot, trying to hobble on, but the pain soon caused him to slump against a slab of granite that protruded from the ground.

Hubbard received the order and, cussing loudly, grabbed the shoulder of the man nearest him, pulling him up and shoving him forward. The scattered clusters of men in Company C were not eager, but most of them left their cover and followed Captain McBee and the two lieutenants, scratching their way up the steep slope. After going scant yards upwards, the men went to ground again, unwilling to remain exposed to the hail of bullets from above. Hubbard did not know that he was the only officer in the right wing who Lieutenant Wood reached before being wounded. The companies to either side never received the order to resume the attack, leaving McBee's company exposed on both flanks, beyond the rest of the regiment.

Chapter 21

On the Slope of Houck's Ridge
Late Afternoon, July 2, 1863

Private Green knelt behind a thick bush, hoping he was hidden. He had been there several minutes when he felt a tap on his back. He turned, expecting to see a sergeant or corporal urging him to keep going. Instead he faced an officer in a dark blue coat holding a sword to his neck. Green didn't understand how the enemy could have gotten behind him until he saw that the whole glade was filling with Yankees coming from the side, not the top of the ridge. The blue-coated soldiers prodded other surprised Confederates with their bayonets, quickly capturing several more Rebs.

Green trudged uphill, followed by a Union private whose dark beard was just beginning to grow.

"Where you Yanks from anyways? You sure come out of no-where's to snatch us up," the Texas private asked without looking back.

"We been fighting on that hill all afternoon 'til we near run out of bullets. Our Colonel told us to fix bayonets and charge. So we did. Caught you fellows cold, did we?

"I reckon. Where'd you say you're from, besides that hill yonder?"

"Maine. Twentieth Maine Volunteer Infantry. You?"

"Texas. Fifth Regiment of Infantry," Green answered. Then he added, "Captured by a man from a place I never even heard of. Don't seem right."

When they reached a small clearing just over the crest of the ridge, the young soldier from Maine shoved Green down on the edge of a circle of Confederate prisoners sitting on the ground. Green landed on his knees, ripping his tattered trousers even more, sharp pebbles puncturing his skin. He recognized three other men from his company who gestured for him to join them. Ignoring his bloody kneecaps, he made his way through the growing band of sullen captives to sit next to the familiar faces.

* * *

Colonel Powell was a large robust man who sported a full beard. His coat collar bore the three gold stars of a colonel in the Confederate army. The bullet that struck him had gone through his chest and left holes on both sides of his coat. Private Smithers knelt beside the colonel, both sheltered by a large boulder, the private not sure if he should leave his wounded commander or stay with him until a litter bearer arrived.

Branches of a bush rustled and parted just a few feet from Smithers. He looked to his left to see a Union soldier aiming his musket at him, while a lieutenant in blue stepped forward and looked down at Colonel Powell. Smithers raised both hands in surrender.

"Lads, I think we have in our grasp none other than General James Longstreet. Can't two Reb generals be this big and hairy."

"Lieutenant, you sure he's Longstreet? What would a corps commander be doing up on this hill, way out front?" a sergeant asked.

"I don't know why he's here, but sure I'm sure, Nathan. Look at his collar. 'Sesh generals wear stars on their collars, like this big boar here. Yup, we captured us Lee's best general."

None of the Union soldiers asked Private Smithers who he had been aiding, so he remained silent.

* * *

Captain McBee and Private Fulton found themselves in a rock-walled cul-de-sac with no path upwards. As they started to retrace their steps to go around the granite obstacle, Fulton unexpectedly stopped, causing McBee to stumble as he bumped into Fulton's back.

The tall private dropped his musket, seeing three Yankee soldiers aiming their bayonet-tipped weapons at him from ten feet away. McBee recovered his balance and saw why Fulton had halted so abruptly. With nowhere to run but straight into three bayonets, McBee angrily grunted, dropping his sword. It clattered and bounced on the rocks, coming to rest between the captain and his captors.

"That's the second damned sword I've lost."

Chapter 22

On the Slope of Houck's Ridge
Near Gettysburg, Pennsylvania
Late Afternoon, July 2, 1863

Three Union soldiers led sixteen captured Texans through thick brush, using a deer trail to make their way up the rocky slope. Near the top of the ridge, McBee looked back at Fulton and quietly said, "When I drop, follow me."

They were in the middle of the line of prisoners, with no guards near them on the narrow winding trail. As McBee started to step around a knee-high rock, he lunged forward and down, rolled a short distance and then quickly scooted under some dense brush. He heard the grating sound of something hard moving over the loose pebbles behind him and then Fulton pushed into his side, finding concealment under the same foliage.

The two men held their breath as the Federal soldiers at the back of the line of newly captured Texans and Alabamians walked past them on the trail. The guards were occupied making sure the prisoners ahead of them kept moving uphill on the uneven path, and never looked to their sides.

McBee and Fulton remained under the bush, still and silent for nearly two hours until dusk. They listened to the sounds of the soldiers on top of the ridge chopping trees to build breastworks. Their only scare came when someone came noisily down the slope and squatted ten feet above them to move his bowels. When he left, the sour stench of half-digested beef and apples lingered in the air.

* * *

Based on the information received from General Hood's staff lieutenant, the twenty men in the Texas Brigade guard detail divided into four groups, each led by a corporal, each vectoring in separate directions to find their regiments. Leading his pack mule, Levi still followed the Fifth Texas men. Soon they increased their pace to the double quick, disappearing into the trees on the side of the large mountain. The booms of cannons and the sharp staccato of musket fire saturated the air and smoke hid much of the scene, causing Levi to wait where he was, having decided that going any closer would take him into the front lines. He pulled the sacks of apples off the mule, sat on a rock and let the mule graze as he listened to the gunfire and gazed ahead at the smoke covered ridge, wondering if the captain and his men were in the midst of the fighting.

* * *

For nearly an hour, Private Polaski Phillips hid in a thicket of brambles on the hillside not far from the creek, hugging the ground during the second and third attacks by his regiment. He sorely missed the guidance of Asbury Lawson, who was now labelled a murderer and a deserter, destined for execution if he was ever captured. When a gut-shot man fell not far behind his hiding place, rolling and groaning in pain, Phillips saw his chance.

He'd decided several days ago that a battle offered him the best chance to slip away from the regiment unnoticed. He'd heard the veterans who'd been through last year's battles musing around their campfires whether absent comrades had died on the battlefield or had been captured. Either way, a soldier missing after a battle was not considered a deserter, so his name wasn't circulated to the provosts. Even better, they were in the Yankee state of Pennsylvania now, not Virginia, and Phillips figured a reformed secessionist soldier would be welcomed.

Leaving his musket on the ground, he scuttled to the soldier and knelt next to him as if giving him aide. Instead of succoring the man, Phillips smeared a thick coating of blood from the wounded soldier's stomach wound all over his own side before he staggered towards the creek, holding both bloody hands over his imagined wound.

Phillips waded through the shallow water, dry-mouthed, but still so terrified of the bullets that continued to ricochet off rocks near him, that he didn't pause to scoop a drink of water into his blood-crusted palms. Once through the creek, the private kept going towards the gap between the wooded mountain and the rocky hill where the Union artillery had been earlier in the afternoon.

After several minutes, the warm sun and the day's exertions prompted Levi to slip down from his stone perch and lean against the boulder so he could nap for a few minutes. The musket and cannon fire faded into a thundering background noise. The mule quit nibbling weeds and stood in its own slumber, blocking the late afternoon sun from Levi's eyes.

Polaski Phillips saw the lone mule not far ahead. Smiling at his good fortune, he angled towards the still animal that was standing next to two lumpy sacks. Several canteens hung from its pack frame. Phillips needed a drink and a man leading a loaded mule would not raise suspicions. He didn't yet know where he would go, other than away from the fighting, but the mule was his for the taking.

"Whoa, Mule," the twangy voice said, the speaker close, but unseen by Levi.

"Whoever you are, stay back from my mule. He's a biter and a kicker," Levi warned as he blinked awake, still not able to see more than legs on the other side of the mule. He stood and pulled the mule's reins to move the animal sideways so he could see the speaker. He recognized the thin man as a soldier in his captain's company, but he didn't know his name.

Phillips was startled to recognize the Negro as Captain McBee's body-servant.

Thinking fast, Phillips said, "I need those canteens to take back to the company. The captain sent me."

152

"Uh huh," Levi answered dubiously.

Phillips stepped towards Levi, pulling his bayonet from the leather scabbard at his belt. The young slave eyed the long triangular blade as he picked up one of the lumpy sacks of apples.

"Capt'n don't know I'm here," Levi said. "He thinks I'm back with the wagon train. Where's your musket?"

"Couldn't hold it. I'm wounded," Phillips said.

"You ain't wounded. You running, that's what you doing. You a coward."

Phillips leapt at Levi, bayonet held out, intent on thrusting it into the Negro's chest. Levi countered by shoving the bulging apple sack at the oncoming blade. The point of the bayonet slid through the cloth, passed between the outside apples and impaled two red fruits in the middle of the sack.

Levi twisted the sack sideways, wrenching the bayonet from the white man's grip. He brought the sack back around and crammed it into Phillips' face, pushing himself forward at the same time. The soldier lost his balance and fell backwards, the sack of apples on top of him and Levi on top of the apple sack.

Levi reached out with one arm, grabbed a fist-sized rock and bashed it against the thin man's skull. The man kept thrashing so Levi hit him a second time, knocking him unconscious.

Levi got up, pulled his short belt knife and walked to the mule, which had stood stoically still during the fight. He cut the straps of one canteen and tied Phillips' hands behind his back. Then he lifted the unconscious soldier and shoved him face-down across the pack frame, feet on one side and head on the other. Finally, he hung the apple sacks from the pack frame, mostly covering Phillips' torso with the sacks, pinning him in place. He left the bayonet sticking out of the sack.

"Reckon it's time to go find the Capt'n," Levi said to the mule as he pulled the reluctant beast forward, following the same path the guard detail had taken over an hour ago. "He'll be wantin' this snake back."

Philip McBride

Chapter 23

Slope of Big Round Top
Near Gettysburg, Pennsylvania
Night Between July 2 & 3, 1863

Around dusk the wounded Rebels who had been left on the hillside by the Union soldiers started calling for water and their mothers, many of them moaning pathetically. With Fulton leading the way, he and McBee crawled from their lair under the bush. Going downhill on their stomachs was easy, not starting noisy little cascades of pebbles was hard. After an alert Federal soldier fired a round that bounced off a rock just a foot above them, the pair slowed their crawls to a snail's pace that made less noise.

By midnight McBee and Fulton had crawled a hundred yards, reaching the creek at the base of the slope. Trousers and coats torn and covered in grime, they slithered through the blackberry brambles to lie in the creek, soaking their tender, scraped knees and elbows in the cool water. Both had left their empty canteens under the bush on the ridge, so they eagerly cupped water into their dry mouths.

"Can we get up and walk now? My knees are killing me," Fulton whispered.

"Not yet," McBee whispered back, resuming his command role. "A smart Yank colonel would have pickets at the base of the ridge."

The two men took another painful hour to crawl from the creek to the tree line at the base of the mountain where the regiment's attack had started nearly twelve hours earlier.

"You boys stand up straight and show me your hands!" a man called softly to them from a deep shadow. McBee and Fulton clearly heard the click of a musket hammer being pulled back to full cock position. They complied with the sentry's order, hands held over their heads.

"I'm Captain McBee of Company C of the Fifth Texas, with Private Fulton of my company."

"Uh huh. What county you from then?"

"Leon."

"Who's the colonel of your regiment?"

"Colonel Powell was when we started the attack, but I heard he and Lieutenant Colonel Bryan were both wounded. I don't know about Major Rogers."

"Good enough. The names is right. You been on a scout?" the voice called back softly. "Hell, the Yanks is up on the ridge t'other side of the creek. Don't need to send a captain to creep around in the dark to find out what we all know. Ain't no reason for 'em to leave since they whipped us." The sentry spat in disgust, unseen by McBee and Fulton.

"Not on a scout," McBee replied. Even nearly whispering, there was an edge in his command voice, peeved at the sentry's insubordinate tone. "We were scooped up on the hillside, but got away. I need to find my company, so call for your corporal of the guard to take us to the Fifth Regiment,"

"Sure thing, Captain. You wait here while I get him," the tired sentry said, not even noticing the captain's irritation.

* * *

"Damned glad to see you, John. What happened to you up there?" Major Rogers asked as the two stood close to each, talking in low voices.

"Got caught in a dead-end. Captured for a spell, but a private and me managed to slip away."

"Good work. We lost a lot of officers today. We need you."

"How about Company C?" McBee asked, his concern evident in voice. "Looked to me like we were the point of the regiment, and got flanked when the Yanks come off the ridge at us,".

"Your Lieutenant Anderson reported heavy losses, a lot of them apparently captured like you. The whole regiment is down by nearly half. Your company may be even worse. You'll have to get the details from Anderson. It weren't a good afternoon."

* * *

When Captain McBee found his company, First Lieutenant Anderson told him that he and Fulton made twenty-eight enlisted, NCO's, and officers present, out of the fifty-two who started the day.

In spite of the major's forewarning, the number of casualties in his company hit McBee like a hammer blow. He slumped against a tree, cursing to himself, aghast that he had lost so many men, only to falter, to fail by not even reaching the crest of the ridge.

"Have an apple, Capt'n," someone said in a hoarse whisper cutting through McBee's silent rage.

McBee looked up at the voice to see a dim figure offering him two round shapes impaled by a stick.

"Levi, what the blazes are you doing on this hill?" McBee asked in surprise, forgetting to lower his voice. More softly he asked, "Why aren't you with the wagons?"

"George is with the wagon. I brung two sacks of fresh apples and some full canteens. Thought you and the men might miss supper."

"Miss supper, huh?" McBee grunted. "Levi, you picked the wrong time to be funny." He looked again at the two skewered apples, realized how hungry he was, and pulled the first apple off what he now saw was a bayonet. The captain took a bite, the tart taste and fruity scent suddenly whisking his thoughts to the bowl of fruit Sally kept on his mother's kitchen table, and that reminded him of Faith. *Where ever I am,* McBee thought, *Faith is right there, always close, waiting to slide in front of whatever I'm brooding over.*

"I brung one of your men back, Capt'n."

McBee looked up, the thoughts of Faith instantly gone again.

"What? Talk sense, Levi. I sure enough need men after today, but you brought apples."

Lieutenant Anderson interjected softly, "Captain, your man Levi met Private Phillips way back in the gap between this hill and that rocky one where the Union artillery was firing at us earlier. Phillips was deserting during the fight on the hillside. Levi was bringing us apples and full canteens. Phillips tried to kill Levi with his bayonet and steal your mule. Levi whacked him with the sack of apples, then a rock, and hog-tied him to the mule and brought him to us. He's tied to a tree over there."

McBee tried to study Levi's face in the dark, but could only see his eyes.

"Did the lieutenant tell it true, Levi?"

"Yessir, I reckon he did."

"You fought Private Phillips, with apples, tied him up and brought him home?"

"Tweren't much of a fight," Levi answered. In spite of the desperation of the evening, McBee felt a flash of respect for his slave's loyalty and audacity, prompting the corners of the captain's mouth to turn up in a smile that no one could see.

"When you going to quit scrapping with white men, Levi? It's likely to get you killed someday. Think you can find the wagons again and fetch us something more than a sack of apples?" The captain added grimly, "Won't need as near as much as yesterday since there's only twenty- eight of us left."

"Twenty-eight, plus me and George, and Private Phillips. It's mighty dark, but the wagons can't be too far back. I reckon the mule and me can find our way, Capt'n. Don't know what rations will be there, but I'll bring what I can get. Look for me in a few hours."

Already thinking again about losing half his riflemen, McBee nodded and Levi walked away to get the mule and be on his way.

Lieutenant Anderson remained near the captain and interrupted his reverie to ask softly, "What about Phillips, Captain? When General Hood hears about him, he'll have him shot. Shot by our own company in front of the whole brigade. And he deserves it."

"Aaron, we lost one out of every two riflemen today. Who knows how many more tomorrow? The men are going to be moody in the morning. They're going to wake up mad and sullen about losing so many of their messmates and not taking that damned ridge. Who knows about Phillips right now?"

"I put Corporal Smith to guard him. Sergeant Hodges helped tie him to the tree. It was already dark when Levi found us, and he came straight to me, looking for you. Levi stuffed a rag in Phillips' mouth when he came to and started hollering, so the men ain't heard him fussing. No campfires, so those not on the picket line are stretched out trying to sleep. I doubt nobody but Smith and Hodges know Phillips is here. At roll call when we rallied up here 'fore you got back, he was just another missing private. You want me to smother him? It'll be quiet and just take a minute. I got no truck with deserters."

The captain looked up at the lieutenant and shook his head no. He wasn't concerned that Anderson had just offered to silently kill one of their men without a court martial, since he himself shared Anderson's disdain for deserters. Nonetheless, that would be more murder than execution, even if it would protect Levi and give Phillips the punishment he deserved.

"Aaron, make sure every man gets a couple of Levi's apples, and spread the word that he brought those sacks of apples to the company on his own. I didn't order him to do that. He may have brought back a deserter, but he's still a darkie, and some of our boys might be thinking to run off themselves, and I don't want any of them making a lot of noise about a slave stopping Phillips. Not to mention a black man beating a white man armed with a bayonet in a fight - with apples." McBee rubbed his jaw, saying, "I sure wish I had seen that."

"Yes Sir, I'll do what you say, but what about Phillips?"

"We may be in a big tussle again tomorrow and need Phillips' rifle. I'd have shot him myself yesterday if I'd seen him running away, but, hell, we all were scared on that hillside. You quietly assign Corporal Smith to stay next to Phillips, like a shadow, and don't give him any cartridges until we start shooting Yankees. I'll decide later on his punishment. Maybe the sorry skunk will redeem himself before we get back to Virginia."

Chapter 24

Camp of the Texas Brigade
Port Royal on the Rappahannock River, Virginia
July 18, 1863

Like nearly every soldier in Lee's army, Captain John McBee looked forward to the delivery of mail. News from home was an elixir to war-worn men, and since Faith had moved to Lexington, McBee was no different. He opened each letter from Faith with an eagerness that belied his normally stern demeanor as their company's captain.

Nonetheless, McBee scowled and crumpled the letter that had just arrived as he strode towards Major Roger's headquarters tent. Halfway there, he stopped, refolded the letter, and slipped it into his coat pocket. He found the regiment's newest commander reading while sitting under the canvas fly that provided shade for the clerks doing paperwork. The captain sat down when the major gestured to an empty folding chair.

"Jeff, I need a sword. I lost the first one at Manassas Junction, and my second one on that damned hill outside Gettysburg."

Major Jefferson Rogers stuck a twig in his book to mark his place and glanced up at his friend, Captain McBee.

"You could start carrying a frying pan instead like Johnny Upton did at Gaines' Mill last summer," the major said. "Must have worked too, since a whole regiment surrendered to us. I won't ever forget him strutting around with those Yankee officers' swords jammed up under his arm, sticking out like a banty rooster's tail feathers while he waved that black frying pan around."

"I remember that, too. He was a sight, and a helluva fighter. But I'm afraid Levi wouldn't let me abuse one of his skillets that way." McBee paused and added wryly, "I can't figure why, since he can't cook worth a damn, but he's particular about his mess ware."

The major grinned because Levi was popular among the staff officers as one of the body-servants who *didn't* burn every meal, and one who usually had a biscuit or corn fritter to offer any officer who had business with his captain.

"Then why don't you go into Richmond and buy a new sword?"

"Because the last one busted my wallet, and I just bought Justin Clay's extra pistol. With your permission, if the brigade's going to be here a few days, I'd like a travel pass to Lexington to get my father's sword. He carried it in the last war with the British before I was born. My mother wrote and offered it. It'd mean a lot to me."

"Sure, John, go ahead. I envy your having family up here. But Lexington's a long ride for a sword, isn't it?"

"I'll catch a ride on a west-bound supply train to Lynchburg from Richmond, and then take the canal packet boat from Lynchburg to Lexington. One day there and one day back," McBee promised.

"General Robertson told us yesterday he expects we'll stay here at least a couple more weeks while General Lee reorganizes the army. Spend a day or two at home with your mother…and her houseguests. I'll try not to be jealous."

McBee didn't acknowledge the innuendo. He suspected his complicated family situation in Lexington was an open secret among the other officers in the regiment. He simply felt gratitude for Rogers' discretion in front of the clerks. McBee fretted every day that the stain on his honor was indelible, and a reckoning lay ahead. Yet, he was also learning that honor had more than one face.

On the way back to his company street, McBee pulled the letter from his pocket and read the short note once more, depressed that the date made the news three weeks old.

June 29, 1863

My Dearest John,

I am frightened as I write this. Young Betsy is burning with a fever that will not abate. She is losing weight and cries until it rends my heart. She takes the milk from my breast, but purges it within minutes. She soils each fresh diaper before Edward can wash the others.

I am trying to be strong of will, but I find I am no longer the brave nurse I was in the soldiers' hospital last year. Our precious daughter is suffering, and the doctor's ministrations and my prayers are not curing her.

Elizabeth and Edward are a blessing in keeping John Junior while I spend each day with his ailing twin. So far the ague that besets Betsy has not afflicted our boy too, Praise be to God.

I read that the army has left Virginia, and I pray every day for your safe return.

Your Faith

McBee walked by Levi who was stooped over the cook fire. "Levi, we're going to Lexington. Pack my valise, if you would. Now!"

"Yessir, Capt'n. The beans ain't boiling yet no how."

Chapter 25

Richmond, Virginia
July 19, 1863

C aptain McBee was pleasantly surprised to find a passenger car attached to the freight train, and that his captain's rank was enough to earn him a seat. McBee made sure that Levi climbed onto the roof of a boxcar before he entered the passenger car and squeezed into the last vacant space on a wooden bench.

The captain sat opposite a middle-aged man with a kindly face framed by dark wavy hair and beard, but no mustache. His mouth, even with lips pressed together, projected a permanent half-smile, while probing eyes sparkled under heavy eye lids.

Next to the portly civilian, a large man with a small waist sat without expression. The handle of a pistol was visible protruding from his belt. His eyes were alert, and no trace of kindness radiated from his countenance. Obviously he was a bodyguard.

While the passengers waited for the black laborers to finish loading the boxcars, the well-dressed civilian scanned page after page of documents until he reached the bottom of the sheaf of papers. He sighed deeply and stuffed the stack back into his leather satchel. Eyes closed, he leaned back for several heartbeats before he blinked a few times and looked casually at the lean officer sitting across from him, their knees touching in the narrow space between the seats. The civilian noted McBee's captain's insignia on his frayed coat collar along with the patched elbows, and the double row of mismatched and tarnished brass buttons.

"I see you are travelling without a sword, Captain. It is my unpleasant experience on trains, where I spend an inordinate amount of time, that infantry officers' swords are inevitably poking about, competing with my feet for the tiny bit of floor space allotted to the living. I've noticed that most officers compulsively caress their steel toothpicks. I suspect they even sleep with them."

"I've slept a few nights on the hard ground with a steel toothpick tucked between my legs," McBee replied courteously, wondering why the man needed an armed keeper. "Makes it hard to roll over, though."

"But you are without one this day," the civilian countered, appreciating the officer's attempt to maintain the verbal repartee.

McBee nodded, if for no other reason than to keep his mind off the image of his infant daughter burning up with fever.

"Lost my sword in Pennsylvania a few weeks back. Before that, I lost one in Virginia at Manassas last year," McBee answered truthfully. "I can't seem to keep hold of the slippery eels when the shooting starts. Doesn't seem to matter what state I'm in."

"Forgive me, Captain, but that's an intriguing admission. Allow me to introduce myself. I am Secretary of State Judah Benjamin. My traveling companion is Mr. O'Kelly."

Benjamin held out a smooth pudgy hand, which McBee took into his big-knuckled grip, giving the Secretary of State a good look at his scarred fingers and his Masonic ring.

"Captain John J. McBee, Company C, Fifth Texas Infantry Regiment, at your service, Sir."

"Well, Captain McBee, your introduction answers the question of your accent. One of Hood's Texans. But don't I hear a trace of Virginia tucked into your Texas drawl?"

"You have a keen ear, Mr. Secretary. I emigrated from Lexington to Galveston when I was a young man."

"Ah, a second son who left home to seek your fortune, I'm speculating."

"As a matter of fact I am the second of three sons. And I did go to Texas seeking my fortune. That and to fight Comanches, as it turned out."

"Did you lose your sword fighting wild Indians in Texas as well?"

"No Sir, it's best to engage the Comanche from somewhat farther away. Not so different from fighting our northern enemies now," McBee touched the pistol holster at his waist. "That's why I will travel without a sword, but not without my Colt."

"Forgive me again, for my impertinence, Captain McBee, but I rarely have the chance to speak with those of your rank; those who've been courageously leading our brave men in the maelstrom of battle to win Southern independence. I've heard generals describe how they lost two divisions, but I have never heard a captain explain how he lost two swords in battle. I am intrigued to learn how you managed to do that, and still remain upright. And, that you are here on this train today, and not in a grave, or some Union prison in Delaware, competing with rats for crumbs of food."

Before he replied, McBee shifted his rump on the hard bench and waited for the locomotive's steam whistle to stop its howling as the train jerked into motion.

"Secretary Benjamin, it's mostly luck, not getting shot or blown apart in battle. No one enemy has ever sought out John McBee to kill me personally, except maybe for one wild-eyed Comanche, but every enemy I've faced has been ready to kill me. Thousands of Union soldiers have been eager to kill me, and every other Secessionist soldier on the field."

McBee let his gaze drop to his boots, before he looked the politician in the eyes and said, "A battlefield is an unnerving place, Sir, truly a slice of Dante's Inferno that has risen from an invisible gash in the earth. A gash split open by the first crash of artillery, there to consume the unlucky, friend and foe alike."

Benjamin softly clapped his palms together, warmly saying, "A Texan with a taste for the classics, and a man of imagery. How delightful. Now, your *Tale of Two Swords*, if you would accede to the curiosity of a man whose stock in trade lies in words, not cold steel."

McBee found himself drawn to the Secretary's boyish enthusiasm, so he began, "At Manassas, the second battle there last summer, we Texans didn't get to Virginia in time for the first one. My regiment came out of the woods in front of a line of Yankees dressed in baggy red-pants and red fezzes. I'd never seen their like before."

Benjamin nodded. "Yes, yes, I'm familiar with the French Zouave craze in the northern states."

"Whatever their name, they fought like red devils, I'll give them that. We let loose a volley that dropped dozens of them. Then we charged with empty rifles, just our bayonets and the hellish scream we've become very good at. Some of them broke and ran. But not all of them."

The Secretary leaned his head forward, held up a palm, and interrupted. "Tell me about the scream. The Rebel Yell our generals keep saying is a weapon as deadly as muskets."

"Nothing but Scottish keening, with a bit of yipping like a coon dog hot on the trail tossed in. It's damned unnerving, even to me. I can see why the Yanks fear it and remember it."

"Ah, Highlanders and hound dogs. What a revelation. Do go on. Some of your foe did not break and run, you say."

"Especially the color guard, they stood firm protecting their flags, while others lost their courage and ran. I saw a big sergeant reloading his musket, was close enough to catch his eye. I held his attention, intending to throw myself down just as he aimed at me. Make him waste a shot. I knew he wouldn't pass up shooting an officer. You know, the sword."

"Yes, of course, the sword. Go on," Benjamin encouraged.

"The sergeant was raising his Springfield when something whacked me hard in the shoulder. Like being kicked by a mule. I fell, yes, I did, just like I planned, because some other bastard in red pants had shot me."

Benjamin was enthralled and added, "I read the reports from Manassas. I remember you Texans pushed the enemy for miles, inflicted massive casualties before you stopped. Since you won the field, how did you lose your sword?"

"Nobody told my Negro body-servant of the great import of his captain's sword," McBee said, his sarcasm perceptible. "Some wounded soldier in my company saw Levi, my servant, at the field hospital and told him that I was shot, maybe dead on the field. The boy came looking, found me and carried me back to the hospital tent. But Levi's just a darkie, so he didn't think to pick up my sword. I'm frankly grateful he was more concerned with hauling my carcass off the field than searching for my sword."

"I surmise then that you own slaves, Captain?"

"A few back in Texas. Before the war I did a good business leasing them out. Had a couple of good carpenters. You, Sir? Are you a participant in our peculiar institution?"

"I was. One can't grow cotton and sugar cane in Louisiana without them. But I divested myself of that burden, most thankfully, before the war, while I was still a senator in Washington City. Being an absent owner of such a complex enterprise was not to my taste. Now, Captain, that's one sword. What about the second?"

"Yessir. That was just a few weeks ago in Pennsylvania. Hood's Division was on the far right end of General Lee's army. We were sent forward to take a ridge. Apparently the generals thought we could roll up the whole Union army once we drove the Yanks from that one ridge. Trouble was, the ground below the ridge crest was steep, really steep, and covered in brush and boulders. My company, and the whole regiment, couldn't maintain our cohesion because of the damned big rocks. We struggled upwards, but our one regiment wasn't enough, and there wasn't a supporting regiment behind us to push once we got all tangled up and stalled in those rocks."

"Yes," Benjamin said dryly, "I've been made aware of the lost opportunity at the Round Tops."

"Round Tops?"

"Haven't you heard the name, Captain? General Hood attacked Little Round Top. That's where you were repulsed."

"Repulsed." McBee stretched out the word as he repeated it. "That's a polite word for losing half our men during three, maybe four, efforts to reach the crest under heavy fire."

"Bloody business, assaulting a well-defended ridge," Benjamin agreed, tactfully sidestepping any blame for the failure.

"Your lost sword?" the Secretary prompted again when the captain in the shabby coat didn't immediately resume his story.

"My sword. On the third push, a high private and I..."

"Excuse me, *high private*?"

"Private Rafe Fulton, an old friend who won't accept a promotion, but a man who the other men look up to, a man I can depend on."

"Yes, I see. A *high private*. An apt term. I would do well to have a high private behind me myself. Do continue."

"Mr. Secretary, Mr. O'Kelly appears to have your back well covered."

The bodyguard shifted his eyes to McBee and nodded almost unperceptively.

"Anyway, the high private and I went up a dead-end blocked by giant granite rocks, and when we turned around, we were facing a pack of Yanks with muskets aimed at us. Fulton dropped his musket, so I dropped my sword and pistol when one of the blue turds looked like he would shoot me if I didn't."

Captain McBee noticed Secretary of State Benjamin raise his chin minutely as he described the circumstance of his capture.

"Mr. Secretary, I may well die leading my men in battle, but I am not willing to be butchered like a hog in a situation where I see no chance to survive if I resist. As to the sword, I suppose some Federal officer is carrying it now, or maybe it's still laying on that hillside in Pennsylvania. It pains me that I paid a pretty sum for that blade in Richmond. Wasn't a spot of rust on it."

"I presume you and the high private became prisoners of war?"

"Yes Sir, we were for maybe half an hour. We escaped while a long line of us were being led up over the ridge. At a bend in the trail we dropped and rolled away unnoticed. We hugged the dirt like ground squirrels until dark. Then we crawled down the hill and made our way back to what was left of our regiment."

Secretary Benjamin now nodded. "Your escape is a story I hope you will relate to your grandchildren someday. I applaud your determination to remain a free man. Now that you are back in Virginia, are you planning to fight the next battle without a sword?"

McBee thought of Colonel Upton's skillet, but decided that story might unduly offend the Secretary's sense of military propriety, so instead he said, "I'm on my way to my mother's home in Lexington to visit family and fetch my father's old sword from over the mantle. He carried it in the last war against the British. When my regiment goes into the next battle, I'll tie his sword's hilt to my wrist. Perhaps the old colonel's spirit is encased in that blade and it will prevent me from again being wounded or captured."

Secretary Benjamin laughed heartily. "Perhaps so, Captain, perhaps so. Nevertheless, t'were I you, I'd keep a firm grip on my Colt in my other hand, and High Private Fulton at my back."

Chapter 26

Lynchburg, Virginia
Evening, July 19, 1863

The heavily used railroad track needed repairs, causing the soldiers and bureaucrats packed onto the crowded benches to bounce and sway. Shortly after the war started, meal service had been discontinued, adding another inconvenience to the interminable six-hour trip.

From Richmond to Lynchburg, John McBee, a Texas infantry captain, and Judah Benjamin, the Secretary of State of the Confederacy, engaged in a wide ranging conversation. Having owned a plantation in Louisiana before being elected to the US Senate, Benjamin guided McBee into expounding on the pre-war agricultural economy in Texas. For his part, McBee welcomed the opportunity to spend a few hours with a learned man discussing the technical aspects of cotton farming, and not the war.

"Captain, I would be honored if you might be my guest for dinner at my hotel," Benjamin said as the train pulled into the Lynchburg station.

"Mr. Secretary, I'll gladly accept your invitation if I might first secure my passage on the canal packet boat going to Lexington. My travel furlough is short and I can't afford to miss the *Marshall's* next departure."

"Certainly, Captain. I am reserved at the Norvell House on Main Street, just three blocks from here. I'll be in the dining room at 8:00 this evening."

"Thank you, Mr. Secretary."

* * *

At the canal boat ticket office, McBee paid for his and Levi's passage, irritated that Levi's ticket cost almost as much as his own, even though as a Negro, Levi would have to find a place among the baggage on the open deck instead of a seat in the cabin. In spite of the cost, McBee was relieved that a boat, a smaller one than the Marshall, would depart at 11:00 that evening and had space available, saving the captain the expense of overnight lodging in Lynchburg.

McBee hesitated a moment, then removed his pistol holster and stashed his sidearm into his carpet bag. The captain expected that the Norvell House dining room's clientele would be high-ranking military officers and affluent civilians, and he didn't want to appear coarse while sharing a table with a member of President Davis' cabinet. McBee regretted he didn't have a better coat to wear to dinner, but shrugged off the matter, rationalizing that the Secretary knew what he was wearing when he extended the dinner invitation. While turning over the valise to the ticket agent McBee asked directions to the Norvell House.

When the pair reached the hotel, McBee tossed Levi a small coin to buy a meal at the back door to the hotel kitchen. Levi deftly caught the coin, pocketed it, and nodded thanks to his captain. When McBee disappeared through the front door, Levi made his way down the alley, but instead of going all the way to the kitchen door, he stopped next to the half-completed frame of a shed being added to the building across the alley from the hotel. Levi picked up a short board, laid it across the top of an open keg of nails and sat down. Then he flipped open the flap of his greasy haversack and pulled out a crumbling piece of fried cornmeal and a chunk of raw bacon.

Levi could see across the alley through a window's gauze curtains into the hotel dining room. While chewing his first bite of the nearly rancid bacon, he saw his captain being seated at the table of a smiling bearded man in a dark green coat. The young black man relaxed against the wall, contentedly invisible in the shadows as Captain McBee unfolded a white napkin and sipped red wine from a fragile-looking stemmed glass.

Watching his master in a room full of rich white people, Levi felt a pride in the captain that surprised him. Levi couldn't remember exactly how long he'd been serving the captain, but he had grown to like the man. His mother had told Levi that the captain had grown up in the McBee household at the same time she had: John, a son of the master, Sally, just another young slave who worked in the kitchen. Until one day, for no good reason, the master's middle son up and went away.

His mother had told Levi that years and years later the grown son had come back to Lexington, just as unexpectedly. He was an army captain needing a man-servant, and Mrs. McBee offered Levi. That put Sally to teaching Levi how to cook so he could go to war to serve the returned son of the long-dead master. One day in the kitchen, she'd told Levi that the captain was somebody special, so Levi better do more than just enough not to get whipped. But she hadn't told him any details.

And now Mama's dead, and won't never tell me how the captain was special to her. Did the capt'n couple with my mama years ago? If he did, did Mama let him, or did he make her do it?

Leaving that ugly question, Levi went another step beyond any of his previous musings: *Could the Capt'n be my father?* That idea seemed too ludicrous for Levi to even consider. But as he sat watching the room full of well-dressed white men and women in the hotel dining room, the young mulatto slave's mind continued to whirl. *If Miss Faith had been my mama by the capt'n instead of Sally, if the twins were my brother and sister, I bet that someday I'd wear a fine coat and sit next to the capt'n in a fancy dining room, like this one.*

Levi knew he was engaged in absurd, futile daydreaming, so he forced his thoughts back to life in the army camp, where he enjoyed his status as the captain's body-servant.

* * *

Adam Samuelson, late of the Confederate army, sat in new civilian clothes at a corner table to the side of the entry from the lobby. He had been covertly watching Secretary Benjamin without staring, by glancing casually around the room as diners came and went, as a man might do looking for someone he knew. Samuelson's blond hair was now dark and his chin was no longer clean shaven; he wore a smartly trimmed goatee beard and mustache. He carried a pocket pistol in his coat and a slim knife with a five inch blade hidden under his coat sleeve, strapped to his left forearm.

Samuelson barely noticed the lean bearded officer when the captain walked across the room, except to mentally sneer at the patched elbows of his uniform coat. Nonetheless, as the waiter seated the officer at Benjamin's table, even though only part of the newcomer's facial profile was visible, that was enough. Samuelson blinked in shock, suddenly aware that he was looking at his wife's lover, the man who had cuckolded him.

The new Federal spy nearly choked on the stringy stewed chicken that he was chewing. He immediately ducked his head as he wondered if McBee had recognized him as he walked through the dining room. Within a few seconds he decided that was unlikely and resumed eating, watching, and thinking:

Why is it that an infantry captain from Texas is sharing a table and engaging in conversation with such a high-ranking Confederate official as Benjamin? What had he not been told in Western Virginia by that damnable Union major, the one who sent him to Lynchburg?

* * *

Levi let his gaze wander among the people he could see through other windows until he glanced at a man eating alone at a corner table. That diner was also studying the other people in the room. As Levi chewed his supper and watched, he decided the man looked towards the captain's table more often than elsewhere. *Why would that be?* The longer he watched the man, the more familiar he looked, but Levi couldn't put the face with a time and place.

Levi shifted about straining for a better look, until he finally stood up for a clear view. Still not sure, he edged along the wall until he was directly across from the window nearest the man's corner table. Finally Levi stooped over and crossed the alley to crouch against the hotel wall. He carefully checked both ends of the dark alley to be sure he was alone. He rose up and peered through the gap in the curtains, and was suddenly certain.

The man had changed his hair color, grown a beard and shed his uniform, but Levi realized that he was looking at Miss Faith's husband. *The same man who took me off the highway at gunpoint last year, meaning to murder me and the captain. The same man who killed Sheriff Cain in Lexington just this spring.*

Levi slid down the wall, his heart beating fast enough to hear. *The man fled north, killing a deputy on the way, but he's back, he's right there on the other side of the wall, eating and eyeing the capt'n. I have to warn him. But I can't get in the dining room. Maybe I should just shout. Maybe throw a rock through the window. Maybe I can go through the kitchen. Put on an apron…*

* * *

"Is your companion Mr. O'Kelly not joining us?" McBee asked after his first taste of the red wine.

"Look around, Captain. The Norvell House knows the importance of its patrons. There are competent watchers at every door. I won't be bothered here." Benjamin paused, adding almost impishly, "So I've encouraged Mr. O'Kelly to seek his own diversions this evening. There's a sporting house just a few buildings away, and Mr. O'Kelly is an unmarried robust man with a boring and often sedentary job."

McBee didn't quite know how to respond, so he picked up a piece of dark bread from the basket on the table.

"Captain, before you depart to Lexington, I'm compelled to broach a new subject," the Secretary of State, suddenly serious, said as McBee spread thick molasses on the bread.

"Day after day I am deluged with inquiries from cowardly sycophants, men from families of influence who look to avoid the hardships of military service by becoming employees of my department. I have no use for them. But I am in need of liaison officers with the military. Men with honorable war records that garner the respect of other officers. Men who understand the military mind, who can accompany the army to observe and report to me as the war progresses."

McBee was now listening intently.

"I think you may be just such an officer as I need," Benjamin concluded. "Furthermore, I believe a promotion to the rank of major would be in order."

McBee was flattered by the offer and it piqued his interest. He chewed the bread and took another sip of wine while he mentally weighed the benefits of the offer. Major McBee sounded good, and being a liaison officer for a member of the President's cabinet certainly would bring him status beyond that of the commander of an infantry company. Against those obvious benefits, he considered his duty to his men from Leon County, the men from home, the men he had led for nearly two years. McBee was reluctantly framing a polite refusal when another diner shouted:

"FIRE! There's a fire in the alley!"

Chapter 27

Lynchburg, Virginia
Evening, July 19, 1863

Frightened diners abandoned their dinners in confusion, although some few astutely noted that the flames were outside, not within the wooden walls of their building. They moved more calmly towards the entry way; others fled in haste crowding the entry to the lobby. McBee imagined the stairs would be full of people rushing to their rooms to save their valuables before taking to the safety of the street. In one smooth motion, McBee gripped the Secretary's elbow and pulled him out of his chair, moving toward the kitchen door at the back of the dining room.

* * *

Elliot O'Kelly, Secretary Benjamin's bodyguard, heard the screams of "Fire!" while he lay on his bed rereading a nickel novel about King Arthur and the Knights of the Round Table. O'Kelly liked to imagine himself as a knight, a big strong knight who preferred a morning-star over a sword; a knight whose immense arm strength could swing the studded iron ball on its chain around his head and smash through wooden shields like splintering kindling.

When he heard the screams, he slid off the bed, scooping up his brass knuckles and pistol off the bedside table. He glanced out the open window overlooking an alley and saw flames and smoke. The bodyguard hurried into the hall and while still putting on his coat, banged on the Secretary's door. When the door didn't open after three long seconds, O'Kelly backed up a few steps and kicked the wood just below the doorknob as hard as he could. On the second kick, the lock broke and he rushed into the room. Empty. Grunting, he turned and trotted down the hall.

The stairs were crowded with people hurrying up to their rooms and he had to shove his way through them. The lobby was equally crowded and chaotic, so O'Kelly stood on a chair scanning the room for the Secretary. Not seeing him, the bodyguard pushed his way across the lobby into the dining room, which was empty.

* * *

Once out of the dining room, Captain McBee led Secretary Benjamin through the kitchen and into the back yard of the hotel, looking for his man-servant. Not seeing Levi near the kitchen door, McBee spied a gate in the wood fence across the back of the hotel property. He pointed it out to the Secretary, who nodded his agreement. Together, they went through the gate into a narrow alley and around the large block, finally emerging onto Main Street across from a livery stable.

* * *

Levi stayed in the shadows of the buildings across the street from the Norvell House until he spotted Samuelson push through the front door and walk briskly away. Levi would have lost him in the throng of people in the street, but Samuelson wore a light pecan-colored hat that stood out in the uneven light from the many windows of the buildings lining Main Street.

Levi furtively followed the tan hat while still watching the front door of the hotel. When Samuelson disappeared into a livery stable two buildings away from the Norvell House, Levi returned to his station across from the hotel entrance, waiting impatiently for his captain to appear as he kept one eye on the door to the livery stable.

* * *

Elliot O'Kelly, a bodyguard who had lost his charge, stood on the sidewalk in front of the Norvell House his gaze flicking on one man after another. He didn't see the Secretary in the confusion in the street, but he did note men carrying buckets of water dipped from horse watering troughs in front of the hotel. O'Kelly took a few steps until he could see the bucket brigade in the alley flinging water at the heavily smoking fire. Even as he watched, the flames shrank as the blaze was splashed repeatedly with water.

* * *

Back in the shadows, Levi watched and smiled, smugly satisfied that with nothing but one lucifer, a greasy haversack, a chunk of bacon, and his dirty shirt stuffed into a barrel of wood scraps, he'd been able to empty the dining room and send Miss Faith's bad husband scurrying.

Then Levi thought very clearly: *I just called him Miss Faith's **bad** husband. Does that mean the capt'n is Miss Faith's **good** husband? Can Miss Faith have two husbands without being a Jezebel?* That disturbing thought gave way to: *Where, oh where is the capt'n? I've got to tell him Sam'lson's here. And we've got to get to the canal boat 'fore it leaves the dock.*

Among the people who were rushing both ways on Main Street, Levi noticed a tall man with wide shoulders walking slowly, his head turning back and forth. *Like me, he's looking for somebody,* Levi thought. The man stopped and waved at someone farther up the street. *Good for you, now where's my capt'n?*

Out of the corner of his eye, Levi saw the big door to the livery stable open and a dark horse being led out. The man holding the halter was on the other side of the horse, only the crown of his tan hat visible over the saddle. Levi immediately began walking after the horse, keeping on the boardwalk, next to the buildings, still searching for his master.

The gold cloth bars on McBee's collar flashed in the light from a window, finally catching Levi's attention as his sweeping gaze kept probing the shadows looking for the captain, growing more desperate as the seconds passed. Realizing that Samuelson, hidden by the horse, was leading the animal towards McBee, the young man-servant dashed into Main Street waving his arms.

* * *

O'Kelly didn't see the young Negro until Levi brushed by, running past him, waving his arms and shouting. The bodyguard looked beyond the running black man and saw the army officer from the train and Secretary Benjamin standing on the sidewalk, directly in the running Negro's path. O'Kelly pulled his pistol, ready to shoot the running figure in the back if he pulled a knife, and sprinted after him.

* * *

Captain McBee saw Levi running in his direction and wondered why his man-servant was frantically waving his arms. McBee was subconsciously aware of a horse being led diagonally across the street coming his way. With Levi blocking his line of sight, he didn't see O'Kelly at all.

* * *

The Secretary noticed the running black man, and when the Negro stumbled and bent forward to catch himself, Benjamin saw Elliot O'Kelly running behind him with revolver held high. Benjamin instantly reacted by dropping where he stood, reaching deep into his coat pocket for his own small pocket pistol.

* * *

Levi regained his balance, pointed at the dark horse in the street, and yelled as loudly as he could, "Sam'lson! Capt'n, it's Sam'lson!"

The tan hat disappeared behind the horse. An instant later, the sharp crack of a pistol rang out from the direction of the horse, the red muzzle blast from the pistol appearing just in front of the animal's neck.

* * *

O'Kelly heard the Negro shout just before hearing the pistol shot. The big man swiveled towards the sound to see a man clambering onto a horse that was trying to rear up. O'Kelly looked back towards Benjamin who he only saw as a dark lump on the sidewalk. As the Secretary's bodyguard watched, a pistol crack and muzzle flash came from the lump, telegraphing in an instant to O'Kelly that his charge was alive and responding to the attack. He turned back to the horseman who was bent low over the beast's neck, kicking his mount in its flanks. O'Kelly fired twice as the horse broke into a run, one bullet hitting its haunch.

Even though the Secretary had just dropped to the boardwalk, McBee remained standing, his attention riveted on his man-servant. He heard Levi's shout and looked where the frantic young man was pointing. He saw the muzzle flash just in front of the horse and heard the bullet hit the wooden wall of the building behind him and the Secretary. Instinctively, McBee leapt off the boardwalk, running as quickly as he could towards the horse while bending down as low as he could without falling forward.

The captain heard two shots to his right side as the wild-eyed horse rushed past him, still too far for McBee to grab at the rider's leg. The horse galloped through the shadows on Main Street and quickly disappeared in the night.

Secretary of State Benjamin stood up, taking in the whole scene around him, as McBee walked back to the boardwalk.

"For a man who makes his living with words, you put this weaponless soldier to shame. Well done, Sir," McBee said.

"Who's Sam'lson?" Benjamin asked, ignoring the compliment. "I don't think the man likes me."

179

Chapter 28

Lynchburg, Virginia
Evening, July 19, 1863

Elliot O'Kelly held his pistol as he watched the street, while Secretary Benjamin and Captain McBee talked. Levi stood ten feet away in the shadows, listening.

"Mr. Secretary, I think that man, Samuelson, may have been after me, not you."

McBee couldn't see Benjamin raise one eyebrow at that, but he did hear the snort before the Secretary said, "I say, Captain, that's rather unlikely, unless perhaps you cuckolded the man."

When McBee remained silent and dropped his eyes, Benjamin laughed. "So I was nearly shot dead on a dark street because my dinner companion dallied with another man's wife? How rich."

With a pained expression, McBee looked up and said, "Mr. Secretary, you are correct. The man who shot at us has fair cause to see me dead. But there's more to it than Faith and me."

"Faith?"

"His—no--my wife. Her name is Faith. She had twin babies six months ago. My babies. One of them is sick. That's really why I'm going to Lexington, not just to get my father's old sword."

Benjamin, with sudden revelation, interrupted. "But her first husband, this Samuelson, unless he's been shadowing you, he couldn't know you'd be here in Lynchburg. He didn't know you'd be in the Norvell House dining room with me."

"You're right about that, Mr. Secretary. The day of General Jackson's burial in Lexington, he killed the sheriff and ran for Western Virginia. Killed the provost lieutenant who was leading the posse chasing him. There's no way he could have been following me around Virginia."

"This Samuelson sounds a dangerous man."

"Yessir, he is, and clever. He also owns a company that smuggles tobacco to Baltimore. The Pamunkey River Freight Company."

"If Samuelson has been in a Union state for the past six months, why would he hazard travelling back to Virginia? He's wanted for murdering a lawman and a provost. Why would he be in Lynchburg tonight at such a risk to himself?" Benjamin wondered.

"Like you said, he couldn't have known I'd be here tonight. I didn't even know I was getting a furlough until yesterday." McBee said. "On the other hand, how long ago did you make plans to come to here? Who knew you were coming to Lynchburg before you got on that train?"

The secretary considered McBee's logic for a few seconds then said, "My travel plans are not secret within my office. Long before I boarded that train, several of my staff knew I was coming here. Any of them had enough time to send a message north, I'm afraid."

"Captain, you seem to have talked us both out of your first assertion that Samuelson was shooting at you, and not me."

"Mr. Secretary, I must board a canal boat within the hour and go on to Lexington. My baby daughter is sick, maybe dying, with fever."

"I too have a daughter, Captain. I understand."

"But I can only stay a day or two. Then I'll be returning to my regiment. Our meeting on the train was pure chance, but your hotel reservation and dinner wasn't chance."

"No, indeed. Like I said, arrangements were made some time ago."

"If Samuelson has turned coat and is now a Union agent and was waiting for you at the Norvell House, he may not be alone. You might want to find other accommodations for the night."

Secretary Benjamin stood mutely for a full minute before he said, "Do you think the canal packet boat to Lexington can squeeze in two last minute and nameless passengers? And might your dear mother, Mrs. McBee, have a spare bed for a statesman? A statesman who would like to remain safely out of sight for a day or two while he kicks open a hornet's nest in his own office. There is a working telegraph in Lexington, I presume."

John McBee rolled his eyes in the dark before he answered, "Of course. You and Mr. O'Kelly may take my seat in the cabin of the packet boat, and I'll join Levi on the deck." Swallowing, he continued, "And I'm sure my mother will be flattered to welcome such a distinguished statesman into her home. Without fanfare, although that will doubtlessly be more difficult for her."

* * *

Captain McBee and Levi sat on boxes of ceramic dinnerware bound for the mercantile store in Lexington. When his stomach growled, McBee idly complained, "All I've eaten today is bread and molasses. And that at the fanciest restaurant in Lynchburg."

"You had red wine, too," Levi said.

"You saw that, did you? Spying on your master?"

"No Sir, I was just eating my supper in the alley. Couldn't help but notice all the folks in the dining room since the windows were wide open."

"My servant was eating a hot supper from the hotel kitchen, while I ate stale bread."

"No Sir. I ate raw bacon and cornbread crumbs from my haversack."

"Huh. Then I want my Davis Dime back. No, never mind. You keep it as thanks for recognizing Samuelson. And where's your green shirt? You had it on. I saw it," McBee looked sternly at his man-servant who now wore a dirty brown jacket, but no shirt under it.

"Gone."

"Don't be evasive. Answer me."

"Burned up in the fire back in Lynchburg."

"The fire in the alley at the hotel?"

Levi nodded.

"That fire was set in a barrel."

Levi nodded.

"Did you start that fire with your shirt?"

Levi nodded and elaborated. "It had enough grease stains on it to catch like pine pitch."

"You trying to get yourself lynched?"

Levi shrugged.

"All right. I'm asking: Why did you set the fire in the barrel in the alley?"

"I saw Sam'lson sitting at a table in the corner of the dining room."

"Now I see. And you couldn't come in the dining room to tell me," McBee said.

Levi nodded again.

"Did you have to burn up your shirt?"

Levi shrugged again, saying, "Didn't have time for nothin' else. Maybe Mizz McBee can find me another one."

Levi gently pulled the last cornpone from the pocket of his jacket, looked at it wistfully, and gave it to McBee. The captain chewed once or twice before swallowing it. Then each man tucked his legs up on the top of his crate and went to sleep. Neither the captain nor his servant noticed how hard a mattress the boards made as the mule pulled the boat along the well-worn path by the canal, rocking it gently like a giant cradle in the moonlight.

Directly under the pair on the crates, the Secretary and his bodyguard sat next to each other on the bare wooden bench in the narrow passenger cabin. O'Kelly held a candle while Benjamin scanned pages in a popular novel by Emily Bronte, searching for the needed words to pencil a coded message to his assistant in Richmond. After completing

183

that pressing task, he closed his eyes and within minutes began loudly snoring in a most undiplomatic fashion.

Elliot O'Kelly fought sleep by looking through the window pane at the mule that pulled the packet boat, counting each of the mule's measured rhythmic steps. Before long his snores challenged those of the Secretary, the sounds emitted by both men irritating the two middle-aged sisters who sat across from them in the cramped cabin.

Chapter 29

Lexington, Virginia
July 20, 1863

The four men disembarked from the canal boat before dawn. Secretary Benjamin put a folded paper in Elliot O'Kelly's hand with instructions to find the telegraph office and send the urgent message to his office as soon as the operator arrived. McBee gave the bodyguard directions to the telegraph office and told him how to find his mother's house.

Captain McBee, this time holding his pistol, and Secretary Benjamin, carrying his leather briefcase in his left hand with his right hand gripping the pistol in his coat pocket, walked the mile from the dock to Elizabeth McBee's house. The streets were empty and the buildings dark. Levi followed behind them, carrying both men's carpet bags and looking back over his shoulder every few seconds.

In the first light of the new day, McBee stopped to open the front gate to the yard, only to groan, "No, oh, no." They all looked at the wreath that hung on the front door. Dull green fir branches were intertwined with strips of black cotton, fragile white roses drooping down, the porch boards in front of the door littered with wilted flower pedals.

Captain McBee rushed to the door, pushed it open with a jerk, and hurried in. He saw Faith sitting in the parlor in a rocker nursing a baby. He looked around the room for the second infant before Faith's sad eyes caught and held his. She shook her head, her mouth held tightly, new tears wetting her cheeks.

"Eight days ago," said a vaguely familiar voice from the kitchen door. McBee looked past Faith to see Edward Bell, hands covered in flour, holding his pistol. "Captain, we buried little Betsy eight days ago. Your mother insisted she be put right next to her own baby Betsy."

From the banister at the top of the stairs, the elder Mrs. McBee spoke, causing John to twist his head around and look up, "It seemed the right place for her. Reverend Brown's cemetery is filling fast these past months. He'll be glad soon enough that we fit her in where she can lie next to her poor Aunt Betsy for eternity. Johnny, she was such a beautiful, happy little baby. I'm so sorry."

While Elizabeth McBee held her son's attention, Faith buttoned her dress bodice and crossed the room to hand John McBee their baby boy. Then she kissed her man hard on the mouth.

"My sincere condolences, to you, Mrs. Samuelson, on the loss of your precious child," Secretary Benjamin said from the doorway, the corners of his mouth slightly upturned as always.

"It's Mrs. McBee, not Samuelson. And who do I have the honor of addressing?" Faith retorted, impudence in her tone, not sure what the man's bare hint of smile meant.

Benjamin inclined his head and shoulders in a quick bow before he answered, "My apologies, Mrs. McBee. I'm Judah Philip Benjamin, your husband's fellow traveler." Looking up the stairs, Benjamin continued, "And temporary companion to your son, Madam. We met on the train from Richmond." Still speaking to Elizabeth McBee, he added, "Might I have your permission to enter your home?"

Faith cut a quick glance at Captain McBee, who barely nodded without looking up as he studied the face of John Junior, who was now six months old, and whose left hand was pawing at his father's salt and pepper beard.

"Please, Sir, excuse our rudeness," Elizabeth said as she descended the stairs. "My son's arrival is most welcomed, but was unexpected. Do come in."

The captain put one arm around Faith's shoulders as he held their child in the crook of his other arm. Looking at Benjamin, he said, "Secretary Benjamin, this is my wife Faith, our son John Junior, and my mother and hostess, Elizabeth McBee. Mother, Faith, this gentleman is Mr. Judah P. Benjamin, the Secretary of State of the Confederacy."

McBee heard a cough behind him. The captain looked back, sighed, and added, "And the gentleman in the kitchen door is Edward Bell, Confederate army veteran and now the family cook and driver."

Faith looked past Secretary Benjamin at Levi. "Levi do come in and put the bags down. It's good to see you. I'm so very glad you came with John."

Levi could only nod, not sure at all that he was glad to be back in Lexington.

* * *

The breakfast of fried eggs and biscuits served an hour later was devoid of any bacon or ham. When Mrs. McBee started to apologize for the absence of breakfast meat, Benjamin raised a hand, saying, "Please, Mrs. McBee, my mother raised me without pork, as is proper in a Jewish household."

"Jewish?" countered Elizabeth.

"Yes, there weren't many of us in Charleston, but enough that one or two groceries stocked kosher foods. But the dining hall at Yale University wasn't so accommodating. I fear I capitulated to the aroma of marbled bacon smoked over apple-wood more than once."

Faith smiled politely as she looked at Benjamin. "My maiden name is Cohen. I well remember the trouble my mother experienced keeping my sisters and me away from pork. I too must admit that she finally lost that war."

Elizabeth fidgeted and blurted out, "Let's not speak further of hogs." *Or of two Jews at my table. How the world is changing. Too fast,* she thought. *Too fast.*

"Tell us, Secretary Benjamin, are we winning *this* war?" Elizabeth asked. "The news from Pennsylvania and Louisiana is not encouraging. The army's failure at that

187

Gettysburg town and the loss of Vicksburg are not small matters, as I understand the news."

"An excellent question and an astute observation, Mrs. McBee. But not a question for me to answer. I'm not a general or military strategist. My department is responsible for foreign diplomacy, primarily seeking formal recognition of our young Confederacy from the governments in Europe."

"And do you tell those governments that we are winning our struggle for independence?" Elizabeth McBee asked.

"Absolutely. Why wouldn't I?"

"Perhaps because there's no pork for sale at the butcher shop in Lexington. Just as there is no cotton cloth for diapers or crib sheets at the mercantile store," Faith suggested.

"Yes, well. Hardships do accompany conflict. We are maintaining armies of hundreds of thousands of men in the field on all the borders of our infant nation. We must divert essentials for their sustenance, sadly often at the inconvenience of civilian families. As to cotton diapers, surely you would not suggest we deprive our wounded soldiers of bandages."

Remembering her weeks of grueling work in the Texas Soldiers Hospital in Richmond where she'd torn her own petticoats into bandages, contrasted to the daily loving chore of cleaning John Junior's dirty bottom, Faith muttered, "Of course not. But you are surely aware that each month we endure new shortages of goods. The lack of essentials has become more than an inconvenience."

"Perhaps *sacrifice* is a better term," Benjamin conceded. "Yet you understand the higher priority must be our military efforts to assure the Confederacy's national sovereignty."

"You mean win the damned war," Elizabeth McBee said.

"Exactly."

* * *

While the three McBees and Secretary Benjamin ate their porkless breakfast and discussed current events, Edward Bell, Levi, and Elliot O'Kelly ate a similar breakfast at the kitchen table. The conversation, however, was not similar.

"That's a big pistol for such a little feller as you," O'Kelly said through a full mouth, looking at the army Colt laying on the table by Bell's plate.

Looking down at the wooden grip of the pocket pistol shoved into the waist of O'Kelly's trousers, Bell countered, "And yours seems a bit short for such a tall fellow as you."

Levi sopped up his runny egg yolk with bread, keeping his eyes down and his mouth shut.

O'Kelly laughed, and said, "How is it a young man like you ain't in the army?"

"I was in Captain McBee's company until I got sick. I'm on furlough while I heal."

"You look well enough to me," O'Kelly said. "And you sure do cook good enough."

Bell retorted, "How come you aren't in a uniform? You look well enough and big enough to pull a cannon by yourself. Save the army the cost of a team of horses."

O'Kelly snorted, amused at the spunk of the slight man. "I'm on special assignment as the Secretary's bodyguard. Next to President Davis, he may be the most important man in Richmond. It's my job to keep him alive."

"Me too," Bell replied. "Only it's Miss Faith and her young'un, and Miss Elizabeth, too. That is, while I'm recovering. Captain McBee offered me to stay here if I'd do chores and look after his family. Until I'm able to go soldiering again, that is."

"Why do you need that big pistol to look after two women and a baby? Ain't there a sheriff in Lexington?"

Before Bell could answer, Levi spoke up, anxious for the talk to move away from the curious situation of the soldier-turned-cook and any possible mention of the death of the previous cook, his own dead mother. He also wanted to talk about the excitement in Lynchburg. "Private Bell, Mizz Faith's first husband is back: Sam'lson. He tried to shoot the Secretary or maybe the capt'n last night in Lynchburg. Me and Mr. O'Kelly saved 'em both."

"Levi, are you saying that the man I'm supposed to be protecting the ladies from was thirty miles away in Lynchburg last night? And shooting at the captain?"

Levi nodded.

"Why don't you tell me how you two saved the captain and Mr. Benjamin?" Bell directed the bodyguard and servant.

* * *

Benjamin napped in the unused bedroom during the heat of the summer afternoon while Edward Bell drove Elizabeth McBee, John, Faith, and John Junior to visit the cemetery. Elizabeth held her grandson while John and Faith held each other's hand. Levi stayed behind to prepare the evening meal, which would include one fried chicken, the hen cut into eight pieces as Sally had taught Levi a decade ago.

O'Kelly sat in the parlor reading about a frontiersman named Hawkeye and his Indian friend named Chingachgook from a dusty, but well-thumbed leather-bound book he found on a book shelf in the stairwell. After reading the first chapter, the big man put *The Last of the Mohicans* on his chest and nodded off.

At the cemetery, Captain McBee stood next to his child's as yet unmarked grave, the mounded earth still bare of grass. The sight distressed John McBee more than even the most horrific battle deaths now did. He had seen so many eviscerated torsos, sundered limbs, and shattered skulls, that the gore now only left him numb. But staring at the dirt clods under which the decaying remains of his helpless infant daughter lay in a doll-sized casket was too much. The new grave, sterile, simple, with an aura of innocence, yet oh so terrible, brought forth tears the captain could not stop, tears from a pain that left him too distraught to be ashamed.

The captain's sobbing was contagious. Soon, visible grief returned to poor Betsy's mother, grandmother, and even Edward Bell, breaking through the fragile protective shells they had each carefully crafted over the past eight days. That Elizabeth cried as much for Sheriff Cain and Bell cried for her brother Zeb didn't matter.

No one spoke during the buggy ride back to Lexington, each of the four taking solace in silence.

Chapter 30

The McBee House
Lexington, Virginia
July 20, 1863

A dam Samuelson watched the crowded buggy drive away from the McBee home. He sat still under a tree, ten feet inside the wood line. He hid up the ridge from the houses on the street, but where he had a clear view of the end house, the McBee house. He saw a Negro emerge from the back door, go into the chicken coop and come out holding a bird. He watched the servant wring its neck and start the process of bleeding, gutting and plucking the carcass under the shade of a beechnut tree.

That should leave just the big bodyguard and Benjamin in the house, Samuelson told himself. *It's time.* He was tired, having ridden all night maintaining a position a hundred yards behind the canal boat. *If I'm tired, so are they, maybe even sleeping while the McBees are all gone somewhere.*

The fugitive boldly walked onto the front porch of the McBee house, barely noticing the disintegrating roses on the dark wreath that hung on the front door. He quickly leaned over and looked in the open parlor window, seeing the bodyguard in a chair facing him, an open book on his chest, head down, chin nudging the book, appearing sound asleep.

Samuelson pulled off his low buckle shoes and carefully climbed through the window. Inside he pulled the long knife from his sleeve, padded across the rug to O'Kelly and without hesitation plunged the sharp blade into the side of the bodyguard's neck. He quickly pulled the stiletto out and pushed it in again as the big man began to thrash, eyes popped wide open in shock.

Samuelson stepped away as O'Kelly fell with a thud from his chair onto the floor. His leg knocked into the small side table, causing the oil lamp on it to rock back and forth. Samuelson grabbed the globe with one hand, preventing it from falling. O'Kelly was on his side, one arm pinned under him, but with his other hand he desperately tried to cover the puncture wounds which were pumping his blood onto the rug. Samuelson stepped on that hand, pinning it and watching the dying bodyguard grow still.

Secretary of State Benjamin rolled from his side to his back when he heard a thump downstairs, but no voices. The nap left him needing to use the chamber pot, so he wriggled off the bed, walked to the corner, and began urinating into the brass pot. Benjamin stood with one hand gripping the back of the straight chair on which his coat was draped, and the other hand guiding the yellow stream into the jar.

The door suddenly burst open. A shot rang out causing a tuft of goose down to erupt from the bed mattress, right where Benjamin had just been lying. The door blocked the Secretary's view of his assailant, yet he reacted instantly, letting go of his member and reaching towards his coat pocket for the small revolver.

Before Benjamin could grasp the weapon, Samuelson pushed the door further open, seeing Benjamin in the corner. The killer noted his victim's unbuttoned trousers and circumcised penis gone turtle. He laughed, aimed at his target's head, and pulled the trigger again. But Benjamin was dropping to his knee and the shot went high.

Samuelson immediately cocked the pistol again and fired, this time the shot punched into Benjamin's shoulder, two inches from his heart. Frustrated now, he pulled the trigger for the fatal third shot, only to hear the pistol hammer strike a spent firing cap above an empty cylinder.

Samuelson looked at his pistol and shrugged at Benjamin. He then menacingly waggled the blade of his dagger still held in his left hand, and took a step towards the man he had been sent to kill.

Benjamin pulled his pistol free, saying, "My turn, you Philistine turd."

Samuelson had started forward, intending to kick the chair aside. When he saw the metal barrel of the little pistol coming up and heard the hammer being cocked, he leapt sideways through the door.

Reaching the doorway, the Secretary fired one round at the fleeing man on the stairs. He missed. Levi ran into the hallway, but was bowled over by Samuelson as he jumped down the last three steps. Samuelson stumbled over the Negro just as Benjamin fired again without effect. The assassin and Levi recovered their footing as the Secretary of State fired a third ball which grazed Levi's arm before it burrowed into the door frame. Benjamin swore softly, but held his last bullet as security and out of concern that he'd accidentally shoot McBee's servant.

Samuelson jerked open the door and bounded down the porch steps, hurdled the white picket fence, and sprinted in his socks into the woods at the dead end of the street.

* * *

It was after dark when Lexington's new sheriff, the doctor, and the carpenter who made caskets drove away with O'Kelly's corpse. The blood-stained rug had been rolled up for scrubbing, and the women, baby, and Levi had all gone to bed.

Captain McBee and Secretary Benjamin sat in the dark parlor, leaving the lamp unlit at the Captain's suggestion. McBee's pistol lay by a half-empty bottle on the table next to his chair. They each held a glass of the whiskey Benjamin found in O'Kelly's carpetbag. Benjamin's shoulder was tightly wrapped and he'd already refilled his own glass twice with whiskey and water. His shoulder ached more than he had thought possible, but the whiskey dulled the pain and loosened his normally restrained tongue.

"Captain, have you considered my offer to transfer to my department?"

"Yes Sir, I'm flattered, but I'm compelled by honor to refuse your kind offer," McBee said.

"Having tonight come face to face with your wife's first husband, your nemesis, I believe I can offer you an inducement for you to reconsider," the Secretary answered.

"I'll earn a promotion to major on my own merits soon enough," McBee said.

194

"I don't doubt that, Captain. The war is nowhere near over. But consider this, if you will: Forgive me for a lack of humility, but I'm an attorney of some distinction. The only reason I'm not sitting on the bench of the Supreme Court in Washington is that the pay is abysmal, and I do like my comforts. I understand how the justice system works, and I am adept at carefully constructing rational arguments that permit judges to momentarily overlook the letter of the law in favor of common sense."

"You're saying you are skilled at getting judges to ignore the law."

"Precisely. At no further cost to you, after the war, I will put that knowledge to work on your behalf. After the war, I will create the documents and make the arguments that will free Mrs. Samuelson from her legal marriage to Lieutenant Samuelson. Should he still be living after the war. I assure you that tomorrow I will be putting in motion a manhunt of significant resources."

"That is a generous offer, Mr. Secretary, but again, no. After the war I'm taking my family to Texas, Samuelson be damned. If I see him again, I'll shoot him on sight and leave his wretched carcass for the wild hogs. And your manhunt won't find him. He'll be in the Yankee state of Western Virginia, again, by this time tomorrow."

"Yes, well, perhaps. Samuelson has proved to be a slippery sort. Nonetheless, I would not discount the possibility he may return here. Even after the war ends."

"Which is why I'm taking my family to Texas. What about you, Mr. Secretary? You need a new bodyguard. One who reads less. I'll accompany you back to Richmond, but then I'm bound for my regiment."

Benjamin sipped his whiskey and nodded, the captain's observation causing him to mourn once more ever so briefly for O'Kelly, who he had liked, but who had indeed liked his books too much.

"That I do, but the toughest brute in Richmond still won't recognize Samuelson. Would you consider selling Levi to me? The young Negro knows the bastard's face and the foul man could yet make another attempt on my life. I would put Levi to work as my carriage driver, another set of watchful eyes while I'm exposed on the streets of Richmond." He thought to himself, *But not more exposed than I was upstairs.*

"I'd pay you more than market value for him," Benjamin assured his host.

"Levi is my mother's property, not mine. She loaned him to me when my man-servant from Texas got sick and died right after my company first reached Virginia." McBee wet his tongue with the dark alcohol and finished his thought. "I need Levi with me until the war ends. Sorry."

"Hmmph. If I may be so bold, the boy is light-skinned enough to be mulatto, and seems to favor you. Might you be his sire? You wouldn't be the only man in our officer corps to have a son taking care of him. The white offspring get to be aides-de-camp and carry messages, while the less fortunate black bastards of our aristocracy cook and clean as man-servants."

McBee could only see the Secretary's silhouette, but he clearly heard the sarcasm in his voice. The son of the Virginia planter took a bigger sip of the whiskey and decided not to take offense at Benjamin's insolence in asking if he was Levi's father. Instead, on a whim, he answered truthfully. McBee repeated the story he had told Faith that first night over a year ago when she had tended his bloody feet, the story he had never spoken of to anyone else in two decades.

"My father, the Colonel, had a taste for young Negro girls. He didn't even try to hide it. My mother never forgave him."

"Your father, the Colonel, was not alone in enjoying that taste, Captain. It's my observation that such is an unspoken perquisite of slave ownership. Almost expected. And cruel beyond measure to wives who must pretend not to notice the familiar features of their servants' children. And did you inherit the Colonel's eye for dark girls?"

"He thought I should have." After a slight hesitation McBee went on. "He gave me a night with one particular girl as a birthday gift. To celebrate my manhood. I was young and scared witless of my father."

Benjamin nodded. "So the colonel was a strict man. Most colonels are."

McBee nodded in agreement, "Still, I knew it was wrong. I knew I shouldn't have been there. So I told the girl we could just sit in the dark a while and then I'd leave her untouched. No one would know."

"That girl was Levi's mother?"

"Yes, and you know what she told me? She said come ahead, there'd be lots more white men after me, so why don't I just enjoy my pap's gift."

"So you pushed your qualms aside and tasted the fruit."

"I did, and I've regretted it since that night."

"And she was correct in her feral wisdom. You were not the only white man to enjoy her?"

"No, I wasn't. Father and his overseer kept her busy until her belly grew too big. With Levi."

"So the boy is a mulatto, and he is either your brother or your son, or the overseer's bastard."

McBee replied thoughtfully as he drank again, "Levi's too smart, too loyal, too earnest, to come from Overseer Jones. He was a mangy mongrel dog of a man."

Setting down his empty glass, the captain said, "But that makes no difference. Levi is a Negro, nothing but a Negro. Even should McBee blood run through his veins, he can only be a slave."

"One drop. Just one drop of black African blood outweighs all of our ivory white European pedigrees," Benjamin mused.

"And that makes Levi a slave, only a slave, at least until General Lee runs out of soldiers and the Lincolnites turn 'em all loose. Then what? I doubt that even loyal darkies like Levi will stay close to their owners. I wouldn't. Would you, Mr. Secretary?"

"No, indeed. But my people have a long history of fleeing bondage. Surely you've read Exodus. Freedom from slavery was a long and difficult journey for my Jewish ancestors. I expect it will be no less so for Levi and the Negro people."

McBee rolled that thought around in his head along with the whiskey and replied, "God sent seven plagues and parted the waters to get the Israelites out of Egypt. President Lincoln is not God, but he has sent six or seven armies to plague the south. And while my men were dying in Pennsylvania just a few weeks ago, one of Lincoln's armies parted the Mighty Mississippi River at Vicksburg and split the Confederacy in two. I think it is not just the Negro people who are facing hard times ahead."

"Hmm, indeed. Again, a man of imagery," Benjamin replied as he sipped from his glass. "Tell me, Captain, are you personally acquainted with your Division commander, General Hood?"

"Yes, I've had the honor to have a conversation with him. We told each other about fighting Comanches in Texas."

"Worthy opponents, the wild Comanches?" Benjamin asked.

"Oh, yes, but first you have to chase them half way across the plains."

"They are a colorful lot from the magazine illustrations I've seen."

"Butchers and barbarians, if that's what you call colorful," McBee said, remembering the fight near Plum Creek nearly twenty-five years ago.

"Back to General Hood, if you don't mind. Does he command the respect of his troops? Do you company captains consider him...exceptional?"

"He's our general. We follow his orders. What else is there? Captains don't question generals."

"You're right, of course," Benjamin replied, letting his voice reflect his acceptance of McBee's reminder of military protocol. "Captains don't question generals. But neither do infantry captains from the frontier drink whiskey in the dead of night with members of President Davis' cabinet."

"I suppose not."

"You know you Texans have a reputation for fierceness in battle. Does that stem from General Hood's leadership, or would you be *Lee's grenadiers* under any division commander?"

"Hood was wounded at Gettysburg, Mr. Secretary. Knocked off his horse by shrapnel exploding overhead, I'm told. I don't look to see him leading our division in the next campaign. So, I reckon we'll learn soon enough if we're Hood's fierce war hounds or someone else's yard dogs."

"General Hood is recovering from his wound. Captain. He will be appointed to another command. I'm asking you for a rare confidential appraisal of the general. Should he be promoted? Could he effectively lead a corps, or perhaps even take on some other important role?"

"Hood's a gambler, Mr. Secretary," McBee said, the liquor having overcome his prudence. "He gambled on me once, with fair reason. I think regardless of the level of his command, he would not be reluctant to take extreme risks. But what isn't, these days? You couldn't even take a nap upstairs without risk."

"*Touché*," the statesman said. "And now I'm going to hazard another few hours of sleep. Without my bodyguard."

Benjamin slowly climbed the stairs, leaning heavily on the bannister for support.

McBee took a deep breath and walked towards the kitchen where he intended to splash cool water on his face. It was still several hours until dawn, and he knew his duty was to stay awake and armed in the parlor. He jumped back in surprise when Edward Bell emerged from a dark corner of the dining room.

"Go upstairs to your wife, Captain. She's waiting on you. Besides, as interesting as it may have been to drink whiskey and tell your deep secrets to the Secretary, it don't make for an alert sentry. I've got the duty detail covered."

"Dammit, Bell, were you listening to our conversation?"

"Every word, Captain."

"Forget it all, Private. Scrub it from your mind."

"Sure, Captain, every word scrubbed away. Now go upstairs to Faith."

He did, and for the next hour he was very glad of it.

* * *

The next morning Captain McBee walked to the bank to withdraw a portion of the funds he had deposited when he first came to Lexington two years ago. A half hour later he walked home, dismayed that the account balance paid out in Confederate currency had barely one quarter of the purchasing power it had a year ago. What he thought would be a comfortable sum for Faith to contribute to the household expenses would last just weeks, not the months he'd presumed.

As soon as he walked into the house, John called Faith and his mother into the parlor. In a few sentences he told them the state of his finances that rampant inflation was causing the value of Confederate money to fall fast. Neither woman was surprised, as they both well knew of the never-ending rising costs of buying staples at the markets.

McBee gave Faith three-fourths of the currency he'd withdrawn, with instructions to barter for whatever they could, and to use the funds to stockpile as much food as they could purchase before further inflation and the normal scarcity of goods through the winter made it even harder to buy necessities.

Secretary of State Benjamin stood quietly out of sight in the hallway listening to Captain McBee, nodding approvingly at the man's foresight and common sense. But mostly Benjamin was remembering the near riot he'd witnessed from his office window in Richmond just a few days before. Led by a woman butcher wielding a heavy chopping cleaver, the mob of hungry women had threatened the police who'd tried to break up the protest.

Only the unexpected appearance of President Davis himself had stopped the crowd. The gaunt, somber president, mounted on his horse, appealed to the patriotism of the women and reached into his pockets offering whatever money he had for them to buy flour and meat. Benjamin had watched, enthralled by the aura of strength and reason projected by the President, but chilled by the prospect of food riots in the capital.

His bad news delivered, McBee left the house to telegraph his business partner in Texas with instructions to sell one of their small parcels of river bottom land. McBee had used that strip of fertile land for cotton production before the war and he'd hoped to plant it in cotton again when he returned home. The captain knew that no telegraph line reached into Texas, and with the recent loss of Vicksburg, getting personal mail across the Mississippi River had become very unlikely. Regardless, he included instructions for the message to be forwarded to a ship's captain in Mobile on whose vessel he'd shipped cotton to England before the war. He hoped the ship was still successfully running the blockade into Galveston. McBee figured the odds were stacked against eventual delivery of the message, but it was all he could think to do to supplement his insubstantial pay as a Confederate infantry captain.

After McBee left the house, Secretary Benjamin sought out the woman he still thought of as Mrs. Faith Samuelson. For once she was alone, making a pie in the kitchen, while the elder Mrs. McBee played with John Junior upstairs.

"Mrs. Samuelson," Benjamin began.

"Mrs. McBee," she corrected him.

"Of course. Please accept my apology, again. May I have a word?"

"If I may finish putting together these fried pies for John and Levi to take."

"Certainly," the Secretary replied as he sat down at the table.

"Well?"

"Do you know that Mrs. McBee recorded your maiden name as Collins in the family Bible?"

"I know. How do you know?"

"The Bible was in the room where I slept, and I looked, of course. Does her disapproval of Jews concern you?"

"Not particularly. Elizabeth is old and set in her ways. But she has a big heart and has accepted me as her son's wife."

"Are you a patriot, Mrs. McBee?" Benjamin asked without preamble.

With her hands in the bowl of dough, Faith answered truthfully. "I'm a woman of Virginia and I pray for my soldier-husband every day. But I abhor slavery. I cannot believe it is God's will for one race of people to enslave another race. Israelites or Africans."

"Hmm. Do you wish for the Confederacy to remain an independent nation?"

"Mr. Secretary, I wish for the war to end and for my husband to return home so we can go to Texas. I frankly don't care whether laws are written in Richmond or Washington City."

"I see. Would you be willing to leave Lexington and take a trip on my behalf to expedite the conclusion of the war?"

"A woman diplomat? Hah! I hardly think so."

"Not a woman diplomat. No. Rather, a woman courier to deliver a private message to someone important in Kentucky, a state that has failed to commit to the southern cause."

"A spy? You want me to serve as a spy for you?"

"No, not a spy. I'm the Secretary of State, my department employs diplomats, as you said. I need a confidential messenger."

"In Kentucky?"

"Yes, as far as I know, that's where the man is."

"Why me? Don't you employ a whole building full of messengers?"

"Yes, I do. But your ex-husband knew when I'd be at the Norvell House in Lynchburg. Someone in my office relayed that information to whoever sent him to kill me. There's someone close to me whom I can't trust. I don't yet know who that man is, but I will in time. Meanwhile, I will soon need to communicate with this gentleman in Kentucky, and I can't possibly entrust the message to anyone in my department who may be a Yankee spy."

"But you can trust me even after Adam - Lieutenant Samuelson - twice tried to kill you?"

"Who better? First of all, I trust you because you hate the lieutenant, with good cause."

"And...?"

"And second, if you are questioned, you can plea that you are in Kentucky to search for your husband, who deserted the Confederate army to change sides, to join the Union army, and left you with a baby. It's plausible and could keep you out of jail."

"Why would I be in danger of going to jail even if I were questioned? And John says Adam is running back to Western Virginia, not Kentucky."

"But no one in Kentucky will know that. And more importantly, your story of chasing Lieutenant Samuelson might prevent the authorities from searching you and your valise."

"Other than the indignity, why should a search of my baggage concern me?

"Because they might not stop with your baggage, and you would have a coded message either hidden in your hair or sewn into a seam of your undergarments."

"A spy. I thought so. No."

"Again, you would not be a spy. A spy observes and commits crimes in a foreign nation. You would be only a messenger delivering words of encouragement to an important man whose true identity must not become known."

"He's a spy."

"He's a Southern patriot in a dangerous situation," Benjamin assured her.

"Why would I agree to do this?" Faith asked as she dumped a handful of sliced apples into a bowl and added a big spoonful of molasses.

"To bring about a quicker end to the war than if the message is not delivered. A quicker end so that the good women of the south can quit spoiling apple pies by substituting molasses for real sugar."

Faith stirred the mix with a wooden spoon while she thought about the Secretary's offer.

"No, Mr. Benjamin, I'm flattered by your offer and your confidence in my abilities, but my duty is here with Elizabeth and John Junior. I couldn't possibly leave my son for such a long time.

"The pay would be substantial. I couldn't help but overhear Captain McBee in the parlor."

"Sir, you seem to have a knack for learning things about our family."

"Mrs. McBee, my eyes and ears are my most valuable assets. I can't turn them off just because I'm a guest here."

"You're a wily man, Mr. Secretary, I'll say that for you." She stirred the apple filling longer than it needed as she thought more about his offer.

"Let me put forth more incentive, Madam. I said the pay would be substantial. Specifically, I will insure it is sufficient to purchase an engraved headstone for your infant daughter's grave, and see you and Mrs. McBee through the war, and perhaps still have seed money for your travel to Texas once war has ended."

"That would be an impressive sum, Mr. Secretary," Faith replied. "I would need to talk to John and Elizabeth. John is a proud man, I'm not sure he would agree. And I'm not sure I could leave John Junior for weeks, even if it meant a headstone for Betsy."

"Mrs. McBee, forgive me, but I'm compelled to point out that Captain McBee is performing the most dangerous job in the army. He's been wounded already, and I assure you that there are more battles ahead for General Lee's army. Your husband will go in harm's way again. A prudent, intelligent woman would do well to see to her own financial needs when the opportunity presents itself. I suppose you and Mrs. McBee could sew uniforms by the piece and sell them to the Quartermaster Department. I hear that many soldiers' wives are doing that to keep bread on the table. But the war will end someday, and then what, should your husband, God forbid, be a fatality or come home with no legs."

Faith shivered at the memory of the soldiers she'd nursed in Richmond the year before, the amputees whose lives were shattered by their injuries. She knew the importance of having money. But she said nothing as she considered the Secretary's request, until she suddenly made her decision.

"Gold coins. We'll need gold in Texas after the war. We need hard coins now. I would need to be paid in gold before I leave Lexington, not Confederate bank notes."

She glanced up and looked the man in the eye before she added, "And you are not to speak of our arrangement to John. After it's done, I'll ask for his understanding when I put a stack of gold coins in his palm."

Benjamin nodded in agreement, as he leaned back in his chair and watched her spoon dark apple filling onto the four circles of pale white dough crust that she had flattened on the table. She carefully folded a layer of dough over the apple filling and sealed the edges of the dough with her fingers.

"Is this how your mysterious coded message will be sealed into the seam of my petticoat?"

"I've never actually seen a message sewn into a petticoat, nor a fried pie constructed. My job is write the messages and eat the pies," Benjamin answered.

Faith smiled at the Secretary's candor, and brushing a loose strand of hair back from her damp forehead, she repeated, "Gold coin. Paid when I accept the message. And I'll sew it into my petticoat myself."

"Agreed regarding the gold coin, but the message is not for your eyes. It will already be sewn into a new petticoat that will be delivered to you. The package will arrive as an unexpected gift from Captain McBee, bought in one of the last shops in Richmond to stock imported French fashions, which few people can now afford."

"But you can?"

"As a matter of fact, yes. One more thing. The route from here to Kentucky is lengthy and arduous. There are mountains to cross. No railway runs in a direct route. No stage line will offer a direct route. Kentucky is controlled by the Union army and you will pass through numerous checkpoints. Your accent will make you suspect. You'll find yourself time and again repeating your purpose for travel. In short, it will be long, difficult, and potentially dangerous."

"May I carry a pistol?" Faith asked.

"I won't be here to stop you, but I would strongly advise against doing so. Discovery would only lead to further suspicion and a probable search of your person, the very thing to be avoided above all other considerations. Your protection will be the sympathy created by your beauty, your youth, your charm, and your burning determination to find your wayward husband who abandoned you with a child and no money. Besides, who would you shoot? You couldn't win a shoot-out with a Yankee patrol."

"How am I paying for the cost of travel, if my wayward husband left me penniless? Which he did, by the way."

Benjamin shrugged. "You sold your jewelry and sold the carriage since he rode off on the family horse."

"Where is my baby?"

"At your mother's, of course."

After some negotiating they agreed on the amount of gold for her service, in addition to the cost of travel. Faith demanded more than Benjamin was accustomed to paying for similar services, but she correctly surmised he both liked her and had no other trustworthy candidate for this particular mission. He then told her the details of what to expect sometime in the coming weeks.

Chapter 31

Mid-September, 1863
From Port Royal, Virginia to Chickamauga, Georgia

Days passed, men talked, and newspapers published stories about the great gathering of steam engines, boxcars, and open flatcars. The rolling stock came from three states to move the 12,000 men and hundreds of horses of Longstreet's Corps. News of the mass troop movement by train quickly spread across Virginia, North Carolina, and Georgia. Any hope of secretly shifting a major portion of General Lee's army from Virginia to Georgia evaporated in the hot southern weather. Speed replaced silence as the matter of prime importance.

Corporal Jason Smith poked the steel point of his belt knife into a crack in the brittle gray board. He wiggled and tapped the hilt with his palm, working the blade deeper into the wood before he sharply twisted his wrist. An inch-wide sliver of pine popped loose from the wall of the boxcar, giving Smith a narrow view of the Virginia countryside.

The welcomed fresh air coming through the tiny gap into the hot interior of the freight car encouraged the young corporal. He used his knife to widen the gap until he could slip the fingers of both hands into it and jerked hard, snapping off a two-foot length of the warped board. Other men in Company C, using bayonets and knives, pried off boards all around the inside of the car. Within an hour only the metal skeleton of the walls remained.

Sitting on top of the same freight car, the troops of Company D hooted and yelled as the train rolled through the small towns of southern Virginia. At every hamlet young ladies waved handkerchiefs and flags at the young men. When trains stopped to take on loads of wood to be burned in the steam engines, women came forward with jugs of cool water, baskets of cornbread, and gingerbread cookies. Sometimes, even small bundles of homemade socks and shirts were tossed to the soldiers.

In the skeletonized car carrying one regimental band, the musicians brought out their brass horns to serenade the ladies. Not to be outdone, the man-servant of a major in a different regiment unwrapped his master's precious fiddle at every stop and played lively dance tunes while he stood on the roof of the car.

* * *

"Where are we?" Smith asked as he and others tumbled out the door of the freight car.

"Don't matter," his messmate Cal Gilbert answered. "Just look at all that food." He hit the ground and broke into a trot towards the long plank tables that were covered with plates of cold sweet potatoes, stacks of cookies, and piles of chicken and fresh biscuits. Even more appetizing to Private Gilbert were the many young ladies on the far side of the tables who held out glasses of water and more plates of food.

Levi climbed off the roof of the officers' car. He was among the dozen man-servants in the regiment who'd left the wagon train to accompany their owners on the railroad journey. The officers rode in the only car of the train that had actually been built to carry human passengers. Since it had glass windows and carried "gentlemen," it was also the only car on which the wooden siding was not ripped off.

Looking from the train roof, the Negroes saw a single separate table set up apart from the long line of heavily laden banquet tables. Several Negro women with their hair covered by colorful turbans stood behind the table, ready to give each of the man-servants a foot-long shingle of wood piled with food.

Soon the fifty Negroes from the four trains carrying the brigade had received their meals and sat under trees eating. No one but the turbaned women remained near the table, which still held platters of untouched food.

Meanwhile, young soldiers stood three deep around the other tables, many hungry men jostling others to squeeze to the front of the crowd to grab what they could. None of the soldiers paid any attention to the Negros' table which held the same welcomed dishes and plates of fresh food, with no waiting and no competition for the last hard-boiled egg or fried drumstick.

The leaders in the community prevailed upon someone from the train loads of soldiers to make a speech. A brash lieutenant climbed onto the platform by the train station and began to speak. He expressed his gratitude to the beautiful and gracious ladies of Sumpterville for the wonderful banquet and aptly closed with a fair description of himself and the men in the Texas Brigade.

"Perhaps, ladies, you have had the honor of listening to better-looking men, smarter men, braver men than me, but I'll venture to say that you have never beheld or listened to a *dirtier* man than George Cheek of Texas. Yours most obediently."

Cheek went on to thank the ladies of North Carolina for the banquet, emphasizing that the farmland of northern Virginia had long been stripped of crops and cattle as the two armies struggled against each other for the past two years. He was extravagant in his appreciation for the delicacies which had not been available to them for a long time. He closed with an assurance that Longstreet's Corps would protect the farms of North Carolina so they might stop this way again and enjoy another feast in the months ahead. With that he stepped down to shake hands with several leading citizens of town.

When the steam engine blasted its whistle signaling their fifteen minutes of respite had ended, Cheek grabbed a turkey leg and a square of cornbread before joining the crowd of soldiers who were reluctantly climbing back on top of and into the train cars.

* * *

Private Polaski Phillips wanted a drink. The feast by the train station two days before in another town had filled his belly, but had been regretfully shy of liquor. Now the brigade trains were parked on sidings in Wilmington, North Carolina. They had been waiting since mid-day for a clear track to make the next leg of the roundabout trip, and the officers had just spread the word to their sergeants that the brigade would spend the night where they were. It was nearly dusk, and bored soldiers had been exploring the town all afternoon.

Since his thwarted attempt at desertion at Gettysburg, Phillips had been under the close watch of Sergeant Moss, who Phillips had seen lifting a bottle or two during his months as a soldier. Neither man had left the vicinity of the train station, but Phillips had talked to other men who had returned from visiting saloons and taverns.

"Sergeant, how about you and me take a stroll down to Paddy's Hollow, down by the ship docks. I hear there're places that're serving up drinks to soldiers for near nothing."

"It'd have to be on the nothing side of near, since I ain't got a single coin," Moss replied. But he was yearning for a drink himself, and set off with Phillips.

The pair visited two seedy saloons where armed barkeepers only served whiskey to soldiers that could pay with Confederate script or hard coins. Rebuffed but not giving up, Moss and Phillips joined a group of penniless soldiers who entered a third bar, this one farther from the wharfs.

When the barkeep asked for money, a big corporal held his belt knife to the man's throat and suggested a tab for all of them would be nice, that they'd pay later. With the point of the blade pricking his neck, the barkeep thought that was a reasonable idea and pulled the first bottles from under the bar.

The number of soldiers in the saloon grew as word spread of the Texans' line of credit. By midnight no bottles remained under the bar or on the shelves behind it, and the crowd of rowdy soldiers packed the building. The owner slipped out the back to fetch the police.

"Private, is them Yankees up the street yonder?" Moss asked Phillips as they left the dingy saloon and saw a group of five men in dark uniforms rounding the corner.

"Constables I'd say, since I see our barkeep right in the middle of 'em," Phillips answered in a whiskey slurred voice. "And they got nightsticks."

"Well, that ain't right, ain't right at all. Rally on me, Boys!" Moss called to the score of inebriated soldiers who were nearby.

Phillips pulled his knife and held it low by his side as men from Texas and Arkansas formed a rough line stretching across the street. With a Rebel Yell they attacked.

The melee lasted only a minute. The five policemen were all elderly, too old to be conscripted into the army, and no match for the Texans. The outnumbered lawmen were punched, clubbed and beaten down by the combat veterans commanded by John Barleycorn.

One constable suffered a broken rib, another was slashed in the side by Private Phillips. Seeing the blood, Phillips quickly sheathed his knife and pulled Moss away from the fight, wanting to distance himself and his keeper from any potential retribution.

The two men found their way back to the train depot where Lieutenant Hubbard spotted them. He grabbed each one under the arm, led them to the right train car and shoved them inside where the two collapsed and began snoring. The train pulled out early the next morning, before an official protest by the city police could be written.

The journey from Richmond to north Georgia that was supposed to take two days instead lasted nine, as the route had to be greatly lengthened to detour around a stretch of the railroad tracks in Tennessee held by Union troops. The Texas Brigade changed trains at eight different towns when the trains of one railroad company reached the end of their line of tracks and another company's train depot lay across town.

The thousands of men and animals in Longstreet's Corps finally disembarked a last time at a place called Chickamauga Station.

Chapter 32

Near Chickamauga Creek, Georgia
September 19, 1863

Captain McBee led his company through the dense woods. Brambles and tangled muscatine vines forced the men to abandon their straight lines and resort to following each other where gaps could be found, pushing forward as best they could. Finally clusters of men began reaching the edge of a field where they halted to regroup.

While the sergeants prodded their troops into proper alignment, the captain studied the field ahead of them. The Union artillery was active, the blasts of the cannons clearly heard, twisting trails of smoke visible in the air.

McBee's attention was suddenly drawn to a moving shape a hundred yards away in the field, coming towards them. For an instant he thought he'd detected a line of Union skirmishers, but the figure quickly proved otherwise. *Damn, it's a woman, and she's carrying a baby, no, two babies, one in each arm. What's that behind her? A dog? No, it's another child, a little boy, and there's another. Damn!*

The woman stumbled and fell, keeping one infant in the crook of her arm, but dropping the other as she reached out reflexively to break her fall. McBee watched as she got to her knees and somehow scooped up the second baby, which was without clothing. She staggered up, looked around for her other two boys and took another step.

McBee couldn't watch any longer. He trotted into the field towards the woman, his sword scabbard bouncing against his leg. Before the captain reached her, Levi passed him, running hard. When McBee stopped in front of the ragged young woman, Levi had already taken one infant and the sack of belongings she'd tied around her neck and flung over her back.

McBee nodded approvingly at Levi before he spoke. "Ma'am, please permit me and Levi here to escort you off this field. It's likely to get nasty in short order. You and your children will be safer under the trees."

The woman looked up at McBee with wide wild eyes, as the two barefoot boys wrapped arms around her legs, tucking their heads in her skirt. McBee saw she was beyond the ability to respond, so he took each boy by the hand and gently pulled them loose from their mother.

"Come on, boys, you're safe now. We're going under the trees," McBee said as he took a step in that direction, dragging the boys with him. At that moment a fountain of earth and grass erupted nearby in the field and showered the little group with dirt clods.

The children wailed at the deafening sound of the explosion. McBee stopped to lift both crying boys into his arms, looking back to see that the woman was following. Levi, holding the naked baby tight against his chest, walked behind the woman.

Two of McBee's soldiers stepped aside to let him and the refugee family through their formation. Several men, fathers themselves and not knowing if they would start their own long sleep that afternoon, swallowed hard as their thoughts leaped to families left behind in Texas.

Ten yards into the woods McBee knelt down and set the boys on their feet. "Go with your mama now, boys. Mr. Levi is going to take you all to where it's safe." McBee looked up at Levi.

"You ain't never called me *mister* before," Levi said. "And that's gonna be some miles back, Capt'n."

"I know. But make sure they're out of cannon range before you leave them. Try to find another house. Somebody who can take them in," McBee directed.

"Yessir, I'll do that. Capt'n, you take care of yourself while I'm gone. Don't you leave me alone down here in Georgia."

McBee stood up and squeezed Levi's shoulder. "Bring some full canteens back with you if you can find some. You know we're gonna run dry before the day's gone."

Turning to the woman, the captain said, "Ma'am, Levi is going to take you away from the fighting. You'll be all right. Do you understand? You and your children go with Levi. Do you have a name, Ma'am?"

The refugee mother of four shook her head without speaking, but she followed Levi as he started off. Both adults carried a baby in the crook of one arm and held a walking boy's hand with their other. Before she disappeared in the trees the woman turned and softly said, "Thank you."

* * *

The Texas Brigade marched forward, advancing towards the sounds of musketry with orders to add their firepower to the troops of General Bushrod Johnson's soldiers. Fifty yards into the field the Texans broke ranks to step around the still forms of a Confederate officer and his horse. From his position behind the company, Sergeant Moss stopped to kneel by the officer's body.

"Lieutenant! This here is a general, and he ain't dead yet!" Moss shouted.

"Leave him," Anderson answered. "Stick his sword in the ground and put his hat on it. The litter bearers will see it and carry him back to the hospital."

From a distant hill Union artillery harassed the attackers. Corporal Smith's eyes were drawn to an eruption of dirt and grass from which he clearly saw a black cannon ball emerge to roll at speed towards them. Smith was the last man in the front rank of Company C, with an open gap of a few feet to his left. He saw the iron ball rise a foot in the air, changing course when it ricocheted off a rock, to come directly at him.

The corporal swiveled sideways to fall backwards to his right, pushing aside the man next to him and grabbing the soldier who'd been right behind him, pulling him aside too.

The cannon ball flew by at knee height, so close Smith could feel the heat radiating from it.

The Texans began encountering wounded and worn-out Confederate soldiers moving away from the battle. The sight of men without visible wounds seeking safety in the rear caused some of Hood's men to hoot derisively at them.

One wounded soldier saw the Texas flag and yelled back. "You Texans'll git your fill. These Yanks are westerners, and they ain't runnin' at the snap of a cap."

For several minutes Robertson's Brigade advanced across another field and through a lightly wooded patch of scrub. From in front of the Fifth Texas, Major Rogers shouted, "Look yonder!"

To the front left of the brigade a long line of Federal soldiers were rising from the ground on the lip of a ravine. Within seconds the blue line evaporated behind a wall of white smoke as the Union regiment fired a single volley.

From his horse General Robertson called for his four regiments to respond by marching to the left oblique, angling their advance to approach the new threat directly. When the Confederate line of battle reached the edge of the wooded ravine, it was empty, the defenders gone. Far ahead, beyond the ravine, a ragged line of dark shapes were visible on a hillside, moving towards the crest. The brigade followed them.

The Federal cannons switched from lobbing solid shot and exploding shrapnel at the attacking Confederates to firing canister, tin cans packed with dozens of small iron balls. All across the brigade's front an increasing number of soldiers fell from being hit by the deadly spray of the canister rounds. When a man fell, the soldiers to his sides shifted slightly to close the new gap, causing an ongoing shrinking of the company formations.

Major Rogers led the Fifth Texas Regiment up the slope, the captains and lieutenants working to keep the 250 riflemen in a two-rank line of battle. A hundred yards from the breastworks made of fence rails that stretched across the hill crest, the Federal troops stood and delivered a volley at the attacking Confederates.

Lieutenant Anderson watched two of the company's twenty-one riflemen fall and a third man drop his musket as he spun around, grabbing his bleeding leg before he slumped to sit on the ground.

The single volley was enough for General Robertson to release his tight rein on the four regiments of Texans and Arkansans. Their battle lines disintegrated as thirteen hundred men broke ranks and charged up the hill, bayonets fixed and shining in the late afternoon sunlight.

The keening Rebel yell hit the blue line before the wave of men in dirty gray reached the hastily-made wall of fence rails. The high-pitched undulating sound, coupled with the snarling faces of the attackers, terrorized half the Federal soldiers, causing them to turn and flee down the far side of the hill. But the other half of the men from Iowa and Indiana held their positions and met their enemies with bayonets and rifle butts.

Lieutenant Hubbard and Corporal Smith were the first two Leon Hunters to hurdle the breastworks, throwing themselves into the confusion on the other side.

Right behind them, Wiley Green and Alamo Brashear jumped together to the top rail of the low wall. Green fired his musket from the hip at the back of a big Union corporal who held his own musket by the barrel and was about to crash the butt down on Jason Smith's head. The Yankee crumpled as dust and blood burst up from his lower back.

Brashear leapt down from the wall lunging with his bayonet at a lieutenant who was calmly cocking his revolver, his arm held straight out, aiming at Lieutenant Hubbard. Hubbard was just three feet away, smashing his sword's brass hilt guard into the face of a Union private. Brashear's bayonet point caught the young Federal officer in the ribs, jostling his arm so that his pistol shot went above Hubbard, but hit the leg of another soldier coming over the fence rails.

Hubbard heard the enemy's pistol discharge near his ear, so he turned and fired his own revolver into the chest of the fallen lieutenant. A second later a rifle butt smashed into the back of Hubbard's neck, knocking him down on top of the Union officer he'd just killed.

At age forty-two, Captain McBee had been outrun by most of his company, so that when he climbed the fence rails, his men were already thick in the melee on the far side. He quickly dropped into the bedlam, firing his revolver at a blue-coated soldier who was on his knees straddling Sergeant Hodges, pummeling the Texan's face with both fists.

215

Hodges pushed the dying man off his chest, grabbed his musket and looked around. The Union defenders were abandoning the fight and running, Confederate company officers shouted for sergeants to gather their men. Sergeants and corporals pushed and pulled privates into rough lines as the riflemen struggled to reload their muskets.

Major Rogers saw the Union artillery battery that had been bedeviling them. He called for his regiment to face to their right, intending to charge the battery, seeing that the cannons were not supported by any infantry. When most of the bluecoats at the breastworks were retiring, the Union artillery captain ordered his six pieces to swivel to face the log wall that was swarming with Confederates. At his command the six cannons fired together, each one spitting out over forty iron balls from two hundred yards distant. The salvo ripped into timber and flesh alike, snapping bones, shredding bowels. Texans and Arkansans died.

Chapter 33

Chickamauga, Georgia
September 19, 1863

The woman followed Levi for over an hour as he kept to trails through the woods. When they came to a road, Levi called a rest until several army wagons came by. After asking a teamster if he had passed any homesteads nearby, Levi led the family in the direction the wagons had come from. The woman didn't speak except once when the child in her arms began to loudly cry.

"Wait. I have to feed the babies."

She settled on a log next to the road and beckoned for Levi to hand her the second infant. For fifteen minutes the babies fed at their mother's breasts. Levi sat on the ground near her with the two older boys, looking away. He found a wrinkled apple in his haversack and cut it into quarters. He gave each boy a slice, kept one, and without turning held one out to the children's mother.

When the woman finished nursing, she handed the naked infant back to Levi while she dug into her sack, pulling out a threadbare square of cotton cloth. She laid the child on the leaves and expertly wrapped the cloth around the child into a diaper, but not before the little girl had peed in the nest of Levi's arm. The mother repeated the diapering with the baby boy, then shook and carefully folded his soiled diaper before thrusting it back into her sack of belongings.

Levi asked her if the babies were twins, and she said no without further comment. After another few miles of walking with frequent stops for the boys and their mother to rest, Levi saw a cabin. The thunder of the cannons and musket fire seemed distant and moving away from the direction he was going, so Levi judged he'd taken the family as far as he needed to.

Levi stopped several yards from the log house and called, "Hallo. Anybody here?"

A barking brown dog ran out from behind the cabin. A hard looking, middle-aged, gray-haired woman holding a big knife cautiously looked around the corner of the building.

"Where's your man?" the older woman asked loudly.

"Gone to the army," the young woman answered.

"Mine too."

Within minutes the two women exchanged names and circumstances and had taken the children into the cabin. The older woman dismissed the Negro guide with a wave of her arm. The young mother stayed silent, but smiled and nodded her head to Levi before she was ushered through the door.

Levi stood in the bare dirt of the yard for a long moment, scratching the dog's ears, considering the closed door of the log house and how low the sun was in the sky. He grunted once at the sorry state of how things were and started walking back towards the dim sounds of the battle.

* * *

"Private, what the hell are you doing? Aim at the damyankees! They ain't flying ducks!" Lieutenant Anderson yelled at Isaiah Johnson his voice cracking in the heat and smoke..

"I'm not going to appear before God with the blood of my fellow man on my soul," Private Johnson shouted back as he held his musket to his shoulder and shot at a cloud. Anderson wondered if the private had gone through the battle at Gettysburg shooting at the sky, but now was not the time to argue about Judgement Day.

"Just stay in line, dammit! If I see you shirking back, I'll shoot you myself and face the Lord with *your* blood on *my* hands," the lieutenant shouted in the private's ear before he moved away.

Major Rogers didn't seek permission from General Robertson when he waved his regiment forward. He'd noted that the vicious canister from the artillery battery on the hill had lessened, the musket fire from hundreds of muskets having taken a toll on the cannon crews.

Captain McBee spotted Major Rogers waving his sword, pointing as he moved up the slope towards the Union battery. McBee ran after Rogers, shouting for his men to follow. Within a few seconds the entire regiment had joined their commander, shifting their line of attack to charge the already devastated artillery battery.

The remaining cannon crewmen turned and ran down the other side of the hill, leaving the six artillery pieces to the attacking Rebs. The officers of other Union batteries, deployed on high ground to either side of Robertson's jubilant Confederates, wheeled their end guns to face the enemy clustered around the newly captured artillery pieces.

The four cannons began sweeping their target with canister, aiming at the Confederate infantry who were milling around the abandoned cannons. While the Texans and Arkansans lay prone and endured the hail of iron balls coming from two directions, Federal infantry reformed their battle lines and stepped forward intent on retaking the captured cannons.

* * *

Levi followed the road back towards the battleground. It was nearly dark when he reached a crossroad where the tents of a field hospital glowed from the lanterns within the canvas walls. The silhouette of a table and a man with a saw caught Levi's eye, and the sudden scream sent a shiver through him. After more than a year of service, Levi had seen several such hospitals and spent hours working in one at Manassas. He didn't mind the blood, but the screams unnerved him.

Remembering his charge from Captain McBee to bring full canteens back to the company, Levi walked along the rows of men waiting for their turn in the tent. When he encountered a soldier already dead, McBee's servant knelt by the corpse and gently pulled loose any canteen he saw and slung it over his shoulder.

"Hey, Boy, what you doin'?" a white litter bearer asked as he and his partner lowered another wounded soldier to the ground.

Thinking quickly, Levi replied, "I brought a lieutenant shot in the side. He's in the tent. Capt'n says bring water back, so I'm taking the canteens from these poor men whose souls have flown away."

Too tired to stop talking even though he knew that the less spoken to a stranger was always better, Levi went on. "Their time here is over and they don't need the water of life no more. But the capt'n's men still do."

The litter bearer grunted, "Can't argue with that, even from a darkie."

In just a few minutes Levi had seven canteens banging on his hip. He decided seven was enough, that to stay longer would probably result in his being put to work hauling broken men and dead bodies in and out of the tent as he'd done last year.

* * *

The Union counterattack to retake the six cannons came before General Robertson could realign his disordered regiments to face the attackers. There was no time for his infantrymen to turn and load the artillery pieces they had just captured to point at the two long lines of Yankees. Rather than be overrun, and taking casualties from the cross fire of the batteries on either flank, Robertson pulled his men off the crest, down the side the hill which they had charged up just a few minutes before.

* * *

Leaving the hospital and returning to the road, Levi followed it down a long slope until he came to a creek crossing. In the moonlight, he could make out the shapes of horses and men drinking and filling buckets and canteens, the line stretching in both directions along the rocky banks of the narrow ribbon of water. Levi left the road and worked his way upstream, past dozens of white soldiers and Negro servants, until he came to the last detail of soldiers who were kneeling by the creek, holding canteens under water.

Stretched out on his belly, Levi pushed one tin canteen to the bottom of the creek and set a rock on top of it while it filled. He quickly had three canteens wedged under the surface, bubbling as water forced the air out of the inside each one. When he'd filled all seven and drunk all he could, he made his way back to the road and spoke to three young soldiers who were starting to walk away.

"Pardon me, but I need to find the Fifth Texas Regiment, Hood's Division."

"Fifth Texas? Hell, man, we're in the Sixth Texas. Cleburne's Division," one dark haired soldier said. "I heard the Fifth was with General Lee. Got roughed up in some Yankee state and limped home like whipped dogs. That's what I heard."

Levi knew he dare not respond as he wanted to, so he sidestepped. "We rode trains from Virginia through the Carolina's and up through half of Georgia to get here."

"Ah, that ain't nothing. When we was let out of prison camp, we rode a train all the way across the whole Yankee nation 'fore they exchanged us in Virginia."

Levi had to grin at the soldier's comeback. In the moonlight he looked darker than the others.

"The capt'n sent me to fetch all the water I could. But the regiment was about to go into the fight. I could wander around all night and not find 'em."

"We're on our way back to the Sixth. Walk with us and we'll get you closer than here anyway," the man said. "Got a name?" he asked as the four men began to walk up the side of the road.

"Levi. I'm Levi. I take care of Capt'n McBee, Company C of the Fifth.

A second man spoke for the first time. "You don't talk like a Texas darkie."

The first man said, "I'm Private *Jesús* McDonald, Company K of the Sixth. The Alamo Rifles."

The third soldier now said, "Jeez, Jesse, you don't gotta give your name to a nigger."

The soldier with the dark complexion twisted to speak sharply at the third man. "I'll give my name to whoever I want. *Mi madre* gave me the name of the Lord, and it's a name I'll spread around whenever I take a hankerin' to."

"Sure, Jesse, don't get riled up. I didn't mean nuthin' by it."

Turning back to Levi, Private McDonald said, "*Señor*, please take no never mind to *mi compadres*, we all come from *San Antonio de Bexar*, where black men are not commonly seen or heard."

I can't remember anyone ever apologizing to me for what another white man says, Levi thought; but he said, "I'm bred and raised in Virginia, not Texas. My capt'n moved off to Texas when he come grown. He fetched me from his mama in Lexington after his man-servant from Texas got sick and died. Didn't know there was a place called Texas 'til the capt'n told me."

Private McDonald talked while the quartet walked, the canteens hanging from the shoulders of all them clanking in the dark. Levi learned the whole Sixth Texas Regiment had been taken prisoners in a state called Arkansas last winter, then near froze to death on the deck of a steamboat going north to a prison camp. What men didn't die in the prison camp were exchanged for Yankee prisoners after a few months, and they really did ride a train across the whole country.

McDonald said the dead men at the camp included his own cousin, a freeborn black man who drove a wagon but was captured anyway, and got real sick and croaked in the pox house. Levi wasn't sure what that meant, but it sounded bad.

Levi shivered in the humid night air and only half believed McDonald's story of how a sergeant named Chalk escaped prison camp. Levi couldn't bear to think that any man would climb in a coffin with a dead man done turned blue. Beyond that he couldn't imagine trusting friends to leave the nails of the wooden box's lid loose enough for him to break out in the night while the coffins were stacked in a shed waiting for the ground to thaw so they could dig the grave. But that's what McDonald said.

The four men separated at a fork in the road after an ambulance driver told them that Hood's Division was somewhere off to the left, while Cleburne's Division was farther along the right fork. Even though a hundred and twenty thousand soldiers were within a few miles of the place where he stood, Levi was alone in the night.

Chapter 34

Near the Viniard House
Chickamauga, Georgia
September 20, 1863

After several times asking directions from men in canteen details he encountered on the dark road, Levi found the regiment bivouacked without campfires. He delivered the canteens to Captain McBee and assured him that he'd left the woman and her children with other civilians safely away from the fighting. McBee instructed Lieutenant Anderson to use the full canteens to replenish the water supply of every man in the company.

Dawn brought a deceptively serene blanket of fog to the early morning activities of the Texas Brigade. Soon all four regiments formed and moved to their assigned positions for the coming attack. Then they waited.

"I swear, unless we're out in the bright sunshine these new trousers and jackets look more blue than gray," Private Gilbert said to Corporal Smith as the men leaned on their muskets.

"Cal, you ain't complaining, are you?" Smith replied.

"Nope, I ain't. Fact is, I'm grateful that English sheep must grow thicker wool than American sheep, 'cause I stayed warm all night. But you tell me, Jason, are we wearing blue uniforms or gray uniforms?"

"Let's call it dark English gray, since we're in the Confederate army, and quit fretting over it. Me, I'm just glad to have trousers that still have a seat in 'em."

"And shoes that got soles without holes."

"Yeah, that too," Corporal Smith agreed. "Here comes Captain Cleveland. I heard Major Rogers was hit yesterday. The Fifth is now Captain Cleveland's command."

"When's the Fifth going to be Captain McBee's command? When he's the last captain standing?" Gilbert asked.

"I reckon so," Smith said. "Ain't but a couple of captains left that's been leading since we left Texas."

"I don't know if I'd like to see our captain out in front of the regiment, waving his damned sword and hollering, *Charge!*" Private Rafe Fulton added to the conversation. "You know how many of our colonels, lieutenant colonels, and majors have been shot down? Too many to count on both hands. And this war ain't over. Hell, this battle ain't over. Nah, I'd rather Father John stick with us and let some younger fireball command the regiment the next time we attack a line of blue-bellies. "

A minute later the four regiments in the brigade marched forward through a patch of woods. When the long battle lines emerged from the cover of the trees, distant Union artillery began pounding them with exploding shells. A few men fell, the unlucky ones who were wounded or killed by the unpredictable flying shards of iron shrapnel.

Soon heavy musket fire erupted from a hill to the right front of the Texans, causing more casualties. General Robertson ordered his regiments to shift their attack obliquely to the right, to go straight at the Union infantry on the heights.

As the Texans angled their ragged battle lines toward the enemy on the hill, they took more and more casualties. Determined soldiers stepped over and around fallen comrades, knowing that to stop would invite even more death. As they had done during their failed uphill attack at Gettysburg a hundred days before and their successful assault just the day before, the men fired their muskets as they advanced, reloading on the move. When Private John Cox fell, hit in the thigh with a Minié ball, Sergeant Hodges stopped only long enough to wrap a dirty handkerchief around the wound.

The brigade reached the slope of the hill and pushed their way to the top. The Union infantry gave way before them, retiring down the far slope. Once the high ground was occupied by Confederates, more Union cannon batteries turned their fire on them. General Robertson quickly saw that his oblique attack on the hill had separated his four regiments from the Division, exposing his men to heavy artillery and infantry fire from two directions. Reluctantly, he ordered his brigade to retire back down the hill to the partial protection of a lightly wooded area.

"Captain, we're taking hits from the flank," Lieutenant Anderson shouted to McBee.

"I see that, but the Yanks are out that way to our front. Don't let the men slack off their fire," McBee answered.

"But, Sir..."

"Lieutenant, if some other regiment in the Division is firing on us, we can't fire back! It's these damned new uniforms. They're too dark." Looking around through the smoke, McBee saw a line of gray clad soldiers to their left rear.

"Anderson, you run like a Texas jack rabbit towards that regiment off to our left. Tell them they're firing on other Rebs. Let 'em know we're Robertson's Brigade in Hood's Division. Go now!"

The fire from their own lines lessened, then stopped after Lieutenant Anderson and a few other quickly dispatched junior officers delivered urgently shouted messages to the commanders of three regiments.

Using his telescope from a ridge three hundred yards to the rear, General Hood saw a large body of men under Confederate flags going the wrong way, retiring from a hilltop just taken from Union infantry. He immediately shut the telescope and spurred his horse in that direction, followed by his staff officers and flag bearer.

From horseback, under his own brigade command banner, General Robertson watched his regiments reforming. They were still taking casualties, but nothing like they had on the exposed hill crest earlier. Robertson's aide-de-camp touched the brigadier's shoulder and pointed at the cluster of riders approaching.

Robertson saluted the Division commander, and quickly explained why he'd withdrawn his command from the hill crest. Hood nodded, about to give Robertson new orders when a bullet ripped into the senior general's upper thigh. Quickly, two men dismounted, slid Hood off his horse and bandaged his leg.

"Go ahead. Keep ahead of everything," Hood ordered as he was lifted onto a litter to begin his journey back to a field hospital.

General Law again assumed command of the Division and promptly ordered Robertson's Texas Brigade to shift to the far left and construct defensive works to protect their flank from a possible Union counter-attack. The Fifth Texas Regiment finished the second day of the great battle at Chickamauga Creek wielding shovels and axes instead of their muskets.

Chapter 35

The McBee House
November 30, 1863

F aith answered the knock at the front door to find the clerk from the freight station standing next to a wooden crate.

"Are you Faith McBee?" She nodded as he held out a pencil and a receiving slip. She signed the form and pulled the door further open so he could wheel the crate into the hall. He plopped the big wooden box down then quickly left, the dolly wheels bouncing loudly down the porch steps.

Edward Bell brought a small pry bar from the carriage house and popped the dozen nails that held the lid firmly in place. Elizabeth McBee stood at the head of the stairs holding John Junior, watching.

Faith saw the folded paper on top of whatever else was packed in the box. She picked up the note and read aloud:

To the Ladies of the McBee Household,

Please accept these gifts sent in my deepest appreciation for the warm and gracious hospitality you bestowed upon this uninvited houseguest. While the gifts may seem most utilitarian in nature and *not the niceties that a grateful gentleman would normally bestow upon a family who opened their home to him in a time of need, I am of the opinion you will find them beneficial for your personal use or for bartering in the months ahead.*

Your Obedient Servant,   J P B

Faith first pulled from the box a bolt of fine dark green wool cloth wrapped around a cardboard spindle. Next she removed an even thicker bolt of green and white calico print cotton, and a bolt of white osnaburg used for lining garments. Then came a small box containing a dozen spools of thread, needles, two silver thimbles, and two dozen bone buttons of varying sizes.

Under those items she found a large folded piece of thick absorbent cotton used for infant diapers, four cotton bed sheets, and two new thick wool blankets.

Next were the food items: Two crocks of honey; four sugar cones; two sacks each containing a pound of coffee beans; a ten pound sack of finely-ground flour; a five pound sack of salt; and several sealed cans of oysters.

In the bottom of the crate were a new large skillet and a pair of new butcher knives with shiny razor-sharp blades.

Sandwiched between the cook ware and the yard goods was a large package tied with cord. Faith set it on the table and unwrapped it. One by one, Faith held up a worn tan dress, a dark brown hooded wool cape, a somewhat frayed silk chemise, two cotton petticoats both showing signs of wear, and one new petticoat. Even the worn garments smelled and felt clean.

The chemise was rolled around a small, heavy chamois sack containing a number of gold and silver coins in varying denominations, some minted in the United States, some Confederate. Inside the bag on top of the coins was a smaller cloth pouch that contained a roll of Confederate bank notes and a note on which was written in the same handwriting as the first note:

Travel to Middlesboro, Kentucky, near the Tennessee border. Wear both petticoats all the time until you check in to a hotel in Middlesboro. At that time replace the two old petticoats with the new one and wrap the old ones in the brown paper. Be prepared to hand over both worn petticoats wrapped together to the clerk at the Harmony Laundry on 2nd Street between noon and 3:00 pm from December 10 until December 15. You will ask the clerk if they can remove a red wine stain. Only give him the package if he answers, "If the stain has not set too long I can use a special soap on it." Keep the package if the clerk says anything else. Either way, start your journey home as soon as you leave the laundry. Burn this note after committing the necessary information to memory.

* * *

The next morning Faith gave John Junior a long tearful squeeze and reluctantly handed the ten-month-old to his grandmother. Faith watched Elizabeth take each deliberate step up and disappear with John Junior into her bedroom. The young mother let out a deep sigh, remembering her tense conversation with Elizabeth after John and Secretary Benjamin had left Lexington.

Elizabeth had immediately voiced her opposition to Faith travelling alone, to embarking on a stagecoach journey without John's permission, to entering a Yankee occupied state, to leaving John Junior behind. Faith agreed it was a difficult decision, but their need for more income outweighed her concerns about the trip to Kentucky. And the trip would not take more than two or three weeks.

To refute Faith's reasoning about their need for money, Elizabeth had reminded the younger woman that she still had the income from her three Negro laborers to support them. Faith countered that the prices of everything were soaring; that even a quart of milk from their new cow sold for seventy-five cents; that selling a single gallon of milk brought in as much as a day's wages from one of Elizabeth's slaves. Faith said she would happily use some of the payment from Secretary Benjamin to buy two more milk cows, allowing Elizabeth to free her slaves without losing the income they brought in. Elizabeth retorted that would be absurd, that each slave had a value of over a thousand dollars.

When Faith had asked what would be the Negroes' value when Mr. Lincoln's army won the war and all the Negroes became free men and women, Elizabeth had left the room.

For three months Faith and Elizabeth had waited for some communication from Secretary Benjamin, their disagreement over the trip put aside. Faith busied herself with weaning John Junior from her breast, mixing mashed cereal with cow's milk to spoon-feed him. Elizabeth worried as she closely watched prices rise at the market every week. Finally, she came to grudgingly agree that the need for more money in the household was real enough and the offered pay ample enough to justify Faith's journey.

One evening shortly before the crate arrived, all four members of the household were in the kitchen enjoying the warmth of the stove. While Edward read an old Richmond newspaper and Faith was playing with John Junior, Elizabeth made her announcement.

"As soon as the message arrives from Secretary Benjamin, I'm going to take John Junior to visit Robert's widow Anna, and my other grandchildren. I've been ignoring them, and it's not too soon for little John to spend more time with his cousins. That will allow Edward to accompany you to Kentucky while the baby and I stay with the McChesneys."

Faith and Edward both snapped their heads up.

Seeing she had their attention, Elizabeth continued, "I do read the newspaper myself, and I've talked to other members of the congregation who've travelled over the gap to see family in Kentucky. It's not an easy road from Abingdon. The stage line goes on south, but not west up and over the Cumberland Mountains, even at the gap.

"The Secretary may be one of the smartest men in Richmond like the newspaper says," Elizabeth audibly huffed a bit as she went on, "but he missed this one. He wouldn't have recruited a young woman to travel alone over the gap if he knew there isn't a stage, and that highwaymen roam the whole area."

"Elizabeth, the Secretary told me that Captain Champ Ferguson's partisans patrol our side of the gap, and the highwaymen fear him." Faith countered.

"Dear, I've no doubt the wretched Unionists and sissyboys who are hiding in the mountains do fear Captain Ferguson. But his company can't be everywhere. Whatever the Secretary may have said, I've been assured that Ferguson spends more time on the Kentucky side of the mountains than on our side. No, you must at least have what protection Edward can provide while you ride up to the gap."

Faith looked at Edward. He shrugged.

"Edward, did you ever learn to shoot that big pistol better than Levi did?" Elizabeth asked.

"Yes, Ma'am. I practice handling it every day. I take it you want me to go with Faith as her little brother? Or her little sister?"

"Little brother, still too young for conscription until next year. You look it. Two young women travelling without a man would be too tempting to many men, outlaws or not."

"Do I go into Kentucky with her? I can't see Yankee soldiers letting me carry a pistol across the border. And without a weapon, I don't know how much protection I'd be for Faith."

"Johnny said you're a fighter. Aren't you?" Elizabeth asked.

"Yes, Ma'am, I am. But do I look threatening to you or anyone? I win fights because I surprise big men who think little men are weak and timid. I'm not either of those. But that's not the same as the sight of a big pistol to make a ruffian think twice when we're walking down a street."

"Faith?" Elizabeth asked.

"I was planning to go alone, but I'd welcome Edward escorting me as far as he can without jeopardizing himself because of his pistol."

Chapter 36

Lexington, Virginia
December 1, 1863

E dward and Faith walked to the stage line office. Unaccustomed to the weight and constricted movement allowed by double petticoats, Faith walked self-consciously to the ticket window on the far side of the waiting room, leaving Edward and their bags waiting near the door.

"I would like two tickets to Abingdon on today's stage, please."

"Yes, Ma'am," the stooped and gray haired clerk answered. "Will you be paying in hard coin or Confederate script?"

"Bank notes."

"Yes, Ma'am." The elderly man consulted a chart of fares to different towns. "That'll be $110. In bank notes."

"How much in coin?"

"Less. Do you have coins? I heard you say bank notes, Ma'am."

"That's correct. Here." Faith removed a stack of bills from her handbag and peeled off enough to pay for the ticket.

"That's a substantial amount of money there. You best not be pulling out the whole thing once you take your seat on the stage," the ticket agent said as he made change.

"Thank you for the advice. I'll be discreet."

"Aren't you Mizz McBee's houseguest? The lady with the twin babies? I seen you at church. Quite a handsome pair of young'uns."

"Thank you, Mr., uh?"

"McGregor, Ma'am. Stewart McGregor."

"Thank you, Mr. McGregor," Faith said with a sudden catch in her voice as she pushed away the image of Betsy in her casket. "I'm Mrs. McBee's daughter-in-law, not a houseguest. My little brother on the bench over there has been hired by Mrs. McBee as her driver and groom. Our tickets, please?"

"Oh, certainly, Mrs. McBee. The boy will be bringing around the fresh horse team any time now and the stage should be arriving from Staunton between ten and noon. Road's dry right now, so I expect it'll be closer to ten. You have a good trip, Ma'am. You should arrive at Abingdon tomorrow afternoon. You'll be laying over tonight at Christianburg Station and you'll need to rent beds at the boarding house there. And don't let other folks see all them bank notes."

"One more thing, Mr. McGregor, We're travelling into Kentucky through the Cumberland Gap. I understand the road is too rough for coaches. Does the stage company offer mounted travel through the gap?"

"Kentucky, Ma'am? The Yankee army's in charge of Kentucky these days."

Faith listened impatiently. The clerk hadn't yet said anything that she didn't already know. His next statement, however, yanked her attention back.

"I think our company still takes folks on the back of pack mules up and over the mountains through the gap. But just a month or so ago our soldiers left the forts up on top of the mountains. And the damyankees moved into them. You can't get through the gap unlest the Yankee soldiers let you through, and they're particular about who comes into Kentucky through the gap since our side is where the Confederacy starts, or ends, I suppose they would say."

"Yes, well…" Faith started, but the clerk droned on without noticing her attempt to speak.

"Still and all, since Kentucky never actually seceded from the Union, it's officially a neutral state, even if the Yankee army runs things. I'm told some civilians still travel to there from here. Don't know your business in Kentucky, but the Yankee soldiers at the fort in the gap will want to know."

"Why I never! You mean to tell me a strange man will inquire of my affairs in Kentucky?" Faith replied, showing alarm she didn't feel.

"Oh, yes indeed." The clerk continued, enjoying his new importance as a bearer of shocking information. "They'll ask why you're going into Kentucky, and if they don't like your answer, well, they'll put you back on your mule and send you back down the mountain the way you come. Be a waste of hard-come-by dollars, that would be. After that, I don't know what travelling is like, but I expect you'll see lots of Yankee soldiers."

"That would be unfortunate, to be turned away," Faith replied. "Are there other trails, unguarded trails, through the gap that don't go by the Yankee fort?"

"Well, Ma'am, sure there are, but that's where no woman would dare ride, even with an escort of two armed men, if you call that boy a man. And your pack mule guide, he won't go off the main road, no ways. That's where the Unionist skunks from Tennessee and Virginny hide out, whole passels of 'em, I'm told. No Ma'am, getting off the main road up and over the gap would invite certain depredation, if you'll pardon my forward speech."

Chapter 37

On the Stagecoach
Between Lexington and Abingdon, Virginia
December 1, 1863

Three other passengers shared the coach with Faith and Edward during the trip to Christianburg. Mr. Matthews was a talkative middle-aged businessman who was certain the war was the sole reason for his current financial difficulties. By the time the stage reached the station, Faith knew far more than she cared to about the hardships being experienced by his family in Staunton. The husband of the couple who sat opposite Faith attempted to speak about his own family's travails, but gave up after his troubles were airily dismissed as trivial compared to those affecting the Matthews family.

Faith kept her head turned while she stared out the window, the hood of her cape allowing Mr. Matthews only brief glimpses of her profile. When she tired of watching the scenery, Faith leaned her head back and shut her eyes, ignoring the babble coming from the man sharing the bench seat. Edward Bell sat between Faith and Matthews and read from the same novel that Mr. O'Kelly had been reading when he met his unexpected death in July. Bell kept the big Remington pistol tucked into her waistband, visible to all.

The ride from Christianburg to Abingdon the next morning was a repeat of the day before, with two new male passengers replacing the couple on the bench across from Faith, Edward, and Mr. Matthews. Faith feigned sleep as Mr. Matthews spent the morning again detailing the litany of woes that he had fully described the previous afternoon.

Faith stood at the clerk's window in the Abingdon stage station to purchase passage for herself and Edward over the Cumberland Gap on the back of pack mules. She listened to the clerk tell her to expect to be stopped by Yankee soldiers in the gap, their luggage possibly searched, and certainly questioned about their business in Kentucky.

He also informed Faith the mule train couldn't leave for another two days because the guide and the animals were still not back from their current trip. They would need to spend two nights in rented rooms in Abingdon. Moreover, the ride to the Cumberland Gap would take two days, so they would be renting beds at Gibson Station after the first day's travel.

The morning air was bitterly cold. Faith could see her breath when she and Edward introduced themselves to Thaddeus Rix, their guide and muleskinner. Faith silently thanked Secretary Benjamin for the foresight of the heavy brown woolen cape that had come with her dress and her own foresight in bringing her kid leather gloves. She hid her dismay that she would not be riding on a lady's side-saddle, but would have to straddle the mule like a man. When it was time to leave, Faith grasped the saddle with a firm grip, put a foot in the stirrup, and with Edward's assisting hand pushing on her rump, she swung up onto the saddle.

While Mr. Rix puttered around with his lead mule tightening all the cinches, Faith stood in her stirrups to immodestly arrange the skirt of one petticoat under her bottom. She had to hold up her heavy cape and dress with one hand, making her efforts even more awkward. When she caught Edward broadly smiling at her, she narrowed her eyes until Bell looked away still grinning.

Once the mules left Abingdon, the road slowly but steadily rose upwards as they left the flat fields of the lower Shenandoah Valley behind and approached the foothills of the Appalachian Mountains. By the time the trio reached Gibson Station late in the afternoon, Faith's legs ached and her derriere and inner thighs were chafed from the leather saddle, her petticoat having refused to stay in place more than the first few minutes of the jarring ride.

The next morning the pain in Faith's legs and her tender bottom almost prevented her from continuing. But she realized she had no choice, other than returning to Lexington a failure, and sending the money and gifts back to Secretary Benjamin. So, Faith unwrapped the new petticoat, and using Edward's pocketknife, cut it into strips and wrapped her legs from knee to groin. Finally, she fashioned a makeshift diaper with the last strip of cotton. The cotton padding felt good against her raw skin and stayed in place, preventing further injury during the second day's ride.

By noon, the trio reached the lower slopes of the mountains. Almost immediately they began traversing switchbacks as the narrow path continued ever upward. During one of the breaks to let the mules catch their breath, the beasts' heaving sides pumping like bellows, Edward Bell approached Rix.

"Do any of the side trails we've been passing also take us over the mountain, but not through the fortified gap?" Edward asked their guide.

Rix grunted and said, "Shore. I'll show you the next one up yonder a ways. But them trails is hard to follow. They loop around back and forth, and just fade out some places. Ain't meant fer decent folks to travel on."

True to his word, half an hour later Mr. Rix stopped again and pointed out a break in the bushes to the right of the trail.

"There's one. It runs along the slope fer a mile 'r so, then cuts down a spell 'fore it loops back up through a ravine and twists through a crack in the rocks and goes over the top. Ain't easy, but it goes around the forts the Yanks is in. You not wantin' to go that way, are ye? 'Cause I ain't."

"How much longer to the fort in the gap?" Faith asked.

"Few hours. We'll get there 'fore dark."

"Mr. Rix, Mr. Bell will not be going through the gap with me. We are of the opinion the Yankees at the station would take his pistol, and perhaps arrest him. You stop at the best place for him to spend the night, while he waits on you for the ride back to Abingdon."

"Yes, Ma'am. I'll be glad to have a friendly gun with me on the way down."

* * *

Lieutenant Jarl Knudsen enjoyed the random arrival of civilians crossing the gap into Kentucky from the rebel side of the Cumberland Gap. Being the son of immigrants from Norway and having grown up on an isolated farm in Wisconsin, Knudsen didn't feel the daily gnawing loneliness for companionship that struck many of his troopers. Yet, lonely or not, he still enjoyed the occasional chance to engage in conversation with the travelers who applied to him for permission to travel into Kentucky.

The lieutenant stood in the door to his small office building and watched the two riders dismount. He recognized the guide, who immediately led the mules to the water trough, then sat down in the shade. Knudsen noted with surprise that the other person was a young woman. An attractive young woman.

When Faith handed her mule's reins to Mr. Rix, she said loudly enough for the soldiers to hear, "Thank you, Sir, for your service. I'll be fine, now. These good men will provide for my safety."

"I think I'll wait 'til you talk with the lieutenant over there," Rix answered.

"As you wish," Faith said as she turned and walked stiffly to the building, carrying her valise.

Knudsen watched his first sergeant approach the guide and speak to him. The guide pushed himself off the log bench and walked back to his mule. He pulled a cloth bag out of one saddlebag and handed it to the sergeant. The sergeant hefted the sack and glanced inside, then looked towards the lieutenant and nodded, assuring his officer that the necessary toll payment of dried tobacco leaves had been delivered.

Faith opened the conversation as she approached the office. "I'm told I'm to speak with you, Lieutenant."

"Inside, if you would, Madame," the officer answered.

Faith went through the door and walked directly to the stove in the corner. She took off her gloves and held both hands over the stove top.

"Lieutenant, that coffee pot smells heavenly. May I have a cup?" Faith asked without invitation.

"There's tin cups on the shelf," the lieutenant replied. After the woman had poured herself a steaming cup of dark coffee, Knudsen pointed to a chair in front of his tiny desk. Being an inch over six feet tall, the lieutenant had to sit with his legs angled sideways, since they wouldn't fit under the desk drawer. He deliberately pulled a printed form from the drawer, dipped a quill into an ink well and asked, "Name?"

"Mrs. Adam Samuelson."

"Your given name?"

"Sir?"

"Your first name?"

"That is not a proper question, Sir," Faith said with both hands wrapped around the warm sides of the tin cup.

The officer set down his pen and looked at the woman seated in front of him.

"Do you want admission into Kentucky?" he asked in curt manner.

"Of course. Why else would I ride a mule up that godforsaken trail all day?"

"Do you understand that you must have my approval to cross the Cumberland Gap into Kentucky? If you continue to take umbrage at my questions, I will deny that approval and you will ride down that godforsaken trail all night. Now what is your given name?"

"Faith."

"Place of residence?"

Having asserted herself as much as the young officer would permit, Faith answered demurely, "Near West Point, Virginia, not far from the Pamunkey River, northeast of Richmond."

"Purpose of travel from Virginia to Kentucky?"

"Family matters." As she spoke, Faith unbuttoned her wool cape and draped it over the back of her chair.

"I need more than that, Madame," the Lieutenant said, not unkindly this time.

"It's delicate, Lieutenant."

"I still need to be told the nature of your family matters that require your travel to Kentucky from Virginia, a commonwealth that is actively engaged in a traitorous act of rebellion against the Union."

"Must I?" Faith implored the young officer. She took another sip of hot coffee.

"Only if you want admission to Kentucky, Madame. I would not pry for personal voyeuristic reasons."

"Very well. I'm on a quest to find my husband."

"Mr. Adam Samuelson?" Knudsen asked, looking down to verify the name.

"Lieutenant Adam Samuelson. Past lieutenant, that is. I don't know his rank in your army. Or even if he's in your army. But he said he was going to Kentucky to join."

"I see. Or rather, I don't see. Would you please elaborate, Mrs. Samuelson."

"If I must," Faith said sighing, hoping to exhibit a sense of shame and resignation.

"You must only if you…" Knudsen began.

"Yes, I know, only if I want to enter Kentucky. I don't *want* to enter Kentucky, but I am compelled to, Sir, if I am to remain an honorable woman, wife, and mother."

"Very well, do go on then."

"It's shameful, but not complicated, Lieutenant," Faith assured her interrogator.

"What's not complicated, Madame?"

"My husband abandoned me, abandoned his son, abandoned his duty in the army, and abandoned Virginia."

"Why did he do all that *abandoning*, Mrs. Samuelson?"

"I don't know," Faith said with a barely stifled sob. "If I knew, maybe I could have stopped him."

"You said earlier that he may be in the Union army now?"

"Yes, that's what he told me the night he left. That he'd decided he was fighting for the wrong cause, was in the wrong army."

"So you believe he deserted the Confederate army, left Virginia, traveled to Kentucky and joined the army here? That's not uncommon. Thousands of loyal citizens from Tennessee and Virginia have done so. But you said you live on the other side of

Richmond, why wouldn't he go north to Baltimore such a short distance away? Why cross the mountains to Kentucky? I don't have to tell you it's not an easy journey."

"His cousin. He has a cousin here. Near Middlesboro. He's a soldier, an officer, in a regiment somewhere in Kentucky. Adam was planning to contact him, hoping he'd know someone who could help him become an officer too. So, I'm going to Middlesboro."

"If I approve your passage through the gap," the lieutenant reminded her.

"Yes, of course, I'm sorry. If you approve my passage," Faith said.

"What will you do should you find your husband, Mrs. Samuelson? You can't force him to return to Virginia with you."

"No, certainly not. I will stay in Kentucky with him."

"And where do your loyalties lie, Madame? With the Union or the rebellion?"

"I've not had to consider that before now, Lieutenant. I'm a good wife and my loyalties reside with my husband. Whether he is in Kentucky or Virginia."

"You used the word *mother* earlier? Do you and Mr. Samuelson have children?"

"I gave birth to twins last January. But our Betsy died of fever a few months ago. Only the little boy is left and he is in the care of his grandmother. I wanted to bring him, but feared for his safety. I do miss him so already."

"But you are prepared to be away from him until the conclusion of the rebellion? Months, years even?"

"Surely not so long as years. Surely not so long. But, yes, I pray daily for the fighting to end."

Lieutenant Knudsen did not respond while he wrote several sentences before he set down his pen. He looked at Mrs. Samuelson and drummed his fingers on the desktop. Finally, he resumed writing, and with a discernable flourish, added his signature to the document.

"I'm reluctantly granting your application to enter Kentucky, Mrs. Samuelson. I'm doing so because I applaud your husband's loyalty to the Union, even if it's late in coming. And I approve of your commitment to your husband. A man needs a loyal wife. I trust your husband will welcome your arrival, should you locate him."

"Thank you, Lieutenant. Is there a stage that leaves from here? I fear my mule belongs to Mr. Rix, the guide.

"No stagecoach comes this high up, Madame. But I will send you along to Middlesboro with the next supply train of pack mules going down. You will enter Kentucky under the escort of the US Army."

* * *

Before he left his office for the night, Lieutenant Knudsen completed the second part of his task as the gatekeeper of the Cumberland Pass. He copied his record of the interview onto a second document, sealed it in an envelope, addressed to a Major Francis in Frankfort. Finally, he put the envelope in the mail satchel that would go down the mountain with the same supply train of mules that would take Mrs. Samuelson to Middlesboro. The sealed envelope would then be taken by courier to the army train depot and delivered to Major Francis within two days.

His daily duties done, Lieutenant Knudsen walked to his cabin, hoping to catch a glimpse of Mrs. Samuelson near the tent she had been assigned as sleeping quarters. He didn't see her, but he did fall asleep thinking about her.

Chapter 38

Near the Border of SE Kentucky & SW Virginia
December 5, 1863

Edward Bell had spent the night shivering in a nest of dead leaves. The morning sight of Thaddeus Rix's mule easing its way down the trail perked up Bell, but didn't stop her shivers. When the pair passed the spot where Rix had shown them the side trail the day before, Bell instinctively stopped and studied the location, looking for recognizable landmarks. Rix again related how the trail meandered along the ridge and made its way over the crest. But he also again cautioned Bell about the Unionists and the men evading conscription who hid in the mountains.

Clomping steadily down the switchbacks until the trail turned into a rutted road, the pair reached Abingdon in just one day. Bell immediately went to the stagecoach station, purchased a ticket back to Lexington, and took a long nap sitting upright on the wooden bench in the waiting room. The stage ride back to Lexington was uneventful, Bell spoke very little and no other passengers were interested in her.

In Elizabeth McBee's parlor, Bell related the story of the journey as she knew it. Mrs. McBee wasn't any more or less worried when Bell finished talking than she had been, but she still nursed a silent fear for Faith's well-being.

Middlesboro, Kentucky

December 9, 1863

Faith's ride down the mountain on the back of an army supply mule was even less comfortable than her ride up the mountain had been. Instead of a regular saddle, she'd sat on a scratchy blanket strapped to a pack frame. Each step the mule took jarred her spine, and threatened to spill her forward onto its neck, and the animal took thousands of downward steps before they reached the plateau where the trail leveled out.

The two-story Baker Hotel sat prominently at the intersection of Middlesboro's two main streets. Rooms were available, but Faith had to spend US minted coins to pay. After a year of occupation by the Union army, her Confederate bills were worthless in Kentucky, even in a town just across the border from Tennessee.

Faith was relieved that she'd reached Middlesboro as soon as she had, with no real difficulties other than the humiliating interrogation by the tall blond lieutenant. In her efforts to allow for the vagaries of public transportation, crossing the mountain pass, and still reach Middlesboro on time for her visit to the laundry, she'd arrived four days before the first date given in Secretary Benjamin's message. She now looked forward to resting during those four days.

She was bone weary of travel, tired of being outside in the cold wind, tired of riding on the backs of mules, or on the hard bench of a stagecoach. Faith was very willing to spend the next few days sleeping, and maybe reading, even on a lumpy mattress in a drafty hotel room. She wished she could write a long letter to John, but she understood that would not be prudent. She intended to do nothing that might endanger or interfere with her making the simple delivery at the laundry, and then going home as quickly as possible.

Faith locked the door, impulsively wedged a straight back chair against the door knob for extra security, and fell backwards on the bed, fully dressed. She was asleep in seconds. At dusk she awoke long enough to use the chamber pot, then she undressed, crawled under the bed cover and slept through the night.

The next day, Faith walked around the town, finding the Harmony Laundry without difficulty. She stopped in a mercantile store, curious if the prices of goods in Kentucky were as inflated as they were in Virginia. They weren't, which prompted Faith to purchase a few small sewing items and a wooden toy horse with moving legs for John Junior, items she could carry in her valise. Thinking ahead to spending the next few days in her hotel room, she also bought a used copy of *Little Dorrit*, a novel by Charles Dickens, a loaf of bread, a thick slice of smoked ham, and a jar of jam.

Finally, Faith went to the stagecoach office to inquire about travel over the Cumberland Gap to return to Virginia. She learned she could repeat her trip in reverse, but there might be a longer waiting time at the army station in the gap. She'd have to wait for a guide from Virginia to arrive with a traveler headed into Kentucky, whose rented mule she could ride down the mountain to Abingdon.

Having performed the chores necessary for her to complete her task in Middlesboro and return home afterwards, Faith returned to her room to rest and read until Monday morning.

Frankfort, Kentucky
December 9, 1863

At the same time as Edward Bell was in Lexington telling Elizabeth McBee about the journey to the Cumberland Gap, and Faith was checking into the Baker Hotel in Middlesboro, Major Francis read at his desk in Frankfort, Kentucky. He held a report from one of the many officers who sent him information detailing who was entering or leaving his jurisdiction of Kentucky.

It was tedious business, trying to keep abreast of the whereabouts of the many men and few women whose travel was sometimes suspect. On this cold afternoon, one name caught the major's eye. He was reading a summary of the interview of a Lieutenant Knudsen on duty in the Cumberland Gap with a woman named Mrs. Adam Samuelson.

As soon as he finished reading it, the captain set down the document and pulled a stack of papers from a desk drawer. He shuffled through the loose pages until he found the notes of his final meeting with Lieutenant Adam Samuelson. After quickly scanning the page to refresh himself of the details, he leaned back, closed his eyes and reviewed what he knew.

The lieutenant twice failed to kill the fat Jew, and the second attempt was in the same house where Samuelson's runaway wife was hiding out with her brats and her lover's mother. That means Benjamin and Mrs. Adam Samuelson know each other, since they stayed in the same house together for two or more nights. And they both have good cause to despise the Samuelson woman's legal husband who is a murderer, and now a failed assassin.

Why would she, a young woman with infant children, travel alone in the winter over a high pass to Kentucky? Her story is clearly a fabrication. She hates her husband. She fled Samuelson and has attached herself to a new man, an infantry captain, and she's glad Samuelson has left Virginia. She wouldn't go looking for him.

No, she was sent. She was sent by Judah Benjamin, a guest in the same house where she's been living. She is on a mission for that damned Benjamin. But why? Why put herself at such risk? She must not understand the danger of her travel to Kentucky.

Benjamin either has something on the woman, or he is paying her a hefty amount of money. I need to talk with Mrs. Samuelson. I need to know if she is a courier for the Jew. If she is a courier, and why else would she be in Kentucky, I need the message she is carrying.

"You underestimate me, you smug bastard. You will regret that," Francis said out loud, even though he was alone in his office.

The major quickly wrote a message and called for the sergeant to take it immediately to the telegraph office. Lieutenant Knudsen was about to have a temporary duty assignment.

The US Army Post at the Cumberland Gap
December 11, 1863

Two days after Major Francis wrote the message, Lieutenant Knudsen read it with mixed feelings. He was pleased to have a reason to visit the town of Middlesboro, to eat in a restaurant and have a drink in a bar, but he wasn't enthused about traveling down the mountain in the winter weather. Mostly, however, he was eager to undertake a special duty for Major Francis, whose middling rank he knew did not reflect the secretive officer's importance in Kentucky.

Middlesboro, Kentucky
December 13, 1863

Lieutenant Knudsen and his escort of two corporals arrived in Middlesboro late in the afternoon, too tired and too late to inquire at the three hotels for a woman guest named Samuelson. Instead, they went to the city jail, which was now being used by a small detachment of army provost guards. The lieutenant checked in with the sergeant on duty who directed the two corporals to an empty cell to spend the night, while he led the young officer to a spare bunk in the sheriff's quarters at the back of the jail.

December 14, 1863

Faith rested in the only chair in her room. Her legs were stretched out, feet balancing on the edge of the mattress in a most unladylike manner. The chair was angled to catch the morning sun through the window to better illuminate the pages of Mr. Dickens' most recent tome.

She glanced up from her book and looked out the window to see three Union soldiers crossing the street. The visors of their blue caps hid their faces from her. The one with officer straps on his coat was taller than the other two, with wavy blond hair that nearly reached his shoulders. He had to be the lieutenant from the post at Cumberland Gap.

Faith smiled to herself, wondering if the lieutenant might have found a reason to follow her to town to make sure she arrived safely. Although their conversation had centered on her search for her husband, the young officer had seemed hardly more than a boy, and rather taken with her. Enjoying what she decided was an unspoken affirmation that she was still attractive at the age of twenty-eight and a mother, Faith returned to Dickens' prose.

The sound of knuckles rapping on her door a few minutes later didn't surprise Faith. Holding her book to her chest, she opened the door ready to respond with a properly reserved, but sincere pleasure at seeing the lieutenant again. She had mentally framed her words of gratitude for his concern for her safety, and even her polite refusal to join him for dinner in the hotel dining room, an invitation she expected to be forthcoming.

Without preamble, Lieutenant Knudsen addressed the woman who stood before him. "Mrs. Samuelson. It is my duty to escort you to the provost office where you will be detained for questioning."

"I beg your pardon?"

"Mrs. Samuelson, you are under arrest."

"Lieutenant, surely, surely not," Faith stammered.

"Corporal Olson will pack your belongings and follow us. But you are to go with me. Now."

With those words, Knudsen reached out an arm and took Faith's right elbow, pulling her through the door. The other corporal clamped his fist on her left elbow and the two soldiers forcibly walked Faith Samuelson to the jail.

Chapter 39

The Jail
Middlesboro, Kentucky
December 14, 1863

The prisoner was homely and dirty, mousy brown hair curling over her ears, yet cut short enough to see the ring of grime circling her neck. Heavy eyebrows nearly met over a long nose, and the trousers and shirt she wore betrayed narrow shoulders, wide hips, and a slat thin torso. Her gaze was dull when she turned her head at the sound of the key sliding into the steel lock.

Lieutenant Knudsen pushed Faith into the cell with her and said, "Disrobe."

"What? What did you say?" Faith replied in shock.

"Take off your clothes. All of them. There's a sheet on the bunk you can wrap yourself in."

"I will not!" Faith retorted.

"Mrs. Samuelson, either you take off your shoes, dress, petticoats and any other undergarments and hand them to me, or I will call the corporals in to strip you. You also will unpin your hair and comb it out with your fingers."

"I, I...Lieutenant Knudsen, why are you doing this? I don't understand."

"Those are my orders, Mrs. Samuelson. You are to disrobe immediately upon being detained. I am to search your clothes. Take them apart at every seam."

"What? Again, why? Lieutenant, why are you doing this? What have I done?"

"You are suspected of being a spy for the Confederacy."

Faith slumped to sit on the edge of the empty cot, her face a mask of despair.

"That's better. Mrs. Samuelson, while you are sitting, pull the pins from your hair and comb it out. Then take off your shoes."

Realizing she had no choice, yet still fighting for dignity, Faith said, "Very well, if I must. But, I will not do this in your presence, Lieutenant, and certainly not his." Faith nodded towards the other cot.

"You and that prisoner get out of the cell. Lock the cell door and leave the room. I'll pile my things by the door. I'm keeping my hair pins to fasten the sheet around me. While you're out please find me a dress to wear. There's money in my valise. Send a man to buy me a dress, if you must. I saw a pretty blue striped one in the mercantile store."

"My orders are to watch you disrobe, Mrs. Samuelson. To make sure you don't destroy any message hidden in your clothing."

"This is preposterous! The only thing being destroyed is the respect and privacy of a lady in a sudden, unfathomable nightmare."

"Be that as it may, unpin your hair, then take off your boots and stockings." The lieutenant shifted from one foot to the other, his tone of voice softer, his growing discomfort apparent, but his determination to follow his orders also clear.

"What about that man? Surely you don't intend to let another prisoner gaze upon me like I'm a peep show harlot."

A snort came from the other bunk. "I guess my disguise isn't so bad. I'm no man. My name is Jane Ferguson. I'm under arrest for being a Rebel spy myself."

"Never mind her, Mrs. Samuelson. You two will most likely have a long time to get to know each other. Now untie your boots."

"You told me when we talked at the gap that you are not a voyeur. Were you lying to me? Please leave the room and allow me a woman's rightful privacy!" Faith pointed to Jane Ferguson.

"If she's a woman, she can watch me disrobe, while you wait out front."

"I don't think Captain Francis would approve my allowing one spy to watch over another. No. Your time is up, Mrs. Samuelson. Untie your shoes and remove them and your stockings. Now, or I call for the corporals. Believe me, you don't want that."

Faith Samuelson McBee seethed in anger, shook in real desperation and contrived indignation, but she complied.

Chapter 40

The McBee Home
Lexington, Virginia
December 20, 1863

Elizabeth McBee's knees ached. She hated to admit it, but she felt all of her sixty-two years. Keeping up with John Junior, who was now nearly a year old, was more of a burden with each passing day. Stooping over to lift him and climbing the stairs with him were painful to her back and joints. Also, the little boy was now crawling and had to be watched continuously.

Elizabeth sorely missed the services of Sally, her enslaved house servant who'd been accidentally shot last January. Edward-Edwina tried to help, but Elizabeth could see the strange young woman's discomfort when asked to handle the baby, the ex-soldier much preferring to stay busy in the kitchen.

More important than her personal comfort, Elizabeth fretted more each day about another matter. The time needed for Faith to deliver her hidden message and return home had passed. She was overdue. Something had delayed her in Kentucky, and Elizabeth was worried.

"Edwina, it's time for you to go find John," Elizabeth told her house servant.

"Are you talking to Edwina or Edward?"

"Quit playing with me, young woman. You know how hard it is for me to think of you as a man."

"Yes, Ma'am. I'm sorry. You want me to go find Captain McBee?"

"Yes, dear. It's time he learns about Faith's journey to Kentucky."

"He won't like it. I'm not sure I want to be the one to tell him," Bell replied.

"It's best he hear it from you. Better than me writing a letter that may never reach him. Besides, letters from home rarely bring good news. These days it seems letters are no different from newspapers, full of the names of people who've died, or lamenting the rising cost of bread."

"I agree with you, Ma'am. He should know about his wife's trip. I'll go. Do you want me to leave today?" Bell asked, looking through the window at the snow drifting down.

"I suggest getting an early start in the morning. Maybe the weather will break this evening."

"Yes, Ma'am. I'll ride the horse, leave the carriage here. The papers say the captain's regiment's been around Knoxville, Tennessee with General Longstreet. No telling where I might have to go to find him. What about you and John Junior? If Miss Faith doesn't show up soon, can you manage? I'll be gone a week or two."

"If I have to, I'll hire help," Elizabeth said. "I know a few soldiers' wives who would welcome any money at all."

The Camp of the Fifth Texas Infantry Regiment, CSA
December 22, 1863

Edward Bell found the Texas Brigade and McBee's regiment with surprising ease after just two days of riding. After a failed attempt at driving the Union forces from Knoxville, General Longstreet had marched his troops to Morristown, Tennessee, not far from the state line of Virginia.

Bell was right. Captain McBee was first dumbfounded, not believing the story Bell told him about his wife's trip to Kentucky. Then he became coldly furious, stalking out of the tent, not even taking the time to put on his heavy wool greatcoat. But he did tell Bell to find Levi, have him pack McBee's bag and saddle McBee's horse and his own mule.

253

Stomping through the snow, the captain called back, "Don't leave. You're going with us."

* * *

Captain McBee stood at attention in front of his friend, Major Jefferson Rogers, who still commanded the regiment.

"Major, I'm in need of a furlough," McBee began.

"John, this isn't a good time. The weather is miserable, the men are played out, rations are scarce. Not a good time for a company commander to go see his wife, leaving his men in these conditions," Rogers replied, remembering McBee's furlough the prior summer. Rogers knew McBee's mother and new wife lived in Lexington, only a two-day ride from Morristown.

"Jeff, I won't be going to Lexington. I'm going to Kentucky to find my wife," McBee blurted.

"Kentucky? The Yankee army is all over Kentucky." the Major answered, waving his arm.

"That's why I have to go. Jeff, there's more to it. Faith was sent to Kentucky by someone important in Richmond. She was sent with a message. She's in danger. I have to find her and bring her back before she's discovered, arrested, and..."

"Hold on, John. Ease up a minute. What message? Who in Richmond? What sort of danger?"

"Jeff, I can't tell you anymore, and I can't wait. Are you going to write me a furlough pass?"

"I don't know. I need to think." Major Rogers looked down at his camp desk and fiddled with his pen. Rogers remembered the young married woman who'd nursed the soldiers from Texas last year in the makeshift hospital in Richmond. It was no secret among the regiment's officers that McBee had become infatuated with her, was now calling her his wife, had even moved her in with his mother in Lexington. Rogers had also heard camp gossip of her first husband, a staff officer in Richmond, turning traitor and fleeing Virginia.

"John, …" The major looked up to see McBee walking briskly away.

"Dammit, just dammit," Major Rogers cursed. *Now the woman had gone missing in Kentucky? Sent by someone in Richmond? And my most senior captain is dead set on fetching her back.*

"My friend, what has that woman done? How deep a hole has she dug for herself? And you?" the major muttered to no one as he reluctantly scribbled a furlough pass for Captain McBee and sent an aide running after the captain to deliver it.

Chapter 41

Middlesboro, Kentucky
December 14, 1863

Jane Ferguson, the ungainly-looking cellmate dressed in blue trousers and a wool shirt, watched as Faith began to disrobe under the scrutiny of the lieutenant. Faith, barefoot, her long dark hair loose and uncombed, sobbed. With shaking fingers, she fumbled with the buttons on her dress.

Her anger growing, Ferguson got off her cot, scooped up her own bed sheet, and took three steps to stand between the lieutenant and the crying woman. She held out the sheet as a screen, staring hard at the young officer.

"You're following your orders, Lieutenant. You're in the cell watching this poor woman take off her dress. Enjoy the show." Ferguson sneered at the tall young officer.

"But…" Lieutenant Knudsen began.

"But nothing," the woman in blue trousers said, cutting him off. A minute passed.

"Here!" Faith threw her brown dress over the sheet to land at the lieutenant's feet. Another minute passed.

"And here!" The two petticoats followed.

"Th… thank you, Jane," Faith stammered as she pulled the sheet off her cot and wrapped it around her torso.

Ferguson looked back over her shoulder and dropped her arms, letting the screening sheet fall and giving the lieutenant a full view of Faith pinning the sheet above her chest, still wearing her chemise.

"That, that under thing, too, Mrs. Samuelson." Knudsen waved his arm at the prisoner.

Wordlessly, Faith turned away, pulled her arms out of the shoulders of the chemise and clumsily worked the garment down past her knees under the sheet and stepped out of it. She left the chemise in a puddle on the floor as she fell onto her cot, reaching for the blanket.

"Satisfied?" Faith's single word was drenched in humiliation and hatred.

* * *

After an hour of quiet sobbing on her bunk, Faith regained her composure, but was still agitated enough to want to move around in the jail cell. She put her bare feet on the floor and immediately pulled them back up, the brick floor too cold to do anything but lie huddled on her cot under the filthy blanket.

"Will he send a man to buy me a dress?" Faith asked her cellmate.

"No. He's too scared of Major Francis."

"Do you think Major Francis is going to question me?"

"Yeah, and he's good at it. He'll batter you down, asking the same questions over and over. He's like a dog hanging on a bear's throat. Just won't let go. Leastways, that's how he was with me."

"Will he hit me?"

"No. He got real close to my face shouting at me. His foul breath was like a fist, but no, he didn't beat me."

"Thank God for that." Faith's relief was evident.

"But, he'll take one thing you say and shake it back and forth until you get so mad or scared that you just blurt out something you swore you'd never tell him. Don't matter how careful or how fixed you are to just stay quiet, before he quits you're gonna blab."

"What did you blab?"

"Me? Hmph. I told him lots of things. Some of 'em lies I made up. Some the truth. A few things I didn't want him to know."

"Are you a Confederate spy?"

"No. I'm telling the truth about that. I ain't. But it's a mixed-up story, and I can see where's it'd be easier to believe I am."

Chapter 42

Near the Cumberland Gap
December 25, 1863

C aptain McBee called for Bell to hold up. As the captain motioned for Levi to bring his mule alongside his own horse, Bell looked back to make sure nothing was wrong. Satisfied that McBee was only stopping to tell his man servant something, Bell resumed watching the trail ahead.

McBee reached under his black wool greatcoat and pulled out a small pocket revolver. He held it by the short barrel and offered the hand grip to Levi.

"Here. Don't shoot your foot."

Levi looked at the little pistol. "What do I need that for, Capt'n?"

"You're covering my back, aren't you?"

"Yessir, I am."

"Good. I'm counting on you. We're going up there." McBee waved towards the dark green heights of the wall of mountains ahead of them. "If we meet other men on the trail, they'll probably be outliers who are hiding on this mountain. They'll most likely want to rob us, or worse. We're not going to let that happen. If I start shooting, you do too."

"Yessir, I will." Levi took the weapon and dropped it in his coat pocket.

"Levi, listen to me. That little pistol's not made to shoot far, so go for the man closest to you on your right side. If a band of men mean us harm, they'll let you pass by before they show themselves. So there may be one man behind you. Don't try to shoot him, just duck down over your mule's neck in case he shoots at your back. The man to your right, uphill of us, will be your target. Hold your arm straight out and point the pistol at the chest of the man you're going to shoot. Show me."

Levi pulled the gun out of his pocket and held his arm out, pointing at a nearby uphill tree.

"Don't forget to pull the hammer back. It won't shoot unless you do that. Show me."

Levi nodded and cocked the pistol.

"Now hold the hammer back with your thumb, squeeze the trigger, and then lower the hammer down real gentle-like."

Levi followed the captain's instructions.

"Good. Cock it again. Now uncock it again. Which side man do you shoot?

"Right side, Capt'n. Why's that?"

"So you won't have to aim across your chest, but mainly so I'll know which man not to worry about, because you're going to shoot him. Last thing, shoot the man twice before you look for another target."

"Won't one shot kill him, capt'n?"

"It might, but probably won't. Shoot him twice to be sure."

"Yessir."

"Bell? You listening?" McBee called.

"Yes, Captain."

"If I say, 'We don't have a single gold coin among us,' you pull your pistol and shoot the man who's been doing the talking. He'll be the leader. Is your coat unbuttoned at the waist? Can you reach your pistol?"

"Sure thing, Captain. I'm unbuttoned at the waist, and if you say 'We don't have a single coin among us,' I shoot the talker."

"Close enough. Then you kick that horse and ride straight up the trail. You shoot any man blocking the trail, Bell, don't wait. Shoot the talker once, then kick your horse and go hard. Me and Levi will be right behind you."

"Wouldn't it be better to ride hard back down the trail the way we came? Faster, safer?" Bell asked.

"Private Bell, didn't you come to Tennessee to tell me that my wife is in grave danger in Kentucky on the other side of these mountains?"

Bell nodded.

"Then why would we turn and ride away from Kentucky?"

"'Scuse me, Captain. I wasn't thinking. Over the mountain it is."

* * *

The little group led by Private Bell climbed steadily, the two horses not quite as sure-footed on the trail as Levi's mule. When they reached the tiny open area where Rix had pointed out the side trail, Bell wordlessly reined his horse onto the new path. McBee understood that Bell was taking them on an untried and circuitous path, but one that would skirt the Union army post in the Cumberland Gap. As Rix had promised, the trail was difficult to follow, twice causing Bell to lead them into dead-end ravines.

The first ravine made McBee nervous, because it reminded him of the day last summer when he and Rafe Fulton were captured in just such a dead-end at Gettysburg. Moreover, the three riders had to turn their mounts around on the narrow trail before they could leave the gulch, which put Levi on his mule at the head of their tiny column. McBee trusted Levi, but he wasn't sure he trusted him to react with the decisiveness that might save their lives should they meet foes on the trail.

McBee breathed easier as he passed Levi at the mouth of the ravine. The captain pulled up his horse to let Bell resume his position in the front. An hour later, Bell stopped his horse in front of another wall of rock, looked back at McBee and shrugged.

"Gotta go back again, Captain. There's no way around that boulder."

McBee nodded and the three of them again pulled hard on their reins to pivot their animals and retrace their steps to leave the narrow rift. As they neared the mouth of the gully, a voice boomed out of the trees ahead.

"Hold right there, and git off them animals."

Levi, who was now in the lead, since they had just turned their horses, slipped his hand into his coat pocket as he heard the captain speak.

"Hallo, ahead. I can't rightly see you in the shadows. I like to see a man I'm talking with."

"You ain't gonna see us 'til you git off your mounts. Git down, I said, 'afore I start shootin'.'"

Levi held his pistol tightly in his pocket, but didn't make a move to dismount. He waited for the captain's reply.

"No need to use any guns on us. We don't have a gold coin among us."

Levi instantly kicked his mule forward, pulled his pistol, cocked it and shot in the general direction of the voice in the trees. Right behind Levi, Captain McBee followed with a second shot, having seen movement in the shadows ahead. As Bell fired, McBee heard the sharp crack of the pistol firing behind him, and felt a bullet whiz past his left ear. As McBee re-cocked his pistol, he saw a figure fall off a half-hidden horse to his left side. Without a visible target, McBee fired again, this time to the right, where his instinct told him another rider hid among the trees.

Levi's mule shied when a mounted figure emerged from the brush directly to its front, blocking the trail. Levi saw the rider leveling a long shotgun towards him. He kicked the mule in both flanks, bellowed a wordless challenge, and fired his pistol again. The big mule jumped forward and collided with the horse that was blocking the trail. The smaller mare stumbled to the side, leaving the mule enough space to push past.

Levi heard a shot ring out right behind him. He twisted to look. The bushwacker dropped his shotgun and clutched his stomach. One more shot echoed through the trees. Levi hunched over his mule's neck, holding on as the animal pushed recklessly through brush and tree limbs. After a score of bounding leaps heedless of the danger, the mule encountered terrain too steep to keep its frantic pace, causing it to slow.

McBee's horse followed the mule that was breaking trail. When the mule reached a small clearing, McBee spurred up next to the pie-eyed beast. The captain grabbed the reins and brought the mule under a precarious control. Bell came up along the other side of the mule and patted its neck. After a few more steps, all three animals stopped.

Levi looked at the captain, his fearful countenance melting into a broad grin. Bell let out a whoop, causing McBee to look back up the hill, thinking the ambushers had followed them.

"Nah, don't worry, Captain. That was a victory yell," Bell near shouted. "We did it! Levi, you did it! You led us out of that trap!"

McBee knew they weren't yet safe, but he patted Levi's knee. "Private Bell's right, Levi. You were the point of our little sword, and you slashed your way through. Two, maybe three of the scoundrels went down. Well done." McBee offered a rare smile to his servant. "Now, let's find a way over this mountain before more of that pond scum come after us."

"Too late for that," a voice with a heavy Tennessee twang said as a line of seven riders stepped out of the trees ahead. Each man held a pistol, shotgun, or carbine leveled at McBee, Bell, and Levi.

"We ain't the same pond scum as them fellers you just shot up. Fact is, we've been dogging them, and you done us a favor if you kilt them all. All the same, I'd be obliged if all ya'll would drop your pistols. Even the nigger. I know he's got one too."

McBee looked towards the voice, about to make a suicidal decision to bring up the pistol that he still held and charge the line facing them. The man who spoke wore a green knitted scarf around his neck, but his coat was gray and faded yellow sergeant stripes adorned the sleeves.

Instead of spurring his horse forward, McBee called, "I've been in Tennessee and Virginia for over two years fighting Yankees and you're the only Confederates who've aimed firearms at me and my men."

"Your *men*?" the sergeant's sarcasm clear. "That boy there that ain't ever shaved, and a nigger?"

"No, not them, these boys are in my personal service. I mean Company C of the Fifth Texas Infantry. Longstreet's Corps. I'm Captain John McBee. And who are you, Sergeant?"

"I'm the sergeant whose men are still ready to pull the triggers of enough weapons to kill you, if you don't let your pistols fall to the ground right now. Because in about ten seconds, they'll be tossing dice over your coats and horseflesh, while I read whatever papers are in your pockets."

McBee sensed the sergeant would do just that, so he dropped his pistol, nodding for Bell and Levi to do the same. A corporal dismounted and gathered the three pistols, stuffing all of them in his saddlebag.

"You're welcome to read my furlough, the pass authorizing my travel into Kentucky," McBee said. "Sergeant, are we now captives of a band of army deserters and renegades, or are we guests under the protection of a squad of Confederate cavalry scouts?"

The sergeant guffawed at that. "Let's say you are the captives of Captain Ferguson's Partisan Rangers. It'll be Champ's decision if you get hung or get fed. You best hope he's in a good mood if you want to be a guest instead of crow bait."

Chapter 43

Near the Cumberland Gap
On the Tennessee – Kentucky Border
December 25, 1863

The severed head still dripped blood as the partisan ranger held it up by its sandy-colored, matted hair. Only one eye was open, and the black tongue filled the gap between two rows of tobacco-stained, yellow teeth.

"Got a rock in mind, Sergeant, or you want this one on a tree trunk spike?" asked the man holding the head.

Edward Bell recognized the gray face of the bushwacker she'd shot less than an hour before. She leaned sideways in her saddle and retched. Levi's jaw dropped and his eyes widened as he stared at the grotesque trophy. McBee squinted at the head, instantly revising his opinion of their captors.

"I reckon that flat rock over there will work just fine," the sergeant answered. "Did you fetch his hat? I hate to see a head out in the sun all day without a hat." The sergeant snorted at his own wit.

"Sure thing. Got it right here."

"How many dead back there, William?" the sergeant asked.

"Three, now. One was still thrashing around in the brush, gut shot."

The man in the green scarf nodded with approval. "Captain, you and your boys did all right. Champ will like the head count." Without further talk, he pointed, and his men filed onto the narrow trail.

"Why leave the head?" McBee asked the sergeant.

"Marking territory, naturally. Tends to keep the undesirables off our piece of the mountains. They ain't nuthin' but cowards and Unionists hiding from the draft. A head on a rock saves a lot of hanging."

"Ever consider painting a 'Keep Out' sign?" Bell asked.

The sergeant laughed again. "Now, that's funny. Imagine a sign out here in the wilderness. I'll be sure and tell Champ you asked that."

* * *

After several hours of riding on trails that seemed invisible to McBee, the group emerged into a clearing dotted with tents, brush arbors, and campfires. The sergeant told McBee to stay with him while the others dismounted and unsaddled their horses. Bell and Levi waited with their animals.

A clean-shaven, handsome man whose lined face was not young, but whose hair held no gray, lounged in a kitchen chair, watching the pair approach. Without introducing McBee and the man to each other, the sergeant described his encounter with the trio. When the sergeant finished, Captain McBee offered his furlough pass to the man who read the document, grunted, and dropped the paper on the ground.

"I'll need that paper back," McBee said, speaking for the first time since arriving in the camp.

"There it is, if you want it."

McBee stooped over to retrieve the paper, only to be kicked in the ribs by the seated man. The booted foot hit solidly, but without a great deal of force. As the blow landed, McBee grabbed the extended leg and fell forward, tumbling the seated man off his chair, landing on top of him. The captain from Texas delivered one punch to his opponent's jaw before the sergeant's pistol butt crashed onto his skull. McBee blacked out.

* * *

John McBee pulled his head up after the second slap on his cheek.

"It's too cold to douse you with water. Look at me." The clean-shaven man was squatting next to McBee. He reached out and pulled McBee to a sitting position. "Have a seat and we'll talk."

"Why didn't you offer a chair before you kicked me?" McBee pushed himself up to stand, gingerly touching the knot on his skull.

"Paper says you're a captain. I'm a captain. Had to show you that you ain't the senior captain here."

"I got that. You must be Champ Ferguson."

"*Captain* Champ Ferguson. And you say you are Captain McBee from Texas and General Longstreet's army. The problem for you is that we're a long ways from that army and a longer ways from Texas. Up here, it's just Champ's partisan rangers. Ain't no mighty General Longstreet or General Stuart with his flashy uniform. Now, sit down and tell me why you're on my mountain. Tell me why I shouldn't hang you and your boys. Or maybe I'll sell your nigger and just hang the two of you."

"I came for my wife."

"Your wife? You're going over the mountains after your wife? Maybe a runaway wife? Seems to be a plague of runaway wives in these parts. I got a cousin right over there by that fire whose wife is a runaway, too. He sent her on a scout dressed like a Yankee soldier and danged if she didn't turn on him. Decided she'd rather be a Yankee whore than a Tennessee Ferguson. I hear she's in a jail in Kentucky." Ferguson spat brown tobacco juice. "Women."

"My wife isn't a runaway. She's...a messenger. A messenger from Richmond sent to Kentucky."

"Your wife's a spy? An agent? What kind of man are you to let your woman do such a thing?"

McBee's neck and cheeks flushed at the insult. "She's a southern patriot, just like you and me."

"Patriotic southern women stay home and raise their sons to be soldiers," Ferguson replied. "Their patriotic husbands don't allow it no different."

"Didn't you just tell me your cousin's wife was a soldier in this outfit?"

"And she got caught, because a woman can't be passed off for a soldier. He shoulda kept her at home. Like you should have."

"I was gone with the army. I didn't know she did it. But that's not any of your business. When Bell, that boy over there, searched me out to tell me, I got that furlough to come fetch her home."

"You know where in Kentucky she went?" Ferguson asked, his curiosity growing.

"Middlesboro."

"Huh. That ain't far. Who's the message for, I wonder?"

"I don't know or care. I'm going to get my wife."

"Not unless I decide not to hang you, you ain't." Ferguson got up and walked to the fire and tossed another branch on it. Then he squatted and poked at the coals with a stick while he thought. After a minute he spoke.

"Tell you what, Captain McBee. You wouldn't sit still for a good thrashing. Got a mean left hook, too." Ferguson said rubbing his jaw. "I'll offer you a swap. I'll send a man into Middlesboro to nose around after Mrs. McBee. I got just the fellow. He was raised there. Knows everybody. If your wife's there, or been there, he'll find out."

McBee nodded. "I'd be grateful for such assistance."

"And while we wait on him, you and your boy go with me on a little raid up into Kentucky. There's a good-size train trestle not far north of Middlesboro that I been meaning to tend to. Now seems a good time."

"Fair enough. But we all three go. The darkie, too. He'll fight." The Texas captain looked hard at the partisan captain.

"Why not? Maybe I'll send the nigger out to scout the bridge. Won't even have to rub mud on his face."

"No. Levi's no Comanche. If you want one of my men to slither up close to the Yank sentries, young Bell goes. He's a natural at deception."

"We'll see, Captain. We'll see," Ferguson said.

"One more thing. It's important. My wife is traveling under a different name. It's Samuelson. Mrs. Adam Samuelson."

"A Jew? You married a Jew?" Ferguson sneered. "You sure you want her back?"

"Let it go, Captain. It's just a name," McBee said.

Ferguson spat again. "Wives."

Chapter 44

The Jail
Middlesboro, Tennessee
December 26, 1863

Faith sat in the cane-back chair, knees and ankles together, hands clasped in her lap. She'd been left alone in the jail's windowless storeroom for over an hour, but wasn't restrained. An oil lamp burned on a small table, providing dim light and a wisp of heat. The room was otherwise empty except for a single matching chair that faced hers.

Faith's bare feet were warmer on the wood plank floor than they had been in the jail cell, but she was still cold. Twice she stood and struggled to wrap the sheet around her more efficiently, trying to cover her bare shoulder without losing the protection somewhere else. She combed at her hair with her fingers and found a splinter on the floor to clean her fingernails. In a whisper she rehearsed the things she planned to say. Finally, she simply sat still and waited.

The Union major who came in stopped in front of the empty chair to look down at Faith.

"I'm here to listen to your explanation of why you came over the Cumberland Gap from Virginia. I've read Lieutenant Knudsen's report of your interview with him. I know that you wove together truth and lies to create a story that would seem plausible to him. But Lieutenant Knudsen is young and inexperienced. He was also most likely drawn to your attractive features. But Lieutenant Knudsen is no longer involved. Your fate rests with me. And you may be assured, I am not young, not inexperienced, and I am not smitten with your charm. You may begin."

Faith thought to herself, *Oh, but you are smitten with me. Otherwise, you wouldn't stand there and make a little speech about yourself before you even sit down.* She remained silent.

The officer had no notes or paper with him. He sat down, crossed one knee over the other, and repeated, "I said, you may begin."

Faith studied his face for a few seconds. His bald head and untrimmed gray fringe of hair gave him the look of a clerk, except for his dark eyes, which struck her as dead pieces of coal. She found she couldn't match his unblinking stare, so she looked towards the lamp.

"I came to Kentucky to find my husband…"

"Stop. Before you continue, I will tell you that your husband, that is, your *legal* husband, Lieutenant Adam Samuelson, works for me."

Faith swallowed and involuntarily shivered when she heard those words.

"If you are cold, I suggest you now tell me the true reason for your journey so you can return to the warmth of your blanket." The major didn't smile.

"Oh, so you know Adam. Can you tell me where he is?" Faith asked, gathering her confidence. "Because I came to find him…"

"Stop. That's two. At three lies I end an interrogation. Lie to me again and I'll have your cover removed and leave you alone in this room until tomorrow morning. You will have noticed that there is no stove, and without even a sheet, you will suffer through the night."

"You're bluffing, whoever you are," Faith impulsively blurted out.

The major stood, picked up the lamp and left the room. Within seconds, two burly soldiers came in, a lantern in the hallway providing the only illumination in the nearly dark room. One man unceremoniously grabbed Faith's hands and jerked her out of her chair, holding her while the other man pulled the sheet away. The two soldiers examined her for a few seconds, grinning at her nakedness, then left the room.

* * *

When the major returned the next morning, he found Faith Samuelson McBee curled in a corner, shivering, teeth chattering, and coughing uncontrollably. The major set a lamp on the table, walked to Faith and dropped a scratchy blanket on top of her. Without a word he went to his chair and sat down. Faith tucked the blanket around her and didn't move further.

"In one minute, the jailers will come in and remove the blanket. Then they'll tie you to the chair so we might continue your interrogation. Or you may walk to your chair right now and speak to me, with the blanket warming you and hiding your private parts. Choose. Tick tock."

Faith took her seat in the cane-backed chair.

"I need water. My throat is parched."

"After you tell me why you came over the Cumberland Gap."

"To find my husband," Faith answered as she coughed.

"That's your first lie of the day, and we've hardly begun. Moreover, you wasted it by repeating a lie you told me yesterday. I thought you were brighter than that." The major offered his first smile. "Consider that pneumonia is not a pleasant way to die."

"Why did you come over the Cumberland Gap?" the man repeated, his arms crossed over his chest.

"All right! I was sent to deliver a message."

"Better. Who sent you?"

"A man from Richmond. I don't know his name."

"That's two. You and I both know his name."

Faith looked into her interrogator's black eyes. "If you know his name, you tell me what it is, so I'll know too." She coughed violently.

"I must hear the word from you."

"So...you don't know. Well, neither do I. And leaving me to die coughing and naked in the cold won't change that," Faith said with quiet intensity.

"You should be on the stage, Mrs. Samuelson. You have mastered the art of credibly projecting false emotions."

"What do you really want from me? You seem to know everything already. Are you just here to wallow in my degradation?"

"I am here to hear you speak one word. A name."

"Why? If you know, why do I have to guess?"

"Because I want confirmation. There is only one man from Richmond who would send you to Kentucky. He was a houseguest where you've found refuge since you fled from your husband."

"Judah Benjamin? You're talking about Secretary Benjamin?"

"Quite so."

"He's the Secretary of State."

"Of the rebelling states. Yes, he calls himself that."

"He must have a building full of couriers and messengers. Why would he send me?"

"Because of me, Benjamin suddenly needed someone not connected to his Richmond office to deliver an important message."

"Why would Benjamin care about you? One more major in the vast Yankee army."

"Ah, that's better. Wit under duress. As an example of cooperation, I'll answer. Because after your husband's two failed attempts on his life, Benjamin finally deduced that I exist, and that I have eyes and ears in his office. Next question: Who in Middlesboro was to receive your note?"

"What note?"

"This note," the major pulled a two-inch-long carefully rolled paper from his pocket and held it for Faith to see.

"I've never seen that paper."

"Truth or fib? It doesn't matter this time, so your answer won't count toward your tally of lies for today. This paper was cleverly sewn into a seam of one of the petticoats you threw at Lieutenant Knudsen."

"It probably has the name of a French seamstress printed on it," Faith suggested. "I bought those petticoats before the war. They were imported from Paris."

"Don't insult my intelligence, Mrs. Samuelson. Clothing manufacturers don't hide their names inside seams. But, Paris was a good diversion. Unfortunately for you, the waist bands are stamped with the name of a garment factory in New York. You should have looked more closely. That's two. With your next, shall we say, fabrication, our session ends and you lose your blanket."

Faith pulled her cover more tightly around her and waited for the next question.

"Again, and for the last time, who was to receive this note?"

"I don't know a name, or even if it's a man or woman."

"What *do* you know?"

"A place."

"Very good. Let me think. Ah, of course. Dirty undergarments in a town where you are a stranger. The hotel laundry service?" the major said with raised eyebrows.

"No."

Suddenly turning grim, the major said, "Enough then. No more chit-chat. What is the place?"

Faith was silent for long seconds while the major glared at her.

"What happens to me if I tell you? Will you release me? Send me home? Maybe ship me off to my *legal* husband? Will anything be any different than if I say nothing?"

"A reasonable query. You're not stupid. But I'm not here to horse-trade with you. When you tell me the place, I'll send men to arrest whoever is there. Your future will depend on my success."

"So my life depends on your good will."

"Mrs. Samuelson, treason and espionage during a war are crimes for which people, including women, are executed. Hanging, usually. Very efficient."

"Are you trying to terrify me into betraying my country?"

"Madame, you did that when you joined the rebellion. I'll be explicit: If you choose to keep the location of your contact to yourself, I won't hurt you. I will, however, draft documents to prosecute you as a spy who has refused to divulge critical information. The likely outcome of your trial will be your death on the gallows. For a final time, tick tock. You have only a few seconds to speak."

"Tomorrow. Send me back to my cell now. I need time to think, time to weigh whether my loyalty to the Confederacy is worth my life, worth my child becoming an orphan." Faith could feel tears welling in her eyes. The major did not change his expression or move a muscle.

"If you insist on my speaking now, my predilection to stubbornness, to defiance, will seal my fate, and ruin your hunt. That's not what you want. I will answer you tomorrow, probably give you the answer you want, but tomorrow morning. I cannot do so now. I can't think clearly when I'm freezing, starving, thirsty, and need a chamber pot." Faith clamped her jaw and tilted her chin up ever so slightly.

The major sat motionless for a full minute, his dark eyes never leaving his captive's face, before suddenly standing and leaving the room. The two guards came in and dragged Faith, wrapped in her blanket, back to the cell she shared with Jane Ferguson.

Chapter 45

North of Middlesboro, Kentucky
December 27, 1863

L evi had never been so cold from the waist up. His bottom wasn't so bad because the heat of the mule's back seeped through the saddle leather and his trousers. He fervently wished they were still back in the raiders' camp on the mountainside, huddled next to a fire, not riding through a snow storm. His coat wasn't near as thick as the caped military great coats which Captain McBee and most of the partisan rangers had, mostly taken off the corpses of Union soldiers.

Levi wore a woolen civilian coat, its shoulders white with a coating of snow, but Levi was also without a vest. He did have knitted mittens on his hands and a ratty gray scarf covering his ears, but he was still miserably cold. Bell was better off, wearing a wool shirt, vest, coat, and leather gloves. She kept her wool blanket draped over her head and shoulders as protection against the snow.

Snowflakes stuck to McBee's beard. His thoughts returned to the miserable march of the Division's stragglers he'd led at the beginning of the year, a duty assigned him directly by General Hood. If his lips weren't nearly frozen into a grimace, he'd have laughed at the contrast between that day and this one.

He'd started the year 1863 by leading a thousand or more infantrymen on an improbable winter march through weather like this day's snow. From dawn to after dusk, he'd pushed reluctant, suffering men to persevere longer and go farther than anyone thought possible. Today, he and his two servants were ending the year as virtual captives of a brutal guerrilla leader, an unstable man whose forty partisan rangers killed men in their beds and decapitated their vanquished foes.

Champ Ferguson knew his column was close to the point where they would leave the horses and go on foot, and it would be dark soon. He halted his mount to let his men pass by in a slow single file on the snow-covered trail. When McBee came close, Ferguson motioned for him to stop.

"I'm sending you and your pair up with my scouts to kill the sentries. Shouldn't be more than two or three of 'em. Your darkie and the boy have killing knives?"

Captain McBee gritted his teeth. "Yeah, they both carry belt knives. For cooking, not slicing the throats of half-frozen sentries."

Ferguson grinned. "How about you, Captain? You ever slit any Yankee throats?"

"No, I command soldiers who stand and fight. Their rifles do my killing."

Ferguson chuckled. "Well, that's honorable, Captain. But tonight you'll use a knife. Got one?"

"Just a pocket Barlow."

"Here, use mine." Ferguson held out the hilt of a dark-bladed sheaf knife.

"We'll need our pistols, too."

"Nah. No pistols yet. It's knives tonight."

"You're testing us, huh?" McBee replied.

"I got to know how far you'll go to save your wife. If we find her, they ain't gonna give her back just because you ask. There'll be killing, and we won't be standing in a straight line waiting for you to holler 'Fire!'"

McBee ignored the rebuke.

"Are we going after both ends of the bridge? You got kegs of powder? I've not seen any pack mules."

"Yup, both ends of the bridge. But no powder kegs," Ferguson confirmed. "We're going to capture the cannons that're aimed to protect the bridge from raiders like us. Come daylight, we're going to turn those cannons around and knock down the bridge with the Yankees' own artillery."

"That could take an hour or more," McBee commented with skepticism. "A bridge trestle is mostly air. Hard to hit a framework of timbers with a cannon ball. By the time the bridge collapses you may be fending off a whole regiment of Yankee infantry."

Ferguson looked sideways at McBee, tilting his head in thought as McBee outlined his idea.

"Why not empty the caissons of the black powder charges for the solid balls and pile them at the base of the girders and set them off. Stack the exploding shrapnel shells right next to the powder. Make one big explosion without warning instead of taking the time and the risk to shoot the cannons several times each."

Ferguson considered McBee's plan, looking for holes in it.

"How would you get the powder to explode? You going to hold a lucifer to them? Not even my men would do that."

"I told you my riflemen are my weapon. Young Bell will put a Minié ball into the pile of powder. He can shoot. You got a reliable Enfield or Springfield?"

"Nah, my boys carry shotguns and carbines, but the Yanks will. We'll have a bundle of them after we take down the guards." Ferguson took off his hat and brushed his hair back.

"All right. We'll do it your way," the partisan leader said, grudgingly acknowledging the advantages of McBee's plan. "But a couple of my men were squirrel hunters. They'll help your boy with the shooting."

"And you should know," Ferguson continued, "my man came back from Middlesboro. There're two women prisoners in the jail the army took over from the sheriff. And a Yankee major's been questioning both of them."

"Names?"

"He couldn't get the names. His aunt's been cooking for the guards and she heard them talking about what a waste of good horse flesh one of 'em was. That ain't my cousin's wife. She's homely. Built like a board. She ain't a mare any man would want to ride. You reckon they's talking about your wife?"

"Could be," McBee answered bitterly. "If she's been violated, I'll kill them all."

"Now that there is something a partisan would say. And do," Ferguson said with a mirthless grin. "What say we go blow up a bridge now. Then we'll visit the jail in Middlesboro. I'm countin' on a big explosion to draw the soldiers out of town before we get there."

* * *

The partisan scout snaked his way back to the others, the snow muting the sounds of his movement.

"Five sentries. Just one artillery piece aimed straight up the track away from the bridge. They're standing and facing out like they're supposed to. The one on the left looks to be nodding off. I couldn't see where the corporal of the guard and the reserves are. They ain't sitting around a camp fire."

"They'll be back a ways," Ferguson whispered.

An hour later the second scout gave much the same information about the Yankee guard post at the far end of the bridge.

"That's more sentries than I counted on. Change of plan. We all go in together. We'll swarm the guard detail at the south end of the bridge. Leave the other end be. Knives only. The snow fall oughta muffle whatever noise we make taking out the five sentries. Then we'll rush the reserve before they know we're there. Might get lucky enough to catch'em rolled up in their blankets. Let some colonel attack the redoubt tomorrow and find a row of bled-out bodies already wrapped in their shrouds." Ferguson didn't see McBee scowl.

Before Dawn
December 28, 1863

"Capt'n, I don't know if I can knife a sleeping man," Levi whispered as they paused to let the last of Ferguson's men to crawl into position. "I don't know if I can put a knife in any man."

"Just stay close behind me. Remember you still have my back. Can't say I trust Ferguson or his men," McBee warned in a soft voice. "They might stab us yet for our animals or our firearms,"

"Nah, I ain't gonna have you stabbed," Ferguson whispered from his spot just a few feet away. "I want to see you kill all them Yankee guards what been violating your woman."

The sergeant, crawling on hands and knees, approached to tell his captain that the men were all ready. Ferguson nodded and waved his arm, the line of dim silhouettes rising and gliding through the falling snow, crouched over, every man carrying a long bladed knife.

Silent, snow-covered phantoms appeared out of the dark, giving the five Union sentries no time to react to the slashing blades. Behind the fallen pickets, the ready reserves huddled in pairs under low-slung tarps or sat against tree trunks draped by their rubberized blankets. A few men awoke in time to futilely raise an arm or kick a leg out against the sudden shapes looming over them. A few men shouted, but none fired their muskets, having depended on the sentries for a few seconds of warning that never came.

Work parties immediately removed from the wheeled caisson every shell and powder charge for the single cannon that guarded the south approach to the bridge. The sergeant led the detail down the precipitous slope to the bottom of the cut where a half-frozen stream gurgled.

McBee, Bell, and Levi picked up two Springfield muskets each and laboriously unbuckled and pulled cap and cartridge boxes from three of the fresh corpses. The trio followed the partisans to the base of the bridge, where McBee and Levi passed off the Springfield muskets to a pair of partisans. McBee pulled out his dirty handkerchief and draped it over the pile of loose powder, weighting it down on the corners with rocks.

Sun rays lit the top of the ridge, but the creek bottom and bridge girders were still in dark shadows when Ferguson's two best marksmen joined Edward Bell. The trio formed a short firing line on the trail a hundred yards downstream from the bridge. The rest of the raiding party waited on their mounts behind the three riflemen.

278

"Now! The handkerchief is your target. Shoot, dammit!" Ferguson growled.

The three soldiers fired. Nothing happened.

"Again! Quickly!" Ferguson shouted as each of the three men picked up his second loaded musket.

The two rangers fired immediately, the bark of the muskets echoing down the canyon. No explosion.

"You sorry shits for soldiers!" Ferguson yelled. "Reload!"

Bell glanced over her shoulder at the frantic partisan commander. She spit on her finger and wet the musket barrel's front sight with a drop of saliva. Without pausing, she lifted the Springfield, cocking it as the butt came to rest against her shoulder. Within a second she aligned the tiny white splotch of the handkerchief with the glistening dot of the front sight, and settled both deeply into the V of the rear sight. Slowly letting out her breath, Bell gently squeezed the trigger.

The Minié ball struck the edge of the loose powder, setting off a ball of red fire and yellow flames that radiated outward. A fraction of a second later the stacked shrapnel shells exploded in a roar that dwarfed the sound of the exploding loose powder. The thick wood beams nearest the powder and shells disintegrated instantly, starting a cascade of falling trestle timbers that spread up and across the whole framework of timbers.

The twin steel ribbons of train rails on top of the bridge hung together, swaying for several seconds, until one after another, the heavy wooden cross ties tore loose from their binding iron spikes and crashed downward. Lastly, the rails dipped and separated from each other, dropping like giant spears hurled by a god, as smoke, dust, and incredible noise engulfed the whole valley.

Champ Ferguson's company of partisan rangers watched the demise of the bridge in awe before they began whooping and yelling in triumph. In high spirits, they kicked their horses along the trail away from the collapsed bridge, hurrying towards the jail in Middlesboro.

Chapter 46

The Jail
Middlesboro, Kentucky
December 28, 1863

Major Francis made a habit of rising before dawn to read the telegrams that arrived during the night. He held the stack of papers that had been left in the outer office, thinking they would require two hours of reading and note-taking. Francis knew his effectiveness as the army's head intelligence officer in Kentucky and West Virginia came from his diligence in daily studying every scrap of information. Therefore, as he did every day, he set to work, intent on giving due consideration to each name and activity mentioned in every telegram from his network of border-watchers and spies all around the state.

Today, however, to his disgust, Francis' mind kept wandering to the sharp memory of the naked dark-haired woman huddled on the floor. He reluctantly conceded his attraction to her alternating displays of fear and defiance. Certainly her features were comely, but watching her internal struggle to fight or give most appealed to him. Even as Francis chastised himself for being drawn to the young woman, after less than an hour of reading, he ordered her taken to the inner room where he'd questioned her yesterday. He'd let her sit alone in the cold room for another hour while he finished reading the telegrams.

A far-off crash of thunder interrupted the major's concentration on the telegrams. He was surprised by the sound, as the air felt too cold for rain. In fact, his last glance out a window the previous day had revealed snowfall. He fleetingly thought perhaps snow had caused an avalanche on one of the mountains north of Middlesboro, but he shrugged off further speculation. Weather didn't interest him.

* * *

Faith shivered in the same chair as before, waiting, wrapped in a rough blanket as before. This time, she did not rehearse answers. This time, she had no intention of obfuscating the facts and misleading the major. Her third miserable winter night in the jail, coughing and clothed only in a blanket, had convinced Faith to tell all. Overnight she'd realized the major would not release her, whatever she told him. She was going to spend the rest of the war in a prison. Her only hope to see John her husband and John her son was to cooperate with the major, to pray for leniency. She would even beg for leniency if necessary.

Major Francis stood in the open door and studied his prisoner's unmoving form. Yesterday her long hair had been merely unkempt, today it was wild and bedraggled. Her grimy feet had a bluish tinge to them, and she rested her left foot on her right, to keep one off the cold floor. Blinking away any further waste of time enjoying the prisoner's telltale signs of internment, Francis walked to his chair and looked down at the dark sunken eyes of the woman. No sooner had he sat than she began to speak.

"My instructions from Secretary Benjamin were to take the petticoats for cleaning to the Harmony Laundry sometime this week."

Major Francis crossed his legs, entwined his fingers together and laid them across his stomach.

"Go on." He pushed aside a fleeting regret that she had not chosen silence, which would have provided him cause to strip her blanket away again.

"I'm to ask the clerk if…"

They heard the booming sound of gunfire from somewhere in the building.

* * *

The bridge explosion had reverberated through the freezing night air, waking up civilians and soldiers for miles around. Speed replaced stealth as the raiding party rode hard down the main road towards the town, intent on reaching the jail and overpowering the guard detail. The forty-four riders galloped into Middlesboro, weapons at the ready.

Captain Ferguson led them directly to the jail, leaving half his troops at the front and sending others to the rear door of the building. Two of Ferguson's men burst through the front door as fast as they could dismount their horses. The first partisan blindly fired both barrels of a shotgun as he crossed the threshold, killing one Union soldier before he was shot dead by another guard. The second raider held two revolvers, which he discharged as quickly as he could, his ten rapid-fire shots taking down two more guards. Then he too was cut down by a fourth guard who fired from the doorway to the hall that led to the cells. Eight more Confederate raiders piled into the front room and rushed the guard in the doorway, easily overwhelming him and pinning him down.

Captains Ferguson and McBee came in and quickly surveyed the scene. Ferguson walked to the captured guard, pulled his belt knife and sliced off one of the man's ears. The guard screamed, his head held down, blood running down his jaw from the raw wound.

"Tell me about the prisoners," Ferguson ordered him, holding up the man's bloody ear lobe.

"Two thieves in one cell, two women in another. Aaah, God, that hurts!"

"Who else is back there?"

"A major from Frankfort. Came to question the women."

McBee pushed by the others, followed by Bell and Levi, all three holding pistols at the ready. They went through the next door into the hall facing the barred cells. John McBee looked at the figure sitting on a bunk in the first cell. It wasn't Faith. He rushed to the next cell to find two men standing by the door, watching him with hope in their eyes. He

282

ignored them. The third and last cell was empty. The Texas captain returned to the hall, saw two rangers standing in the open back door. Near the end of the hall, Ferguson was going through the only other interior door.

* * *

As soon as he heard the gunfire, Francis stood and jerked the blanket off his prisoner as he pulled her up. He grabbed her long hair, pulling her head up as he turned her to face the door. When Ferguson pushed the door open, the Union major was standing behind the naked woman, his pocket pistol cocked and aimed.

His first shot hit Captain Ferguson in his right forearm, causing the partisan leader to drop his pistol and jump back into the hall.

John McBee shoved Ferguson aside and burst through the door. Faith swung her arm, knocking Francis' wrist up, sending his second shot into the ceiling. Edward Bell and Levi crowded through the door right behind McBee, guns ready.

The sight of Faith, nude and filthy, a bald man with dark sunken eyes holding her hair, affected the intruders as Francis had hoped. For a brief instant John McBee paused in disbelief, even as he held his cocked pistol pointed at Faith's captor. Bell and Levi froze, Levi's eyes glued to the sight of the first nude woman he'd ever seen.

Francis jerked his arm back to hold the pistol against the woman's temple.

"Stand aside. The woman and I are leaving. I'll need a horse."

"No. You leave this room, the men in the hall, Champ Ferguson's men, will shoot you dead. And in all that gunfire, my wife will get shot, too. Or worse for you, they'll take you prisoner, cut off your ears, then your head, and put it on a stake in the street. Your only hope of staying alive is to surrender to me."

"Then what?" Major Francis asked.

"Then I do what honor demands of me," Captain McBee replied.

"I'll expect a parole."

"I'll deliver you to Richmond."

Major Francis thought quickly if there was any better hope for him. There wasn't. And it was long way to Richmond. He nodded, set his pistol on the table, and released his grip on Faith's hair.

Without hesitation, instead of reaching down for the blanket, Faith McBee, still naked, picked up the pistol, cocked it, and shot Major Francis in the thigh. Twice. As the Union officer collapsed, Faith's husband rushed to her, his embrace lifting her feet off the floor. Faith held onto the pistol.

Levi's feet wouldn't move until Bell hit the back of his head. "Get the blanket, you dumb ass. Cover Mrs. McBee."

Levi jumped forward, scooped up the blanket and draped it over the nude woman's shoulders while she was still wrapped in her husband's arms. John released her just enough to pull the blanket snugly around her.

"Oh, Miss Faith," Levi said, "We done crossed mountains to find you. Don't you go running off again. The capt'n gets all out of sorts when you do such things."

Tears forming, Faith looked at Levi, Bell, and her husband. "Levi, I promise I won't. Ever."

"Faith, let me have the Yankee's revolver," McBee gently ordered as he let go of his wife.

"Oh no. This pistol's mine now. By God, I've earned it. I'm not letting go of it until this war's over. And maybe not then."

Edward Bell crossed the few feet to where Major Francis writhed on the floor, groaning, trying to staunch the bleeding from the two holes in his leg. Bell kicked him hard in the groin before she knelt next to the officer and wrapped her own scarf around the major's wounded leg.

Ferguson's sergeant came in, looked down at the captured major, grinned an evil grin, and left the room.

Faith held the blanket tightly. "John, I need clothes. That man cut mine to ribbons. And there's another woman here. In the cell. She's Captain Ferguson's kin."

"Private Bell, please escort Faith to where the other woman is, and find her some clothes and shoes. Quickly, if you will. Time is short." McBee reluctantly shifted his attention from his wife back to the dilemma his prisoner now presented.

"Levi, get the major up. We're taking him with us."

"No, you ain't taking him anywhere, but maybe a hanging tree, after I cut on him some," Champ Ferguson said from the doorway, holding his bandaged arm.

"Captain, we can argue, and even fight over this piece of mule dung, but before long this jail will be surrounded by Union infantry out to settle accounts for the bloodbath you left behind at the bridge. It's time to go."

"You're a smart one, I'll give you that. Always thinking. All right, we'll take him and go." Ferguson ordered his men out of the jail and onto their horses.

Jane Ferguson soon delivered to Faith the only clothing available in the building: the uniform trousers, shirt, jacket, socks, shoes, and hat from the smallest of the guards slain in the front room. Faith kept the wool blanket to use as a cape.

Chapter 47

Middlesboro, Kentucky
December 28, 1863

Lieutenant Knudsen watched the long column of cavalrymen approach at the gallop. He saluted the colonel who reined in his horse in front of the jail.

"Report, Lieutenant," the colonel ordered.

"Four dead troopers inside, Sir. Two men prisoners still in their cells, two women prisoners missing. As is Major Francis."

"And nearly two dozen dead soldiers with their throats slashed at the south end of a bridge that's been blown to bits," the colonel added. "At least no train was on the bridge when they blew it up. Who's Major Francis? Is he with the infantry garrison here?"

"No, Sir. He's in the…a different department. He came down from Frankfort to question two women suspected of spying for the Rebs."

"The two missing prisoners, I gather. They must be important. The trip from Frankfort to here isn't easy."

"Yes, Sir."

"Is Major Francis your superior? Are you a member of his staff?"

"Yes, Sir. I control border crossing at the Cumberland Gap post. I report to Major Francis."

"Would you recognize the two women, Lieutenant? Have you ever seen them?"

Knudsen involuntarily blushed at a vivid memory of Mrs. Samuelson undressing. "Yes, Sir."

"Then you go with Captain Fox in pursuit of the damned partisans who did this. Bring the women back. Can't have spies in skirts operating all over southern Kentucky."

"Yes, Sir, my horse is saddled."

* * *

Four hours after he had led his band out of Middlesboro, Champ Ferguson watched his troopers pass by until he was next to the sergeant at the back of the group. Ferguson spoke quietly to him, then kicked his mount into a trot and returned to the front. Jane Ferguson, riding in the middle of the pack, noted the captain's special effort to give orders to the sergeant, unheard by others.

An hour later, Ferguson halted the men in a clearing halfway up a ridge, motioning for Captain McBee to join him.

"I'm going to set up an ambush for the Yanks that'll be on our tail. I'm sending the sergeant and his scouts to take you and the prisoner over the top back into Tennessee. We'll join you in camp after we see off them fellas who'll be chasing us."

McBee said nothing but gave a casual salute to Ferguson, relieved that his party wasn't expected to take part in the ambush. The sergeant wearing the green scarf rode forward and sent three men ahead, then with three more riders, fell in behind McBee, the two rescued women, the Yankee prisoner whose hands were tied, and McBee's black and white servants.

After Captain Ferguson left with the larger group to return to his chosen ambush site, the smaller group resumed their trek up the switchbacks, climbing the ridge. Jane Ferguson worked her horse forward until she was right behind Captain McBee, as close as she could get on the narrow snow-covered trail.

"Captain, don't turn around to look back. Can you hear me?" Jane asked in a low voice.

"Yes, I hear you. What is it?"

"The sergeant's got orders to kill all of you. Champ don't like other men disagreeing with him like you did back at the jail. And he wants to kill the Yankee major. "

"How do you know that?"

"I saw him whispering to the sergeant right before we split up. My husband's Champ's cousin. I been around him for years, I know how he thinks. Those three men up ahead will come back soon enough. Nearer to the top there's a little glade. The sergeant and the men behind us will spread out. Then all seven of 'em will open fire without sayin' nothin'."

"Ma'am, why are you warning me?"

"I reckon I like your wife's spunk. And that you come over the mountains to fetch her home. My man didn't do that for me. Champ was surprised to find me back in Middlesboro."

"Three guns to their seven, with women and a prisoner. Not good," McBee said.

"They won't shoot me. Champ wants the glory of bringing his cousin's runaway wife back to him. But you best do something before they do, or you'll be buzzard meat before dark."

"Right." At the next sharp turn in the trail, McBee pulled up his horse and called loudly for Levi and Bell to turn around and follow him. When the sergeant's horse was within two yards, McBee spoke to him.

"Sergeant, I've been thinking. I owe Champ for leading me to that jail to find my wife. I'm worried about him. The Yanks are most likely chasing us with at least a full company of cavalry. I'm taking my boys back to help him. Why don't you come with us? We'll add seven guns to the ambush. The women and the prisoner should be safe enough with your three scouts until we get back."

"Can't do that, Captain. Neither can you. A man who don't follow Champ's orders don't live too long."

"Sergeant, you don't give me orders. Me and my men are going back to add our guns to Champ's ambush." McBee nudged his horse to take a step forward. The sergeant didn't say anything, but started pulling his pistol out of its holster.

McBee raised his voice to a near shout, "Besides that, we don't have a gold coin among us."

"What the hell do I care if…" the sergeant said as he lifted his revolver.

He didn't finish because Captain McBee shot him in the face.

Hearing the code phrase, Edward Bell already had pistol in hand. She squeezed her horse past the captain's mount and the fallen sergeant. Pushing by the sergeant's wild-eyed horse, she fired a round into the chest of the next partisan in line while the trooper was still scrambling for his revolver.

McBee kicked his mount to make two lunges uphill off the trail before he jerked the reins hard to the side causing the horse to plunge down at the two remaining riders at the end of the line. Both had weapons ready.

The lead man discharged his shotgun into the chest of McBee's horse. The animal's inertia carried its falling weight into the shooter's horse. McBee pulled his feet free of the stirrups and fell onto the rider while the man pulled back the hammer to fire the shotgun's second barrel. McBee discharged his pistol an inch from the soldier's neck, severing the raider's spine. The dead man's finger reflexively jerked against the trigger, firing the shotgun over McBee's head. The remaining partisan also shot at McBee, grazing his back.

Seeing no room for his mule, Levi leapt off and pushed by the horses down trail from him, pistol cocked and arm extended. He saw his captain come crashing out of the trees into the soldier's horse and the exchange of gunfire.

Levi took a final step and fired two quick rounds at the last rider. The first bullet missed. On the second shot, the partisan's nose disappeared into a spurt of blood, right before he slumped and slid off his horse.

McBee's back seeped blood through his two coats. He ignored the burning pain while he mounted the dead sergeant's horse. Bell and Levi collected the pistols of the fallen partisans, giving each of them a second weapon. Major Francis had disappeared during the shooting, Faith taking one hasty shot at him as he kicked his horse into the trees.

Bell patted Levi's back. "Levi, I believe we've become McBee's Mountain Warriors. You were downright fierce just now."

Levi nodded. "You too, Mr. Edward, you too."

Captain McBee looked to his wife.

"John, the Yankee major rode off and I couldn't stop him."

"Don't worry. He's a long way from safety, has no weapon, and his hands are tied."

McBee next approached Jane Ferguson. "Thank you for the warning. I'm sorry I couldn't think of a way to extricate us without killing those men."

"Don't give that a thought, Captain. They were all murderers."

"Well, I still regret it. Fact is, I do owe Champ for freeing Faith. Just the three of us couldn't have done it. Look, I don't want to fight his three scouts who're ahead up the ridge. Do you know some other trail we can take to get over the top?"

"There's a river canyon we've used. North of here, but before the main gap trail. It's slick with ice in weather this cold, and going over the crest beyond where the river starts will be tough. I might can find it if we stay heading north and downhill across the ridge. There won't be a trail from here, though."

"Does that mean you're going with us? Not back to your husband?"

"After you killed the sergeant and his men, Champ wouldn't leave me alive. I've got a sister in Virginia who'll take me in, so I'll lead you up the river canyon and over the top out of Kentucky."

"Then let's go, You lead." McBee called for Bell to follow Mrs. Ferguson. "Faith, you stay in the middle. Levi behind Faith. I'll stay in the back."

Chapter 48

Cumberland Mountains
Southeast Kentucky
December 28, 1863

The fir trees threw long shadows across the swiftly flowing river. Suddenly the whole canyon was engulfed in darkness as the ridgeline swallowed the last bit of the sun. The roar of the narrow river rapids made it impossible to hear.

Jane Ferguson looked back expectantly at Captain McBee, wordlessly seeking his permission to stop in the deepening gloom. When he waved his arm downward, motioning for her to dismount, she gratefully did so.

"We'll wait until dawn to go through the canyon." McBee stiffly slid off his horse and offered Faith outstretched arms to help her to the ground.

"John, I need a fire," Faith said, visibly shivering as she tugged her blanket tight.

"My love, we can't. Too many eyes are searching for us. The mountainsides are so steep, it's impossible to hide a flame. You'll have to settle for sharing a blanket with me tonight. When it's not my watch, that is."

Captain McBee insisted two of them keep watch together in shifts. One sentry stayed next to the still-saddled horses, the other across camp, closer to the river. While the captain and Jane Ferguson took the first watch, Faith and Private Bell lay down on their sides huddled together with a blanket under them and two over them. Levi wrapped himself in his own blanket and settled in a foot away from Private Bell.

After an hour, Faith softly snored, with her arm thrown over Bell's hip, pressing against her back from head to toe. Edward awoke when Levi's shoe heel moved a rock that clicked against another stone. Bell could see Levi's dark shivering form and thought she could even hear his teeth chattering.

Bell extended her arm and touched Levi's back. He jerked and sat up, looking wildly around.

Bell whispered, "You're freezing to death. Scoot this way. Get next to me. We'll both be warmer."

"Ain't nothin' warm about me, Mister Bell."

"Then shift over here. Come on."

Levi scooted, until he was close enough for Bell to throw her arm over him. She tugged him another half-foot, until she was close enough to put the front of her knees against the back of Levi's. Pressed next to Levi's back, she almost instantly felt his body warmth, and within a minute or two Levi stopped shivering, her warmth reaching his back.

Faith continued to snore, so Bell took a chance and whispered, "What did you think?"

Levi didn't respond.

Bell nudged him with knees. "I know you're awake. What did you think?"

"'Bout what?" Levi hoarsely whispered.

"You know darn well, about what." Bell paused until she heard another snore behind her.

"About seeing Miss Faith without clothes on." Bell nudged Levi again.

"I can't talk about that."

"I thought your eyes were going to pop out of your skull. You never seen a naked woman before today?"

"No."

"Want to again?"

"Stop it, Mister Bell. I got to sleep. Black men get hung for seeing less than I seen today."

"Levi, don't you know that I'm not a man."

"I know you is a boy, not yet a whole grown man. But you're a good hand anyhow."

Bell waited again for Faith to snore.

"Levi, without clothes, I look like Miss Faith, not like you."

Levi snorted. "Nah, you don't. Miss Faith has, has…"

"Bosoms. So do I, just not so, uh, so apple-like as Miss Faith's."

Levi twisted onto his back and started to sit up, turning his head to look at Bell.

Bell held him in place with her arm. "Stay put, Levi. You're my front warmer. I'm not going to hurt you."

Faith's snoring abruptly ended. "A rock's digging into my side. Turn over with me so we won't lose the blankets." They all three rolled over. Within seconds Faith's snores resumed. Bell fell asleep snugly sandwiched between Faith's back and Levi's front. She woke once and groggily noted something firm pressing against her bottom, noticeable even through her trousers. She smiled contentedly and dropped back into a secure sleep.

After four hours, the captain shook Bell and Levi. Without speaking, they stood their watch until the first glow of predawn.

December 29, 1863

As soon as Captain McBee could count five fingers at the end of his outstretched arm, the party resumed their slow and deliberate ride along the river bank. It began to snow again.

When the trail disappeared, Ferguson dismounted and handed her lead rope to Bell. Using a drift wood branch as a probe, Ferguson took slow steps through the snow between the edge of the icy river bank and the slick rock canyon wall. After she'd gone thirty yards, including up and over a boulder that reached into the water, Ferguson returned.

On foot, leading their animals, the group advanced behind Ferguson. Bell's horse balked at climbing over the boulder. While Bell tugged on the lead rope, Faith took off her hat and swatted the animal's rump. The horse jumped forward, its front feet reaching the top of the big rock, but its rear feet scrabbling frantically against the slick side. Unable to find traction before losing its forward momentum, the horses' rear legs slid into the water, its torso falling backwards to crash through the ice into the swift frigid water.

Bell let go of the rope to avoid being pulled down by the horse. The frantic animal piteously thrashed in the icy water, trying futilely to regain its footing on a broken leg. In less than a minute, the beast succumbed to the cold and lay still.

Faith, Levi, and Captain McBee waded through the broken ice, leading their mounts around the boulder, brushing by the horse carcass. Faith shuddered as she stepped over the dead animal's broken leg that stuck out unnaturally.

As soon as they climbed out of the foot-deep water onto the snowy riverbank, the captain dug spare socks out of his saddlebag for Faith, while Levi did the same for his own freezing feet. The worn seams of the captain's boots had allowed enough water to seep in to soak his toes, but having no more socks, he said nothing. Bell rode double behind Levi, grateful to benefit again from his body warmth and even more grateful to wrap her arms around his chest and hold onto him.

The four animals and five riders made their way without further mishap up the canyon until the river became a stream, then a trickling creek until the water disappeared altogether high on the side of the mountain ridge. After a mid-day break, to spare Levi's mule, the captain told Bell to ride behind Faith on her horse. The pair rode in silence for some time, until Faith finally spoke as she watched the trail ahead.

"Apples, huh? Since the twins were born, I've thought they're more the size of pears."

"I wondered if you were really asleep last night, Ma'am," Bell replied.

"I'm accustomed to waking up before one hungry baby cried loud enough to wake the other. It was much easier to nurse one while the other slept."

"Yes, Ma'am." To shift the conversation away from Faith's deceased daughter, Bell quickly added, "And pears seem about right. You're a fortunate woman. Me, I'm stuck with a pair of cherries."

Faith laughed loudly, prompting Jane Ferguson to look back and scowl at the noise.

"You're young. Those cherries may yet ripen into lovely plums," Faith said softly.

"I used to be grateful I was small. Cherries made it easier to go through the days as a man. Now, now I'm thinking plums might be better."

294

"I doubt Levi will mind, either way," Faith suggested, startling Bell.

"Miss Faith, about last night, about Levi. Do you think a white woman and a black man can…"

"Put those thoughts aside for now, dear. It's too cold and we're too far from home to be fretting over the hard ways of the world. You come back to Lexington with me, and let Levi go back to the war with his captain. Once the fighting ends, once this damned war is over, I suspect many things will be different than before."

"Yes, Ma'am. I hope so."

* * *

"Captain, do you think Champ is still behind us?" Ferguson asked when the party stopped at nightfall.

"I doubt it. I don't see how he could get away into the mountains after his ambush and chase us at the same time, without the Yanks catching him again. He'll be cursing me, but I don't think he's on our tail now."

"Then can we build a fire?"

"No. I may be wrong about Champ not following us. And there's other bands of gunmen loose in these hills. You know that. And a Yankee cavalry patrol might have found our trail through the canyon and followed us, or maybe they sent a troop of cavalry over the Cumberland Gap to try to intercept us on this side of the mountain. Remember, they think we have that bald-headed major. Faith said he must be an important officer."

Bell walked up. "The captain's right. Another dark, cold night of shivering is just the thing. Me and Levi'll take first watch, Captain."

December 30, 1863

The party spent another freezing night, their misery worsened by an unceasing cold wind. At dawn they began their slow ascent to the crest.

They didn't linger on top of the picturesque ridge, even though they could see in both directions for miles. The wind was chilling and they didn't know who might be watching. The exhausted riders spent a long tense day of working their way down game trails on the Tennessee side of the mountains, still fearful of being caught by Ferguson's men.

The next day Captain McBee's party emerged from the foothills without having encountered any Union pursuit, renegade outliers, or Rebel partisans. During the last afternoon of their ride, Faith and John rode next to each other bringing up the rear, while Ferguson led the way and Edward Bell and Levi followed her.

"How much longer?" Faith asked her husband

"I think we'll reach Morristown before dark."

"No, not this road. The war. How much longer will the war last? I want my husband back."

"I don't know. Maybe a year. Maybe less. There does seem to be an endless supply of Yankee soldiers and a shrinking number of us to fight them." Faith had no reply to that.

"John, what about Secretary Benjamin?" Faith asked a few minutes later. "Should I write him? I took his money. I think he deserves to know I failed to deliver his message."

Captain McBee reached out to firmly grab his wife's elbow. "Faith, don't write him. He deserves nothing from you. Give him no reason to resume correspondence with you."

"But, John…"

"Faith, he sent you, a married woman, a baby's mother, my wife, into the wolf's lair. He had no right to do that, a point I will personally deliver to him soon enough."

"You won't hurt him, will you? You could go to jail."

"No, I won't hurt the fat bastard. He's too important to the cause. I won't hurt him. Much."

"His gifts and his money truly will help us survive this winter. I am grateful to him for that," Faith said.

"Faith, Benjamin may smile all the time and have a paunch, but he's the hardest man I've ever met."

"Even harder than Champ Ferguson?"

"I believe he is."

"Then I won't write him."

The pair rode in silence until Faith changed the subject again.

"Do you know Edward Bell wants Levi to court her?"

"What?" The captain guffawed. "Bell's a …"

"Young woman," Faith finished for him.

"But, Levi's a…"

"Young man."

"But he's a Negro."

"He may be your son. Does that matter to you?"

"Yes, dammit, but they can't…not with each other."

"John, I think they understand that. For now. But I don't know about after the war ends. Levi may not be willing to put Edwina at such risk, but the coals are simmering between those two. If they do spark after the war, you and I will support them, even if we have to take them with us to Texas."

The captain looked sideways at Faith. "It wouldn't be easy for them, even in Texas. They might have to go all the way to Mexico."

"John, will you talk to Levi about, about his choices when the war ends."

"Faith, he'll remain a slave when the war ends."

"No, he won't. If the Yankees win, they'll free all the Negroes. If the South prevails, which I don't see on the horizon, you'll free him."

"Mother owns Levi, not me."

"Then you'll buy him from Elizabeth, and free him when we reach Texas. If he and Edwina then need to go on to Mexico to be together, he'll be free to make his own mind about that. Will you speak with Levi? Speak with him in a fatherly manner?"

"Faith, I don't know if I can do that. I'm not sure what that even means. Old Isaiah wasn't given to fatherly talks. Regardless, Levi's still my bound servant. He does what I order him to do, without question. Like all the men in Company C. That can't change. Maybe when the war's over."

"I'll accept that, my captain. Will Levi be in much danger when he returns to the army with you?"

"Less danger than he's been in the past week," he answered truthfully. "Levi should live through the war unless he's unlucky or stupid. Our servants don't fight in the trenches. They don't charge the enemy. Only the Yankee army gives black men weapons and puts them on the firing line like they're white men."

"The Yankee army and Captain McBee. Or was that not a black man who twice charged in shooting to save you back in the mountains? Like a son would do," Faith replied, expecting the last comment would likely irritate him.

"What about you, John. Will you not be stupid or force your luck? Please."

McBee looked at his wife and gripped her hand. "Faith, I'll do my duty to my men. I have no choice. And you wouldn't want me if I did otherwise."

Faith leaned across the gap between the two horses and kissed her husband's bearded face.

"You are an honorable man, John J. McBee. Sometimes I wish you weren't."

The pair rode in silence until John pulled his reins to halt his horse. Faith did likewise, not caring if the others distanced themselves ahead.

"Faith, I'm not an honorable man. In fact, honor has evaded me all my life. I left home looking for honor. I fought Comanches in Texas searching for honor. After twenty years, I came back to Virginia as a soldier, still searching for honor. Through all that what I've learned is that I have no idea what honor is." The captain paused to pat his horse's neck.

"I understand duty. I understand sacrifice and leading by example. I've tried this year to redeem what honor may still be buried deep down in me. But I don't know. The war's not over. My regiment will go back into combat when the winter ends."

McBee looked ahead, then turned to look Faith in the eye. "Most importantly, your first husband is still out there somewhere, hating us. He may be a murderer, but he's still your lawful husband. He has every right to kill me."

The captain from Virginia and Texas sighed deeply and concluded, "And as you brought up, Levi is still a slave. I suspect honor will remain elusive for John McBee."

Faith again leaned sideways in her saddle to kiss her husband, wisely saying nothing more.

January 1, 1864

In Morristown, in spite of the holiday, Captain McBee bartered two pistols for a dress and cape for Faith, a wool vest for Levi, a new scarf for Bell, a man's civilian coat for Jane Ferguson, and a new spare pair of socks for himself. Tickets were secured for Edward Bell and Faith McBee to ride the stagecoach north to Lexington. Jane Ferguson rode her horse behind the coach as far as Abingdon, where she struck off by herself to find her sister's home farther east.

On the first day of 1864, the captain and his body-servant rode south to rejoin their regiment.

Philip McBride

Afterword

The character of John McBee was inspired by a real Confederate officer, John J. McBride, a man who did command Company C of the Fifth Texas Regiment during 1863, including the battles at Gettysburg and Chickamauga. McBride was born and raised in Lexington, Virginia before he moved to Texas for health reasons, settling in Leon County in 1842.

The character of Levi is also based on a real man, Levi Miller, who was of mixed ethnic heritage. Miller was a slave belonging to the McBride family, before he was taken off to war to serve as Captain McBride's body-servant.

Several of the names of the new recruits to Company C in *Redeeming Honor* are straight from the actual roster: Andrew Dunlap, John Hailey, Polaski Phillips, brothers named Alamo and Napoleon and brothers named Edward and Zebulon, whose last names I changed.

I put significant effort into keeping the military history in *Redeeming Honor* accurate. The intrigue is fictional. That said, this second book in the McBee trilogy takes a leap by including two historical characters whose fame, or infamy, remain on the edge of Civil War mainstream lore.

First, Secretary of State Judah P. Benjamin was an enigmatic figure who served as the Confederacy's Secretary of War early in the conflict, then took on the mantle as Secretary of State. Benjamin was one of President Davis' closest advisors, and although Benjamin burned all of his official and personal documents when he fled Richmond with President Davis, he is thought to have also run a secret spy operation during the war.

Benjamin was born Jewish, raised in Charleston, South Carolina, and attended Yale University until he was dismissed for causes that remain cloudy. He settled in New

Orleans, where he married a teenage girl from a wealthy Creole Catholic family. Benjamin and his new wife owned a plantation, where he was a slave owner and raised cotton, while he practiced law. He was elected to the US Senate where he served until secession fever infected the south and he resigned to return to Louisiana. During the war, Judah Benjamin was considered one of the brightest minds and most influential men in President Davis's cabinet, even while enduring discrimination over his Jewish heritage.

Benjamin's wife, with their daughter, lived abroad, separated from Judah, during most of their marriage, including the years of the Civil War. Her absence opened the door for unsubstantiated, but detectable hints of a questionable sexual orientation on Judah's part. All in all, the historical Judah P. Benjamin was influential, affluent, intelligent, witty, and mysterious, all perfect character traits to add intrigue to a plot.

The second historical figure introduced in *Redeeming Honor* is Captain Champ Ferguson who was the homicidal leader of a band of southern partisan rangers who operated in northern Tennessee and southern Kentucky. The real Champ Ferguson was such a bad actor that he was one of only two Confederate officers who were tried and executed after the war by the US government for their war crimes. The other officer was the superintendent of the Andersonville prisoner of war camp.

General Thomas "Stonewall" Jackson did have a second funeral in Lexington, where he lived before the war, working as a professor at the Virginia Military Institute. After an enormous crowd watched his first funeral procession in Richmond, the general's flag-draped coffin was transported by train and canal packet boat as described in my book. Jackson's remains reside in the Lexington city cemetery to this day

An unknown number of women did hide their gender and serve as soldiers in both the Union and Confederate armies. Lieutenant Laura Williams, a Texan, was one. She is named, but is not a character in *Redeeming Honor*. Jane Ferguson, who does play a minor role in the story, was another. Edwina Bell is fictitious.

302

As is the case in my first two Civil War novels, many, but not all, of the military vignettes in *Redeeming Honor* come directly from soldiers' memoirs or published histories of the Texas Brigade. The winter march of stragglers led by Captain McBee was indeed led by Captain John McBride. The public demonstration by JEB Stuart's cavalry, which the infantry in Hood's Division watched as part of the audience, did occur shortly before Gettysburg. The Texans did race for the many fallen hats of the cavaliers.

My favorite true snippet occurring during the Gettysburg campaign will always be the group of women in carriages fording the Potomac River while the Texas infantry crossed at the same time at the same ford, many of the hundreds of soldiers having doffed their trousers and ankle-length drawers.

Also during the march, General Hood did authorize a "gill" of liberated Pennsylvania liquor to each man in his division, causing one memoirist to record that the Texans ate breakfast in the state of Virginia, dinner in the state of Maryland, and went to bed in Pennsylvania in the state of inebriation, four states in one day!

The long nine-day train ride to Georgia before the battle of Chickamauga was a popular topic in the Texas soldiers' memoirs. The men did rip the plank siding off the freight cars to let in air and allow them to see the countryside. A banquet was laid out for the train-riding infantry in Sumpterville, North Carolina, and the humorous text of the thank-you speech by a lieutenant is presented as recorded. The Texans' brawl with the police in Wilmington, North Carolina happened, thankfully with no fatal injuries inflicted on the aging policemen.

Finally, during the battle at Chickamauga, a fleeing woman with infants and small children in tow did cross the path of the Texans' advance, a sight so pitiful that a soldier included it in his memoir decades later.

As with my first two Civil War novels, I relied heavily on memoirs of soldiers who were in the three Texas regiments in the brigade. What follows is a list of the memoirs that allowed me to understand the flavor and feel of being a soldier in the Texas Brigade 150 years ago, and the modern history books that kept my history straight.

Memoirs:

The memoir of Robert Campbell, Company A, Fifth Texas Infantry: *Lone Star Confederate, A Gallant and Good Soldier of the Fifth Texas Infantry*, edited by George Skoch and Mark Perkins. Published in 2003.

The memoir of Chaplain Nicholas A. Davis, Fourth Texas Infantry: *The Campaign From Texas to Maryland With the Battle of Fredericksburg*, edited by Donald E. Everett. Memoir first published in 1863.

The memoir of William A. Fletcher, Company F, Fifth Texas Infantry, *Rebel Private: Front and Rear*, Introduction by Richard Wheeler. Memoir first published in 1908.

The memoir of Val C. Giles, Company B, Fourth Texas Infantry, *Rags and Hope: The Recollections of Val C. Giles, Four Years With Hood's Brigade, Fourth Texas Infantry*, edited by Mary Lassell. Published in 1961.

The memoir of Colonel Robert M. Powell, Fifth Texas Infantry, *Recollections of a Texas Colonel at Gettysburg*. Edited by Gregory A. Coco. Memoir first published in 1884.

The memoir of John W. Stevens, Company K, Fifth Texas Infantry, *Reminiscences of the Civil War: A Soldier in Hood's Texas Brigade, Army of Northern Virginia*, by Judge John W. Stevens. Memoir first published in 1902.

The memoir of Captain George T. Todd, Company A, First Texas Infantry, *First Texas Regiment*. Notes and introduction by Harold B. Simpson. Memoir first published in 1909.

The memoir of John C. West, Company E, Fourth Texas Infantry, *A Texan In Search of a Fight: Being the Diary and Letters of a Private Soldier in Hood's Texas Brigade,* by John C. West. Memoir first published in 1901.

Letters from John M. Smither, William H. Lewis and Colonel R. M. Powell, *Touched by Fire, Letters From Company D, 5th Texas Infantry, Hood's Brigade, Army of Northern Virginia, 1862-1865,* Edited by Eddy R. Parker. Published in 2000.

Hood's Texas Brigade, Its Marches, It's Battles, Its Achievements, by J.B. Polley, Author of "A Soldier's Letters to Charming Nellie." Memoirs first published in 1910.

Four Years With General Lee, by Walter H. Taylor, edited by James I. Robertson, Jr. Published 1996.

The memoir of Lieutenant Campbell Wood, Adjutant, Fifth Texas Infantry, Unpublished. *Hood's Texas Brigade: Lee's Grenadier Guard*, by Colonel Harold B. Simpson. Published in 1970.

History Books:

Hood's Texas Brigade: A Compendium, by Colonel Harold B. Simpson. Published in 1977.

Gaines' Mill to Appomattox: Waco & McClellan County in Hood's Texas Brigade, by Colonel Harold B. Simpson. Published 1963.

Hood's Texas Brigade in the Civil War, by Edward B. Williams, Published 2012.

Lt. Col. King Bryan of Hood's Texas Brigade, by Michael Dan Jones, Published 2013.

Philip McBride

History Books:

Jeff Davis's Own, Cavalry, Comanches, and the Battle for the Texas Frontier, by James R. Arnold. Published 2000.

Chickamauga and Chattanooga, The Battles That Doomed the Confederacy, by John Bowers. Published 1994.

Judah P. Benjamin, The Jewish Confederate, by Eli N. Evans. Published 1988.

Lee's Lieutenants, Gettysburg to Appomattox, Volume 3, by Douglas S. Freeman. Published 1944.

Gettysburg, The Last Invasion, by Allen C. Guelzo. Published 2013.

Rebel Yell, The Violence, Passion, and the Redemption of Stonewall Jackson, by S.C. Gwynne. Published 2014.

Gettysburg, by Stephen W. Sears, Published 2003.

ABOUT THE AUTHOR

In 2013, McBride completed his first novel, *Whittled Away*, a story centering on the Alamo Rifles, a company from San Antonio which served as Company K of the Sixth Texas Infantry Regiment, CSA.

This novel, *Redeeming Honor*, is McBride's third Civil War novel, and is the second of a three-novel set which will follow the Fifth Texas Infantry Regiment from 1862 until the final surrender of the Army of Northern Virginia in 1865.

Since 1999, author Philip McBride has been a regular contributor to the *Camp Chase Gazette* magazine, writing over eighty articles about Civil War soldiers and the hobby of Civil War reenacting.

McBride is a retired teacher, high school principal, and school district administrator. He is an avid consumer of military historical fiction. He and his wife Juanita live in Lockhart, Texas, a small farming town in central Texas.

The author welcomes comments or questions about his novels and Texas in the Civil War, and may be contacted at ptmcbride49@gmail.com.

McBride publishes weekly posts on his blog, which is centered on things relevant to writing Civil War fiction, as well as random current events and his grandchildren.

His blog can be found at: http://mcbridenovels.blogspot.com/

Philip McBride

24033726R00195

Made in the USA
Middletown, DE
12 September 2015